The Princess Breakers

J Simon

Books by J Simon

The Princess Breakers

Fossilized Gods
Lithified Saints
Petrified Devils

Zwirner

RatHeart

Majra
Songs of Sa'bahr
The Great Celestial Machine of Saithan

http://majra.org

* * *

ISBN-13: 979-8587819177

First paperback edition.

I

Axiom: Nothing ever goes right. Corollary: Things can always get worse. Take the Market at Kairay. Quaint, right? Merchants lead heavily-laden donkeys around the edge of the Market, setting up their stalls, braving dust and sun and wind to sell spices and fruit, worked bronze and shaped wood. Surely nothing could go wrong there? Allow yourself the generous privilege of being enlightened, by me. Some time ago, I rented a space in the Market. The rental papers somehow got filed wrong and ended up proving— conclusively—that I was dead. The soldiers agreed that it was probably a mistake even as they arrested me for commandeering a dead woman's space. I tried to prove that I wasn't a corpse by doing a fun little dance, which corpses—excepting cases of extreme post- mortem flatulence—are rarely known to do. It didn't work. The city still charges me nice and regular, even though I haven't bothered showing up in months. Now they just arrest whoever's closest and send me the bill.

"Going into business together! Wow! This is going to be great!" Vindi announced, rubbing her hands together. I glanced sidelong at her. Manic grin, disordered hair, twin ceramic horns that— despite being installed by a mad wizard when she was six—didn't seem to do anything. In other words, the usual.

"Delusional," I decided. "I love you like a sister, Vindi, but are you even paying attention? Nothing goes right. Ever. Remember when we were kids, and we set up that fruit stand? I'm still not sure how I cut myself so badly on a grape."

"Try to remember the good times," she said encouragingly.

"That's assuming there are good times to remember."

Vindi led me on a winding path across the dry, hot Market. Nehra the wine merchant made the sign against evil as I passed. I stuck my tongue out at her—just in time for the wind to whip up and coat it with dust. Of course.

"When I think of the Grape Incident," Vindi said, "I think of the medics that eventually arrived. I'm sure they didn't mean to drive their donkeys through a wedding parade, but my, that was a delicious cake that fell out of the sky and into my lap."

I sighed, shading my eyes against the sun. "Oh, I remember them, too. Keep in mind that I was actually fine until they came galloping up—lost control of their donkeys—and trampled right over me. Upon which they panicked, backed up, and ran me over again. You want to know the best part? Emergency calls aren't free. I got to pay for my concussion, along with a laceration shaped like a pooping rabbit that's visible to this day."

"WHAT?!" Vindi yelped. "How did I not know about this??"

"I'm very careful about how I dress when I go swimming."

"Well, you still have to remember the good times," Vindi said, ducking under a rope studded with the dully clanking bells of Nahssa the Tinker. "Like how generous I felt when I decided to do something nice for you, and settle ownership of the cake on a coin flip—heads you win, tails I lose."

"Whereupon the coin promptly shot up my nose and lodged there," I agreed. "Yes. I remember. Take my word for it—nothing ever goes right."

Vindi smiled. "I love you like a sister, Saraya, but aren't you being just a little arrogant? When things go wrong, we ordinary folks keep our mouths shut and deal with it. You'd have to think you were a pretty big deal to imagine *the universe itself* had a vital, panting interest in thwarting you at every turn."

"My bad luck is real," I said simply. "Your father says so, and he's... well, the wizard Avashti says so, too."

"Sure, it's real. But don't let that be your excuse. Don't let it stop you from having fun with the people who love you." Vindi shimmied as if she was bursting with so much joy and wonderment that she just couldn't contain it all. "Going into business together! This is going to be great!"

"Delusional. It's now my mission in life to travel the world quacking like a duck and pointing at a picture of you until your face has become the clinical definition of 'insanity' in every culture in the land."

"A duck?" she said, distracted.

"Ducks are famous for being insane!" I insisted. "Admittedly, my copy of our children's primer did get kind of messed up when I dropped it in that puddle, but I'm pretty sure the part about ducks was solid." I paused. "I'm less certain that the proper etiquette for greeting returning soldiers involves mooning them, ever since I got stabbed in the—"

"I dropped my primer, too," Vindi said thoughtfully. "But all that happened was it clobbered one of the Leaf Riders on the head. Poor thing was so concussed, it kept granting me wish after wish, thinking each one was the first." She noted my scowl and flushed. "Well, they were *small* wishes," she said defensively. "On the plus side, I accumulated nearly enough seeds to make a pomegranate!"

"Delusional," I repeated, shaking my head.

A wind kicked up as we crossed the Market, threatening rain as it tossed the branches of the great trees back and forth. We only get one or two real storms a year, and this looked like it could be one of them. The city of Kairay winds across the desert like a deranged and wriggling serpent, following as it does the course of the river that gives it its name. Here, life is possible—even easy, depending on the generosity of the annual floods. The Kairay river is bracketed by twin rinds of forest that are inhabited by bright colorful birds, butterflies of ridiculous size, and keen-eyed little Leaf Riders who leer at passers-by and giggle in a disturbing fashion. The heart of the city is its Market, and the heart of the Market is a soaring artifact of ancient and powerful wizardry—the Grand Emporium. In a city where buildings of mud, brick, and stone rarely top three stories, the Grand Emporium rises like a hornet's nest made of rock, its interconnecting chambers and senseless winding staircases rising at least forty stories above the dusty streets below. No one knows who left it there or why, but over the centuries, all of its lower-level rooms have been claimed by merchants. The Grand Emporium has become a noisy and colorful place—in many ways, the beating heart of Kairay itself. Vindi led me right up to this towering monolith, the heat falling to an almost bearable level in the depths of its shadow. I glanced at Vindi. The spaces here were tremendously sought-after, the rents almost beyond belief. Only the wealthiest of merchants could afford to have shops here.

"Oh! I almost forgot," Vindi said, taking something from her pocket. "I got you something to commemorate the world-altering day we became business partners. Do you like it?"

She handed me a bracelet. I studied it. It was a silver-colored metal, but not silver. It was about as fat across as my spread hand, and inscribed with a few simple but elegant symbols.

"A portable lightning rod?" I said, trying it on my left wrist. "I like it! I have to say, spitting in the face of the gods right when we're about to have a storm really appeals to me. Bring it on, universe!"

Vindi rolled her eyes. "Do you have to be so dramatic? You haven't been struck by lightning in almost four months."

"Two," I corrected her.

"Oh, come on! You can't count what happened when I persuaded you to fly kites with me. That one didn't even blow your eyebrows off!"

"I love it," I said, holding my arm over my head and recklessly brandishing the quasi-silver bracelet at the impotent clouds. "Not the most efficient suicide device, but it'll do."

Vindi looked at me strangely. "Suicide device?"

"I'm starting a collection. Look!" I rummaged around in my pocket, proudly showing her a silk cord barbed with sharp little knots of metal. "Anteyvan strangling cord. Took all the money I had—and a few forged documents claiming I was a fellow museum—to get it out of their collection, but I managed."

"Why do you even *have* something like that?" Vindi asked, making a face. "I mean, isn't it illegal to even own it?"

"No. Well, yes, but that's all right. I mean to keep a bunch of fun and interesting suicide devices on my person at all times, specifically so I can refuse to use them and show the universe what's what. YOU HEAR THAT?" I shouted, shaking my fist at the sky and attracting puzzled looks from passers-by. "I'M SMARTER THAN YOU, I'M STRONGER THAN YOU, AND I'M BETTER THAN YOU!"

"It's all right," Vindi said soothingly. "The bad, mean cloud is gone now. And, ah, how many suicide devices have you collected so far?"

"One," I said, tucking the cord back into my pocket, "but you've got to start somewhere."

"Whatever you say." Vindi adjusted my position with little tugs and pushes, then gestured grandly at the space in front of us. "Anyway, here we are… the future location of our shop! What do you think?"

I shot a dubious look at Vindi. The Grand Emporium towered over us like a cliff, and every one of its bottom-level rooms was taken. A little to the left was the shop of Sabah the Jeweler. Her shop occupied a nice clean chamber which was bordered on the right by a dizzying spiral staircase at least twenty stories high. Sabah herself wore simple but flattering garments of blue and white, set off by a single ostentatious display of wealth—the shimmering, iridescent ring of a crystal rim pinned over her heart.

"It's a wonderful location," I admitted, "but I'm not clear on how you mean to get rid of Sabah. Are we going to *murder* her or *seduce* her?"

"What?" Sabah asked, alarmed.

"Not there," Vindi said, grabbing my shoulders and physically turning me. "*There*. The space under the stairs! All we have to do is dig it out and it's ours!"

I looked. There was, indeed, a slight gap under the stairs. It might have been tall enough for a worm, if that worm was especially depressed and slouched a lot.

"Right. Dig a nice deep pit and drop all of our possessions down it *just* before the floods arrive," I said laconically. "Seems sound to me."

"You worry too much," Vindi said. "If you drown, I'll charge customers to poke your bloated corpse with a stick. We can't lose!"

"You've really thought of everything," I admitted dryly. "Fine. I'll admit, for the sake of argument, that floods are fun and the world is made of love. We're setting up here, and no amount of bad luck can change that." I started counting on my fingers. "One. Two. Three."

"Quit it! Nothing's going to go wrong. When have I ever led you astray? Well, other than the time I literally led you astray and accidentally dropped you down a thirty-foot sinkhole. But that doesn't count. I mean, I spent the rest of the day tossing all kinds of supplies down to you! Which, admittedly, hit you on the head and knocked you unconscious, but you have to look on the bright side. The rescuers I summoned may have been bad at tying knots, but they could really sing!"

"Five. Six—"

"You can't set up there," Sabah the Jeweler said regretfully. "That space—the staircase and everything under it—belongs to me. It's in my rental agreement."

"What? Really?" Vindi said, startled.

"Really."

"Well, what of it? It wouldn't hurt to let us stay, would it? I know! We'll pay rent! Do you accept dancing as currency?"

"Vindi—"

"What if I made *Saraya* dance?" she said cunningly.

Sabah the Jeweler sighed. "The thing is, letting you stay *would* hurt me. Part of what I sell is the *experience*. When people buy jewelry, they want a shop that's spacious, quiet, and a little private. Having another shop crammed into the grounds? Not so good."

"Oh, come on! It'll be fun!" Vindi wheedled. Sabah just shook her head. Now that I saw her up close, her clothes were even finer than I'd realized, while her crystal rim—a pearlescent gemlike ring about a thumbnail across—shattered the dim light into a hundred sparkling rainbows. I idly placed a hand across one of the many stains on my oft-washed tunic.

"You'll *love* having us as neighbors," Vindi pleaded. "We'll pay our rent on time, I promise—"

"—assuming that your definition of 'time' is neither linear nor circular but bird-shaped," I said helpfully.

"—we smell great, and also, we're quiet and meek and well-behaved!"

"By which she means that we tell only the most *elegant* dirty jokes," I said, "call each other the most *elevated* and *inspiring* of obscene names, and engage in highly cultured slap-fights while making extremely graceful fart sounds with our armpits."

"Plus, I'll cut you in for half of the 'poking-Saraya's-bloated-corpse-with-a-stick' concession," Vindi said encouragingly. "You can't lose!"

Sabah the Jeweler shook her head. "I like you. I really do. But it wouldn't be right for my business."

"You'll change your mind. Maybe not today. Maybe not tomorrow. But soon enough." Vindi glanced at me. "This is a temporary setback, that'll all. Please don't blame it on some supernatural boogedy-boogedy that's out to get you."

"What, this?" I snorted derisively. "*This* hardly counts as bad luck at all. Being turned away at the start, it just seems so *obvious*. The universe is really losing its touch if it can't torment me worse than that. Here's what could have happened: Sabah was out when we visited, so we never found out we couldn't set up here. We labored for days digging a huge pit, then spent further days meticulously arranging all of our junk—"

"'Pre-loved goods'," Vindi corrected me.

"—and when she finally spotted us, Sabah called the guards to drag us away. In a single moment, day upon day of emotional investment and back-breaking labor was turned into so much trash." I paused, cocking my head thoughtfully. "And also, one of the guards turned out to be allergic to Sabah's perfume and started spasming wildly, horrified to see himself beating me with his cudgel but helpless to stop. *That's* how it could have happened."

"Is she always like this?" Sabah the Jeweler asked mildly.

"You have no idea."

"Or—hear me out!—it could have happened like this," I said, inflamed with a dubious sort of macabre enthusiasm. "We got our shop set up just fine, but a roc with digestive problems flew past and took a super-colossal dump on our store, leaving behind two things: A huge, stinking crater and the world's most disgusting mystery."

Vindi winced. "Why do you always have to be so gross? Rocs are amazing. We saw one once, remember? Its wings almost blotted out the sky! The world is full of wonderment and mystery."

"Exactly," I said. "Therefore, we disrespect the world itself if we merely stare at its amazements in dumb surrender. These things are *real*, and the greatest way to honor them is to really *think* about them, to know them, to ponder their secrets in all their dirty, filthy, disgusting glory. Rocs are gigantic, *and* they're real. Real animals poop. Therefore…"

"Fine! I surrender! Now stop making me think about it!"

Looking resigned to her fate, Sabah the Jeweler finally managed to get a word in edgewise. "I'll say this one more time: You can't stay here. The issue is closed, over, and done. So you'll leave, right?"

Vindi smiled. "You actually think getting rid of us is going to be that easy?" she asked. "You really don't know Saraya, do you? Failure doesn't make her give up. If anything, it makes her try twice as hard."

"You have to show Reality who's boss," I explained. "So the world knocks me down. So what? Reality only wins if I don't get up again. Or, on the occasions when my tendons snap for no reason, if I fail to roll over and flop around all angry-like." I smiled at Sabah the Jeweler. "But then, I'm not the only one around here who's admirably persistent. Vindi's too deluded to quit. Ever."

"What's deluded about it?" Vindi asked. "My luck is as good as yours is bad, pretty much by definition. And a person who always wins literally has nothing to lose. Why *not* keep fighting?"

"So you see, Sabah, you might as well—" I paused, looking back at Vindi. "Wait. Are you admitting that I'm better than you, since I risk more?"

"Hmm. Well, if you think about it, a person who always loses *also* has nothing to lose, since she didn't have anything in the first place," Vindi mused. "She doesn't *risk* anything by taking a stand. When you do it, it's a shrug the size of the universe. When I do it, it's an act of heroism spanning all of time and space. You're welcome."

"Could I make you go away if I gave you money?" Sabah asked desperately.

"YES!"

"NO!" Vindi glared at me. "We're going to keep coming back, keep pleading, keep wearing you down until you let us put our shop here."

"Was it a *lot* of money?" I plaintively asked Sabah.

"If you invested it, in time, yes," Sabah said evasively. "So long as you agree that time is shaped like a bird."

"Well, we'll go… for now… but you're missing out," I told her. "It would be a lot of fun, letting us put our shop here. You could watch us slowly go crazy as we spent all our time trapped in a sunless pit, growing mushrooms on our faces." I paused. "Our faces if we're lucky."

Vindi glared at me. "Plus, given that we'll be down in a pit, Saraya will be looking up your skirt all day long," she said. "If you're a pervert, you'll enjoy it. If not, you'll enjoy calling the guards to come beat her up. Talk about a win-win!"

Sabah looked like she was trying not to smile. "Fare well, then. Ah… not that it has anything to do with anything, but what exactly are you going to sell?"

"Junk," I said. "We're junkmen. We can't afford better."

Vindi punched my arm. "What we sell is *solutions*. Pure ingenuity. If we can improvise a cheap answer out of junk, well, wouldn't that be better than paying ten times more for something purpose-built?"

"Not if your 'solution' smells awful and breaks right away," Sabah noted.

"She's good," I said, impressed.

"Go. I think I see a customer."

"We'll be back," Vindi promised. "We'll change your mind or die trying!"

"We could die *trying*?" I asked, distracted. "From just talking to her? How?"

"Tongues get stuck places. It happens. Ask anyone!"

"GO!" Sabah the Jeweler shouted.

"Tomorrow!" Vindi cried, waving. Shaking my head, I followed her across the Market.

* * *

There are no bridges across the Kairay river. By tradition, children ferry people across, braving that muddy expanse on whatever loosely hammered-together collection of planks seems least likely to sink. We didn't actually need to cross, but Vindi gave a coin to a little girl anyway, paying her to take us downriver the lazy way. Trees soared overhead, blotting out the sky with vast interlacing canopies of green, while their great beards of moss and epiphytes dangled almost all the way to the river. A bright yellow bird darted low across the Kairay, trailing smoke. As we watched, it burst into flames, plummeted, and hit the water with a loud 'plunk'.

"That was… a very small phoenix?" Vindi said hopefully.

"Nope," said the taciturn little girl, one arm draped across the tiller. "Regular bird. Ate a salamander. It happens."

"The world is full of wonders," I said maliciously. "Speaking of which. Was it really a good idea to pay for a boat ride? The last time I saw more than two coins in one place, it was such a shock that I started flopping around on the ground and speaking in tongues."

"I love you and treasure your safety," Vindi decided. "Therefore, to protect you, I'll do my absolute best to ensure you remain dirt-poor."

"Gee. Thanks."

"Anyway, money is easy," Vindi said dismissively. "Remember when we were girls, and you got mad at me for some reason, and you threw a beehive at me when my back was turned?"

"I still don't know why they all swarmed after *me*," I muttered.

"What about *my* suffering? I had wax on my ass for half a month. Every time I sat down, it took forever to pick off all the coins I'd sat on. Money is easy."

"I like money," I said. "It's a physical reminder of how the world works for other people. Other people go to the races and bet on donkeys. So do I." I smiled nostalgically. "Did I ever tell you about my first bet?"

"You lost?" Vindi commiserated.

"Actually, no. I won. Right up until I jumped up and down with joy and accidentally punched the winning rider in the face. It

9

made him so groggy, the judges assumed he was on something illegal and disqualified him. I lost everything on a winning ticket. True story."

"Money is *possibility*, crystallized into material form," Vindi said. "As long as it's a physical object, coins and gems and such, it's meaningless. It's important to remember that. When you find your world getting all tiny and dull, always seeing the same things, always doing the same things, you can precipitate those useless chunks of alloy into *experiences* that will make your world big again."

"Easy for you to say," I said sourly. "When you own as few coins as I do, you have time to learn their individual names, hobbies, and secret aspirations. What can I say? I get attached to the sparkly little bastards after a while. Haven't you wondered why I hold a quick funeral every time you make me buy something?"

Vindi eyed me speculatively. "So… if I forced you to spend a coin, you'd weep uncontrollably as you mourned its loss, whereupon I could collect your tears and distill out the salt, which I could then sell to get back the original coin!"

"That seems unnecessarily complicated," I noted. "Not to mention capricious and cruel. I'll admit it… I'm impressed."

"I charge more for ferrying crazy people," the little girl said flatly. Vindi shut up, settling for making faces at me for the rest of the trip. I tried to get back at her by miming the act of a small bird bursting into flames, but it's a hard thing to convey through gestures alone. The little girl spotted me, upon which I pretended I was just brushing my hair. Not sure I pulled it off.

We finally landed at a spot well east of the Grand Emporium and made our way homeward. The farther we got from the river, the drier it became. The trees got smaller and sparser, the ground dusty and cracked. There were far more buildings jammed together far more densely. The people… well, they weren't exactly poor, but they weren't any better off than we were. We finally came to a crumbling three-story spire built from mud brick. That's the problem with baking your building materials out of straw and mud: Freak rainstorms tend to melt it—and this building obviously hadn't been repaired in years.

"I guess Dad isn't back yet," Vindi mused, studying the shuttered windows.

"Delirious! The child is delirious!" cried a large man with a wild beard as he hurried through the crowd, earning numerous odd looks as he elbowed his way toward us. "We all know wizards aren't allowed to have families. She's an unrelated urchin whom I allow to live in my house solely because her blood is useful for *so many things*."

"What about me?" I asked, amused. "Why do *I* get to live in your house?"

"I wouldn't say that you do. You *infest* the place, and my efforts to exterminate you have yet to be crowned with success."

"It's good to see you, too, Avashti," I told the wizard. He dug through a weird detritus of glowing metal and rune-inscribed stones in his pockets, finally pulling out a perfectly normal key. "Good trip to the Temple of Souls?" I asked. "Say, settle a bet for us. Assuming that zombies can't die, if you really wanted to make one go away, I figure you'd have to eat it. My question is what sort of unspeakable horrors might rise from the latrine a couple of days later."

Avashti ushered us inside. He was careful to shut the door before sweeping Vindi into a crushing hug.

"You want to be more careful," he told her. "If anyone found out I have a daughter…"

"I'm not sure I can keep it quiet much longer," Vindi said, glancing sidelong at him. "I make mistakes. Things slip out. You want to make sure I look *realistically* deranged when they do, so that no one pays attention to the things I'm saying. Keeping me drunk all the time would probably be easiest. How much beer can you afford?"

"I'm not going to do that. Well. I *may* not do that. Just how loose-lipped would you say you are?"

"How much beer do *I* get?" I asked brightly.

"None," Avashti said. "No one believes what you say *sober*. Why mess with what works?"

"I know there's a flaw in your reasoning somewhere," I said, disgruntled.

Avashti led us through a lower level crammed with weird and inexplicable things: Metal tortoises that unfolded their shells into wings made of gold and took off buzzing around the room; gearwork golems that sorted rice grains by size and color in a frenzy of pointless industry; maps made of stone on which dragon figurines spun aimlessly until they fell over sideways. Wizards almost never get what they want on the first try, but they always get *something*. If may be wrong, demented, broken, or useless, but you've got to keep it somewhere. Avashti tiredly climbed the stairs to the second level, Vindi and I right behind him. It was a lot quieter up there—almost sane. Avashti led us to the dining area, which was little more than an alcove with a big rectangular table and a bench on either side. In the wall next to the table was a large square window. It was little more than a gaping, empty hole—no glass. You'd think a wizard could afford a few luxuries, but I guess you look a lot more Mysterious when you have bats stuck in your beard and bugs in your teeth.

"Here," Avashti said to Vindi. He dug some curved metal plates from his pocket, each about big enough to cover the tip of his thumb. "Try these."

Vindi took off a set of identical-looking earrings and replaced them with the new set. Nothing happened. Nothing changed.

"Do you feel different?" she asked me.

I shrugged. "Not really."

"I don't think it's working," Vindi said judiciously. "If part of my soul were being reflected into you, you'd be dancing by now."

"For the last time," Avashti said irritably, "that's not what it does. I committed some terrible deeds when I was younger…"

"I know," I said. "You've told us before. Lots of times. Could I pay you to *not* tell us again? On an unrelated note, do you have any money I could borrow?"

"I like it," Vindi chimed in. "I mean, not the story, obviously. But the fact that he trusts us with the burden of his regret and pain? That's a mark of true love."

"Torture equals love?" I said, impressed. "You know, there's an off chance you're even more messed up than I am."

"I committed some terrible deeds when I was younger," Avashti repeated. "I was arrogant, overconfident, reckless in my power…"

"Here it comes," I said, resigned to my fate.

"It's all right, Dad. I'm making a trust circle with my arms," Vindi said. "If you feel the need to unburden yourself, literally, by throwing up…" She held her arms up right next to my head. "Here will do. Try not to miss."

Avashti sat heavily on one of the benches. "My beloved daughter Vindi, my precious little girl… of course I wanted her to live a charmed life, an exceptional life. Is that so wrong? My first attempt involved installing those ceramic horns. They didn't work."

"Stylish, though," Vindi said, flicking one to elicit a ringing chime.

"The second thing I tried… also didn't work, though it does

explain why I have a limp to this day. But my third attempt?" Avashti gazed at his hands. "Amazingly, I succeeded... but at a devastating cost. Vindi's *good* luck came by sucking all the fortune out of her closest friend, dooming that poor little girl to a life of miserable *bad* luck."

I shrugged. "It isn't a bad thing, having a wizard feel guilty about what he did to you. I still remember how you used to buy me honey *any time I asked!* I generally managed to choke on it, sure, causing me to flail wildly and accidentally throw the rest of it into Vindi's mouth, but what a way to die!" I paused, eyes widening as I realized that I could swiftly and flavorfully expand my collection of suicide devices. "For, uh, no particular reason, are there any jars of honey in the pantry?"

"Nine years I've been trying to undo what I did," Avashti said heavily. "Your luck, Saraya, is still being transferred to Vindi. I haven't been able to stop that. The earrings, though, reflect your stolen luck back to you, returning you to normal. Well, *close* to normal. With each new set of artifacts, I get it a little more right. I'd say you're now getting three-quarters of your luck back. Maybe four-fifths. But I need to do better. I need to be perfect... and perfection requires years of precision, care, and attention to detail."

"Uh-huh," I said. "By the way, Vindi has decided to murder-seduce Sabah into giving us her space at Market. I'm not sure which will come first, but it's going to be hilarious either way."

"I am NOT!" Vindi said, glaring at me. "But just so you know, I'd seduce her first. Don't be gross."

Avashti managed a faint smile. "Girls... don't be like me. Be careful, prudent, and above all, pragmatic. There are... consequences... to being otherwise."

"You do magic for a living," Vindi said disbelievingly, "and you're lecturing us about *being more grounded*?"

Avashti tapped his fingers on the table. "The more powerful and unpredictable something is, the more wrong it can go," he said. "I used to think I was a special talent, greater and more amazing than anyone who'd ever lived. I thought that wild, flamboyant, risk-taking magic was the only kind worth having." A far-away look came into Avashti's eyes. "Why take forever to do things right... when you could just do *something*, and fix what was horribly broken about it afterward?" The gleam faded from his eyes. "Take it from me. Do things right. You'll be less miserable in the long run."

"I think he's incredibly convincing, telling us to be all pragmatic and grounded," I said wryly. "And this from the man who likes to jam wizardly artifacts up his nose and pretend to sneeze out fireworks."

Avashti's eyes narrowed. "The Work of Ages is greater than any man. If the ineffable power of wizardry requires me to blow glowing, sparkling snot at you for its own unknowable reasons, who I am to refuse? I am but a vessel for forces greater than myself, which for some reason demand the enthusiastic deployment of incendiary boogers."

"Speaking of which. Musical flaming nose-lizards. Will you do them for us tonight? Please?"

"Bah. A wizard obeys no commands," Avashti declaimed. "Don't tell the bird how to fly, and don't tell me how to set you on fire."

We didn't have to wait long for dinner. Avashti mixed rice, vegetables and spices into a curry that was, yes, magical in its near overwhelming flavor. I sat by the window, watching people go by, while Vindi made plans for our shop.

"We're keeping an awful lot of junk… I mean, pre-loved goods… out in the shed," she said suddenly. "Do you think we should sleep out there tonight? You know, to protect the merchandise?"

"Vindi, it's junk," I said flatly. "The biggest risk isn't people stealing it. It's people breaking in so they can leave *more*."

"We'll be famous before you know it," she said airily. "Our reputation will spread."

"For better or for worse."

"Hush! We've already had our first paying job, haven't we?"

"A job which we failed at," I agreed. "Neither of us could figure out how to fix Rivi's wizard-lamp."

"But we got paid," Vindi argued. "Plus, now Rivi has a pocket wine press the exact size and shape of a broken lamp! Way better!"

I smirked. "I think she paid us to go away, mostly because you wouldn't stop apologizing for our failure. What the weeping and wailing didn't accomplish, the copious snot-bubbles finished."

"And *I* think she paid us to go away because you wouldn't stop demonstrating her new wine press on every fruit in the house."

"Dates taste better when they're crushed," I explained. "Eating them, you know you've beaten them in a fight."

"Girls!" Avashti said tiredly. "Will you shut up if I promise you fireworks?"

"Yay!" Vindi cried.

"That depends," I said cautiously. "Remember the time you had a sneezing fit and couldn't stop setting my eyebrows on fire?"

Avashti tried to keep the smile off his face. "Ah, yes. A regrettable accident. Too bad you keep reminding me of it. One of my most shameful memories."

"Then why are you laughing?"

"I have a weird reaction to shame. It's part of the Great Work. Inadequate mortal minds such as yours could never understand."

"Yup. He's as grounded as they come," I said to Vindi.

"Hush," Avashti said. As Vindi and I avidly watched, he turned and started stuffing something up his nose.

* * *

Ask most people to imagine what bad luck *really* means, and they'll go on about poverty and infirmity and abandonment and all of the splashy, big-ticket stuff you've heard so much about. Then there are the little things. The simple things. The things that are so basic, you don't even notice them until they're gone. Take sleep. A couple of years ago, I got a mosquito stuck in my ear. *For six days*. Not long afterward, my ear provided the nesting site for a family of extremely tiny, extremely untalented trolls that *loved* to sing. Then I started sweating a savory, meaty oil which attracted flies, which in turn attracted bats, which streaked past my face at wildly exciting if unpredictable intervals. Then, for one memorable year, I suffered from sporadic but explosive diarrhea due to the world's first confirmed allergy to moonlight. Sleep seems like such a simple little thing, but try losing it for good. That way lies madness, and evil puppets. Anyway, my luck may be better than it was, but I'm still nervous about going to bed, and I still put it off for as long as I can.

By the flickering light of a lantern I ran my finger down the bookshelf in my room, trying to decide what to read. Perhaps a travelogue, packed with colorful stories about yawping barbarians who had heads for feet and olives for eyes. Delightful stuff. Not the stories, mind you... the physical proof of how much money you can make by lying just as hard and fast as you can.

As I sat there pondering my options, Vindi poked her head through the door. I'm not sure how I could tell, but I think she was trying to be sneaky.

"Saraya!" she hissed.

"Vindi," I said wryly. "Do you really need to whisper? Your father's up on the third floor blowing stuff up in his laboratory, and you're too lucky to get caught anyway."

"Which means that I have it worse than you."

"*This* I have to hear."

Vindi came in and sat on my bed. "What's life without risk? What's the fun in sneaking around if you know you can't be caught? I *wish* my life were as packed with incident as yours."

"You can have it."

"I can have your life?" Vindi said sweetly. "Wow, thanks! No fighting back, now. I haven't stabbed anyone in *ages* and I'm all out of practice."

"I love you, too," I said wryly, "but no way do you have it worse than me. What's life without risk? If I sneak around, I WILL be caught. Absolute guarantee. No risk at all. I might as well stomp around beating drums with both hands while shouting 'I'M BREAKING THE RULES!!!'"

"It doesn't *always* work that way," Vindi said, smiling. "Remember those two months we spent at boarding school, before we got expelled?"

"Technically, *I* got expelled. You were graduated eight years early *and declared a living god* on account of a clerical error."

"Good times," Vindi said nostalgically. "The point is, while we were there, I got caught *constantly*." She paused. "It's not my fault they kept accidentally writing *your* name on the punishment orders."

I shook my head ruefully. "So you say. I'd still like to know exactly what you told them... but... that's neither here nor there. What do you want?"

Vindi looked embarrassed. "It's stupid, I know, but I wanted to go back to the Grand Emporium and look at the space where our shop is going to be. Imagine... in just a little while, we're going to be shopkeepers! You and me! We're real adults now, with jobs and everything!"

"That's assuming that Sabah will come around."

Vindi shrugged. "Why wouldn't she? People are nice. Things work out. And if we don't get to put our shop there, it'll be somewhere else. I'm going to go and take another look. Want to come?"

I glanced at my bed, which was lurking in the corner

pretending to be all soft and innocent. "I suppose you could hire me to come with," I said, "for a really-quite-reasonable-if-you-think-about-it fee."

Vindi smirked. "Fine. I'll just go without you, then," she said, though she didn't budge. She stood there, lantern-light glinting from her horns and eyes, waiting.

"This isn't a game, Vindi," I said patiently. "I know I've tried to explain this to you before, but it's dangerous out there at night. Your luck isn't what it used to be. There are muggers hiding in the alleys. Murderers. Clowns. All sorts of things."

She shrugged. "I'm going. Which means that whatever happens to me will be *all your fault* since you had a choice, and cruelly forced me to go alone."

My shoulders slumped. "Fine. I'll come with, if only so I can have a plaque inscribed 'I TOLD YOU SO!' nailed to my chest at our funeral." I picked up my favorite (well, *only*) walking-stick, one that was capped with the snarling bronze head of a jackal. "I guess you're right. People are nice. Even muggers amuse me when they're running away with jackal-shaped bruises all up and down their collective asses."

"That's the spirit!"

It wasn't nearly so dark once we got outside. The sky was clear and the moon and stars were out. Luminous spiders hung in the bushes, and lantern-light poured from the windows of most houses. Also, Vindi had a cheap brass necklace that she claimed was one of her father's failed experiments.

"It glows with a nice, even light! Well, I mean, it isn't *now*, obviously, but it *could*. In theory. Though sometimes it just bursts into flames for no reason."

"Uh... sure. Whatever you say."

Vindi and I headed toward the looming black mass of the Grand Emporium, visible even at this distance. Vindi more or less skipped and danced her way down the road, humming and daydreaming, tossing her lantern from hand to hand with each step. I clutched my jackal-headed walking stick, eyes sweeping the blackness in search of threats.

It wasn't long before we reached the base of the Grand Emporium. There was Sabah's shop, boarded up and shackled with rusty chains and a bucket-shaped lock. There was the spiral staircase, and the dark dusty crevice beneath it.

"Looks the same as it did this afternoon," I said.

"But now it's *dark* out!" Vindi said, gently punching my arm. "Everything is new, everything is different! There has to be *some* romance in your soul. Look again at the place our shop will be. Tell me what you feel in your heart."

"Seriously? I feel an infectious new rhythm, forcing me to dance to the pulse of the night."

"Yay!"

"Literally. Thanks to an undiagnosed infection, I feel a mad whir of heartbeats that'll dance me around like a broken puppet until I die, alone and unloved, under the unblinking eyes of the mocking stars."

"Shows what *you* know," Vindi said, satisfied. "You think you're being all morbid and off-putting, but let me tell you something: Nothing, and I mean *nothing*, is more romantic than dying well. You're about to dance yourself to death in a frenzy of uncontrollable passion. I envy you, I really do."

"Dying well appeals to you, does it?" I asked, fishing around in my pocket. "How much would you pay me to strangle you while I recite love poems?"

"You're hopeless," Vindi said affectionately. "Tell you what. Now that we've done what we came for, anything else you want to do, I'm in. Oh! I know! We could go for a swim in the river!"

"Pass. I still haven't found my clothes from the last six times."

"We've got to do *something*. We came all this way!"

I found my eyes drawn to the soaring bulk of the Grand Emporium, which from this angle seemed to blot out half the sky.

"Well..." I hesitated. "There's this thing about scary high places. They tend to have ants."

"I like ants," Vindi said. "They always bring up such *interesting* things when they're making an anthill over a buried cache of ancient secrets just waiting for me to discover it. But do go on."

"When I'm high up, and I trip—because you *know* I'm going to trip—and I start to fall, screaming, over the edge, and I just barely catch myself... well, that's when the ants start walking over my fingers, tickling me until I can't stop laughing and screaming and screaming and laughing and slipping and screaming and—"

"You're immortal," Vindi said suddenly.

"Excuse me?"

"Dying wouldn't be bad luck, not if it freed you from an

unrelenting cavalcade of fresh new horrors. If your luck really is perfectly bad, you can't ever die. You're immortal!"

"Please don't test that," I begged her. *"Please."*

"It was just a thought."

"But *now*," I hurriedly said, gesturing at her new earrings, "with two-thirds of my luck back, or three-quarters or whatever, I'd be willing to go all the way to the top of the Grand Emporium. I mean, seeing Kairay from that high up? That would be something new."

"For me, too," Vindi said thoughtfully. "Huh. You know what? You're on. Let's go!"

We started by climbing the spiral staircase next to Sabah's shop. Half of it was fully exposed to the air, which made half of our trip simultaneously terrifying and exhilarating. I stayed as close to the center as I could. Then, about halfway up, the stairs just… stopped. Ran right into a flat stone ceiling and ended. By the light of Vindi's lantern we wound our way through that maze-like warren, working our way up and down and around and back until we found another spiral staircase and finally emerged on the very top of the Emporium.

"Wow," Vindi said quietly.

The view from the top was something special. I chose a place sort of near the edge and sat down. Vindi made a point of sitting a full pace closer to the dropoff than me: She looked extremely uncomfortable, then furtively scooched back until we were even.

The city of Kairay spread out below us. Houselights sparkled like a skein of tiny bright gems strewn across the night. The river was a winding ribbon of reflected starlight within the deeper black of the forest. Stars shone above us, and a teasing wind added just the slightest spice of worry that it might pick me up and send me plummeting to my spinning death. The moon looked much closer than normal. I don't know. Maybe it was. I stared at it and imagined I could see bizarre and senseless fairytale palaces.

"I wonder what would happen if you jumped over the edge holding a bedsheet by the corners?" Vindi mused.

"Depends. If *I* did it, I'd jump too high, get my head stuck in the moon, and humiliatingly lose my clothes and dangle there naked for a full three weeks before plummeting to my shameful death. On the other hand, if *you* did it, I sincerely hope a handsome prince happened to be passing by so as to break your fall when you landed on him and squashed him flat."

Vindi snickered. "Why a handsome prince? I'd be a lot more

likely to survive if I landed on a profoundly fat pillow merchant who happened to be hauling sacks of his merchandise and wearing the world's puffiest shirt."

"I like my stories to be happy," I explained. "If someone's going to get squashed, let it be someone who deserves it. In stories, princes are always going around demanding to marry girls after seeing them just once. Talk about superficial! And creepy."

"Creepy?"

"Image the exact same story, but with a veiny old man in the starring role. Doesn't seem so romantic now, does it?"

Vindi put her hand to her heart. "I promise, the next time I plummet to my death from atop a mysterious wizardly artifact more than forty stories high, to scream 'I'M A BEAUTIFUL SEXY MYSTERIOUS WOMAN DEEP IN ENCHANTED SLEEP WHO CAN'T CONSENT TO WHATEVER YOU CHOOSE TO DO TO ME!' Whoever comes running, I'll land on *them*."

"You're too good to me," I said, amused.

"I know."

We stayed there, talking as the stars wheeled by, eventually lapsing into a companionable silence. When Vindi's lantern ran low, we reluctantly made our way back down. We got lost immediately, of course, and the weird, twisting, winding path we took was completely different from the way we'd gone up. We finally—finally!—reached the ground, descending a sweeping, curved staircase on the opposite side from where we'd started. I was surprised to see dozens of people waiting for us, carrying so many lanterns that it hurt my eyes just trying to look at them. It didn't make any sense. Burning enough oil to provide *that* much light would be crazy expensive. Literally. You'd have to be hooting, growling, bonking-your-own-head-with-a-gourd insane to spend that much on oil.

"As I have said, so must it be," intoned a tall, gaunt man with an enormous white mustache. He stepped forward, gesturing to the two of us. "I told you they would be here, and here they are."

"Who the hell are you?" I demanded.

"Mind your manners, child."

My eyes narrowed. "Tell us who you are and why you're here, and as an extra-special reward, I'll let you choose which orifice I impale with my walking stick. Here's a hint: *Choose your nose. Every alternative is worse.*"

"Technically, you said he could choose *any* orifice," Vindi noted. "What if he chose one of *yours*? Attack him if you want, sure, but I think you'd be honor-bound to aim for your own butt."

"Thank you *so much* for your contribution," I snapped.

The tall man gazed at me, unimpressed. "I am Darshik, wizard. I know, at a close approximation, everything. All knowledge in the universe belongs to him who understands the secret language of Eternity and the sly deceptions of Forever. I am that man. I know you as you don't even know yourselves. I know your transgressions. I know your sins. I know your passions, your regrets, and your secret shames."

"My father says—" Vindi paused. "—that he knows the great wizard Avashti, who says you created a book of prophecies by accident and have been coasting on it ever since. He says you haven't *done* anything for thirty years. He says a flatulent frog would be as much of a wizard as you are now."

Darshik scowled. "If you require a demonstration—"

"Oh, do be quiet, Darshik," a woman said, not unkindly. "You're scaring them."

My eyes were starting to get used to all that light. I now saw that the animals around us weren't donkeys, but something I'd never seen before... real, actual horses. Horses are too rare and expensive for even the wealthiest merchants, and here were *dozens* of them. They were weird-looking creatures, with stupid elongated faces and big bulging eyes. Their harnesses bore a circular seal depicting an elegant wading bird—the insignia of the royal family. In the lead chariot stood the woman who'd spoken, plain and cheerful-looking and simply dressed. Seated next to her, a lovely young woman gazed at us with uncomfortable directness. Her clothes were encrusted with pearls, gems, crystal rims, and animal figurines of solid gold. At a casual guess, her clothes were worth more than the Grand Emporium... and the lives of everyone who worked there.

"Come here," the lovely young woman said, making a face as if speaking to us was something distasteful. I looked at Vindi. Vindi looked at me. Slowly, reluctantly, we obeyed. "I am Princess Gamal," she said coolly. "My husband is the second child of Her Lordship, the most esteemed Shavala II, making him second in line to the throne of Kairay."

"And I am Princess Shivaka," the other woman said, a hint of merriment in her eyes, "the *eldest* child of Her Lordship, which... let me see, math can be so confusing... would make me *first* in line, wouldn't it?"

Princess Gamal gazed expressionlessly at her. "Pray do wear warmer clothes when you go out at night," she said softly. "What a tragedy it would be if you took sick and died."

"You poor girls. You're probably scared to death," Princess Shivaka said warmly. "Well, let me set your minds at ease. We're not going to arrest you, imprison you, or call for your heads. There's absolutely nothing you can do or say that would endanger your fate or that of anyone you love. Relax."

"Should we be so quick to relinquish the protections of polite society?" Princess Gamal wondered. "Is it really a kindness, letting them misbehave without consequence? How are they to *learn*?"

"One of us is my mother's heir," Princess Shivaka said merrily, "and one of us is not. I'll let them decide for themselves whose word they will heed." She glanced at the wizard. "Thank you, Darshik. You may go."

The gaunt wizard faced Princess Shivaka, unimpressed. "And my payment?" he asked. "You will declare the Crescent Way to be cursed, give the Annubial your blessing, and fund a new amphitheater where the Estin meets the Kairay?"

"You may go, Darshik."

He gazed at her for a moment longer, bowed, and walked away. Princess Shivaka got out of the chariot and sat down on the ground, beckoning the two of us to come join her. Princess Gamal stayed where she was, holding a colorful silk cloth to her nose. I looked at Vindi. Vindi looked at me. Slowly, cautiously, we edged closer. As soon as we reasonably could, we sat down across from Princess Shivaka.

"Do you want more bowing and scraping, or can we cut the crap and get down to business?" I demanded.

"Saraya!" Vindi said, shocked. "They're *royalty*!"

"So what? Being all polite and submissive never helped me any. When the powers-that-be decide to hurt me, no amount of groveling and scraping is going to stop them. It'll just make me feel worse about myself when I die." I stared defiantly at Princess Shivaka. "So how about it? What could you possibly want from the likes of us? What's so important that you had to rouse an ostensible wizard out of bed to find us?"

"Oh, I like her!" Shivaka said, clapping her hands together.

"So do I," Princess Gamal admitted. "It's so much more

satisfying to order the torture of one who's richly and thoroughly *earned* it. Tell me more about how great you are, child."

Vindi's nostrils flared. "I don't care how big you think you are. Leave Saraya alone."

I glanced at her, puzzled. "Uh… you want to maybe let me fight my own battles? You have a lot more to lose if things go wrong."

"*I* have more to lose? Really?" Vindi gave me a lopsided smile. "Saraya, the fact that I always win… it means that I'm free. Free to be my deepest, truest self, because *there aren't any consequences to anything I do*. At least, that's how it used to be. Now? Well, maybe I do have something to lose. But I don't think I'd like myself very much if I clung to my personal safety instead of standing by you."

"So you're just as brave as I am? I'm not special at all? Not different, not unique, not better-than?" I shook my head. "Congratulations, life, on figuring out yet another way to kick me in the balls I don't even have."

"Very touching," Princess Gamal said impatiently, still holding that colorful silk cloth to her nose. "Can we get on with it? I never knew there could be such *smells* in the world."

"I think they're fascinating," Princess Shivaka said.

"The smells?"

"The girls," Shivaka clarified. "Vindi, Saraya… when I promised you safety—I meant it. Speak freely in my presence. Always."

"Fine. What the hell do you want with the likes of us?" I said bluntly.

"I'll get to the point," Princess Shivaka said. "I have all the people I'll ever need to tell me how wonderful I am, or sell me bejeweled trinkets, or prance around for my amusement…"

"Which, should they fail to prance *high* enough, calls for the judicious application of heated spikes," Gamal said helpfully.

"What?"

"Wishful thinking."

Princess Shivaka gave her head a little shake. "What I *don't* have are some good junkmen… people inventive enough to solve problems in a cleverer, more roundabout way than would occur to a dedicated craftsman. Well. I *had* junkmen, but they retired. I would like you to take their place."

"You're lying," I said flatly.

Gamal gazed at me through hooded eyes. "Just a reminder. Speaking thus, in public, in front of me, rates a death sentence."

"I will protect them," Shivaka said carelessly.

"Yes. For now. But accidents happen. People die. Will you still be here in a year? Death warrants don't expire. Essentially, they're flipping a coin to decide whether their heads will stay on their shoulders or not. Do you really want to offend me, girl?" she asked, toying with the gilded table knife at her belt.

"But Shivaka *is* lying," I protested.

"So what? It's the accusation that matters, and the fact that you had the temerity to say it to her face. Truth is irrelevant."

"Fine," I said, disgruntled. "You don't want me saying it to her face? I'll wait until she turns around and say it to her ass." I cupped my hands to my mouth: "YOU'RE LYING!"

"Please explain," Princess Shivaka said calmly.

"You say you want junkmen. You could have hired anyone in the city, anyone at all... and yet you ask two girls so callow, so inexperienced, they don't even have a shop yet? Why us? Why now? Why would you use a wizard to find us, and how did you even hear about us in the first place?"

Princess Shivaka smiled disarmingly. "I know you'll think I'm silly, but I didn't ask Darshik only to find me some new junkmen. I asked him to find someone... well, someone I'd *like*. Someone, were they of my own social class, I could call a friend. He found you."

"Senseless," Princess Gamal muttered. "Half the money I spend when I buy something is expressly to make the seller go away, afterward. It's called the social contract, and it rescues us from having to socialize with our inferiors."

I shook my head. "It's a trap. It has to be. Of course, I've immediately stepped on every mousetrap I've ever set, so maybe I should jump up and down on *this* one so it'll go off as quickly as possible..."

"Will you come back to the palace with me?" Shivaka pleaded. "I have a special contract ready and waiting. All you have to do is sign it, and you'll find yourself richly paid indeed—just to be on retainer! Any actual jobs will pay even more."

Vindi looked at me. I looked at Vindi.

"I... think I want to prove that I can make my own life, forge my own career, *without* help from above," Vindi said, sounding surprised at herself.

"Me, I'd rather stay away from people who could have my head off at a whim—" I glanced at Gamal. "—especially those who've stated their intention to do so at the earliest possible opportunity."

"I understand," Princess Shivaka said, standing up. "I can wait, for a time. If you change your mind…"

She pulled a medallion from her pocket, one bearing the same graceful wading bird that adorned her chariot. She handed it to Vindi. "Know that you can come to me for any reason, at any time. Show that to the guards and you'll be brought straight inside."

"You're giving them a *real* one?" Princess Gamal asked, her brow furrowing. "I don't know why I even bothered ordering all those joke medallions that mean—'execute immediately'. Sometimes, you aren't any fun at all."

Princess Shivaka waved merrily, stepping onto the lead chariot. The horses, obeying some impulse I couldn't see… to get away from Gamal, maybe?… broke into a thundering run. With a great deal of noise and clatter, the whole procession swirled around us in a minor cataclysm of thunder and dust and was gone.

"That was… different," I mused.

"I wonder how many handsome princes they have back at the palace?" Vindi said speculatively.

"Bah. Who cares? Pay a blacksmith to eat roses until he pukes and he'll literally explode with beauty. It's exactly the same thing as a Handsome Prince, plus, you're saved the trouble of having to marry it."

Vindi looked amused. "How much would I have to pay *you* to eat roses until you barfed?"

"Less than you think, but more than you have."

"That's fair," Vindi said thoughtfully. As we walked away from the Grand Emporium, I playfully snatched her brass necklace. Vindi tried to grab it back, but tripped and came up short.

"Ha!" I cried, settling it around my own neck. "It looks like luck is favoring *me* for once!"

And that, of course—with a predictability bordering on the inevitable—was the exact moment the necklace chose to burst into flames.

II

At the breakfast table the next morning, Vindi looked like she was going to explode. She was vibrating slightly and kept making strange little noises, as if she was privately convinced that Princess Shivaka might pop up out of the ground and demand her friendship at any moment. If the clouds had parted and a gigantic disembodied hand reached down from the heavens to give her an 'all-righty' sign the size of a mountain, I think she would have nodded politely and gone right on daydreaming about princesses.

"They're not coming back," I said flatly. "The only reason something so extraordinary would happen to me is so my disappointment would be twice as bad. Rejection doesn't cut half so deep unless you have hope."

"You got off easy. Take it from me," Avashti told his daughter. "There's no such thing as a good princess. Their whole lives, they've been given absolutely everything and told they deserved it. It wouldn't even occur to them that commoners are anything but possessions or playthings. She pretended to be nice, for now, because doing so serves *her*. Just wait until she wants something!"

"You're both wrong," Vindi said. "A good person born in the wrong place is still a good person. Princess Shivaka genuinely enjoys making people happy—I can feel it. I'll bet she sends Handsome Princes on impossible quests all the time, spraying them in every conceivable direction so they can fall in love-at-first-sight with commoners like me!"

"Can you tell when she's joking?" I asked Avashti.

"Princess Shivaka might come back," Vindi said stubbornly. "You don't know. There might be a Handsome Prince who's destined to fall in love-at-first-sight with me. It could happen. If there's one true thing about the world, it's that things never stop happening. They could be good things. You don't know."

"They could also be bad things," I argued. "For example, your prince's eyes might fall out."

"Even better! Now I know he loves me for me."

"What are you talking about? How could he love you when he doesn't even know you? He only ever saw what you look like!"

"He saw me knitting a sock which expressed the true goodness of my innermost soul," Vindi decided.

"But I'd trip on his rolling, gooey eyes (remember them?), and flail around for balance, only I happened to be holding a scythe for some reason, and—completely by accident—cut both his feet off. Now he finds socks to be a cruel reminder of the life he once had, and hates anyone who makes them."

"True," Vindi said, "but—since he already promised to marry me—I extract fifty caskets of gold in exchange for letting him out of his promise. I retire happy and rich."

"Huh." I glanced at Vindi. "Can I come over for dinner?"

"Whenever you want," she said generously. "You can stand outside the window and watch me eat."

"Girls!" Avashti roared. "Stop being whimsical. Learn from my example. Be straightforward and pragmatic."

"By the way," I said blandly, "have you finished that machine that draws down lightning to strike yams as a way of ensuring they'll never turn evil?"

"One, a new way of cooking yams is greatly to be desired. Two, any effect on vegetable morality is more a desirable side-effect than the point of the machine. Three, when it comes to machines designed to incinerate yams with the glory and might of nature itself..." He hesitated. "You'll have to be more specific. I have my fingers in a lot of pies right now."

"Right. We'll be straightforward and practical, like you. Grounded. Whatever you say."

"See?" Avashti said. "Was that so hard?"

The wizard excused himself and went up to the third floor to work on... whatever it is he works on up there. Weird banging and clattering noises echoed down from above, along with the occasional round of impassioned cursing. Vindi continued gazing pensively out the window for what seemed like hours. I couldn't get her to go anywhere or do anything. I finally got her to admit *why*—the moment she went to the privy might, in theory, be the moment the princesses came back.

"*Please* go," I pleaded. "Holding it in this long can't be healthy.”

"I'm fine.”

“See, if *I* waited this long, they *would* show up… at the exact moment I couldn't hold it any longer and ran in circles around them experiencing a sort of speechless personal explosion.”

“Don't you dare,” Vindi breathed.

“Aw, hell. They'd understand. Shivaka would, anyway. We all look the same with our trousers down.”

“I'm not sure that's true. In a just world, Princesses would be far too refined to do… that. They'd sublimate their wastes through the skin in a sort of glorious golden glow.”

“Huh,” I said, rubbing my chin. “I wonder what would happen if you held a match to it?”

Vindi rolled her eyes. “Fine! I'll go. But if they show up, you have to stall them with something really distracting. Sing and dance, cut off your own head, whatever works.”

“That's an easy decision,” I said, amused. I draped the Anteyvan strangling cord around my neck. “What sort of facial expression do you think I should use—eyes popped and tongue lolling out, or a frozen rictus of horror? Aw, you like it,” I said as Vindi make an involuntary 'yuck'-face. “At least my *demise* will be stylish!” I frowned. “Right up until someone sneezes and drops my head in a bowl of soup. I may have to think about this.”

By the time Vindi came back, she'd had a terrifying thought: The only place the princesses had ever seen us was the Grand Emporium. What if they were looking for us there, right now? So we speed-walked across Kairay as clouds swirled and thunder rumbled. I was still wearing Vindi's quasi-silver bracelet on my left wrist, which was practically daring to the clouds to hit me with lightning. At first, I tried to hide it by sticking my hand behind my back, until I realized that—far from preventing a lightning strike—I was only giving it a more convenient path to my butt. I held my arm awkwardly out to the side instead. Vindi gave me an odd look but said nothing.

“I suppose you'll want to stop here for a while?” I asked as we passed near the river. Huge fluffy seeds filled the sky, and dozens of birds with incredibly long, red-and-teal plumes for tails weaved magnificent multicolored circles through the air, snatching the finest, fattest fluff for nesting material.

“Can't stop,” she said tersely. “Can't keep the princesses waiting.”

I frowned. Vindi's habit of stopping to gaze moon-eyed at moments of heart-rending beauty can be really annoying, but at least I'd gotten used to it. Seeing her walk right past Wonderment Incarnate was jarring—like trying to climb a step that wasn't there. Or that time Avashti finally removed the boulder I always stumbled on when I went to the privy at night. The next time I went, I tripped twice as hard, over-correcting for the now-missing barrier my feet expected to find, and went flying—face-first—into the privy. But maybe that's a story for another time.

"You *sure* you don't want to watch?" I asked. "Looks like the Leaf Riders are upset about something. Wanna bet on whether they mount their butterfly steeds and go joust against the birds?"

"Later," Vindi said tersely, not even looking back.

It wasn't long before we reached the Market. We slipped past the stalls of the outer merchants and swiftly approached the looming wall of the Grand Emporium itself.

"Ah!" Sabah the Jeweler said, spotting us. "I thought you'd be back. My answer is still—"

"Have you seen any Princesses?" Vindi demanded.

"Oh, certainly," Sabah said without batting an eyelash. "Dozens of them. They said you look terrible and should buy lots of jewelry from me right now. Also, they said you shouldn't haggle, but pay whatever I want. They'll reimburse you later. No, really!"

"I guess we might as well stay here," Vindi mused. "If they show up on the other side of the Grand Emporium, we'll hear the commotion—right?"

"Either that, or Ebo got his beard stuck in the potter's wheel again."

"No, we'd be able to tell. You know, from all the high-pitched screaming? We want to be listening for the rumble of chariots and horses."

"Horses?" Sabah asked skeptically. "So your Princesses ride mythical monsters, do they? Couldn't you at least choose something *plausible*, like sphinxes?"

Vindi and I sat on the lowest step of the spiral staircase and just waited. When it became clear that we weren't going anywhere, Sabah suggested that we assist her—as a way of "evaluating our sales techniques", she said. Uh-huh. I'm sure it didn't have anything to do with exploiting a ready source of free labor. The thing is, Vindi was far too preoccupied to help out. I sighed. I've never been good at selling stuff, but then, debasing myself for the people I love isn't exactly an unplowed field. Taking a deep breath, I started calling out pitches to passers-by… praising Sabah's jewelry, as well as the cleverness and virility of anyone smart enough to be seen wearing it. People walked past, ignoring me. My eyes narrowed. Without any conscious thought on my part, my tone shifted.

Sabah the Jeweler winced. "Saraya… would you *please* stop screaming insults at my customers?"

"It's getting their attention," I pointed out.

"A little too well. I like my customers one at a time, not in angry, torch-wielding mobs."

"Come on," Vindi said. "We'll go around to the other side."

And so we did, whiling away the long day by climbing around the abandoned middle level of the Grand Emporium. Vindi also asked a number of merchants whether they'd seen any princesses. This elicited a number of odd looks, as well as any number of sales pitches. Interesting, how everyone we talked to *just happened* to discover princess-attracting properties in all the stuff they usually couldn't sell, and at ten times the price.

It was getting dark by the time Vindi and I returned home. According to the neighbors, no one had been looking for us there, either. Vindi looked disappointed, but didn't say anything.

The second day went about the same as the first. The third went about the same as the second. I sometimes saw Vindi gazing at Princess Shivaka's medallion, but it always disappeared into her pocket the moment she noticed me looking at her. After the first quarter-month, Vindi finally started getting back to her old self. We traveled here and there around Kairay and had some minor adventures. We made grandiose plans for the things we'd do once the floods were past and we finally opened our shop. We figured out complicated new ways to make the detritus of Avashti's failed wizardry burst into flames, which made him shake his head in mock disappointment even as he brought us more.

The second quarter-month brought drenching rains, which meant indoor festivals with feasting and dancing and all manner of distractions. Given her reputation, Vindi had no end of young men begging to be her dance partner. Given my reputation, I had an open and undisturbed path to the buffet. Mostly, I sat next to Avashti and watched young men dance with Vindi, and loudly critiqued their performances. Avashti never laughs out loud, but his beard creased and his eyes crinkled until they almost disappeared. Even Vindi had to bite her cheek to keep from laughing at some of her would-be suitors.

The third quarter-month brought deep and widespread flooding, which occasioned citywide celebration and holiday-making since it was impossible to do any work. Vindi invited me to come swim in the Kairay, which had drastically overflowed its banks and was now more or less everywhere. I think she wanted to get a look at my rabbit-shaped scar, but I wore so many clothes that I spent the whole time gasping for breath and struggling not to sink. Showed her. When I got out and went to fetch the stuff I'd left on shore, I found that the quasi-silver bracelet had been struck by lightning no fewer than three times. Some people might consider it a stroke of luck that I hadn't been wearing it at the time. I consider it a warning, the aggressive act of a cocky and overconfident sky demonstrating what it *could* do to me at any moment.

"OH, YEAH?!" I shouted, shaking my fist at the sky. Vindi covered her mouth, struggling not to laugh. "WELL, UP YOURS, CLOUD!!"

The fourth quarter-month brought new growth and flowers, which meant all manner of outdoor festivals, music, and even more dancing. One of Vindi's partners, remembering what had happened the first time, muffled his ears under a bedsheet wound so tight that he couldn't hear my critiques. That one, I thought approvingly, showed promise.

A few days after the last festival was finished, we finally had a morning dawn clear and dry. Avashti had already set out our breakfast by the time I reached the table, though it would be a while before we were permitted to eat. Vindi always has to arrange everything just *so*, moving around the components of our meal to form artistic, beautiful images that—she claims—will effervesce into a harmonious radiance of pure joy in our stomachs. Which I like to use as an excuse to belch in her face—"but it was a *happy* burp!"—in order to give back some of the joy and love she's given me. To my vast irritation, she just smiles serenely and takes me at my word.

"And… done!" Vindi cried, adjusting a curved slice of pear. "Now it's smiling!" She hesitated. "Which would make eating it tantamount to devouring joy itself out of the world. Uh-oh."

"What would it be like, getting to eat something without having to compose a damn poem about it, first?" I muttered.

Avashti shrugged. "My meals used to go much faster. No one took any time at all trying to make me happy." He smiled. "That someone cares about me so deeply… well, perhaps it can be annoying on occasion, but would I want to change it?"

I glanced covertly at Avashti. "*I* do things for you, too, you know. Just last year, I whittled you a pipe."

"And I intend to take up smoking any day now, as a means of thanking you."

"You can't. I made it with a sealed-off bowl so you couldn't actually use it. Smoking is disgusting. But if it's the thought that counts, I'm a hero."

"Hooray for Saraya!" Vindi cried.

"Was that sarcastic or genuine?" I asked suspiciously, but Vindi just smiled.

We'd just about finished breakfast when a curious but somewhat-familiar sound echoed up from outside the window. Along with the shouts of startled passers-by and the rumble of chariots came the peculiar whinnies of horses.

"They came back!" Vindi cried, almost flying to the window. "Oh. Well, one of them did."

I joined her at the window. A minor carnival of chariots and horses was just pulling up outside, all bearing the insignia of the royal egret. Princess Gamal sat in the lead chariot, cold and beautiful and perfect. I didn't see Princess Shivaka. Vindi ran down the stairs to see what was going on; Avashti and I hurried to follow.

Today, Princess Gamal was adorned in enough feathers and gold to look like a bird that had died in a freak smelting accident. She sniffed, trying not to look at anything, apparently displeased to be surrounded by such mundanity. Behind her stood the wizard Darshik, his vast white mustache as impressive as ever. The three of us stopped just outside the tower door, unsure what we were supposed to do.

"I am Princess Gamal," Gamal announced, "a humble servant of Her Lordship, the most esteemed Shavala II. I have come here at her behest. I would speak to Her Lordship's loyal servant, the royal wizard Avashti."

Avashti hesitantly stepped forward. "Begging your pardon, but I resigned that position years ago."

"Plus, he isn't actually a wizard," Darshik said nastily. "What are those *things* behind you? Are those *children*?"

"Experimenting on smaller people is more efficient!" Avashti snapped.

"Of course it is. *I* believe you."

"Trip ass-backward into any books of prophecy lately?" Avashti sneered. "Oh, wait, of course not—making one would require *doing* something, which is quite contrary to your unvarying policy of staring skyward like a helpless toad under a descending boot."

Darshik scowled. "I don't need a wizard who *resigned in disgrace* telling me what to do."

"Ah! You admit I'm a wizard!"

"I do not!"

"Yet I agree with you in one thing," Avashti said. "You don't need me telling you what to do. Since my advice would be coming from an actual wizard, there's no chance you'd *understand* it."

"That's it!" Darshik cried, digging around in one of his robe's pockets. He pulled out a painted wooden wand with a curious resemblance to a bloody pickle. Avashti hurriedly grabbed a wand of braided metal from his own pocket. They pointed their respective weapons at each other. There was a dramatic pause. Belatedly, a tiny curl of smoke rose from the tip of Avashti's wand.

"Seriously?" Darshik asked. "That's almost more embarrassing than an experiment that didn't work at all."

"Opinions differ," Avashti said. "For example, there's you, and then there are those of us who are *right*."

Princess Gamal had been staring straight ahead, as if hoping she could make every objectionable thing in the universe go away if she just ignored it long enough, but she finally seemed to tire of waiting.

"You, Avashti. You say you resigned?"

"That's right," he said guardedly.

"You can't," Gamal said crisply. "You serve at Her Lordship's pleasure, now and forever. Her pleasure is that you obey her commands. And so you most certainly shall."

"Not that I'd refuse… but… just out of curiosity…?"

Princess Gamal sighed, looking slightly bored. "We, all of us, live to serve Her Lordship. Those who do *not* serve Her Lordship, therefore, have chosen not to be alive. The swords of Her Lordship's soldiers would be swift and unerring if they were forced to demonstrate to a traitor the consequences of his actions."

"I see," Avashti said unhappily. "And what does Her Lordship require of me?"

Princess Gamal glanced sidelong at him. "Nothing much. You

must simply retrieve one item from the Cave of Wonders."

Avashti blanched. "I can't go there! No one can! It would be death to try!"

"There's a reason she didn't ask someone *valuable* to go," Darshik needled him.

Princess Gamal's eyes narrowed. "You've had time enough to consider your options. The chariot behind me. Get on. Or are you refusing to serve?"

Soldiers stepped toward Avashti, hands moving to their swords. Sweating and unsure of himself, the wizard took half a step back.

"I wouldn't be any use to you," he said desperately. "I wouldn't even be able to stand, much less go hunting for treasures. Due to a magical accident, I'm literally allergic to authority."

"Not this again," Darshik said derisively. "You've had a dozen years to come up with a better excuse, and you're still clinging to *that* one? Just how stupid do you think we are? More to the point, how stupid are *you*?"

"Take him," Gamal said, sounding bored. A pair of soldiers grabbed Avashti, who immediately started to sneeze. Darshik smirked and applauded Avashti's performance. The soldiers dragged him to a chariot and threw him on as he started to cough, his face turning red from the exertion. Gamal raised her arm, and the whole procession thundered off in a cloud of dust. In moments, we were alone.

"They're going to kill him," Vindi said, quiet and pale. "They're going to kill my father."

"We have to do something," I said, hands twisting together. "But what?"

"We can... we can..." Vindi suddenly looked up, her face alight with a wild look of hope. "We can *ask for help*!" She pulled Princess Shivaka's medallion from under her shirt. "We tell Shivaka everything that happened. We put ourselves at her mercy. We beg for her to intervene with her mother."

"Huh," I said. "You know, that actually might work? Tell you what. We'll split up and I'll go in first. That way, after Princess Shivaka gets done laughing at me and instructing her guards to kick me in the butt *extra* hard, it'll be even more ironic and gut-wrenching when she instantly agrees to help *you*. The universe eats that kind of crap up."

"No," Vindi said, putting her hand on my arm. "We go in

together, and we ask for help together.”

“Damn it, Vindi, I’m trying to do the right thing! You know that nothing ever goes right for me.”

She smiled serenely. “I’m a glowing perfect being of luminous beauty and endless grace. Say it. Say it and I’ll let you do things your way.”

“Fine. You’re a—” I took a deep breath. “You’re a perfect luminous grass-eating beauty, or whatever the hell you just said. Are we good?”

“Nope!” Vindi grinned. “I lied. We’re in this together, whether you like it or not. Let’s go!”

“Not so fast. We need to get ready.”

Vindi stared at me. “Get *ready*? For what? My father’s dying —we don’t have *time*!”

I looked Vindi up and down. “Yeah, I’m kind of thinking it might help if we didn’t appear before a royal princess all filthy and stinking.”

“Oh!” Vindi said, startled. “I see what you mean. On me, it would be a bold new fashion statement, but on you, well, you may have a point. Let’s go.”

Glowering at Vindi, I led her back to the tower house.

* * *

Crossing Kairay takes a lot longer if you try to follow the extravagantly winding river. We didn’t bother with that. We went straight west, crossing back and forth between sun-blasted desert and shade-dappled understory a dozen times or more.

“Ow,” I said, pausing as we left the desert one last time.

“What is it *this* time?”

“I got sand in my eye. Which, admittedly, in the desert, isn’t the biggest shock of all time. *Not* getting sand in my eye would be the bigger surprise.”

“I got sand in my eye, once,” Vindi reminisced. “Well, I *thought* it was sand. They turned out to be seeds… which sprouted, drinking water from my eyes as they grew, and bloomed, and wreathed my head in beflowered beauty. Long story short, I wandered into a masquerade party and won the grand prize by accident. Still, let’s not lose track of what’s important. Sand is nothing. Think of how bad it would be if you got a *monkey* stuck in your eye! Life is good.”

“A *monkey*?” I demanded.

“You know, those ugly little people-shaped buggers that stand

36

around sticking their fingers in unhygienic places? Monkeys?"

"I know what monkeys are!"

"Then why did you ask?" Vindi asked, the slightest hint of a smile touching her lips. I growled at her, and her smile widened.

It was past midday when we finally reached the west end of the city and the royal palace known informally as the Lair of Lapis. Well, I assumed we'd reached the palace. I've never actually *seen* it. The place is surrounded by hedges that tower over fifty feet high, and I'd never participated in the childhood game of sticking my head through the hedge to try and get a peek. Not with my luck. Do you know what hedges are? They're practically *made* of splinters.

There was a great opening in the middle of the hedge, an arch of sandy stone over thirty feet thick. The number of soldiers marching around in front of it was deeply impressive.

"So much for our plan to sneak in," I said fatalistically.

"What are you talking about?"

"They're carrying swords. Swords have this thing they do. They stab me. Remember that soldier who mistook me for his sister and tried to hug me, forgetting that he had an unsheathed sword in his hand? I think our new plan had better call for a lot of bleeding on my part."

"Oh, stop being so melodramatic. Excuse me!" Vindi called, pulling Princess Shivaka's medallion from around her neck. "I have… well, this."

A guard came over. He looked at the medallion, looked at us in surprise, then looked at the medallion again.

"Wait here," he said, and strode off. He returned with a much older man, whose shirt was encrusted with so many medals I was surprised he didn't topple over from the sheer weight of them. Mustache twitching, he examined the medallion. Finally he looked at us.

"You're not assassins, are you?"

"Congratulations on asking the stupidest question in human history," I snapped. "Yes. Yes, we're assassins. How fortunate for everyone here that you and you alone were keen-eyed and sharp-witted enough to *ask us whether we're criminals*. What do we get for being the first people, ever, in recorded history, to answer in the affirmative? Medals for honesty?"

"You get executed."

"We're not assassins! Really! We're humble supplicants,"

Vindi said, shooting me a sharp look. "*Please* let us in."

I frowned at her. "Why are you acting so deferential?" I asked. "I thought that falling ass-backwards into success after success freed you to be your true inner self."

"Believe it or not, but my true inner self, deep down inside, happens to be polite."

"I have definitive proof to the contrary."

Vindi smirked. "Well. You're a special case. I learned long ago the best way to deal with *you*."

The old soldier harrumphed, holding the medallion up to the light. "It's a good thing you have this. I've been instructed to—"

"Come on. Admit that his medals are tacky," I told Vindi. "I mean, how does he even *have* so many? Kairay hasn't fought that many wars. Kairay hasn't fought that many *battles*. Tell me, sir, do you award yourself a medal for wiping if it's enough of a struggle?"

"Please, sir," Vindi pleaded. The old soldier examined the medallion one last time, as if longing to find an excuse to bung us out —or me, at least.

"Take them to the Dark Passage," he decided.

A squad of soldiers immediately formed a square around us. Vindi and I exchanged worried glances, but there was little we could do but let them herd us through the great stone gate.

The first thing I saw on the other side was a garden of countless terraced levels…

Let me rephrase that. The entire palace grounds, for as far as I could see, *was* a meticulously groomed garden of countless terraced levels. We walked on a road of artfully rippled white sand, marring it with our footprints. Looking back, I saw servants hurrying out with feathers to erase first our, and then their own, tracks.

The next thing I saw, as we rounded one last towering hedge, was the Lair of Lapis itself. It was huge, bristling with towers and domes and soaring spires. I hoped that no one had accidentally trapped a thunderstorm inside one of those domes during construction—they were so vast, the storm would presumably still be there. The palace was incredibly colorful, clad almost entirely in its namesake stone. The walls were a staggering, rich blue broken by streaks of impossible green. Have you ever dreamt about living inside a giant gemstone? Me neither, but I have a feeling that's about to change.

The soldiers passed us into the custody of the palace guard, who took us inside. Everywhere I looked, there was staggering wealth on display: Solid-gold statues, solid-gold armor, solid-gold (and presumably unusable) furniture (gold being soft enough to leave a mark when you bite it, I was seriously curious what my ass would do to one of those chairs). Still, the echoing enormity of the place pulled off the amazing feat of making all that gold look *small*.

"They're doing it wrong," I mused.

Vindi glanced sidelong at me. "What?"

"Leaving all this gold just sitting here. Remember those paintings Avashti helped us make by sticking explosives inside bricks of dye? The experience of *making* them is something we'll treasure forever. But the paintings themselves? They're always there, always the same. They've practically become part of the walls at home. When was the last time you looked at one? When was the last time you really *saw* one?"

"It's been a while," Vindi admitted. "What does that have to do with this?"

"Leaving all this gold just sitting here, they'd stop noticing it after a while. It should be something they explode and melt down and throw at each other. It should be an *experience*."

"Maybe it's not for them," Vindi said dubiously. "Maybe it's for us. A show of wealth, a demonstration of power, meant to terrify and intimidate everyone who comes to them."

"That's even worse," I said, disgusted. "I think we have no choice but to teach Kairay's nobility a lesson by carting all this gold away and leaving a minor mountain of donkey dung in its place."

"Saraya!"

"No, no, I'd be doing them a favor! Because..." I hesitated. "Because it would be something they'd never seen before. Something new and different and amazing. They wouldn't be able to stop playing with it!"

Vindi smirked, though she was unable to keep from glancing at our impassive escort. "Tell you what. You do all the lifting, and I'll keep watch. That's a fair division of labor, right?"

A middle-aged man suddenly stepped in front of us. He was wearing sleeping robes even though it was midday: His clothes were stained, his hair sticking out strangely, his eyes sailing wildly around their sockets. From the deference the soldiers paid him, he must have been someone important.

"Guests?" he said to himself. "We have guests? Why didn't anyone tell me? They could have sent a message." He tried to smile at

Vindi, but the right side of his face didn't seem to work, and it came out weird and kind of sad. "People used to send messages using birds, you know. It seems like an awful lot of trouble. You'd have to catch the bird, tie it up, write a message on it, then have a servant deliver it. Seems like there are two or three extra steps involved. For example, why not use a *speaking* bird? Then you wouldn't have to write your message on it. Then you could... I..."

He seemed to lose his place. Looking baffled, head drooping, he shuffled off and disappeared down a hallway.

"All hail Prince Dakar, husband-consort to Princess Shivaka," a soldier said quietly.

Vindi glanced hesitantly at him. "Has he always been... like *that*?"

"No. Only since that damned fever. It's been three years now." The soldier sighed, shaking his head. "His *body* came back..."

Not long after, our escort finally brought us to a pair of huge wooden doors. They were made of ebony polished to a shine and inscribed with swirling, curliqued lines of gold. Even I had to admit that they looked good—solemn and elegant, even. The soldiers opened the doors for us, indicating that we were to proceed alone. I took a deep breath and strode inside, Vindi following. The doors slammed shut behind us, and both of us stopped and stared at the jungle swamp we'd somehow walked into.

The room was both sunken and flooded, the earthen floor planted densely with vegetation that was like nothing I'd ever seen. There were trees and vines everywhere, soaring all the way to the glass ceiling twenty feet overhead. Some bore clusters of intensely colorful fruit. Some had flowers. Some just *were*. Vines and lianas and epiphytes cloaked everything in about eighteen layers of explosive, exuberant, all-conquering life. Elsewhere, plants—trees?—with the biggest leaves I'd ever seen offered clusters of yellowy-orange, crescent-shaped fruit. Brilliant white flowers cut brightly through the gloom, and plants like stinky vermilion spikes bristled from the swampy ground. A narrow, winding path led us deeper into the room. There, on a domed islet of earth in the center, Princess Shivaka waved merrily at us. Her robes were tied up around her elbows, but they were both dirty and wet from the gardening she'd obviously been doing. Princess Gamal stood behind her, as lovely and cold as ever, a colorful cloth pressed against her face as if to keep out the riotous scent of mud and life that surrounded us. Her gown was made from countless thousands of crystal rims, the pearlescent rings shattering what light touched her into an endless rippling wonderment of rainbows.

"Your highnesses—" I began.

"She's mouthy, this one," Princess Gamal noted. "That could be a problem."

"Oh, leave her alone," Princess Shivaka said.

"Is it wise, though, convincing her that she can say whatever she wants without consequence? She might start flapping that delectable tongue of hers when you aren't around to protect her." Princess Gamal licked her lips, looking right at me. "My last feast, of fat, succulent flamingo tongues, failed to satisfy. I wonder if you might be courageous enough to recommend a new sort of tongue for me to stab out of its owner's mouth?"

"That's enough," Shivaka said crossly.

"Don't blame me if they have to be taught respect at the end of a crossbow quarrel."

"You are safe here," Shivaka told us. "Speak freely in my presence."

"We need help," Vindi said. "Our... friend, the wizard Avashti, at the request of Her Lordship Shavala II, was ordered to enter the Cave of Wonders."

"I see," Shivaka said quietly. "If he's already inside, you know there's nothing we can do. Wizards have been dumping their failed experiments down there for centuries... and, sometimes, weapons of such devastating power that no one can be permitted to have them at all. It *should* be impossible to escape from the Cave. Anything less would mean that it could be plundered for its wonders... and its horrors."

"I understand," Vindi said quietly. Nodding once, Princess Shivaka snapped her fingers. A servant popped up, seemingly out of the ground itself. I studied the walls and ceiling, wondering how many soldiers I'd overlooked, and what sort of weapons they might have trained on me. Shivaka spoke quietly to the servant, who sprinted off with reckless abandon.

"Avashti may still be here. We must trust to hope," she said grimly.

While we waited, Shivaka knelt down and stuck her hands in the mud, performing some arcane gardening task. Princess Gamal just watched us, picking her perfect teeth with a golden toothpick. Vindi and I stood there, fidgeting and feeling more than a little self-conscious.

"I wonder," Princess Shivaka suddenly said. "Even if Avashti *has* been sent inside already…"

"Your highness?" Vindi asked hopefully.

Shivaka tapped her lips thoughtfully with one muddy finger. "I wonder if it would be possible to tunnel in from the side?"

"Right," I said laconically. "I'm sure no one's ever thought of *that* before."

"In case you didn't notice," Princess Gamal informed her sister-in-law, "that was sarcasm, otherwise known as the first and inevitable prelude to her revealing herself as a wide-eyed anarchist and trying to bite our heads off. If she wasn't so pathetic, I might even be worried. You could have prevented this. I want you to know that. You still could, if you authorized me to engage in just a *teeny* spot of torture."

Princess Shivaka sat back, mud dripping from her hands. "Surely, it's been thought of before," she told me, "but no one else commands the resources that we do. A band of brigands could dig for twenty years and never make a scratch. I command the royal engineering corps."

"Actually," Gamal said drily, "*I* do. It's one of the few things your mother gave me. Let's discuss my payment, should I choose to help you. Darshik was telling me, the other day, about a legendary wizard-weapon… what was it called… ah! The Shaker Of The Pillars Of Heaven. Pay me that."

"Why would I make such a foolish promise, when we may not even need you?" Princess Shivaka asked disdainfully.

The servant finally came back. Vindi and I held our breath as Princess Shivaka looked over the note he'd brought.

"Avashti has already been dispatched to the Cave of Wonders," she said grimly. "We might be able to intercept him before he's sent in… but it's not looking good."

"So you *do* need me," Gamal noted. "I want the Shaker Of The Pillars Of Heaven."

"No. No weapons."

"Bah. I have ways of enforcing my decrees. If the wizard emerges without my payment, he goes right back in. One of your guards is my loyal servant, bought and paid for. I won't say which one, but he or she will push the wizard back down the pit and laugh doing it."

Shivaka looked troubled. "I can't let you have such a terrible thing. But... if you must have payment... there *is* an artifact of perception and balance, one that never should have been cast into the cave in the first place. The Lens of Becoming."

Princess Gamal looked disgusted. "How am I supposed to use *that* as a weapon?"

"Take it or leave it."

"I think it sounds fair," Vindi offered.

Gamal fixed her with an unsettling gaze. "Do you imagine, child, that I care what you think?"

"How about it?" I asked Vindi in a loud whisper. "Would it be worth it?"

"What?"

"Me punching Gamal in the face. Shivaka would stop her from killing me... *if* she could stop laughing long enough to speak the words."

"How about you don't punch her at all?" Vindi asked.

"I'm not in love with the idea."

"Just bend over and back up toward her, farting constantly, until she shrieks and tries to run away and smashes her head into the wall. Then she'd have to order the *wall* executed, which would be endlessly amusing to watch."

"Ah," I said wryly, "but she's so used to gold and treasure, with my luck she'd rush forward when I started farting, eager to see something new and different. I'd probably end up with her head lodged firmly up my—"

"Fine. I agree. I'll take the Lens of Becoming as my price," Gamal said, disgusted, "if only so I can get away from *those* two."

"I'll send riders out immediately," Princess Shivaka said. "If we can catch the wizard before he enters the cave... well, that would obviously make things much easier. Would you like to go with them?"

"Yes, please," Vindi said immediately. I shook my head. What could we do but slow them down? On the other hand, if Vindi alone rescued him, I'd never hear the end of it.

"I'll go," I said. "I guess."

III

I guess that horses are reserved for royal use, because the chariot that carried us thundering across Kairay was pulled by donkeys. People still dove out of the way, children ran after us shouting for candy, and the superstitious shouted wishes and threw threads from their clothing at us. Supposedly, if any of the threads were hit by donkey dung, their wishes would come true. I suppose that's *one* way to reconcile yourself to the inevitable.

"Come *on*, Saraya!" Vindi shouted over the rushing wind. "Stop cowering in the corner. I know you've never seen *this* before!"

"I am not cowering," I said crisply, crouching nice and low with both arms over my head. "I am reacting rationally to the fact that I have hair. Hair gets stuck in things. Like rapidly turning chariot wheels, for example. Call me silly, but I have an aversion to having my head popped off. It makes it noticeably harder to eat pie."

"Whoopee!" Vindi shouted, giving the public her best and most jubilant royal wave. "Hold on," she said, sobering. "*I* have hair. I have a head. Why aren't you trying to save *me*? Don't you love me?"

"Of course I do," I said, exasperated. "I just figured, you'd *want* to die a thrilling, romantic death. To make it even more perfect, I'd fall to my knees next to your headless body and shake my fists at the heavens and scream 'NOOOOO!' and swear to avenge your death, which would mean spending the rest of my life as a shadowy figure who occasionally leaps out of the shadows and shouts insults at chariot wheels. You're welcome."

Vindi snorted with suppressed laughter. "You can talk your way out of anything, can't you?"

"I wish. Remember the time I *did* tackle you out of the path of a runaway chariot?"

"It wasn't going to hit me."

45

"True. Since it swerved to miss you and hit *me* instead. And also, it turns out that you have incredibly sharp elbows and a tendency to swing them wildly when tickled, as I found out to my detriment."

"Oh, come on," Vindi said, experimentally swinging her arms back and forth, "my elbows aren't *that*—"

We hit a huge bump, I popped up in the air, and her elbow connected solidly with my nose.

"I'm sorry! I'm sorry!" Vindi cried.

"Then why are you laughing?!"

"I'm not!" she chortled. "That is, I was reminded of something funny that happened the *last* time I was filled with regret and shame. Heh."

I dabbed at my nose. Well, I wasn't bleeding. Getting sloppy there, universe.

Our chariot thundered past the eastern edge of Kairay. Before us, a dusty track wound across the desert, ending halfway up a rocky promontory. There, a dark hole plunged into the earth. As we arrived, I saw that a locked cage covered the entrance, and signs in thirty languages surrounded it, repeating variations on 'STAY CLEAR OR DIE'. I spotted two chariots, some donkeys, and a number of soldiers. I didn't see Avashti. My heart leapt into my throat. Were we too late?

The chariot slowed and finally rumbled to a stop. Our soldiers went to talk to the ones already there. A second chariot pulled up behind us. The wizard Darshik stepped down, looking displeased as he brushed travel dust from his crisp white robes.

"Where's Avashti?" Vindi said quietly.

Darshik pulled a ratty old book from his robes. It was made from a single endless sheet of hammered papyrus, folded back and forth and back and forth until it could fan out into more than a hundred pages. He opened it, consulting a page stained with weird, looping, spidery writing.

"Should you find yourself in the Cave of Wonders…"

"We won't," I said flatly.

"Saraya!" Vindi said, shocked. "We have to save Avashti— whatever it takes!"

"No, we don't. Our obligation is to save as many lives as we can. Two is more than zero. Given a choice between saving us two, and saving absolutely no one at all, the choice is clear. We have to save us two. We will not go down there."

"I can't believe I'm hearing this!"

"What would Avashti tell you to do?" I asked gently. "What would he *want* you to do?"

"Sometimes, loving someone means ignoring everything they say and punching them in the face as hard as you can, and then dumping her into the Cave of Wonders and jumping down after her, and apologizing to her later, except that, if she really loves me, she'll understand and I won't have to."

"Keep your elbows away from my nose," I said warmly.

Darshik ponderously cleared his throat. "But if you *do* find yourself in the Cave of Wonders," he said inevitably, "the key to your escape is threefold…"

"Escape?" Vindi said, looking startled. "I thought the princesses were going to dig in from the side? And as long as we brought the Lens of Becoming, they'd let us out?"

"Vindi," I said patiently, "how many master thieves, cunning adventurers, and well-equipped nobles have gone down there? And how many have returned? I'll give you a hint. It's the same as the number of heads I'd have left if that chariot wheel had been just a little more belligerent. Who cares if the princesses dig in from the side if we don't live long enough to meet them there?"

Darshik glanced at his book. "First," he said, "befriend your murderer. Second, don't even dream of escaping. Third, since there is no escape, you may as well flip a coin to choose your path. That is all."

"Don't tell *me* what to dream," Vindi said warmly. "Dreaming about escaping, sure, not my first choice when I have any number of Handsome Princes clamoring to star in my fantasies, but I will *not* be told what I can and can't—"

"You rob them?" I guessed.

"What?"

"The Handsome Princes. You daydream that you're a dashing, daring brigand, and you rob every Handsome Prince who comes by, and you shriek with laughter as you pour stolen gems and gold over your head? Then you abduct a poor-but-clever tinker's apprentice who has more qualifications for making you happy than the fact that the dice roll of his birth happened to come up all sixes, and who for some curious reason never gets around to escaping from you? That's what you dream?"

"Well, it will be, now," she said thoughtfully.

One of the soldiers finally came back to us. "It's too late," he said flatly. "He's already inside."

"No," Darshik said, not even bothering to look at his book. "They pushed him into the pit, but he caught the edge and managed to hang on. He's still there. He won't fall for another…"

Vindi was off like a rabbit. "NO!" I cried. "He's lying! *Darshik* is Gamal's spy! He's the one who… Vindi!"

I ran after her. Vindi reached the metal mesh of the locked cage. As startled soldiers looked on, she leapt at a sizeable hole on the left side and attacked it like a rabid weasel. She popped through quicker than she expected, and had to windmill her arms to keep from falling down that pitch-black hole in the earth.

"Dad…?"

"Vindi!" I shouted, flinging myself at the same hole she'd gone through. The metal grabbed me, scraping the skin from my ears as I shoved and twisted and finally popped through.

"Vindi, listen," I said. Just then, a soldier stepped up to the cage. Without hesitation, he reached through the hole and gave Vindi a huge shove.

"Oh, hell," I said quietly. "Gamal lied. She's got *more* than one."

Vindi shouted, arms spinning as she started to fall. I grabbed for her—and felt someone shove *me* in the back. I teetered on the edge for one breathless moment, shouting wildly, and then I plummeted into the depths.

* * *

The fall wasn't as bad as it looked. The shaft slanted a little, so I tumbled and slid instead of falling the whole way. I landed next to Vindi, hitting bottom with a grunt. The traitorous soldier must have flung a pair of lanterns after us: One clanged off my head, hitting me so hard that I bit my tongue, and bounced neatly into Vindi's waiting hands. The other hit me between the shoulders and shattered, setting me on fire where I couldn't possibly reach it.

"Not *again*!" I cried. Vindi rushed over to put me out. I have to say, her technique had improved a lot, given that she no longer tried to *punch* the fire out. But then, she *had* had an awful lot of practice.

"Are you all right?" she asked me.

"I'm fine. Mostly. What about you?"

"Saraya…" Vindi sat back, pulling her knees to her chest. "It's my fault we're here. I was the one who believed Darshik. I was the one who ran straight to the pit."

"Could've happened to anyone," I said gruffly. I forced myself to smile. No. In this place, at this time, for her, I needed to do better than that. I threw my head back, laughing a careless laugh.

"It's a goddamned adventure," I said. "It's fun. I'm glad we're here."

"Better," Vindi said. "I almost believed you that time."

I shrugged. "Well, it doesn't matter. We're here. Doesn't matter how. Doesn't matter why. Let's see what we've got, all right?"

Vindi raised her lantern. We were in a cave, plain and simple. It was dry and dusty and otherwise unremarkable. There was only one way onward, a craggy tunnel slanting generally down. As for the pit itself, the walls looked a lot more sheer from below. We obviously wouldn't be getting out that way without a *lot* of help.

"If wizards are constantly throwing stuff down here, where is it?" I said, scuffing my foot over the dusty but otherwise clear floor. "Shouldn't there be a huge mountain of shattered magical junk right about here?"

"Maybe one of the failed experiments was a little bit alive," Vindi said, her eyes aglow with barely-suppressed horror. "Maybe it assembled all of those broken pieces into a working body, and now it's a living landslide of rune-inscribed rocks and singing swords. Maybe it scavenges for parts so it can make itself even bigger. *And all it needs now is a head!*"

Vindi pointed over my shoulder and screamed. I spun around, heart beating so fast that I may just have to swallow a tiny trophy to commemorate the moment. The cave behind me was dry, dark—and empty.

"You should see the look on your face," Vindi snickered.

"Have I ever told you how much I hate you?"

"Constantly," she said happily. "But I know better. People that you *really* hate, you just ignore. Therefore, people you merely *claim* to hate, you must feel passionately about—in a good way, presumably, since we're talking about me."

"Well, what if I said that I loved you?" I hazarded.

Vindi cocked her head. "I actually don't know how to respond to that. Do you need to burp?"

Shaking my head, I beckoned for to follow me into the tunnel. The floor was mostly flat and the way was fairly easy, and we made rapid progress.

"Who's there?" a rasping voice suddenly demanded. A pale,

worried face popped up from behind a boulder, his wild beard matching his disheveled hair.

"DAD!" Vindi cried, leaping into Avashti's arms. He held her tight, allowing her to bury her face in his shoulder.

"Good to see you," I said, awkwardly patting the wizard's arm. He reached over and pulled me into the hug. Which, you know, was an unjust violation of my personal autonomy and all that. Somehow, I forgot to protest.

"I'm glad to see you," Avashti said, finally letting us go. "I'm *furious* to see you, too. This isn't a game. My plan for keeping myself alive was tenuous enough, but now…"

"We found you," Vindi said. "That's all that matters."

Avashti smiled ruefully. "Since you so intelligently thought to ask, I'll tell you how I got here. I never even saw Her Lordship, Shavala II. Only Princess Gamal. Well, her and that daft prince, Dakar, who spent the whole time asking statues what they thought of his wig (which he was wearing on a cord around his neck like the world's shaggiest necklace). He seemed genuinely sad when he told them that he'd have to have them beheaded for the unforgivable insolence of remaining silent. I really don't think he knew I was there. I'm not sure he knew *he* was there."

"Dad…?" Vindi prodded him.

"Ah, yes. Anyway, Gamal told me I had to retrieve a mighty wizard-weapon called the Firmament-Reaver. Said it was my only way out." Avashti shrugged. "Going deeper into the cave, alone, when the lantern they threw after me had broken… that would be a death sentence, wouldn't it? But I figured, if I failed to return for a few days, they'd send someone else to make the attempt. So I waited near the entrance, husbanding my strength, biding my time, so I could join forces with whoever came next." He shook his head. "I didn't think it would be *you*."

"Then… should we wait here?" Vindi asked. "See if they send someone else?"

"No," Avashti said quietly. "I was willing to wait for an ally, even to the point of starvation, but I could never watch *you* waste away and die. We have to go in."

"Suits me," I said. "You have magic, right? That should help."

Avashti looked uncomfortable. "Without my paraphernalia… my plan books… a mere month or two to prepare…"

"Right. Forget I asked. If we see anything weird or glowy, Vindi and I will leap into action and start weeping hysterically. Hopefully it'll be so embarrassed by how pathetic we are that it'll slink off in the other direction."

"Nothing will hurt you," Avashti swore. "I will be your shield."

I looked him up and down. "I'll feel a lot better about that if you weren't made of such soft, squishy meat."

"Saraya!" Vindi said, shocked.

"Fine," I said, disgruntled. "Avashti will live forever, dancing squirrels are going to tailor poofy golden gowns for the two of us, and the moon is made of cake. Happy?"

"No!" she said, aggrieved. "Why did you have to tell me about the moon? Now I know that a big, delectable cake is always hanging where I can see it but never reach!"

I stared at Vindi. "Can you tell when she's joking?" I asked Avashti.

"I've never asked," he said delicately. "Ignorance, I find, is a wonderful thing. For all I know, all sorts of wonderful things could be true. Hard, cold reality might be altogether less congenial."

"You're wise, I'll give you that," I muttered, peering down the tunnel. "We'll find what we find, I guess."

The cave turned a little as it descended, but there wasn't much more to it than that. Before long, we came to a great rectangular doorway carved from the surrounding stone. Oddly, I could see better than I had at the entrance to the cave. Were my eyes adjusting, or was something else going on?

"Extinguish the lantern," I told Vindi.

"No!"

"Look, it'll be fun," I said, exasperated. "This cave has been a real disappointment in the romantic-adventure department, you know? No spinning blades shooting at our heads, no pillars of fire erupting from the earth, no riddle-asking statues barfing acid on us when we ridicule their insipid wordplay instead of actually trying to come up with an answer. But *being lost in the dark*—well! That's the stuff of stories. Specifically, the one that begins, 'you wanna know how Vindi died?'"

"I have complete and total faith in you," Vindi said. "Specifically, I have faith that your conception of me is *slightly* more complex than 'raving idiot who will do absolutely anything if you tell her it's romantic'. Since I *know* you're smarter than that, I also know that you were joking just now. Allow me to demonstrate by laughing in your face as hard as I can."

"*I* can get her to obey," Avashti said. "You just have to know how to do it." He walked around in front of her, a look of enlightened innocence on his face. Vindi watched him suspiciously. "All I have to do is get her to admit that my staggeringly vast intellect cannot be denied, and she'll have to— NOW!" he shouted.

I'd snuck up on Vindi while Avashti distracted her. Now I grabbed the lantern, licked my fingers, and pinched off the wick. The light grew less, but didn't go away. A dim illumination came from beyond the doorway, emanating from… somewhere. It was steady, too, with none of the flickering, leaping shadows created by firelight.

"I can't believe that worked," Vindi said sourly. "I'm putting you both down for three and a half points of revenge."

"But we were *right*!" I protested.

"Immaterial. If we survive this, check your beds for spiders. Big ones." She did a mental calculation, lips moving slightly. "Medium ones."

"I'll go first," Avashti said grimly, and led us through the doorway.

What lay beyond was a vast chamber, half wild cave, half carved gallery. Among rippling terraces of flowstone and stalactites like forests of hanging stone straws, there were treasures beyond match or description. Gilded orbs, studded with gems and inscribed with bizarre runes; weird spinning orreries of white and black pearls; domes assembled from emerald and topaz and all manner of gems, shattering the light into endless overlapping nimbuses of magnificence.

"The Cave of Treasures," Vindi whispered.

"Have you noticed how clean and precisely arranged everything is?" I said. "Has it occurred to you that we may not be the only ones down here? Keeping in mind that people are literally made of meat, and that true desperation is only four or five meals away, there may be consequences to this fact."

"I volunteer to be eaten first," Vindi said dramatically.

I glanced at her. "By cave people, or by *us*, should we begin to starve?"

"I'd never do that to you," Avashti promised.

"Me neither," I said. "I don't have a fork, which would make the process incredibly unpleasant for both of us."

We moved slowly across the Cave of Treasures. A nearly endless number of side passages honeycombed the walls: This place was a cave, and wild, and *big*. It would be very easy to take one wrong step and wander forever, if not for the weird sourceless light that showed us the way forward.

We passed into a new gallery. It lacked gems or gold, but was plenty impressive nonetheless. Sealed inside of huge transparent crystals were the great weapons of wizardry past. Just looking at the first one, shaped like a ball of metal tentacles all grappling with each other, somehow filled me with the dread certainty that life was fragile and soon to be broken. I started to sweat as I beheld the faceless wooden statue next to it; somehow, it felt more like *it* was looming over *me*. A little farther on, a small metal casket radiated the sheer devouring cold of The Death Of All Things.

"The Cave of Power," Vindi said, shivering.

"Yeah, I think I'll avoid having any picnics here," I said. "Nameless Horrors From Beyond really take the zest out of eating Vindi's face."

"How could you!" Vindi said, scandalized. "Faces are hairy and gristly and covered with ears and noses and stuff! Start somewhere soft and meaty." She smirked. "How about you bite my ass?"

I put my hand to my heart. "I swear, the moment I find a fork, you can guess where I'll stick it."

"Girls, girls," Avashti said tiredly. "Could you try being pragmatic and reasonable, like me? *Obviously*, it doesn't matter which part of Vindi we start with, so long we dance the pieces around like joyful merry puppets first, so they dissolve more harmoniously in our stomachs."

I stared at the wizard. So he actually had a sense of humor. Who knew? It's the quiet ones you have to watch out for.

If anything, the Cave of Power was perforated by even more side passages than the Cave of Treasures, but only one path was illuminated. Following it, we came to a gallery that sobered us immediately. Arrayed in neat rows, shining and clean, were skeletons —thousands of them, almost too many to count. Ragged scraps of clothing showed that some had been soldiers, some had been peasants, some had been well-equipped explorers. All had come to the Cave of Wonders in search of power and wealth, and all had met exactly the same fate.

Something I'd taken for a pile of rags suddenly stood up, not ten feet from where we were standing. I swore. Vindi yelped. Avashti held his fists in front of him as if he knew what to do with them.

The thing… the person?… moved toward us with a slow, trundling gait, taking great care to always keep its body turned to the left. Whatever it was, it certainly wasn't human. Through gaps in its ragged black robes, I could see wheels and gears and mechanisms of solid gold spinning endlessly, powered by little mechanical men who wound cranks and pulled chains. They, in turn, were powered by even tinier, dust-mote-sized mechanical men ensconced in their chests, and as for *them*… well, we may never know unless your eyesight is far better than mine. The bizarre mechanical being finally looked up at us. I think. It didn't have eyes. Where the face should have been was a rotating orb of fool's gold, eaten away into spectacular cavities of squared-off facets which sparkled endlessly.

"Good day," it said. The voice didn't come from its head. It came from dozens of rotating cylinders in its chest. They bristled with stubby metal wires, almost like the guts of a music box, and the notes they played merged into a strangely melodic sound, like the music of lost wind chimes.

"What the what?" Avashti said.

"Ah. An explanation, perhaps, would be in order," the thing said. "I am called Archon, or, at least, that's what I call myself. That last statement, although not explicitly a joke, is susceptible of engendering amusement. I will pause now and wait for you to laugh. Excellent."

"What are you?" Vindi asked, fascinated.

"I am an antenna. People, as you know, believe things. These beliefs, by sheer random chance, refract and reflect and accumulate into what are called gods. So-called 'wizards' approach these gods and ask them for favors. The gods may answer. They may not. The wizard takes credit for any success, pretending the result was his own doing."

"Never heard anything so stupid," Avashti said gruffly. "Broken in the head, I'd say. No wonder the damn thing got dumped down here."

"Gods are too capricious. Too random. I was built to be an antenna for belief, to channel humanity's collective power into something more predictable, more controllable. Sadly, I failed to meet my master's requirements. I wielded no power, granted no wishes. So I was sent here to maintain this place, to keep it clean and ordered. I find satisfaction in doing so. I am much happier than I was before."

"And… er… would you help us escape, maybe?" I asked.

Archon's gears hummed quietly. "That query was intended to engender amusement? Evaluating. No. Permit me to explain. There is nothing here that can sustain your kind. Nothing to eat. Nothing to drink. Soon, you will die. Be comforted knowing that you, or what remains of you, will be made clean and ordered, by me, as I have for all these others."

"Why do you keep facing left?" Vindi asked.

"Bigger fish," I murmured.

"What?"

"We have more important things to worry about," Avashti explained. "When the devil comes to claim your soul, you don't spend your one and only question asking about the hilarious mole on his backside."

"That kind of depends on how big it is," I said judiciously.

"I am an antenna," Archon chimed, already answering Vindi. "I am sensitized to the combined thoughts and beliefs of the fifty thousand humans beings in the city of Kairay. My mind-prisms and thought-refractors, angled like *this*, pick up only the highest, purest, most intellectual—"

Vindi snapped her fingers, waving her hand on Archon's right side. It turned to see what was happening—and ended up facing right instead of left.

"—most depraved, debased, and altogether *fun* impulses you creatures have," it continued in a voice that was somehow smoother, oilier, and altogether *slicker*. "Call me Adversary. What the hell. Call me Beans In A Jar if it makes you happy. Unlike my prissy better half, I'm all about the fun."

"Then you're not going to kill us?" I asked hopefully.

"On the contrary. An aversion to murder is a matter of ethics, and ethics, needless to say, are a real pain in the ass I don't have. Archon would just wait for you to die. Pfft. *I* mean to kill you. Specifically, I intend to pump your heads so full of pleasant dreams that you actually die of bliss. So how's about it? How would you like to fun yourself to death? Just tell me what you want to fantasize about, and we're off! Sex is always popular. Not sure why, but hell, if it gets the job done, I'm not going to question it."

I looked Archon/Adversary over. "I say we hold it down and hit it with rocks until we get a personality that wants to help us," I said.

"Wait! What was the first thing Darshik told us?" Vindi asked. "Wasn't it… 'make friends with your murderer'?"

"That pathetic excuse for a wizard?" Avashti said contemptuously. "Someday, I'm going to get my hands on that book and make a few creative edits. He's gotten so lazy. So obedient, doing *anything* the book says. Be funny to watch him prance around naked for the rest of his days. Well," he mused, "naked except for the tiny hats. Hats which are going to get progressively taller and fancier"

"What's so funny about that?" I asked.

"He's not going to be wearing them on his *head*."

Vindi smiled at Archon/Adversary. "I want to be your friend," she said simply.

Adversary laughed at her. Loudly. I grabbed it by the robe and spun it around until it was facing left again.

"You desire to be my friend?" Archon said. "Evaluating. No. This is a ploy intended to extract assistance."

"Yes, I want to escape," Vindi said patiently, "but I'm interested in you, too."

"I evaluate that statement's truth content at less than three percent."

"Evaluate again. I'm interested in even the weirdest, most exasperating creatures in existence." Vindi jerked her thumb at me. "I'm friends with *her*, aren't I?"

"Hey!" I cried.

"New information acquired. Evaluating. Intriguing… you appear to be afflicted with a martyr complex. The more logical course would be to cease being her friend."

"HEY!"

Vindi sat cross-legged on the cave floor. "Tell me about yourself."

"Why? An exchange of personal information would seem to serve no purpose." Archon paused. "Although, I do have to admit, the fact that you have horns intrigues me. Do you gore people with them, or do they serve strictly as a mating display?"

"Talk to me and find out."

So they talked, surrounded by gleaming white skeletons and that weird, sourceless light. I may have to apologize to Revi the Tinker and her endless stories about her darling children. In less than thirty heartbeats, we had a new contender for World's Most Boring Conversationalist. Archon's world extended to caves, cleaning, and organizing. The end. It had a real talent for metaphor, I have to admit, as long as you don't mind describing absolutely *everything* in terms of flowstone. Vindi seemed to genuinely enjoy their conversation, which indicates a real zest for pain. Then again, given that she was friends with *me*, I wasn't sure I wanted to walk too far down that road.

"…and when I was little and had to sweep up the seed pods around the house, I'd make a game out of it," Vindi explained. "I made a maze for Saraya and me to explore! I swept the pods into lines —not straight, mind you, but crazy interlocking spirals—and there were gaps which we were allowed to cross if we jumped just right…"

"Which doesn't go so great when you jump and hit your head on a butterfly and knock yourself unconscious," I noted drily.

"They worked for *me*."

"Organizing items by a rotational symmetry, instead of using a grid?" Archon asked, fascinated. "Intriguing. Perhaps friendship is not pointless. I compute a six-point-three percent chance that exposure to new and different perspectives will trigger unforseen ideas in the recipient. Thank you. You have given me a new sense of purpose. I will organize these skeletons into spirals the moment you've died!"

"All right. My turn," I said, yanking the mechanism-creature around so I could talk to Adversary.

"How about it?" I asked. "Are we friends, or what?"

"You just want my help," Adversary pointed out.

"Obviously. That's what friendship is. Pure transaction. Favors, food and fun, traded in a never-ending orgy of avarice and want. So tell me, friend, what do *you* want?"

"Me?" It was hard to tell, but I had the impression that Adversary was sizing me up. "I have a gripping desire to hear you sing old drinking songs. Loudly, and badly. Have you ever heard 'love' rhymed with 'mug'? You're about to."

"Sounds great. In return, I want a diamond-encrusted stick I can use to menace Vindi, as a means of simultaneously threatening her and looking fabulous. Don't worry. I *promise* I'll sing the whole time you're away fetching it for me."

"I would never question you," Adversary said smoothly. "In fact, questions are completely unnecessary. All of my accusations are statements of fact. You are a lying, devious traitor who has no intention of keeping her promise. I *knew* there was something I liked about you."

"C'mon," I said, sitting down and patting the ground beside me. "Let's talk."

"Sounds dull."

"I'm about to start sinning like crazy," I said. "Do you really want to miss *that*?"

"Another promise?"

"Say, rather, that you need to decide whether to take the calculated risk that I'm telling the truth."

"Very well. I agree—for now."

So Adversary and I 'talked', although it wasn't so much a conversation as a verbal sparring contest as we each struggled to gain the upper hand over the other. Spar and parry, insult and counter-insult, fake humility into reversal, and then—POW! Just like that, I had Adversary tied up nice and neat in an implied contract to be my servant for life, at least until it reversed the whole thing back on me, the worm.

"You think you've won, don't you?" I panted.

"Given that it's a simple fact of the universe, yes, I do think that," Adversary replied.

"Go to hell," I said, and spun it around until it became Archon again.

"I doubt hell would be to my liking," Archon said delicately. "I have calculated the probability of hell at less than zero-point-two percent, but if it does exist, it will almost certainly be full of screaming, naked humans."

Avashti raised an eyebrow. "That seems weirdly specific."

"What else could it be? Naked humans cannot be organized," Archon said delicately. "No matter what you do, their dangly bits just *dangle*."

"Oh," Avashti said. "So this would be *your* version of hell."

"Obviously. Humans, according my calculations, enjoy being naked."

"Enough of that," I said. "Turn around. I want to talk to Adversary again."

"I'd really rather not."

"Don't make me take my clothes off and dangle at you," I snapped. Cowed, Archon turned.

"Nicely done," Adversary said. "You may just be clever enough to deserve my help, after all."

"Oh no," I simpered, "I'm just a pathetic worm who's no good at—" I paused. "Sorry. I like pie, and Vindi's really susceptible to self-deprecation, so I've fallen into the habit of... you know what? It doesn't matter."

"You really think you have me figured out, don't you?" Vindi said, amused. "It's a good thing I haven't learned anything about *you* over all these years." She pulled a coin out of her pocket and started flipping it. "Heads says you have to carry me everywhere for the next three weeks. Tails, I have to carry you. Ready?"

I froze. Sure, I always lose, but that doesn't mean I refuse to gamble. In fact, I kind of have to. Refusing a bet would be tantamount to giving up, curled up in a ball and crying. But it can't be that way. Stick your tongue out at Destiny. Show it that you still haven't given up, and won't, not ever. Show it that it still hasn't broken you. On the other hand, losing a bet can have unfortunate consequences. That's not always fun.

"Do you really *want* to gamble?" I hazarded. "It's... boring. There are so many things you could be doing that are way more fun."

Vindi smirked. "Oh, I suppose I could be persuaded not to make you bet... if you agreed to carry me around everywhere *now*."

"You're a horrible, horrible woman," I said, bending to let her climb up on my back. "Avashti? You want to help me, maybe?"

The wizard smiled. "At a casual guess, I may be the most intelligent being in the history of the universe. Watch me prove it by refusing to get involved."

"Thanks a lot."

"You're welcome," he said, bowing. "Oh, and also, learn from the example of my quaint humility. Self-deprecation is our only protection from ourselves."

"Whatever you say," I grumbled as Vindi kicked my sides and tried to make me gallop. "Come on," I said to Adversary as Vindi continued to spur me on. "If you really mean to help us, now's the time."

"Very well. Follow me, please."

Adversary make a long, slow circuit of the skeleton room. The side passages were numerous, crazy complicated, and veiled by a devouring darkness. Adversary didn't take any of them, but followed a long and winding path that ended up, finally, right back where we'd started.

"Did that have a point?" I demanded.

"Not really, but at least Vindi got to ride longer."

"You're despicable, you know that?"

"I may not be susceptible to blushing, but please know that I enjoy your praise. Lay down here, if you will. All three of you."

Adversary indicated three spaces directly in line with the rest of the gleaming skeletons. I hesitated… but surely that rather ominous positioning was an accident based on his lack of understanding? I reluctantly lay down on the floor.

"Did I mention, if you help me escape, I'll drop all *kinds* of fun stuff down the pit for you?" I hazarded. "Pornographic books, for one. Lots of 'em."

Avashti frowned. "I thought I'd locked that cabinet."

"What?"

"What?" he said, suddenly evasive. Vindi took the space next to me, and Avashti lay next to her.

"Close your eyes," Adversary said. "Good. Listen to my words. Listen to my voice. Don't think. Don't speak. Accept that what I'm saying is true. Accept that what I'm saying is—"

I leapt up with a primal scream, hovered in the air for about three times longer than seemed likely or possible, and kicked Archon/Adversary in the chest-equivalent. It shot across the room as though it had been hit by a diving roc, smashed into the far wall and exploded into golden shrapnel.

"Hurray!" Vindi cried, leaping up. "You've saved us all!"

I frowned. "You don't feel even the slightest bit sorry for Archon, who was only doing its job?"

"You're a hero! You're the best ever!"

Avashti sat up. "You're such an inspiration," he said warmly, grabbing random bits of wizardry from his pockets and assembling them into a weird sort of harness. "This should summon and control a roc, but—you know what?—I don't feel up to flying it. Saraya, I think *you'd* better do it."

"Stop. This is too much fun. This is too perfect. Something's wrong."

"How could anything be wrong?" Vindi asked. "We're about to escape, and you're the reason why. I love you, Saraya."

"Stop. Darshik said we shouldn't even think about escaping." I paused. "Wait. No. He said we shouldn't even *dream* about— oh, crap." I gazed miserably at my celebrating friends. Being their hero felt so cozy and warm, like being attacked by huge-eyed fur sprites on a biting cold night. But then, I've never been one to shy away from the harder things in life. Outside observers probably think I've gotten used to standing up to fate and doing what's right, no matter how much it hurts. Nope. It still stings just as bad, every single time. Sometimes literally, when there are hornets involved.

With a wrenching effort, I forced my eyes open. I was lying on the cold stone floor, skeletons to my right, a slumbering—if smiling— Vindi to my left. Just beyond her, Avashti was in much the same state.

"Wake up," I said, reaching over to shake Vindi.

"C— can't," she yawned. "Using pie to bait a trap for Saraya. Heh heh."

"WATCH OUT, SARAYA!!!" I bellowed. Vindi sat bolt upright, gasping and looking around with wide eyes.

"Avashti," I said, poking him in the side. "Avashti. Avashti. Avashti."

"Nnnn," he protested, feebly batting at me. I kept poking him. At long last he sat up, yawning enormously. "Such a pity. I was having the most *wonderful* dream."

"Were Vindi and I in it?"

Avashti paused, a hint of a smile touching his face. "…yes."

"So you've escaped Adversary's trap," Archon said, making sure to stay facing left as it shuffled over to us. "I'm glad."

"You didn't want us to die?" Vindi said, pleased.

"Not like *this*. Adversary positioned you here on purpose, knowing how much I hate having nothing to do. Now you'll die in weird positions and random locations as you struggle to escape, and your remains will require all *kinds* of work for me to organize!"

"After all this, you're still not going to help us?" I asked.

"That statement was meant as humor? Evaluating. No. You are correct. I will not."

"Then will Adversary help us?"

The mechanism-creature turned to the right. "I don't want you to escape, either," Adversary told us. "The most fun I have is when I vicariously enjoy the fun I impose on mortals. Well, until it overwhelms them and they pop."

"Come with us," I said impulsively. "Come out into the world. There's all *kinds* of fun to be had out there. All kinds of things to organize, too."

"Yeah!" Vindi said excitedly. "We'll all three—four?—of us run a shop together! We'll grant people's wishes in weird and disturbing ways that make them wish they'd never wished at all. Then we'll grant *that* wish in a weird and disturbing way, and you'd better believe we'll be having fun *then*!"

"No," Adversary said, hesitating slightly. "The world above is too… complicated. I would rather stay down here, where sins are simple and direct and come one at a time, and enjoy watching people enjoy themselves to death. I call it 'the circle of life'. Here, close your eyes. I'd like to try again."

"You can't beat me," I told it. "I know, at a deep instinctual level, that anything fun is fake—*because it's fun*. If I kick you in the chest, and *don't* break my foot and immediately fall over crying, I know something's up. I'm going to figure you out, *every single time*. Give up now, Adversary. You've already lost."

"I'm not sure I like you any more," Adversary complained, turning to the left. Suddenly, I was facing Archon again.

"What about you?" Vindi asked. "Don't *you* want to come back to the surface with us?"

Archon paused. "The world is a strange and disorganized place. Here, I know the rules. I know what I need to do, and it works the same way every single time. Up there? My predictions would be rendered worthless the first time someone stuck a fig up her nose for no reason."

"I only did that *once*," I said self-consciously.

"Oh, come back with us!" Vindi said. "We'll help you. It'll be fun!"

"My answer is still 'no'," Archon said. "I must admit, I am curious about some of the things to be found up there, and I know that Adversary is as well, but… it's safer here."

"You need our help."

"I do not. You need mine. Would you like to know the exact odds that I'll help you escape, or would you prefer to continue with this rather endearing mortal affectation known as 'hope'?"

"Useless," Avashti muttered.

"Indeed," Archon said. "The very point I've been attempting to communicate. But I find myself subject to a curious infestation of this 'friendship' delusion that your kind places so much stock in. I will not help you," Archon said, "but neither will I hinder you. No matter what artifacts you move, borrow, or take, I will only watch."

It turned, becoming Adversary again. "But if you wanted to be a real friend," it noted, "you could try your escape drunk and naked."

"Would that help us?" Vindi asked.

"Let's just say that *one* of us would be laughing a lot harder."

I led the way through the Cave of Power and back toward the Cave of Treasures, the others trailing behind me. The ancient wizard-weapons still made me shudder as I passed them: It was some time before the chill passed and I felt comfortable speaking again.

"What we need to do, basically, is find a wizardly artifact that'll help us find our way to the princesses," I reasoned. "We'll never find a way through all these side passages alone. We need help if we don't want to wander forever."

"We also need the Lens of Becoming," Vindi pointed out. "Might as well start there. I mean, a lens, that shouldn't be too hard to find, right?"

"You're thinking rationally," Avashti said gently. "We're in the realm of wizardry. Logic has no place here. It could look like, or be, absolutely anything at all."

"It could be a giant dancing pancake that loves me?" Vindi asked excitedly.

Avashti gave her a pained look. "Do you *have* to be whimsical, even now?"

"It could be a giant dancing pancake that suffers from chronic back pain because it dances so much," I suggested.

Avashti hid a smile. "See?" he told his daughter. "Saraya can do it. Is it really so hard to be realistic and down-to-earth, like the two of us?"

We wandered through the Cave of Treasures. Most of the artifacts waited in silence, but the orrery of white and black pearls continued to whirl around in endless circles.

"What about that one?" Vindi asked, fascinated. "Is that anything?"

"It most certainly is," Avashti said, amused. "It's a pile of worthless junk designed to look impressive while doing precisely nothing."

"But it looks so wizardy!"

"Look at the markings around the base," Avashti said. "Astronomical. It's a calendar. Plus meteorological. It describes—or prescribes?—the weather. It's a weather machine. But the curvature of the base is all wrong. It would never be able to focus energy up in the sky to cause rain or whatever. Shoddy design. Junk. It never worked."

“So how did it get here?”

“Let’s look a little closer.” Avashti jabbed at a pearl, which promptly fell off and hit the floor with a crack. The structure behind it was a lot simpler than the gaudy surface. “There you go,” he said. “The original device was made from brass and glass. When the wizard realized he’d failed, he panicked and told King Stupid that it wouldn’t work without a godawful mess of pearls glued all over it. That bought him some time, but he couldn’t stall forever. Eventually, his bluff was called. His life was ended, too, I’m guessing, if he got dumped down here with his misguided invention.”

I gave Avashti an appraising look. “You really know your stuff.”

“Why do you sound so surprised?” the wizard asked, hurt.

“A lifetime of experience being disappointed with almost everyone almost all the time. But enough about my dating life. Can you find the Lens?”

Avashti shuffled past the arrayed wizardly artifacts, muttering to himself as he examined them. “Useless. Junk. Stupid. A six-year-old with his finger up his nose could do better. Pathetic. Garbage. Just… why?”

From time to time, Vindi was overcome with curiosity and demanded to know *why* such-and-such a device deserved his scorn. Avashti always had an answer, and I continued to be impressed by how much he knew.

“Well, knowing everything *is* my profession,” he said modestly, bringing my opinion of him crashing back down to ground level.

It was Vindi who spotted a smaller gallery splitting off from the Cave of Treasures. This new cave was far more heavily decorated with stalagmites and columns, and the wizardly artifacts scattered throughout were made of simple, practical materials, not the glorified gilded garbage that royal wizards seemed to favor.

“Hmm,” Avashti said, picking up a walnut so heavily inscribed with heiroglyphs that none of its original surface was left. “Interesting. This one might even work as intended. Not helpful with our current problem, though.”

“What is it?” Vindi asked eagerly.

“Isn’t it obvious? Even Saraya could get this one.”

“Yup. Completely obvious. What’s the matter, Vindi? Why aren’t you smart like Avashti and me?”

"Look," Avashti said helpfully. "There's a jackal head on each end—always eating, never eliminating. Add in the vents along the middle, and that means…?"

"It lets you… feed jackals… to walnuts?" Vindi guessed.

Avashti's shoulders slumped. "It's meant to magically empty a person's stomach so they can keep eating without end. Must have been a hit at the really decadent feasts."

"Hold on," I said. "What would happen if a normal person with an *empty* stomach used it?"

"I don't like to think about it," Avashti said delicately.

"It would turn them inside-out, wouldn't it? Mine," I said, tucking the Walnut of Inversion next to my Anteyvan strangling cord.

"Saraya, that's dangerous. It could kill you."

"Which will make my brave refusal to actually *use* it—in the face of a taunting Universe, no less!—all the more of a punch in its giant ethereal balls," I said. "Ha! Take *that*, Reality!"

"Is she always like this?" Archon asked, intrigued. "Such an aberrant personality would seem to compel observation."

"So come with us!" Vindi said merrily. "Stare avidly at her while she slurps her soup. She'll love that!"

Archon gazed at me for a long moment. "Regretfully, I cannot. I doubt the other fifty thousand of your kind would prove nearly so amusing. They might rather tend to throw things at me. Like rocks."

Avashti sorted through several more of the wizardly artifacts in the side gallery, frowning a little as he puzzled out what they were for.

"Now, *this* one is interesting," he mused. The device he picked up looked sort of like a windchime, but with slabs of differently shaped- and colored- crystals dangling from leather straps. The top was made of concentric collars of different metals so heavily inscribed with runes that little of the original surface was visible. Avashti held the top of the thing up to his face and squinted with one eye, sighting along it toward Vindi.

"What is it?" she asked.

"A wizard's wizardry. With this, I can focus on anything wizard-made… observe its power… bend it… *adjust* it?" Avashti studied the device. "*This* is the Lens of Becoming. It has to be."

"Great!" Vindi said. "Then all we have to do is find an artifact that'll help us find the princesses!"

Avashti avoided her eye. I avoided her eye. Archon chose that moment to practice mortal-style friendly laughter. What it came up with was *really* disturbing.

"We've looked at every artifact here," I gently told her. "According to Avashti, none of them are worth anything." I shook my head. "I guess it couldn't be that easy to escape, or people would have been running in and out of this place non-stop for the past thousand years. Who knows where the princesses will break through? In a cave this big, the odds of finding them before we starve to death… well, they're not great."

"I'm not scared. We'll make it. What was Darshik's third piece of advice?" Vindi asked.

"Don't listen to Darshik," Avashti said promptly. "Oh, sorry… that's *my* third piece of advice. And my first. And my fourth."

"What's the second?" I asked, pretty sure I'd regret asking.

"'Watch your step if you march in a parade *behind* the donkeys'."

"Like him or not, Darshik has been right so far," Vindi said patiently. "What did he want us to do next?"

"He said there was no way out," I said darkly. "He said we might as well flip a coin to pick our path. What a jerk. *I* know there isn't any hope, but you don't have to dance around laughing while you tie a bow to the fact. Talk about a total failure of class."

"That!" Avashti said, snapping his fingers. "That's what I've been trying to think of for years! Congratulations, Saraya. Thanks to you, I just came up with my official nickname for Darshik."

We ventured into one of the side passages and started trying to find our way out of the Cave of Wonders. We needn't have bothered: This was a *cave*, a labyrinth of passages that split and rejoined, plunged and soared. Archon/Adversary followed us, humming eerily, satisfied that it would take a *lot* of work to get our bones all cleaned up and squared away after we dropped dead of starvation. The gentle glow emanating from it meant that we didn't have to use the precious little oil left in our lantern, but that was about the only thing it did for us.

"Are you going to help us or what?" I finally demanded.

"That statement was meant to engender humor?" Archon mused. "Calculating. Results uncertain. To be safe, I suppose I should emulate all possible reactions." Archon laughed heartily, which was weird. Then it wept uncontrollably, which was weirder. Then it slapped its knee-equivalents and started dancing, which I don't even want to think about.

"Vindi... Saraya..." Avashti looked up, his face stark and pale in the gloom. "When the time comes, I'll crawl off on my own. My heart couldn't take it, having to watch you suffer. It will be... easier, I think. For all of us."

"So morbid," Vindi complained.

I snorted. "Morbid, I can live with. Literally. I mean, what's wrong with being realistic? It's the whole giving-up part that offends me."

"You're not crawling anywhere," Vindi assured her father.

"True," I said. "Crawling is out. If you're going to abandon us, the least you could do is entertain us with some sassy high-kicks on your way out."

We came to a junction of three different passages. "We've been here before," Vindi groaned, pointing to a red-streaked band of flowstone.

I grimaced. "Darshik was right. In this place, you might as well flip a coin and let *it* choose your path. At least you might get lucky, step into a pit, and die *fast*."

Avashti winced. "Could you *not* mention that charlatan's name where I can... hold on."

"I'm having difficulty comprehending mortal motivations," Adversary complained. "First, you were *against* dying. Now you're for it? Make up your mind!"

"Please don't let's not," I said maliciously.

"I'll tell you what," Adversary said. "If you let me kill you now, I promise that—when I make you talk, later, by flapping your jaw up and down like a puppet—I'll only make your corpse say *tasteful* things."

"NO!" Vindi shouted, horrified.

"Very well. Tasteless things it is." Adversary's gears spun a little faster. "Humans are so weird. Do *you* understand them?" It turned, becoming Archon. "Less than point-zero-six percent of the time," Archon replied sadly, "and what I *do* understand, I generally wish I didn't."

"I think I have something," Avashti said slowly. "Flipping a coin to choose your path... why, it would be ridiculous. Obviously. You'd have to have incredibly good luck for it to work."

"Good luck?" Vindi asked, started to get excited. "If I burned my earrings, would everything go back to the way it was back in the old days?"

"Sadly, no. Wizardly artifacts tend to be… sturdy. They aren't that easy to destroy. But we do have another option." Avashti raised the Lens of Becoming to eye level, its many crystals chiming gently as they glanced off one another. "If I can adjust your earrings," he told Vindi, "and redirect Saraya's stolen luck to one of *us* instead of back to *her*… either you or I would become the luckiest bastard the world has ever known."

"And what would happen to me?" I asked.

"Your luck would be every bit as awful as it was back in the old days, at least until we completed our escape and I put everything back to normal."

"Enough gabbing," I said simply. "Do it."

"I'll protect you," Vindi said confidently. "I always did back then, didn't I?"

"Yeah, like that time a bat flew into my hair, and you flailed away at me because good luck meant that throwing punches at my unprotected face couldn't possibly go wrong. Except that it was a *really* adorable bat, so that *lucky*—in that specific case—meant missing it and clobbering me. Is that the kind of protection you're talking about?"

"You didn't *die*," Vindi protested. "And you got your sense of smell back in less than a year. I really don't know what you're complaining about."

"Are you sure you want me to do this?" Avashti said quietly.

"Perfectly. Do it."

Avashti dangled the Lens of Becoming at head-height, looking at Vindi through its various crystals. Frowning, he moved closer and closer to his daughter until he was practically standing on her feet.

"Only focuses at super-close range," he apologized. "Let me see…" He went into a trance of sorts, speaking in a rhythmic murmur that occasionally rose into a louder chant. Sometimes he swayed. Sometimes he traced inexplicable symbols with his hand. Sometimes he shuffled his feet in a dance as slow, yet as inevitable, as the universe. I started to feel strangely warm. My skin began to tingle. A sudden chill flushed through my body. And then, all at once, the sensations stopped.

Avashti lowered the Lens of Becoming. "That's it. Your luck is now mine. I think."

Vindi frowned. "How do we know if it worked?"

"Allow me," I said graciously. "I'll flip a coin. Heads, you're my slave. Tails, we flip again. Agreed?"

"Sure," she said, amused. I reached into my pocket, only to find a ragged hole where my money had been.

"I'll flip this rock," I said, grabbing what turned out to be an eyeless, colorless cave scorpion. Still plenty good at stinging, though.

"Gah!" I cried. My voice rang through the corridor, rousing a minor explosion of cave bats. I could have understood *one* of them getting tangled in my hair, but all eleven?

"I'd say my luck is right back where it was always destined to end up," I said drily.

"Don't be so negative!" Vindi said, picking the bats out of my hair one by one. "Poor little critters. Avashti? You're up. Get us out of here."

Avashti glanced at the various passages, murmuring numbers under his breath. He took out a coin, kissed it, and flipped it three times.

"That way," he said confidently.

It was a fairly nondescript journey, in that I only fell down a *few* sinkholes. Sure, a couple of stalactites just happened to break loose as we passed and beaned me on the head, further causing me to hallucinate that cave scorpions were delicious pancakes—after which I crammed as many as I could into my mouth—but that could have happened to anyone.

After a long and meandering journey, we reached a point where the cave split six ways. Avashti's coin came out. He flipped. It shot straight into my eye.

"ARRGH!" I shouted, staggering wildly.

"Permit me," Archon said. It reached out and poked its mechanism-finger hard into my *other* eye. "There. Now they match. Mission accomplished!"

"That… wasn't… what I… wanted."

"Mortals are so capricious," Archon complained.

"Wait," Vindi said, holding up her hands. "Listen."

We fell silent. A muted scraping reached us, coming from the other side of the stone wall on our left.

"We did it!" Avashti said, astonished. "The royal engineering corps is going to break through right about here. We even got here first!"

"You're not going to die?" Archon mused. "A pity. I will take my leave, then. I have some innovative ideas about organizing artifacts into concentric circles that I want to put into effect immediately."

"You're weird," Vindi said, hugging the mechanism, "but I like you."

"Is this gesture intended to communicate aggression?" Archon asked, alarmed. "Calculating. I surrender!"

"You're weird," I agreed. "But I like you, too. Half of you, anyway."

Archon turned, becoming Adversary. "Oh, don't stop," it said to Vindi, who was still hugging it. "We're sinning, right? This is some form of human sexual deviancy, isn't it?"

"Just go with it," I whispered.

Vindi hastily let go. "You could still come with us, you know. See Kairay. Experience the surface world for yourself. If you didn't like it, you could always throw yourself back down the pit."

"There is a certain temptation to the idea," Adversary admitted, "but it will pass once you've gone. The outside world, I think, would prove a messy and disagreeable place. *You* folks are worth knowing— especially Saraya, who now owes me six unbroken lifetimes of indentured servitude—but I don't imagine anyone else would be as entertaining as you."

"Come with us. Just *try* it," Vindi urged the mechanism.

Adversary turned, becoming Archon. "You are an irrational, illogical, obstreperous young being," it told her. "As it happens, I have calculated that there is a ninety-nine point eight percent chance that I would find any particular human to be extremely irritating. As indeed I do… except for you. You are merely thirty-six percent as objectionable as your fellows."

"I love you, too," Vindi said wryly.

"Nonetheless, I will stay here, in the only home I have ever known. This is my proper place."

"I understand," Vindi said. "I'll miss you."

"Me too," I admitted. "Half of you, anyway."

"Understood. And now, permit me say goodbye in an appropriately human fashion."

Archon/Adversary threw back its head-equivalent and laughed, a wild and shrieking cackle that went on and on. Before Vindi or I could say anything, it strode away down the corridor, still shrieking with laughter. Vindi hastily lit our one lantern before the mechanism-creature's gentle glow left us entirely. That weird, cackling laughter grew fainter and fainter until it vanished completely.

"Archon?" Vindi called.

"Adversary?" I added. We waited, letting the echoes of our shouts slowly die. No answer. It was gone.

Vindi sighed, turning back to her father. "Well, we've gotten where we need to go. You can put Saraya back to normal, right?"

"I suppose," Avashti said. "You know, a man could get used to this. No matter how often you farted, I never once smelled it."

"Speak for yourself," I said darkly.

Avashti raised the Lens of Becoming and once again went through his ridiculous rituals. My skin once again flushed hot and cold, tingly and prickly.

"Oops," Avashti said, cutting off in mid-chant.

"What? What happened?" I demanded. "In my experience, that word usually comes just before '—wrong one!' and just after 'Let's pull that bad tooth, shall we?'"

"I made a mistake," Avashti said, sounding as if he could hardly believe himself. "Instead of *altering* the earrings, I *moved* their power. I didn't even know that was possible."

"Moved them?" Vindi asked, touching her earrings. "What do you mean? They're still there."

"No, no. I moved their *power*. The earrings are useless. Empty vessels that do nothing. Their power has been transferred to your horns. Your horns are the artifacts, now."

"Can I fly?" she immediately asked.

"What? No!"

"They're not very good artifacts, then. Go on. Fix Saraya. Redirect her stolen luck back to her."

Avashti concentrated once again, doing inexplicable things with the Lens of Becoming as my vision blurred and tripled, darkened and brightened. At long last, he sighed and lowered the peculiar artifact. I didn't feel any different, so I tried picking up a rock. It was just a rock.

"Yeah, I think we're good," I said.

The sounds of digging were growing steadily closer. We moved over and sat against the far wall, waiting for our rescuers to arrive.

IV

The moon was bright overhead when I emerged from that claustrophobic little tunnel, the stars pulsing to their own celestial music. The moon! The stars! Sure, they were out to get me, too, but I felt a surge of affection toward them as a pair of soldiers pulled me from my almost-tomb. I mean, the moon and stars *are* very far away: Now matter how fast they throw a dagger, it would take hours to get here. I almost pitied them for being frustrated in their ongoing desire to assassinate me. Almost.

"Whew! How many days were we down there?" Vindi asked.

"One," Avashti said, climbing out behind her.

"Huh. Seems like a lot longer."

"C'mon, Avashti," I said. "Outwitting magical machine-men who alternate randomly between good and evil makes a girl lose track of time. You're a wizard. Why didn't you know that?"

Avashti rolled his eyes. "It's true that my job is to know everything—*except* things so stupid, it would actually be undignified to know them."

I looked around. We were fairly low on the rocky promontory that housed the Cave of Wonders. All around us were piles of dirt, abandoned gantries, and discarded tools from the dig. An arc of soldiers stood close behind us, though I doubted they'd done any of the actual digging. Before us stood a chariot yoked to three horses all in a line. Princess Gamal sat primly with her hands folded in front of her, her face imperturbably lovely in the lantern-light. Princess Shivaka stood just behind her, red-faced and a little jumpy.

"We got it!" Vindi announced, gesturing to Avashti. "The Lens of Becoming! All yours."

Princess Shivaka managed an awkward smile. "Yes. Well. The thing is…" She trailed off, glancing at Gamal. "Why don't you tell them?"

"Oh, no," Gamal purred, "by all means, go ahead."

"I'd really rather you did it."

"I know. That's why I won't. Call it my treat for the day."

Princess Shivaka cleared her throat. She smiled nervously. She didn't seem to know what to do with her hands. "We… may not have been completely truthful with you," she said.

"Translation," Gamal said, "commoners exist to serve. It's their purpose. Tricking the disobedient into serving is the greatest kindness we can do them, because it restores to them their sole purpose in life."

Princess Shivaka wrung her hands. "The thing is… what *couldn't* I do if I had perfect luck all the time? What Avashti wrought by accident all those years ago may be the most powerful tool in human history. Try as I might—no matter how many wizards I hire, no matter what fees I pay them—I haven't been able to duplicate it."

"Translation: You have something we want, and we are your lords and masters. Therefore, it belongs to us. Feel free to protest, in which case you will shortly be dead, in which case it will *still* belong to us. Nice how that works, isn't it?"

"So," Shivaka said, her face growing even redder, "we're going to transfer Saraya's luck to me, which will leave her… well… actually, I prefer not to think about it. You will give us the Lens. And the earrings."

Startled, Vindi glanced at her father. "Didn't you say…"

"Careful, now," he whispered.

"I thought you were supposed to be one of the good ones," I said, stepping in front of Vindi. "I thought you were supposed to care about lowly nobodies like us."

"You don't understand," Shivaka said, her voice breaking. "I need it. Once I have your luck…"

"Enough of this," Gamal said, snapping her fingers and pointing. "They have something of ours. Take it."

Soldiers grabbed the Lens of Becoming out of Avashti's hands. He let it go without protest. Soldiers hulked out of the shadows toward Vindi: Managing to look realistically scared, she took off her earrings and handed them over.

"The three of them, too. Take them," Gamal commanded, gesturing toward us.

"No!" Shivaka said, her face red. "Let them go!"

"Be sensible," Gamal said. "This is complicated enough. We *have* to take them prisoner, at least until we complete the transfer and make sure everything worked correctly."

"No. We've hurt them enough."

Gamal's lips curled into a venomous smile. "I see. You're afraid. Princess Perfect is happy to declare war on her enemies… but show her the corpses and she'd have to really *think* about what she'd done, have to confront the consequences of her own actions. You're fine with stealing that poor girl's luck for yourself, as long as it's done out of your sight. The idea of actually having to see the drained and empty husk scares you."

"Let them go!" Shivaka said angrily. Soldiers stepped aside. Avashti walked straight ahead. Vindi and I followed. I made faces at the soldiers, but they didn't react. So unsatisfying. Instead, I hocked up all the phlegm I could in a long, slow, noisy rasp, and spat it straight at Gamal. Oh, I don't expect I got within ten feet of her, but the horrified shock on her face was worth about a hundred outraged soldiers.

"The moment my sister dies, I will hunt you for sport," she said, her voice shaking.

"The moment you touch me, I'm going to stick my arm up your—"

"SARAYA!" Vindi said, shocked.

"—and dance you around like a puppet."

We continued down the hillside, the soldiers watching impassively. The tiny pool of light behind us grew smaller and smaller. At last we heard the rumble of the princesses' chariot moving off, taking a different route than we were. The soldiers formed up and marched after it. That left just the three of us stumbling in the moonlit dark, shivering against the shockingly cold desert night.

"Didn't you say my horns were the artifact, now?" Vindi whispered. "Not the earrings?"

"Indeed," Avashti said quietly, "and the moment they figure out they only have *half* of what they need, they'll be coming for us."

"Then what are we going to do?"

I patted her arm comfortingly. "We're going to die," I said reassuringly. "Or, at least, I am."

"Saraya—" she said despairingly.

"No, no. It makes sense, right? If I die, there won't be anyone to steal luck *from*. The whole thing will be over instantly. I've chosen how I want it to happen, too: Avashti uses his magic to make thousands and thousands of delectable pies come to life and attack me. I'm smothered to death under a heaving mountain of delectables that constantly erupts with geysers of berry juice and molten-hot deliciousness!"

"Do you have to be whimsical, even in death?" Avashti demanded. "Can't you do *one* thing with dignity?"

"We're not going to let you die!" Vindi said fervently. "We're not. Tell her!"

"Well…" Avashti stopped walking, a conflicted look on his face. "No. Saraya isn't going to die. Which means that we all have to go to the Temple of Souls. For some reason."

"Why?" I asked.

"Because I said so."

"Not good enough. I repeat: Why?"

"Obstreperous girl-thing! Stop defying me!"

"Why?" Vindi demanded, her eyes dancing as she faced her father.

"Girls…"

"Why?" we said together. Avashti groaned, burying his face in his hands.

"I shouldn't even tell you there *is* a Secret of Wizardry, much less what it is," he said, almost to himself. "After you'd completed an eight-year apprenticeship, a six-year assistantship, and a five-year probationary period I might *consider* it… but…"

"Dad?"

Avashti finally looked up. "Fine. Fine. Here it is: What Archon/Adversary told you is essentially correct. Human belief refracts, at random, into gods. Wizards ask those gods for favors, and take what we're given, no matter how bizarre or wrong or riven with unintended consequences it may be. Some wizards try to move people around and alter the way they believe, in order to change the gods themselves. Others, like me, try to write legal documents so precise that the gods *have* to give us exactly what we want." He managed a rueful smile. "Most of the gods can be found at the Temple of Souls, well south and east of Kairay. We need to go there. We need to try and fix this thing with Saraya, once and for all. The thing is…" He winced. "All of my documents and forms, everything I've spent years perfecting to a nicety, everything that ensures we can actually *deal* with the gods, is at home in our tower. But the princesses have horses. They can go a lot faster than we can. Do we head back into town, stop by the tower… and risk getting caught… or do we go straight to the Temple of Souls in a bid to arrive first, albeit empty-handed and helpless?"

Vindi and I looked at each other. "Do the gods… make sense?" Vindi cautiously asked. "Can we talk to them? Can we make friends with them?"

"Not hardly. For coagulated blobs of human belief, they're about as inhuman as it's possible to get."

"We go back into town and make for home," I decided. Avashti didn't look happy, but he didn't contradict me. The three of us resumed walking.

It was hours before we finally reached Kairay—almost certainly well after midnight. Here, a new challenge presented itself: Even on the outskirts of the city, trees blotted out most of the stars and made it that much harder to see. Just when we needed to be at our stealthiest, we were forced to shuffle down the exact center of the biggest and widest roads we could find just so we didn't trip and break our necks. With my luck, I wondered, would I step wrong and break my own neck first—or would everyone else simultaneously trip onto me, thus breaking it *for* me?

"Saraya!" Avashti whispered hoarsely. "Pay attention! You almost stepped on a squid sprite."

"A glowing one, or a flying one?"

"Well, the bioluminescent striping suggests that—" Avashti made a frustrated noise. "It doesn't matter! Just watch where you're going!"

"Sorry. Can't. I have a lot of thinking to do. Specifically, I need to figure out the best way of positioning myself so my corpse will be useful to Vindi."

"Don't say that!" she said heatedly. "You're useless! Ask anyone!"

There was a fraught moment of silence. "I'm smirking," Avashti told us. "You can't see it, but I'm smirking. Pray tell, would your corpse be useful to *me*?"

"Depends. Do you need a big, floppy puppet for anything?"

"That's… not a gift I'd care to receive. Can I refuse it?"

"Sorry. The terms of my will are *extremely* specific."

"I see. In that case, I think we'll have to keep you alive just a little longer."

Crossing Kairay has never taken so long. At least, it's never *seemed* so long. Every step surely brought us closer to our enemies. My imagination insisted that every patch of darkness was bristling with watchful eyes… *and there was darkness everywhere*. At long last, a familiar tower house rose before us, a stark silhouette cutting across the starry night. Making a happy noise, Vindi started to run toward it.

"Stop!" Avashti hissed, grabbing her. "That's just where they'll be waiting for us!"

Slowly and carefully, we crept up to the wall of the tower house and listened. There was the usual muted commotion from all the failed wizardry packed into the first floor, but nothing else. Avashti crept around back, beckoning us with outsized gestures. There, he laced his fingers into a basket: I shoved Vindi into a bush so I could be the one to risk going in, and let Avashti give me a boost to an open window. I pulled myself up and tumbled inside, finding myself in the utter darkness of a small storage room. I held my breath and listened: I heard the usual roar and clatter of Avashti's machines —nothing else. I opened the door and slipped into the main room, which was incredibly noisy with all of the golems and mechanisms going about their inscrutable business. My grasping hand found the downstairs lantern. I managed to light it. Slowly, cautiously, I looked around. Still nothing. I went to the front door and opened it, waving Vindi and Avashti inside.

The tower house seemed to be exactly as we'd left it. Avashti ran up to his third-floor laboratory two steps at a time. Vindi and I stopped on the second floor and hurriedly packed for a journey of who-knew-how-long, grabbing money from under the secret board in Avashti's room and food from the pantry, clothes from the floor and blankets from our wall chests. Avashti trudged back down from his laboratory, carrying a teetering stack of folded books and heavily marked papyrus. Vindi and I exchanged glances and started stuffing even *more* necessities into our packs. It would be all Avashti could do just to haul such a huge stack of documents: Vindi and I would have to carry food and supplies enough for all three of us.

At last we were packed and ready, if tired. Vindi made us huddle in the pantry to wolf down as much food as we could manage. Finally, carrying two lanterns dimmed almost all the way down, we set out from the tower house. The trees became even taller and closer together, the road plunging into utter darkness.

"We're taking the river?" I whispered.

"I'd rather," Avashti murmured. "If the blisters on my feet got any bigger, I'd end up infested with mice when they mistook my blisters for temples and came to worship."

"That's a vivid way of putting it," Vindi said wryly.

"Won't the princesses be watching for us on the river?" I asked.

"At this point, my dear, we have to assume they're watching for us *everywhere*."

"There are a lot more roads than rivers. Their forces would be stretched thinner. Also, on land, I can run. On the water, about the best I can do is drown artistically."

"Don't say that!" Vindi hissed.

"All right. I'll drown pathetically."

"Stop it!"

I sighed. "Fine. On water, about the best I can do is strap squid sprites to my feet and rocket into the canopy on a blast of obscuring ink. Trust me! It works!"

"That's better," Vindi said wryly. "Also, I hate you. Is it normal to feel that way about someone you love like a sister?"

"From personal experience, I'd have to say 'yes'."

"Also," Avashti said, "please consider my blisters and how much I'd whine about them if you forced me to keep walking."

"Say no more. The river it is."

I turned up my lantern as we reached the waters of the Kairay. Dozens of "boats" were pulled up on shore where children had left them, but they all looked much the same... like leaking, sinking, queasily hammered-together messes of splintering boards. There was one actual boat, but a little girl was actually sleeping propped up against it: Since the first kid to arrive got their pick, I guess that was what it took to ensure she'd have the best boat tomorrow.

"All right," Vindi said, "we wake her up and ask her how much it would cost to— hey!"

I took the girl gently by the shoulders. Avashti took her feet. We moved her aside and she didn't even wake up. Vindi hastily slipped some coins into the girl's pouch, and then we launched the boat and got underway.

Rivers, I understand, are dangerous even at the best of times, what with hidden snags, sand bars, armor-plated murderfish, you name it. Add to that the probability that we were hunted fugitives, and it was even more crucial that we keep a careful watch. For the record, what we actually did was point at each other and ourselves in an exaggerated way, holding up numbers of fingers which presumably meant something. Then we all fell asleep.

I vaguely remember waking a number of times. We bumped up against some tree roots and stalled there for a while; sprites like curious, gently-glowing cotton-seeds drifted down to stare in wonderment at the weirdness of the big, oafish creatures which had stumbled into their realm; vines reached eagerly toward us, only to retreat when they found that we were carrying neither flowers nor nectar; and at one point the sky rumbled and the quasi-silver bracelet on my wrist tingled as if anticipating a lightning strike, even though there wasn't a cloud to be seen.

I woke as the sun cleared the horizon. We'd drifted out of the city and well into the hinterland. Scrubby trees bracketed the river, and the desert beyond was harsher, emptier, more barren than the lands around Kairay. Vindi and Avashti woke as well, and I regaled them with the story of how I'd stayed awake and kept watch all by myself, all night long.

"Uh-huh," Vindi said skeptically. "Then why is there a line on your forehead, as if you'd been sleeping face-down on the edge of the boat for the past six hours?"

"Listen," I said urgently, "can't we agree that my lies are far more beautiful, just, and—in a deeper sense—*true* that the blandishments of mere reality? Don't let that bitch Reality win just because she's right. Don't let her tell you that things are true just because they're so. You can start by believing me."

"Uh-huh," Vindi said with a maddening smirk.

It got hotter as the day got underway. And then hotter. And then hotter yet. We ended up using our blankets to form a makeshift tent just so that the desert sun wouldn't shrivel us up like slugs in a salt mine. It wasn't exactly comfortable, but on a positive note, we didn't die. As the day stretched past noon, I noticed that the trees were getting taller and thicker, even forming a decent canopy overhead at times. Mountains appeared in the distance, or rocky hills, or whatever you call those things that are craggy but not actually all that high. The Kairay river headed straight into a cleft between them. It looked narrow at first, but as we got closer it broadened out vastly.

"The Valley of Thunder," Avashti stated.

A rickety house hove into sight, built from sun-baked mud. Strange boxy vehicles stood nearby, along with a stable holding several bored-looking donkeys. Avashti stuck our one paddle into the water, bending us slowly toward shore.

"People live here?" I said, amazed.

"Every time I come, there's a different person on duty," Avashti said, "so one would be forced to assume there's a whole city nearby."

"Or it's always the same person, and you're just really bad with faces," I suggested. "Here's a question. Do you recognize *me*?"

"Based on the fact that there is no mercy in the universe, yes, sadly, I do."

"I'm Princess Shivaka," I said. "No, really. I'll prove it. Give me all your money and I'll nobly return it to you untouched." I paused. "But first you have to give it to me. And Vindi."

"Yes, do!" Vindi said hopefully.

Avashti rolled his eyes. "One might wish he could die in a foreign land without the brazen taint of whimsy to make his demise even more pathetic… but we're not always given a choice, are we?"

Bumping up on shore, we pulled the boat out of the water, shouldered our packs, and headed for the building. There wasn't a door. Inside, a single barren room boasted a rickety table at which sat a surly, red-faced man.

"What?" he demanded.

"I'm a wizard," Avashti said. "I seek to hire passage across the Valley of Thunder."

"Ten grains."

"That…" Avashti hesitated. "That's almost *too* good. It's certainly less than I paid last time."

"Too hot to haggle. Take it or leave it."

"Oh, I'll take it!"

We were led out to one of the weird squared-off vehicles, which turned out to be little more than a sealed, windowless box on wheels. The red-faced man hitched a pair of donkeys to the front of the cart and then closed us up inside. It was very hot and very dark in there, and the vehicle sat unmoving for a choice slice of forever. What could the red-faced man even be *doing* that would take so long?

"I don't get it," I panted. "Why put us in a box? Why not leave us in the open air?"

Avashti shrugged. "I have my suspicions. Namely, I suspect that there's nothing special about the Valley of Thunder, and concealing that fact is their way of convincing us that we're being protected from all kinds of threats. Thus, we keep paying them, and their livelihoods are sustained. Frankly, as long as we get where we're going, I couldn't care less."

The cart creaked and dipped to one side as someone, presumably the red-faced man, climbed on top. After a few moments he snapped the reigns, the donkeys muttered to themselves, and we *finally* got underway.

Vindi felt like talking. Of course. Generally, I am the soul of courtesy when telling people to shut up (as proven by the fact that I no longer sassily shake my hips when singing the 'please shut up' song), but I didn't even get the chance to start setting down a beat with my mouth this time. The cart hit a HUGE bump just as I opened my mouth, and I ended up slamming into the side of the box and getting a splinter in my tongue.

"And another thing," Vindi said. "Why don't more people dress their babies up as adorable animals? There are only so many years when we can humiliate children without them getting all sulky and launching armed rebellions against us. Why not use that precious opportunity to make life more fun for *everybody*?"

"Mmpha," I said disdainfully.

"See? Saraya agrees with me!"

"MMPHA!"

"Really, Saraya?" Avashti said, shaking his head. "And here I thought you were the rational one. I'm disappointed in you."

"Mmpha mmpha mmpha!"

"And another thing," Vindi said. "We should be working harder to teach the Leaf Riders to make adorable little pies for us. Sure, everything they cook tastes like tree barf, but you have to make sacrifices if you want the world to be a better place."

"Mmpha!"

"See? Saraya agrees with me!"

The cart rolled to a stop. I finally managed to get rid of the splinter by the rather disturbing expedient of licking my own hand repeatedly. I'm sorry to report that my skin tastes like dust and failure.

"Stopping like this… is it normal?" I asked Avashti.

The wizard frowned. "Well… no. But I don't know that it's worth getting worried about."

Someone moved around outside the cart, trying their best to be all quiet and sneaky. Even so, it was impossible to disguise the sound of clopping hooves as the donkeys were led away. Clearly, they'd been disconnected from the cart, leaving our boxy prison sitting alone in the middle of the desert.

"What about now? Can we panic *now*?" I asked facetiously.

"Huh," Avashti muttered. He started pulling at the boards that covered his side of the cart: Vindi took the other side, and I took the back. In moments, we'd each opened a gap large enough to look through. I also managed the rare feat of spearing my hand with a splinter that so precisely speared a previous splinter that it actually split it open like a blooming flower, but that's a story for another day.

"Nothing," Avashti said, peering through his gap.

"I see the river," Vindi said, peering through hers.

I looked through mine. Some distance behind us, pairs of donkeys drew a trio of boxy, closed carts just like ours. They were following on the same road, and would reach us before too much longer.

"There are three carts behind us," I reported. Avashti and Vindi rushed to peer through my gap, Avashti swearing voluminously the moment he saw them.

"We were so careful for so long," he said bitterly. "And after all that, it turns out they were waiting for us *here*."

"What? Who?"

"Princess Gamal's soldiers. Who else would need so many carts? They must have been lying in wait. Knew we wouldn't come near if we spotted them, so they paid the driver to betray us, then waited just out of sight. Once they reach us…"

"Nuts to that," I said, prying at the boards across the back of the cart. They were loose, and got substantially looser as I pulled at them. "They can't catch what they can't find. I say we make for the river and hide in the trees."

"They'll still catch us—it'll just take longer," Avashti said fatalistically.

"They can't kill Saraya," Vindi said suddenly. "They need her alive, so they can drain her luck. They'll have instructions not to hurt her."

"There you go," I said. "You go first. I'll follow behind. Whatever they send after us, it won't be arrows."

"It is more dignified, sometimes, when Death is inevitable, to lean back in your chair, wait patiently for His arrival, and toast His health when he stops in," Avashti mused.

Several boards broke free in my hand. Vindi kicked the edge of the hole, rapidly making it bigger.

"Sure," I said, "but I prefer to jump at Him with onions in each hand, shrieking with laughter and with my underwear yanked up over my head, in the hopes that Death will be so shocked and embarrassed that he'll actually forget to kill me. Then I'll dance around a little, causing him to hide his face in shame, whereupon I'll run like hell and get away clean. To hell with dignity. To hell with Death. If they get us, I want them to know they've been in a fight. It may be statistically impossible, but I intend for them to end up with more bruised testicles than they actually have balls."

More boards broke free in Vindi's grip. I handed Avashti his pack. He smiled at me.

"You do have a way with words," he admitted, and slipped out the back of the broken cart.

We ran for the river as fast as we could. The three boxy carts stayed firmly on course, rolling slowly and inevitably toward our abandoned one. The drivers had to have seen us: Their weird reluctance to let outsiders see the Valley of Thunder might be our one saving grace, if it made them hesitate to tell the soldiers what was going on.

"Come on!" Vindi panted, darting into the shrubby undergrowth. Avashti and I followed: All three of us plunged into the forest, with little thought for the thorns that tugged at our clothes, the burrs that leapt at us with all six fat little arms akimbo, or the tiny spider-striped fey that chittered as they angrily shook their fists at us. Finally, the Kairay river appeared before us, muddy and smooth, careless of our worries.

"Did we do it?" Vindi panted. "Did we get away?"

"Go back and look," I suggested.

"I have a better idea. I'll strap you to a really tall pole and wave you back and forth, and you can scream your report at the top of your lungs."

"No talking," Avashti snapped.

"So we don't attract bad guys?" I hazarded.

The wizard mulled it over. "Sure. That's also a good reason."

We hurried downriver as fast as we could. It wasn't easy without a path: We had to push through bushes, shove vines aside, and step carefully around fairy hives. Occasionally we stopped and listened, but we never heard any sign of pursuit. Not that that meant anything. The soldiers may have decided to simply keep to the road and wait for *us* to come to *them*.

Avashti pushed a branch aside. "If we can just make it to...

huh."

We stumbled into a most unusual clearing. Six enormous, blocky grey boxes loomed over us, standing ten feet tall at least, with weird grey tubes sticking out one side. They looked weirdly familiar. In fact…

"They look like the way I drew elephants when I was five," Vindi said, puzzled. She walked over and touched one of the bizarre structures. It was covered with rough cloth which had been brown before someone painted it grey.

"They're decoys," said a woman's voice, strong and rich, with just the slightest tang of arch overconfidence. It took me a few moments to find her: The observation tower blended into the canopy, well-concealed under a camouflage of vines and leaves and other vegetation. The woman who'd spoken wore leather hunter's gear and an amazing cloak that shone with all sorts of iridescent colors. She also, rather incongruously, had a crystal rim pinned over her heart. It was irregular and flawed, something I hadn't known was possible, but it still had to be worth a fortune. She had her feet up on the railing of the observation tower, smirking at us as she picked her teeth with a dagger.

"Decoys?" I said cautiously. "You have a thing for elephants?"

"Ha! Not hardly, my lass. The name's Ramla," she said, somehow managing to bow while still sitting down. "Ramla the Great, if you will, and just Ramla if you—like everyone else in the world—will not. Why would we want elephants? I'm taking my rotation on watch, just like everyone has to, so I can move the decoys around and make them all life-like if I spot a roc."

"You catch *rocs*?" Vindi asked, eyes wide. "Do you tame them? Do you *ride* them? Do young lovers sing to each other while soaring high above the clouds? Oh! I just had an *incredible* idea for a wedding!"

"Sounds hilarious," I said, grinning. "Who gets to take bets on how many members of the wedding party are swept off the side and lost forever?"

"Don't tell them the truth," Avashti told Ramla. "Some dreams are all the more important for being really, really stupid."

"The truth?" I asked, puzzled. "I thought you didn't know anything about the Valley of Thunder."

"I don't. Well, I didn't. But I have eyes, and—unlike certain people I could mention—I know how to use them," he said gently.

"Go on."

"Look at her clothes. They're all leather, and unusually thick, at that. Almost like the skin of the world's biggest animal, wouldn't you say? Look at her cloak. Made of colorful, veined fibers—like a fragment of the world's biggest feather. I have no idea how they do it, but they must be luring rocs down to hunt them."

"Aren't you the clever one, my lad!" Ramla said heartily, sliding down one of the tower's support poles. So help me, she managed to strike a heroic pose all the way down. "Hunting a roc, now, there's something I'd like to see! No, we lure them down because they're clumsy fliers, they are. Every time they dive, there's a small but real chance they'll smash into the ground hard enough to break their own necks. Then we don't have to do a thing! After they're dead, why, we can pick over the corpse at our leisure. *So* much meat! *So* much leather! *So* many feathers! It doesn't work often—but it works often enough."

"That must be one hell of an impact," I said, impressed.

"Well and truly said, my lass! Why do you think they call this the Valley of *Thunder*? But enough about me. You're obviously not locals," Ramla said keenly. "You need help, yes? A local's sure knowledge and practiced guidance, perhaps? How much would you pay for *mine*?"

"Less than you expect," Avashti said guardedly, "but about twice as much as you deserve."

"Genius!" she cried, shouting with laughter. "I like it! You, you, you, come with me. I'll take care of you, sure enough!"

"What about the decoys?" Vindi asked. "I mean, not that I want any rocs to *die*, but aren't you supposed to be watching them?"

Ramla winked expansively. "Can I tell you something, my dear? Standing watch is boring as hell. If I can make a little money by abandoning my post… Ha! I promise not to tell if you don't!"

Ramla walked down a faint trail through the forest, not even looking to see if we were following. Her walk was practically a swagger, as if she owned everything she saw, or at least, as if everything she saw should feel enormously complimented by the mere prospect of being owned by her.

"Can we trust her?" I whispered.

"She's fun!" Vindi said. "She knows how to *live*."

"The loyalty that money buys may not be the finest or the

best," Avashti noted, "but it still *is*. I'll add a fifteen percent kicker if she agrees not to betray us."

The two of them fell in line behind Ramla. After only a moment's hesitation, I brought up the rear.

The trail wound back and forth through increasingly dense forest. Oddly, I didn't recognize most of the abundant life that surrounded us. Weird pink flowers stretched toward us, their petals pulsing like grasping hands. Huge trees stretched over the river, dangling what looked like long beards of moss—which, as I watched, suddenly snatched a fish right out of the water and tossed it onto the tree's roots, presumably to serve as fertilizer.

"We're nearing the Temple of Souls," Avashti said, noticing my expression. "Gods... *do* things, sometimes, for inscrutable reasons all their own. If they have any reason at all. Prepare for stuff to get weird."

"And everything was so normal up until now," I said drily.

"Ah! We're nearing the city of Qamara!" Ramla called back to us. "Are you rich, my dear friends? Does money pour from your pockets in a never-ending stream? Do you have trouble falling asleep due to the mad excess of golden crowns always orbiting your dear little heads? Ha! I didn't think so. Conceal yourselves, then. There are too many people here for you to bribe, and I'll be damned if I spend any of *my* money on you."

We pulled our blankets out of our packs and fashioned them into makeshift cloaks, complete with hoods to cover our faces. Ramla nodded and pronounced our efforts good enough. After we'd marched a little farther, the forest parted and we came to Qamara.

It was, quite possibly, the single most spectacular city I'd ever seen. Not because it was big. Not because it was lively. Because the whole thing was built into the gigantic skeleton of a long-dead roc, which was nestled in the crater left by its titanic impact years ago. Smoke curled up from the empty eyes of its skull. Orb-shaped houses nestled in the hollows of its neck vertebrae. Crude windows had been hacked into leg bones that, like the limbs of all birds, were hollow. Only under the overarching ribs did I see the squalid shanties of a more normal, if poor, town. It couldn't have held more than two or three hundred people, but what a place to live!

"Good day to you, Bhadir, and a fine day it is, too!" Ramla cried, spotting a squat merchant with a huge beard. His clothes were poor, little more than a shapeless assortment of leathers, rather incongruously pinned together with half a dozen misshapen crystal rims. Even broken and scuffed and pierced by cords, they glittered like iridescent, endlessly colorful pearls formed into rings.

"Ramla," he said suspiciously.

"Look what I've brought you, Bhadir... three new slaves! Cheap! Cheaper than cheap! Whatever you're thinking, you can buy them for half that, so long as what you were thinking was twice a fair price! What do you say?"

"I've had enough of you and your money-making schemes," he said sourly. "Sell your slaves to someone else."

"I was joking," Ramla told Avashti as we moved on, "or at least, the scam would have ended up with me buying you back at half price, so it amounts to the same thing."

"Somehow, I'm not comforted."

"Ah! But I serve you now and for always, I do!" Ramla pledged, hand to her heart. "I love you dearly. Well, I love part of you, specifically, the area just above and outside your hip where my promised fee is jingling in your coin pouch. If you truly want to—"

She suddenly shut up, wrenching her gaze down to the muddy path under our feet. Puzzled, I looked around. There, above us and off to the left, something like a ball of lightning drifted toward us. I stared at it. Lightning... on a clear day? Yet there it was, frazzled hairs of electricity reaching out to touch the upper leaves of the trees it passed. They instantly curled up, turned brown, and burst into flames. I noticed that the quasi-silver bracelet on my left wrist was pulsing in time to the thing's flickering light. As it drew closer, the entire left side of my body began to tic, which was both uncomfortable and embarrassing.

"Don't look at it," Avashti hissed, his own eyes fixed on the path. "They're endlessly curious about people, but *only notice those who pay attention to them.*"

"You mean it's *alive*?" Vindi demanded.

"Hush. Don't look at it. Don't think about it. Don't even admit that it's there."

"Like I'll be able to *stop* thinking about a mysterious, nameless zappy-friend possessed of an unstoppable attraction to me," Vindi said wryly. "Tell me what it is."

"No!"

"Tell her!" I whispered urgently as the quasi-silver bracelet started painfully zapping me, causing my left hand to flap about and fiercely pinch whatever was closest—which is to say, some rather delicate parts of my own body. "Tell her so she can get bored with it and move on to obsessing over something less deadly!" The ball of lighting was now roughly twenty feet over us, circling slowly and starting to drift toward Vindi.

Avashti frowned. "Well… I guess that makes sense, sort of. If you must know, it's a firecat."

Vindi looked startled. "It's a *cat*?"

"Maybe. Maybe not. The gods must've been drunk off their asses the day they made firecats, that's all I can say."

"Anything that makes Saraya foam at the mouth like that can't be *all* bad," Vindi mused, watching the left side of my face tic uncontrollably. "Look at how red she's getting. I think I'll call it Pinky!"

"DON'T NAME IT!" Avashti calmed himself, forcing his eyes back to the path. Pinky was ten feet up, if that, and closing fast. "If it touches you," Avashti said, "it'll discharge all of that electrical power into your flesh. The good news is that *we* won't have to worry about it any more, since it won't exist."

"The other good news is that we can poke through your charred and smoking corpse looking for diamonds," I said. "I mean, that's how diamonds form, right? If not, I need to apologize to some thunderstorms."

With a visible effort, Vindi forced her eyes down to the path. The four of us walked through Qamara as fast as we could. Pinky drifted along behind us without a care in the world. Despite her best efforts, Vindi kept glancing at it. I balanced her out by grimly disbelieving everything in the world. Finally, Pinky seemed to lose interest and drifted away, to Vindi's obvious disappointment.

"Well done!" Ramla cried. "And, as it happens, we're here! In you go. In you go!"

We'd gone a significant way up the crater wall. The entire roc skeleton—and most of Qamara—lay spread out below us. Ramla's home was a simple mud-brick shanty, small and indifferently cared for, with tufts of grass sprouting from the walls. I didn't see any neighboring houses. Either she *really* liked solitude, or no one else could stand her.

We filed inside. The main room didn't feature much in the way of furniture, but someone had dug a fifteen-foot-deep pit across the floor. The walls of the pit were sheer and straight and showed innumerable marks of pick and chisel.

"What's this?" Avashti asked.

"Look. See what's at the bottom?" Ramla asked.

"Well…" Avashti crouched down, his hands on his knees. "There's *something* down there. A froth of mud, and… silver bubbles? I don't understand."

"Look closer. All of you."

Vindi crouched next to her father, peering into the pit. I stayed near the door, arms crossed over my chest.

"What's the matter, lass—don't trust me?" Ramla said, smiling wolfishly.

"Let's review," I said, counting on my fingers. "You abandoned your post, accepted a bribe, tried to sell us for slaves, and did *nothing* about the deadly firecat that almost fried Vindi. You want to talk trust? I have complete and total faith in you. Specifically, I have faith that you're a dastard and a worm and will betray us at the first possible instant."

"Ah, but you're wrong there!" she cried. "I'll wait for you to *stop talking* before I betray you!"

"Huh?" I said intelligently, just before she sprang forward and slammed her shoulder *hard* into my midsection. Before I could do anything, she'd shoved me all the way across the room and into the pit. Ramla gave Avashti a huge shove, and then Vindi, and I had to dodge out of the way as they came tumbling down on top of me. Well. You know how these things go. On the down side, I guessed wrong and dodged *into* Vindi. On the bright side, I did manage to break her fall. With my head.

"This doesn't even make sense!" Avashti cried, looking up at Ramla. "My money's down here with me, and my pack and all my gear. You do realize that, don't you?"

"Oh, you'll escape sooner or later," Ramla said mildly. "They always do. But you can make me some money before you go, ha! I'm going out. They always scream for help, for a while at least. Damned annoying. Goodbye!"

She left. Disgusted, Avashti picked up one of the silver bubbles and examined it. It proved to be a snail with a gleaming, metallic shell. As he studied it, it suddenly exploded into a minor nightmare of squiggling, grasping, hair-fine tentacles which tried to grab him. He shouted and flicked it away… right onto my arm.

"OW!!!" I cried as something sharp stabbed into my flesh. The snail dropped to the ground. I gingerly rubbed the red mark it had left. A single drop of blood oozed out.

"Well, I'm calling for help," Vindi said grimly. Taking a deep breath, she started yelling. And yelling. And then, just to change things up, she threw her head back in a wordless scream. No one came. Either we were too far from town to be heard, or Ramla's nearest neighbors had become totally inured to her prisoners' screams. I wasn't sure which was the more disturbing thought.

"OW!!!" I shouted, knocking a snail from my other arm. I saw that there were dozens of them, perhaps hundreds, slowly and inexorably oozing up my legs, climbing toward exposed skin with terrible inevitability. No matter how many I brushed away, there were always a hundred more behind them. Meanwhile, I couldn't stop scratching where I'd been stung the first time. A red welt had swelled up there, growing bigger and shinier by the moment.

"There has to be a way out," Avashti mused, digging through Vindi's pack. "We could do something with this bread. Set it on fire, maybe, and send up smoke signals?"

He continued to look through Vindi's pack, but I was too preoccupied to help. I had two extremely itchy welts on my arms, with more coming as snails continued to sting me. The first welt was starting to burn, and I mean that almost literally. I've been hit by lightning plenty of times, and believe me—this was worse. Pain seared through my flesh. Tears streamed down my cheeks. I pressed on the welt, hit it, rubbed it, tried to find *anything* that would help. It got so bad that I actually started wishing that my arm would fall off, just to save me the misery. The pain—the pain was worse than being on fire, and I *just couldn't make it stop.*

The welt abruptly broke, clear liquid oozing out. I hopped from foot to foot, still waving my arm. The pain receded slightly. That one appeared to be done, my body having finally dealt with whatever the snail had tried to inject under my skin. Only two or three dozen to go. Plus all the snails that were still climbing my legs.

"We have to get out of here," I said hoarsely. "*Now.*"

"We're working on it," Avashti replied.

Something about the popped blister caught my eye. The dead skin was forming into a shiny ring, shrinking and hardening into a hollow, gemlike loop. I stared in disbelief. There was no mistaking it: It was a crystal rim.

"*That's* where they come from?" I said, my voice rising.

"You didn't pack any actual rope?" Avashti asked Vindi.

"Saraya won't let me. She says, if a brigand wants to tie her up, why make it easy on him? Let him bring his own damn rope."

"You remembered!" I said, touched. "It's the same reason I never go skinny-dipping. Why make things easy on pervert fish that like to look?"

"Enough!" Avashti snapped. "We don't have anything here that can get us out. Help will have to come to us. What can we summon, fetch, or steal from outside? *Think*."

I scratched the many welts on my arms, trying to ignore the fire that was even now spreading and intensifying from the bigger ones.

"One thing we can get for sure is a firecat," I pointed out. "Set Vindi loose. Tell her that murdering me is Pinky's way of saying that it loves her *thiiiis* much. They're attracted to people who think about them? She'll think about Pinky so hard, she'll yank it through fifty miles of solid rock if that's what it takes."

"Summoning death isn't *exactly* what I had in mind… but…" Avashti rubbed his chin. "Electricity is very close to magnetism. We know this. With her passion and your skepticism… if we could trap the firecat in an endless circle…"

I didn't hear what he said after that. The next of my blisters was on its way to popping, and for a timeless while I was in too much pain to see, hear, move, or think. When I finally came to, lying helpless in the mud, I found that I'd been stung a dozen more times. This was not going well.

"Can we… *please*… get out of here?" I said, my breath ragged.

"Almost ready," Avashti said, putting the finishing touches on a device of weird looping wires and metallic mechanisms he'd taken from Vindi's pack. "All right, Vindi. Do your thing. Bring us a firecat."

"I can't. Saraya will make fun of me."

"I will not!" I protested.

"Will too. I bet you won't even inspire me by flapping your arms and crowing like a chicken."

"You're right there."

"Saraya," Avashti said tiredly, "flap your arms and crow like a chicken."

Eyes narrowing, I did so. Vindi just smirked, the bitch.

"I love you, Pinky," she said quietly. "Yes. All pets are deserving of, and capable of, being loved. Just by existing, they increase the sum total of love in the world…"

In the few precious moments I had before the next blister began to pop, I picked snails off of my legs by the dozen. Instead of tossing them aside, I tapped them against my belt buckle until each one, one by one, disgorged a tiny shimmering bead of slimy blackness into my hand. Soon I had a wad of slime and black specks the size of my thumb. If just *one* could cause pain like a waking death, what could a hundred do? Very carefully, I took a sheet of papyrus from my pack, wrapped up the Gooey Orb of Snail-Snotted Doom, and tucked it into my pocket next to the Anteyvan strangling cord and the Walnut of Inversion. Just watch me *not* kill myself with it! Your move, Universe.

"…but a *non-corporeal* pet would be best of all," Vindi mused. "Flesh is limited. Ether is not. The amount of love an incorporeal pet could contain is without limit or end."

"And yet you consistently stop me from murdering dogs and replacing them with infinitely more love-absorbent ghost dogs," I complained.

"I want a firecat," Vindi continued. "I *have to have* a firecat. I must see Pinky again. I must. So pretty… so special… so unique…"

My quasi-silver bracelet began to tingle, threatening to zap me again. I hastily whipped it off and stowed it in my pack. At almost the same moment, a ball of lightning drifted over the pit, frayed fingers of power scorching everything they touched. Avashti leapt back, swearing, and yanked Vindi back with him.

"Disbelieve it!" he barked at me.

"Love *is* powerful," I told Vindi. "In fact, it's the most terrible and destructive force in the universe. Watching someone trip and fall face-first into the privy? *Hilarious.* Watching someone you love do the same? *Terrifying.* Love transmutes joy into grief. That's all it is. That's all it does. Pets die. That's what they do. Just by existing, they increase the sum total of grief in the world."

The firecat drifted away from me. Vindi came over to stand next to me. "Love," she said, and the drifting ball of lightning wheeled around to come toward us.

"Grief."

"Love."

"Grief."

Avashti cautiously held his contraption of looping metal wires over the firecat. Trapped and held by the device he'd crafted, it started going around faster and faster until it was little more than a circular blur of blazing light. The magnetic field it generated seemed to do the trick: The metal contraption hovered in the air above it. Avashti threw a blanket over the wires, then cautiously climbed aboard his weird flying vehicle. It held his weight. He was abruptly hovering in midair, held up by the weird device he was standing on and the blazing firecat that orbited below. By leaning this way or that, he could even fly his vessel in whatever direction he chose, at whatever speed he preferred.

"Get on! Hurry!" Avashti said, dropping down to about waist-height and holding his hands out. Vindi made it on the first try. One of my blisters popped as I jumped, and I tripped and fell face-first in the mud. Even as snails stung my neck, arms, and even an exposed patch of leg, I managed to stagger to my feet and make a pathetic, blind little jump, arms raised overhead. Hands caught mine. Someone pulled me up, grabbed me, held me close. Blinking tears from my eyes, I glanced at my arms, which were now studded with amazing, gleaming, gemlike crystal rims. Well, for all my suffering, at least I was about to become incredibly rich.

"I can't believe that worked," Avashti said as we flew up and out of the pit, pausing to hover in the middle of Ramla's little house. "It's not level-headed, rational, or pragmatic at all. It's the sort of ridiculous improvisation I try to stay away from. I'd better not take any lessons from this. It might draw me away from being the modest, level-headed, conservative wizard I am today." He paused. "Though it's nice to have it *confirmed* that I'm the best in the world at absolutely everything, a fact I've always been far too modest to admit."

Vindi grinned. "Dad…"

"She's kidding!" he shouted to the universe at large, more by force of habit than anything else. "We're unrelated! She's actually a weird and deluded troll I found under a bridge, who I've sewed into the skin of some poor girl's corpse so as to better fit into society while I experiment on her!"

"Do you *have* to be like that?" Vindi said reproachfully. "There isn't even anyone here."

"Walls have ears," Avashti said darkly. "Sometimes eyes. On rare occasions, thumbs. Don't ask."

"What now?" I said, glancing dubiously at the whirring ring of light that was still, somehow, holding us up. "Is it safe to get off this thing?"

"Let's see how far we can take this," Avashti said. "There are certain advantages to showing off your power. I try not to take any of them, being humble and meek and all that, but it's not easy to stop people from being impressed by me. Ramla may be treacherous, but she knows the Valley of Thunder. Let's see if we can find her."

He leaned forward and we shot toward the door—which happened to be closed. Vindi flung her arms out and knocked it open. Avashti ducked. Vindi ducked. I took a mud wall full in the face and was knocked unconscious, which I'm going to take as a blessing. By the time I came to, Vindi still holding me up, the rest of my blisters had popped.

We flew over the city of Qamara in a slowly widening spiral, the firecat whirring in its endless ring below us. People ran out of their homes, pointing and shouting, almost as if they were seeing something unusual. There! I spotted a certain flamboyant cloak huddled next to some much plainer ones. I tugged on Avashti's arm and pointed. Avashti leaned to the left, and we soared effortlessly through the air to where Ramla was throwing the dice with a group of fellow degenerates.

"Ahem," Avashti said. Ramla looked up. Her eyed widened in surprise. Her companions ran for their lives, but she just bowed to us, a seemingly genuine smile spreading across her face.

"You escaped!" she cried, delighted. "Ha! Knew you had it in you. Brilliant! Congratulations, too, on all the money you just made. You get to keep all those crystal rims for yourself, as payment for your trouble!"

"*And* we get to kill you," I said. "Fair's fair."

"Saraya!" Avashti said warningly. He turned back to Ramla, our hovering conveyance drifting around her in a slow circle. "You owe us your life, it's true, but we'll settle for three days of total and unquestioning service."

"Two days," I argued, "and a leg. I want one of her legs. Don't really care which one. In fact, it might be funnier if we made her choose."

"I accept your offer," Ramla cheerfully told Avashti. "Three days of service it is! For starters, do you want help finding all those crystal rims you lost?"

"What the...?" I hastily looked at myself. My arms were covered with ring-shaped scars, but all the crystal rims were gone. They'd fallen off, every last one, while I'd been soaring unconscious over the city.

"Oh, come *on*!"

"As it happens, we need a guide more than we need riches," Avashti told her. "We need to get the Temple of Souls… *before* Princess Shivaka or Princess Gamal. You see—"

We suddenly tumbled forward, falling out of the sky. Avashti landed on his feet. Ramla caught Vindi. I managed to introduce my face to a pile of mud which, to be fair, may have been the dirt equivalent of nobility. (What can I say? Vindi always tells me to look on the bright side. It's pretty underwhelming, isn't it?). The firecat that had been holding us up all this time was quite simply gone.

"Pinky?" Vindi cried. "PINKY!"

"You stopped thinking about it," Avashti theorized, "so it lost interest and left. Not the best timing, either, with so many soldiers still in the area."

"No magic conveyance to fly us swift and straight to the Temple of Souls?" Ramla said. "I like it! We'll do things the hard way, then. Our accomplishments will be fifty times more impressive, and earn fifty times more beer in the re-telling! Let's go!"

"Can you bring Pinky back?" Avashti asked Vindi. She tried. She stood there, face screwed up, fists clenched, actually shivering with effort. Nothing happened. Avashti sighed. "Well, we'll try again later."

"Wait. Before we leave, there's one thing I have to do," I said, and kicked Ramla in the butt as hard as I could. She yelped and flew sprawling into the same pile of mud I'd so recently frequented.

"I like it!" I said heartily. "Let's go!"

Ramla glared at me, rubbing her backside as she got back up. Avashti rolled his eyes but said nothing. It was Vindi who reached behind her back to offer me a secret but celebratory hand-slap. Together, the four of us headed back across the roc-bound city.

V

Once I got past its rather astonishing setting (an! actual! roc! skeleton!), I found Qamara to be kind of depressing. The city had obviously seen better days. More than half of the houses stood empty and abandoned, while the few shops that were open offered a paltry selection of fish, fruits, and vegetables—things that could be grown or harvested on the cheap.

"Where is everyone?" Vindi asked.

"They're all out pretending to be elephants so as to lure in more rocs," I suggested.

Vindi nodded thoughtfully. "That makes sense. Do you get paid more if you're fat?"

"Nope. Only if you stop bathing and turn naturally grey," I suggested.

"I have to apologize on their behalf," Avashti told Ramla. "They can't help what comes out of their mouths, given that they suffer from a crippling mental defect known as 'whimsy', also known as 'stupidity, but let's all agree to pretend it's funny'."

"You won't have to worry about all the rocs we lure in," Vindi told her father. "I'll weave you a hat made of flowers!"

He stared at her. Ramla stared at her. I stared at her.

"You know," Vindi said. "Because flowers attract butterflies? Which taste bad? So the rocs won't actually eat you?"

"That's supposing that rocs have pretty keen eyesight," I pointed out. "Odds are, the roc would swallow him right down, the butterflies would give it the world's worst case of indigestion, and it would barf him back up again hard enough to puncture the sun."

"I still saved his life," Vindi muttered.

"Anyway, where is everyone?" I asked Ramla.

"Ah!" Ramla said, putting a hand to her heart, "I wish you'd seen Qamara when the roc first crashed, some ten years ago! What a place it was then. There was meat enough for everyone, there was, and

97

so much fat that folks covered every available surface with candles—
why not!—and leather for days, and more feathers than anyone knew
what to do with. These days, there's not much left but firecats and
bone soup. Lots of residents have moved on to newer crashes, newer
towns. It's a shame. Qamara was where I grew up. *I* haven't given up
on it." She paused. "Plus, I've been banned from most other cities for
crooked gambling. Which I consider an outrage, since I only cheated
to teach them a lesson! Namely, that cheating is a fun and easy way to
make money, and that they should hire me to teach them my
techniques.   Which, incidentally, I'd sell *you* at a huge discount.
Ninety percent off!"

"How much were they originally?" I asked suspiciously.

"It depends. What's ten times more money than you actually
have?"

We came to a town square that, in fatter times, had probably
been a market. Now it was just a dusty, forlorn place where a handful
of townsfolk sat, glumly waiting for something to happen.

"Ah! Friend Bhadir!" Ramla cried, gesturing dramatically to
the bearded merchant. "I've been captured by evil outsiders! Help
me! Rise up and kill them!"

Bhadir looked sourly at her. "No."

"I promise you wealth! I promise you riches! Just draw
your… wait, you've sold your sword? Ah, but you still have the
option of jabbing them with a pointy stick! The power to earn
incredible riches, and—incidentally—save me is yours!"

Bhadir snorted. "If they're depending on *you* for help, it's
them who'll want saving."

"Hopeless," Ramla muttered as we walked on through the
market.

"Are you done inciting your friends to murder us?" Avashti
asked sourly.

Ramla laughed uproariously, slapping a hand against her knee.
"Ha! I knew I liked you! Joking about wanting a broken, useless,
soulless quitter to guide you. Let me tell you something: You want
someone bold, someone brave, someone who'll never give up. Why,
that sounds like me!" she said. "Will I try to escape? Will I try to
avoid giving you three whole days of my life for free? If the only cost
is a handful of words, you bet I will! And afterward, I'll serve you all
the more faithfully to make up for my betrayal. Everyone wins!"

"I understand," Vindi said, nodding eagerly. "When you're

taking a tiny risk that costs nothing… well, why *not* throw a stick at the moon? The odds of cracking it open and being showered with candy may be vanishingly slim, but there's literally no cost!"

"Unless the stick clobbers the person standing next to you on the way down," I said sourly.

"Even better!" Ramla cried. "The person throwing the stick just needs to stand next to someone who deserves to be clobbered! Everyone wins again! And now, as the unbroken moon sails past, I pledge my service, my loyalty, and my life to you. Make of it what you will."

It didn't take long to cross Qamara and climb the crater wall on the far side. Soon, we'd reached a set of well-worn tracks… the cart road across the Valley of Thunder. Ramla followed it south. Exchanging uncertain looks, the rest of us fell in behind her. The mountains (hills?) surrounding us grew a bit higher, a bit more craggy and dry. The road seemed to go on forever, and as the shadows slowly grew longer, I wondered where we were going to spend the night.

"Ouch!" I sucked in my breath as the quasi-silver bracelet zapped me with a shocking little jolt. I glanced back. Far behind us, a rather familiar ball of lightning followed at a sedate and untroubled pace.

I glared at Vindi. "You're thinking about Pinky again, aren't you?"

"No! Well, yes. But not on purpose."

"Can you try *not* thinking about it? Please? For me?"

Vindi snorted. "Have you ever tried *not* thinking about something? Pops right into your head, doesn't it? If you want Pinky out of my head, distract me. Pretend to be a chicken." She cocked her head, looking at me. "And don't forget to be delicious. In the past, your chicken imitations have been sadly one-dimensional."

"Ba-kwak," I said in an ominous rasp, my eyes narrowed to slits.

In due time, we were once again reminded of the Valley of Thunder's namesake. High up the right-hand mountain was a roc crash from days long past, now just a jumble of gleaming white bones interspersed with the crumbling remains of houses. We kept walking, winding in and out of the craggy hills as the abandoned roc-crash vanished behind us. As the sun began to slide behind the mountains, we came upon a much newer crash, the roc's cloak of feathers almost completely intact. If it hadn't been for the smoke rising from its empty eyes, I might have thought it was just sleeping.

"The city of Davasi," Ramla announced. "True, I've been banned, but I don't think they meant it. Let's go!"

"Can we hire a cart there?" Avashti asked impatiently. "All this damnable walking is giving me blisters large enough to develop their own civilizations. Very shortly, my blisters will learn to talk, and then we'll all be in trouble."

"Let's keep walking!" Vindi asked. "Maybe you'll develop *singing* blisters!"

Avashti rolled his eyes. "I hate to ask... mostly because I suspect your answer will be just as aggravating as the original assertion... but how would singing blisters be better than *non*-singing blisters?"

"Aside from soothing you to sleep at night with tender lullabies? Why, they could enter contests and win you prizes!"

I snorted. "Oh, come on. Where would Avashti keep all the trophies?"

"Tiny trophy-cases nailed to the tips of his shoes. Duh."

"You've got me there," I admitted. "Question withdrawn."

Avashti sighed. "I have to put up with this *all the time*," he told Ramla.

Ramla led us down a side road toward Davasi. I glanced back. Yes, Pinky was still there, though nearly lost in the distance. Doubtless the firecat would lurk safely down-valley right up until I fell asleep and started dreaming that I *wasn't* being set on fire, just for added irony. Here's a question: Does knowing how you're going to die indicate a failure of originality on the part of the universe, or does it actually increase the anxiety and tension of waiting for it to happen?

"Almost a year Davasi has been here," Ramla told us. "That's where we'll stay the night. How much money have you got?"

Avashti looked at Vindi. Vindi looked at me. I shrugged. "We're not *not* penniless," I said honestly.

"That's what I thought. Don't worry—I'll take care of everything! Cloaks on and mouths shut. Follow me!"

Once we'd fashioned our blankets into hooded cloaks again, Ramla led us down into the city of Davasi. We headed straight for a great spherical building of mud and brick which had been crammed into a hollow vertebra just behind the skull. It was very crowded and very loud inside, though there was no furniture—just one big open floor. I did see a bar off to one side, which seemed to be doing plenty of business. What was this place… a tavern? Or perhaps a dancehall between dances? I felt underdressed in my plain brown cloak: Everyone else seemed to be wearing their evening best, their outfits fashioned from giant feathers that flashed striking iridescent colors in the dim torchlight. Not that the universe would allow me to be fashionable even if I tried: If I showed up wearing feathers, the new fashion would be nudity. And if I showed up nude, the fashion would be to point at me and laugh. What I'm saying is, none of it really matters. Since I'm going to be out of step with the world anyway, I might as well make my nonconformity the purest possible expression of who I am. Smirking, I flipped obscene gestures at everyone around us with both hands.

"And a merry day to you, too, sir!" I said to a gentleman who couldn't seem to stop staring at me. "Sorry… my muscles just seize up and do this from time to time. Whoops! Here I go again! It may look like I'm flipping you off repeatedly, but I assure you, it's just seizures."

"Mouths *shut*," Ramla said through cheerfully tight lips. "Follow me. And… ah! Here we go!"

She led us across the crowded floor. I still wasn't sure what was going on, except that many people were sitting together in tight rings. Craning my neck, I saw dice rolling and money changing hands. Realization dawned.

"Room for one more?" Ramla asked, elbowing her way into one of the circles.

"Ramla," said a sour-faced woman who wore a great sunburst of overlapping feathers fanned out behind her head. "Not sure I want to be throwing against you. Not after what happened last time."

"Are you accusing me of cheating?" Ramla asked cheerfully.

"If you *were* cheating, you know what would happen to you."

"And if I *weren't*, you know what would happen to the person who falsely accused me."

"I've never said anything against you," the woman said. "Won't, either. Not until I've got proof."

"Then we're agreed! If it can't be proven that I cheated, it's the same as conclusively proving that I didn't! But just to save us some time, why don't you give me your money now? Kidding! Kidding!"

Glaring at Ramla, the sour-faced woman left the circle. Ramla eagerly rubbed her hands and reached for the dice.

"I need to get in on this," I said to Vindi. "Do you have any money I could borrow?"

Vindi looked at me strangely. "You want to play? With *your* luck? Do you actually think you can win?"

"Do snakes need sleeves on their jackets?" I shot back.

"Only for purposes of fashion."

"Conceded. Like a snake proudly showing off its epaulets, I don't gamble for the normal reason—to win—but for my own purposes."

"Go on."

I shrugged. "What more is there to explain? I have my little rituals. When I see people betting, I ask for the odds. Just that. With luck like mine, I like to hear the numbers with my own ears, spoken by someone who believes in them. What can I say? It gives me a vicarious little shiver of what life must be like for everyone else. Excuse me, sir. What do you get for shooting a six over a nine?"

"Seven plus three," he said absently.

"Look," I told Vindi. "Goosebumps. This is my favorite part —when the world is golden with possibility. Before the losing starts. Putting actual money at risk… you could call it a physical symbol of my defiance against fate, proof that I haven't been broken yet. Me, I just get a kick out of how things can always get worse. Reality can be so inventive if you give it the chance."

"Give your heart what it sings for, I guess," Vindi said wryly. "Even if what it sings for is really stupid. Tell you what. I'll bankroll you if you let me bet against you."

"That might be a very good idea for both of us."

So I gambled, while Vindi bet steadily against me. I lost and she won, of course, my tiny supply of coins evaporating instantly. Vindi passed me some money so I could keep going. I shrugged and kept playing. I lost my new stake almost immediately—which meant that Vindi kept winning. She passed me more coins.

"You know," she said contemplatively, "we don't want *my* wealth to count as good luck for *you*. If it did, I'd probably lose everything at the end just so you could be screwed over in the most ironic way possible."

"That's true," I admitted, "but what can we do about it?"

Vindi put her hand over her heart. "I hereby swear, upon my life and soul, that I'll only use my wealth to taunt and punish you… *never* to make your life easier!"

"Yeah, sounds like my luck's about the same as always," I sighed as she passed me more money.

The doors suddenly burst open: As gamblers looked up in confusion, a host of soldiers in Kairay colors poured inside.

"Attention!" barked their leader, the old soldier with the chestful of medals. "We require food, drink, and a place to rest. We require it now. We also require information regarding any foreigners you've seen."

I tried to shrink further under my hood. Close by, a feather-bedecked man scowled worriedly, leaning close to the woman who was with him:

"I don't like this. Letting them see what we've got with their own eyes… what's to stop Kairay from sending an army to strip our rocs bare and leave us with nothing?"

I scurried over to Vindi and Avashti. "We have to go," I said urgently.

"Tell me something I don't know," Avashti said under his breath. "Oh, wait, you can't. It's not my day of the week for pretending not to know things so as to appear loveably fallible."

"Pragmatic, modest, *and* sensible. You, sir, are adorable."

We started backing toward the door, only to bump up against Ramla, who had a peculiar smile on her face.

"Let's get out of here!" Vindi whispered. "Hurry!"

"Ah! But my deliverance has been handed to me, hasn't it?" Ramla said, enjoying herself greatly. "Three whole days of freedom, and at no expense at all!"

"Ramla…" Avashti said warningly.

"Don't think of it as another betrayal," she said warmly. "Consider this: A story with fifty times as much danger is fifty times more interesting and will bring fifty times more beer when you tell it to your friends. Essentially, I'm getting you drunk. Love me!"

With a single swift movement, she yanked Avashti's hood down. Before he could react, she yanked down Vindi's and mine, let out a piercing whistle, and ducked out of the way. The old soldier spun around. His eyes widened.

"GET THEM!" he roared. Gamblers shouted and dove to either side. Their path now clear, soldiers surged toward us.

"I AM A WIZARD—A WIZARD OF FIRE AND PAIN!" Avashti bellowed. "APPROACH ME IF YOU DARE, MORTALS!"

The soldiers stopped in their tracks, eyes wide, caught between their superior's orders and a lifetime of superstition instilled by their elders' gleefully disturbing stories. Red-faced, the old soldier pointed at us.

"He's bluffing. I've been assured by Darshik that he's harmless. Get him. NOW! That's an order!"

"Beg for death!" Avashti shouted. "Beg! If I feel merciful, I *may* grant your wish. Also, Darshik is dumber than a ten-day egg *after* the hippopotamus sat on it!"

The soldiers exchanged nervous glances. None of them seemed eager to charge Avashti, but they weren't about to let him escape, either. It was a stalemate… at least until they worked up the nerve to attack. If we wanted to scare them off, I realized, we were going to need something big, showy, and over-the-top.

"Vindi!" I hissed. "Summon Pinky! Hurry!"

"What?" she said. She seemed to be in shock: I couldn't be sure she'd heard me at all.

"Pinky," I said, enunciating clearly. "Your firecat. Summon him. Now."

"I… what?"

One of the soldiers worked up the nerve to edge toward Avashti. Red-faced, Vindi grabbed a nearby flagon and flung it at his head. It bounced off his shoulder, its contents spraying all over the place, and he hastily stepped back in line. A few drops hit torches and burned up with a hissing flare. I was impressed. Most liquor is too wet to burn: This stuff must have been incredibly potent.

I sidled over to Vindi, tugging on her sleeve. "Are you going to summon Pinky or not?"

"I… what?"

"All right. Time for my backup plan. Which is… um…" My eyes fell on the smouldering spots where the flaming liquor had landed. "Hmm. Tell you what. Give me the money you just won. All of it."

Something of her usual spark came into Vindi's eyes. "But it's *mine*!"

"I know. And I need you to give it to me."

"I don't think you understand how money works."

"Vindi…" I growled. Vindi made a face, but finally poured a stream of coins into my cupped hands.

"You'll bring it back when you're done, right?" she said wistfully. "I mean to surround the tower house with an impassable wall of flowers so that Dad, unable to get in, will fly into a blind rage and try to strangle beauty itself. Such fun!"

"I'll… see what I can do."

Avashti and the old soldier continued to exchange promises and threats, the other soldiers looking as if they wished they were anywhere else. I had time, if not much. I slipped through the crowd, quickly finding the sour-faced woman Ramla had driven out of our gambling circle.

"There's something I need you to do for me," I said, going on to explain what I had in mind. She stared at me, aghast.

"No. There's no way. I will never, ever—" She caught sight of the money heaped in my cupped hands. Her eyebrows rose. "On the other hand, they say trying new things is rewarding. Give. All. Now."

I hesitated, but if I waited for her vocabulary to expand to two-syllable words, her demands might get even more outrageous. Sighing, I poured the money into her hands. She nodded once and put it in her pocket. We headed over to the bar, where I asked the tavern-keeper for a flagon of the most potent stuff he had. Here I encountered another problem: Despite her newfound wealth, the sour-faced woman wouldn't *pay* for the drinks. I had to open my pack and barter away most of my food to get what I needed. Then it was simply a matter of using the booze to soak the woman's sunburst headdress of feathers. She was still wearing it at the time, but I made a good-faith effort to avoid dumping too much of the stuff down her neck. Considering that the temptation to throw it in her face was almost overwhelming, you surely must concede that I deserve a medal.

The deed was finally done. I pointed out where I wanted her to stand, and she took her place. I drifted back toward Avashti. The situation had progressed… or deteriorated. Soldiers surrounded him in a loose arc, though none had actually dared grab him yet. He was shooting off minor fireworks, mostly silver sparkles and snapping flashes of light, to hold them at bay. Vindi hid behind her father, unwilling to abandon him even when all hope was lost.

"AHEM!" I coughed, pointing vigorously at the sour-faced woman. Avashti glanced at me. I made whooshing and explosiony gestures at her, then grabbed a torch and waved it around a little before pointing at her again. Avashti seemed to get the idea.

"You presume too much," he declaimed. "My patience wears thin. Enough warnings have I given. The time has come to unleash my full and awful power!" He paused. "And by 'awful' I mean, 'inspiring awe', not 'kinda yucky'. What I *should* have said—"

"NOT THE TIME!" I bellowed.

"Right." Avashti made a slithering, mystical gesture. "Kalama-ZAM!" he bellowed, pointing at one of the soldiers. The soldier ducked. Standing behind him, of course, was the sour-faced woman. At my signal, she turned slightly, causing the edge of her booze-soaked headdress to touch one of the torches. The whole thing went up in flames with a gigantic WHOOMP. It was epic—if you weren't watching closely, it looked like her entire head burst into flames. Screaming wildly, she sprinted directly at the clustered soldiers. They broke, shouting hoarsely as they ran for cover. I can't say I blamed them. Avashti and Vindi and I reached the front door at almost the same moment and spilled out into the night. Not a single soldier came after us. Not yet, at least.

"Come on!" I cried, jogging down the track I vaguely remembered would get us back to the road. "Hurry!"

"Just… give me… moment," Avashti panted, bending over to rest with his hands on his knees.

"Well met, friends!" Ramla cried, popping up behind me.

"AAAGH!"

"No need to shout for joy," she said, poking me in the side. "Yes, it's me! Really! And you," she said to Avashti, "you didn't tell me you were a wizard!"

"You saw him flying," Vindi pointed out. "Wasn't that kind of a tip-off?"

Ramla snorted. "You were *all* flying. Anyone can fly. It's easy. Just jump out of a tree. Done! I figured he'd bought that thing off some big-city artificer. But an actual wizard?" She glanced sidelong at Avashti. "Can you get those clowns at the Temple of Souls to obey your commands?"

"You know that much?" Avashti said cautiously. "You know about… them?"

"The gods? You could say that. Some years ago, I met a god with a flock of birds for a face, made an intemperate wish and ended up with a talking butt. Not *my* butt, just a disembodied one that followed me around everywhere. Had a hell of an attitude, too. Took me three years to lose it."

"I can do better than that," Avashti said modestly, tapping himself on the chest. "I know the words to make oranges rain from a silver sky. I know the words to turn up into down and down into up, and to confuse people so totally that they don't even realize there's been a change. I know—"

"So if you asked the gods for gems and gold and all that, you'd actually get it?" Ramla said eagerly.

"I don't see why not," Avashti said. "Gold should be easy. It's only made of one thing, isn't it? Not like mushrooms, which are fiendishly complicated and *will* try to kill you."

"I like it!" she said heartily. "Come on. I'll guide you to a place where we can rest. Maybe the soldiers could find it, but without me for a guide, they'll wish they hadn't! Ha!"

"Um…" Vindi hesitantly raised her hand. "Just wondering, well, why we should trust you, after you betrayed us *again*?"

"Dear child," Ramla said affectionately, "use your head. I didn't betray you. Exposing you was a *distraction*! I got the soldiers looking at *you* so they wouldn't see *me* setting my dear friend's head on fire. That's right, it was me! *I* saved you all! *I* got us out of there!"

"What are you talking about?" I cried. "*I* did that!"

"Trying to steal credit for my brilliant plan?" Ramla said, amused. "Ha! I like it! She has spirit, this one! Don't worry. I won't tell them how you huddled weeping in the corner while I did all the work."

"It wasn't you!" I protested. "It was me!"

"Sure it was," Ramla said, winking hugely at Vindi. "It was my intention all along to heroically save you, you know. First, I thought to myself: 'Ramla, take on a dozen soldiers all by yourself, sword against sword! It'll be easy!' And so it would have been, but I needed a way to actually be *less* impressive, so that fewer soldiers would flee weeping into the night where they'd have a better chance of catching you." She grinned rakishly. "So I threw a flaming woman at them instead. Yes, ideas really do come to me that easily. I'm just that clever!"

"IT WASN'T YOU!" I turned to Vindi, who was actually nodding in agreement with Ramla. "Vindi… you have to believe me. If Ramla was the one who did everything, where did your money go?"

"A good and proper question," Ramla said. "Given that I didn't spend any of it, where *did* Vindi's money go? I saw you drinking an awful lot while you were hiding in the corner. Who bought all of that for you?"

"You got *drunk* while Ramla was saving us?" Vindi

demanded.

"No!" I cried. Just then, I stepped on a millipede, causing me to whirl my arms around crazily until I staggered and fell over. Of course the millipede bit me on the nose, turning it nicely swollen and red, and also, I bit my tongue when I hit the ground.

"Lithen—" I popped back up, hiccuping loudly. "I ah NOTH dunk. NOTH!!"

"How could you?" Vindi demanded.

"She… what… but…" I sighed, shoulders slumping. It was all monstrously unfair, which is to say, everything was back to normal and nothing I could say would change it. Not that I intended to give up the fight that easily, but if constant losing has taught me one thing, it's how to bide my time. I tried to smile. I don't think it came out right.

"Follow me, my glorious friends!" Ramla said cheerfully. "I know! Let's pass the time by singing songs about our respective triumphs. You three go first. Done? Right! Being as modest as I am, I try to avoid literally singing my own praises, but I guess I don't have a choice. Here we go!"

"Wait, wait," Vindi said as Ramla led us down a side path. "Aren't we going to stay on the road?"

"Not hardly," Ramla said graciously. "We'll leave that horror to our sword-wearing friends, thank you very much."

"Horror? What horror?"

"Night worms!" she cried.

"Oh, yeah. Those," Vindi said faintly.

We didn't actually sing, since that would have been a sure way for our pursuers to find us. Give thanks for the little things, I guess. Once we'd put some distance between ourselves and Davasi, Ramla decided that it would be safe for us to make a light. We all stopped while Vindi got a lantern out of her pack: Then, following Ramla's lead, we meandered seemingly at random up this path and down that one. Her explanations, when they came at all, were as cryptic as they were cheerful: "Carnivorous moles!" "Screech bats!" "Moths… that crave BLOOD!" "Ah, my girl, I see that someone hasn't learned to fear… SLIGHTLY OBLONG ROCKS!!"

We finally reached a fairly clear area where we could spread out our blankets and sleep under the stars.

"We'll stay here tonight," Ramla decided. "Tomorrow morning, we take on the soldiers face to face!"

"*What?*" I demanded.

"Ha! We can't just leave them to hunt us down at their leisure, can we, my stupid, ignorant friend? We have to seize the initiative and deal with them once and for all!"

"And how are we going to do that?" I demanded.

"It'll be easy!"

"Right. Sure. But how, specifically, do you intend to stop them?"

"By being six times cleverer than they are, my lass!"

"Just go to sleep, Saraya," Vindi said, stifling a yawn. "We can talk about it in the morning."

"Vindi…" I pulled her aside as Ramla chose a spot and settled down. "Can we talk about Ramla?"

"Just give me some time, all right? After what you did tonight, I'm not sure I want to talk to you right now."

I smiled tightly. "Let's just say…" I took a deep breath. "Let's just say that it doesn't matter who got us out of there tonight."

In the dark, I could see Vindi's silhouette as she turned toward me. "So results don't matter, is that it?" she said sharply. "Funny how that works. She does everything, you do nothing, and suddenly results don't matter. I see."

"Listen," I said, anger boiling up inside me. "She wants us to find the soldiers tomorrow morning. Right. Great plan. What *exactly* are we going to do when we find them?"

Vindi shrugged. "Ramla knows what she's doing."

"We're all going to die. You know that, don't you? Whatever half-formed mental vomit she intends to spew at them, it's not going to work. Reality delights in making things go wrong in ever more inventive and amusing ways." I snorted. "When it's *me*, at least. Who knew that a scheme to paint the walls of my room a *slightly different color* would end with the invention, at my expense, of rocket-propelled hornets?"

"Yeah, well, that's how things go for you. Ramla's plan won't fail."

"Right. Fine. I see. I fail, so I'm worthless. Ramla succeeds —you think—and now she's your best friend. Doesn't that say something about *you*, that you value the happenstance of success over some pathetic little nothing like friendship or love?"

"I don't like her more than you," Vindi said evenly. "But sometimes, when you act like this, it's a little hard not to."

She turned on her heel and walked away. I just stood there,

with only the cold and distant stars for company. I finally returned to the clearing and lay down, trying to find a position where I could avoid lying on a rock, a millipede, or a scorpion. Well, two out of three isn't bad.

"Saraya," Avashti murmured, scooching his blanket over until he was right beside me. "For what it's worth, *I* believe you."

"There was one thing in my life that was always good, bright, and fun," I said bleakly. "No matter how things went, she never abandoned me. As little sense as it made, she was proud to call herself my sister. I kept waiting and waiting for her to go away, but she never did. And now…"

"Would it amuse you if I set my beard on fire?" Avashti asked. "I mean, I'm not going to, but I think the fact that I made the offer shows a level of compassion and sympathy that, quite frankly, sets me apart from the run of ordinary human beings."

"You're being annoying on purpose, aren't you, to distract me from thinking about *her*?"

Avashti shrugged. "My magnificence has many facets, it's true. Try not to worry. You may not be shiny, but neither do you tarnish. She will remember that, in time."

"Thanks," I said sourly.

"Don't worry so much. Once we reach the Temple of Souls and fix your problem, Ramla won't be forced to stay any more. Want to bet how fast she runs in the opposite direction?"

"Winning by default, because I'm the only option left—just what I wanted," I said wryly. "Wait. How can you be so sure we're going to fix my problem? You could never fix me before, and that was when you had all the time in the world. Now that you're being chased by angry soldiers…"

Avashti sighed. "We're going to fix this because we must."

"Nope. Not good enough. Nothing ever goes right. Things can always get worse. What if we fail? If things go right, great. But we need a fallback plan in case they don't."

Avashti shook his head. "Don't worry about it. Darshik is pathetic. Even if he had the Lens of Becoming *and* Vindi's horns, he couldn't transfer your stolen luck to Princess Shivaka. I think. For a while." Avashti paused, seeming to follow an intriguing line of thought. "He'd need help, that's for sure. Knowing that I'd succeeded where he failed, he'd probably try to force *me* to perform the actual transfer. And if he had Vindi… if he could threaten her with all manner of tortures… well, I'm not sure what I'd do."

"Maybe we could do something with that," I said, stifling a yawn. "If you were the one actually doing the transfer, couldn't you just make *yourself* lucky again?"

"It wouldn't work," Avashti admitted. "Darshik may be stupid, but he's not dumb. Anything that didn't make Princess Shivaka luckier, he'd know."

I stared at the mocking stars. "There has to be *something* we can do. Someone's going to end up doubly lucky, and I'm going to end up tripping face-first into the wrong end of incontinent dogs again. We know this. How can we use it to our advantage?"

Avashti didn't answer for a long time, so much so that I thought he'd fallen asleep.

"Saraya…" He hesitated. "Maybe… with your permission… we could make Shivaka even luckier, at the expense of making your luck even *worse*."

"Huh? How would that help?"

"It might just be possible… refracting it, amplifying it, twisting it around and splicing it back into itself… to give you the world's first case of luck so bad it's good. To make the universe so eager to punish you that it would make *any* wildly unlikely thing happen, so long as it meant a short-term and humiliating come-uppance for you. You could arrange for all sorts of bizarre coincidences by setting them up to make you suffer as much as possible."

"Love it," I said drily. "Sounds like exactly what I need."

"I shouldn't have mentioned it," Avashti said contritely. "It would be too complicated, too difficult for even *me* to pull off. We'll get to the Temple of Souls and solve your problem the right way. Trust me."

I pointed my finger in what I hoped was Avashti's direction. "No. This is good. We'll hope for the best, sure, but start working out an alternative plan. Take all the time you need. We have to have a fallback."

"Mmph," Avashti said, and fell silent. Asleep, or working things out in his mind? I couldn't tell, and in time, I fell asleep, too.

* * *

The next morning, we headed back toward Davasi. I still didn't see much point in throwing ourselves into the arms of our pursuers, but no one was listening to me. Ramla and Vindi walked ahead, Ramla telling wild stories about her escapades, Vindi laughing uproariously. Avashti walked with me, but he wasn't much use as a conversationalist. In fact, he was so absorbed trying to figure out the good/bad luck problem that I occasionally had to grab him by the shoulders and steer him back onto the path.

"We're getting close!" Ramla announced, striking a casually heroic pose. "Cloaks on and hoods up, people!"

Once we were covered up, she led us onward. The soldiers had camped just outside of Davasi. They had the same three carts I'd seen before, but with the boxes hacked off so they were little more than wheeled wooden platforms. The carts were pulled up in a rough circle (triangle?) with the donkeys tied up outside of it. Although I stood on my tiptoes and craned my neck, I couldn't see what the soldiers themselves were doing.

"Follow me!" Ramla said confidently. Swallowing my misgivings, I fell in behind Vindi.

The soldiers looked up as we neared. The old soldier came out to meet us, his uniform encrusted with so many medals that any blacksmith would have shaken his head in despair at all that wasted effort. So much more efficient to make one BIG medal the size and shape of a man, if that's the effect you're going for.

"You'll have to keep back," he told Ramla. "We're looking for some people who, ah…" He trailed off as he spotted the three of us standing behind her. "Those cloaks look familiar."

"Ah, my friends!" Ramla cried. "I saw you last night, I did, and I saved you, throwing myself in front of that flaming woman so that you could escape!"

"I don't recall having seen you before," he said shortly. "But those cloaks…"

"Sure, sure," Ramla said, her voice dripping with sarcasm. "These are the people you're after, right? Because anyone you were looking for would surely come straight back and throw themselves at your feet the first chance they got. That would be the smart thing to do. I don't know. I guess it is." She walked over and grabbed my hood. "I can show you their faces. Do you want me to? Some people —Hi!—are so utterly devoid of intellect, they can't admit the most basic facts of the universe without having it smushed in their faces like a baby with a piece of cake. Are you like that? Do you have to be shown? Is logic not enough for you?"

She started pulling. I made a quiet, desperate noise as my hood began to slide away from my face.

"That won't be necessary," the old soldier said sourly. "It's obviously not them. What do you want, anyway?"

"Ah! Therein lies the tale. Having saved your life from the Woman of Fire, I now propose to convey you safely across the Valley of Thunder, fast as fast can be, and all for a nominal fee! What say you?"

"We already paid," the old soldier said peevishly. "We aren't going to pay again. There's a track here, and we have experienced people who know how to drive donkeys. What do we need *you* for?"

Ramla burst out laughing, bending over backwards until it seemed like she was about to fall over and start rolling on the ground.

"Oh, believe me, you won't make it far without something to hide you from… *them*."

"Who?"

"*Them*! Let me tell you a story…"

Ramla launched into a tale about semi-invisible monsters who delighted in driving men mad, but I could see from the impatient set of his face that the old soldier wasn't buying what she was selling. It was going to take more than showmanship and lies to persuade him: He was the sort who required evidence.

Moving slowly and casually, I pulled the Gooey Orb of Snail-Snotted Doom from my pocket. Still wrapped in its papyrus shell, the gelatinous goo contained over a hundred black specks each representing a snail sting I'd avoided. I sidled over to Avashti.

"Put one of these on a coin," I said under my breath, "and drop it as close to them as you can."

He glanced at me, startled. I nodded emphatically. Shrugging, Avashti took a gleaming silver coin from his pouch and attached the speck that I gave him. Just as well I didn't try it myself, since it would have gone spectacularly wrong if I had. I still remember the *second* time Vindi wandered into the path of a runaway cart, and I sprinted across the road to shove her out of the way. I bet you think the cart ran me over, don't you? No such luck. The driver spotted me at the last possible instant and—in total desperation—brought the cart to a dead stop just as it was in the *process* of running me over, with its full weight resting directly on my face.

Avashti dropped the coin and then walked away, seeming not to notice its loss. A soldier spotted the free money just sitting there. He glanced at his companions. He bent to pick it up.

"OUCH!" He sucked his finger, hastily stepping back into

line.

"Try as you might, you won't escape... *them*," Ramla was saying, her eyes wide. "No, no, go ahead if you want. We've lived in the Valley of Thunder all our lives. We can see... *them*... without going insane. You? Maybe you'll be lucky. Maybe you'll die of fright first."

The old soldier scowled. "If you think to extract payment from us with your wild tales..."

The soldier who'd been stung was starting to look extremely uncomfortable. I could sympathize. He had to be itching like crazy. The only question was what would happen when the pain set in.

"...see you to your destination for just a few insignificant coins!" Ramla was saying.

"Agggh..." The soldier panted, staggering and almost falling. Tears streamed down his cheeks. He started to wave his hand around, and then slap it against his face, and then scrape it against the edge of his armor as he sought something—*anything*—that would help the pain. The old soldier whirled to stare at him, astonished. Almost in slow motion, the injured soldier crumpled to the ground—and started screaming, interspersed with fits of gasping and crying. Then he started laughing hysterically, beating his fist on the ground as he alternately laughed and screamed and screamed and laughed...

"QUICK—KNOCK HIM UNCONSCIOUS!" Ramla bellowed. One of the soldiers hastily complied, which was probably for the best, since his blister had just burst and he was on the verge of making a swift recovery.

"Well done! He'll be sane when he wakes up." Ramla glanced sidelong at the old soldier. "But you won't make it far without my help. *They* have the taste of your minds now, and they like it. *They* will be coming for you. I can help. I can save you. Best of all, today only, I'll give you sixty percent off my normal fee!"

"We won't pay *much*," the old soldier said unwillingly.

"I'll take it! Let's be off, then. I'll drive the lead cart. You and you," she said, pointing at Avashti and Vindi, "drive *that* one and *that* one. Follow me *closely*, and... uh..."

Avashti sneezed thunderously, over and over again, with such ponderous regularity that it seemed like some weird kind of joke.

"What's he doing?" Ramla asked blankly.

"Are you all right?" Vindi asked, worried.

"Stop stalling. Climb up and drive the cart," Ramla instructed the wizard.

Avashti fell to his knees, still sneezing. As his hood shook, I caught a glimpse of his face, which was worryingly red and beaded with sweat.

"Stop," I said. "Something's wrong."

"Well and good," Ramla said, irritated. "You and you—" She pointed at Vindi and me. "—drive *that* cart and *that* cart. I don't much care what you do with *him*."

Ramla walked to the first cart. Avashti's weird fit stopped instantly. He rested his hands on his knees, sucking in deep breath after deep breath.

"What was that?" I asked, worried.

"Allergies," he explained, climbing weakly onto the third cart.

"Oh, come on. You expect me to believe that?"

"Don't much care what you believe. It's the truth."

"So *that's* dealt with," Ramla said, raising her voice to address the collected soldiers. "And now, my dear friends, I'm going to take care of each and every one of *you*. Climb aboard! We ride!"

"How does she *do* it?" Vindi murmured appreciatively. I had a few answers, but was constrained from saying them by an irrational preference for keeping my throat clear of axes, daggers, swords, and other foreign obstructions. Ramla had already taken the driver's seat on the first cart. Vindi glanced at her father, obviously worried about him, but Ramla had directed her to take the second cart. Slowly, reluctantly, she obeyed. I climbed onto the third cart, taking my place next to Avashti.

We drove our little train of carts down the dusty road, the donkeys clopping placidly along as we headed deeper into the Valley of Thunder. I couldn't get over the fact that there were eight or nine murderous and armed soldiers *who wanted to do unspeakable things to me* hardly an arm's reach from where I was sitting. Maybe Vindi was right. Maybe Ramla *was* impressive, in her own despicable way.

Avashti cleared his throat. I glanced at him, only to find him staring fixedly behind us. I looked back... and there was Pinky, floating sedately in the dusty distance, like a star that had descended to earth and discovered that it *liked* filth.

"By the gods, Vindi, not *now*," I said despairingly. I tried to disbelieve everything in the universe, which wasn't easy when *part* of that universe was the wooden plank I was sitting on, which had decided to poke splinters into my butt every time we went over a bump.   Somehow, I managed.   Pinky slowly fell farther back, disappearing for long stretches behind one mountain or another.

Ramla abruptly turned her cart, leading us down a side road. It wasn't long, quickly taking us to a clearing by the Kairay river where yet more blocky elephant decoys had been assembled. The man who'd been assigned to keep watch took one look at three carts full of heavily armed soldiers and took off at a dead run.

"What are *those*?" the old soldier demanded, pointing to the decoys.

"No idea. Just found them here," Ramla said easily. "But they'll do nicely, won't they, as boxes to hide in so that *they* can't see you? All you have to do is attach one to the top of each cart and then hide inside. Better than those old boxes you were trapped in before. Roomier! You folks get to work. My friends and I will rest up for the hard drive to come."

Shrugging, the old soldier picked out three of the elephant decoys and barked orders to his troops. They didn't have the proper tools, but the air was soon filled with pounding, chopping, and swearing as the soldiers labored to mount the decoys on the carts. Very soon, as far as the local megafauna was concerned, we would be driving a trio of tasty mobile snacks across the desert. Cream-filled, even.

"What's our endgame, here?" Avashti asked quietly. "What are you going to do to the soldiers?"

"Ha! Pretending you're too stupid to figure out the obvious?" Ramla said appreciatively. "I like it! Me, I'm going to take a nap. Wake me when it's time to leave."

Avashti shrugged. "I can't argue with that." He headed in the opposite direction, laying down behind some patchy bushes. I sat down on a fallen log, watching the soldiers work. After a time, Vindi came and sat next to me.

"You see it now, right?" I asked Vindi. "Ramla's a murderer. It's pretty obvious she means to kill the soldiers. Anyone who gets in her way has to go."

"Give her some credit," Vindi shot back. "She's gotten us this far, hasn't she?"

"Debatable."

Vindi rolled her eyes. "She's not going to kill anyone. She probably knows something about the local birds that we don't. Maybe they aren't the kind of roc that eats people. Maybe they're just…

curious."

I glanced at her. "How many kinds of roc do you think there are?"

"Well, it's just logic, isn't it?" Vindi said uncomfortably. "There's more than one kind of bird, right? Surely there has to be more than one kind of roc. Somewhere far away, I bet there's a pseudo-roc that's like a super-gigantic flamingo, walking around on legs taller than the tallest trees, dipping its beak into the ocean to filter out sharks and crocodiles and other stuff that would otherwise be too small to notice."

"Huh," I said, becoming interested despite myself. "And maybe the people there set out stone decoy crocodiles in hopes that a flamingo-roc will eat one and die, giving them free meat and feathers and so on."

"Can you imagine what a cloak made out of *those* feathers would look like?"

"No one could accuse their warriors of being too subtle."

"Now I know what I want to wear, today and for the rest of my life," Vindi said enthusiastically. "Even better if they're a collapsed civilization on the brink of total savagery. Can you *imagine* the slaughter-girl costume you could make using *those* for raw materials?"

"Yeah, I don't know if I want to be messing with flamingo-rocs," I mused. "Birds have a tendency to get caught in my hair, panic, and poop at the exact moment I look up. Extrapolate that to the size of a flamingo-roc, and I think you'll agree that catching one would be far more trouble than it was worth."

"Disgusting as ever, I see," Vindi said, amused.

"The *world* is disgusting. You're the one who lives in a bizarre slice of reality where meat appears bloodlessly out of nowhere and birds don't poop." I cocked my head thoughtfully. "But then, if they *didn't*, they'd just swell up bigger and bigger until they exploded, splattering everything in the vicinity with a stinking fecal slime. What do you know? Extrapolating from *your* premises is twice as gross as the real world!"

"I'm going to go check on… something," Vindi gagged, heading off to observe the ongoing construction. I watched her go, unsure how I felt. Was I still mad at her? Well, yes. But maybe not as much as before. Why did she have to go around being *herself* instead of kicking puppies, murdering monks, and just generally prancing around being evil and despicable? In a way, it showed just how inconsiderate she was. If she really loved me, she'd make it *way* easier to hate her.

When the carts were finally ready, Ramla cheerfully ordered the soldiers to get inside, which they did.

"Don't come out no matter what," she said. "If you hear any screaming, it's just *them* trying to fool you. All right? All right!"

She jumped up on the first cart and started driving. Avashti and Vindi took the second, and I climbed up on the third. It was a little weird, driving a giant fake elephant across the desert, the muffled conversations of eight or nine hidden soldiers my only company. The mountain-hills seemed to be getting drier and more desolate: I certainly didn't see any more cities or roc crashes. After a while, the road curved away from the river, crossing open desert. The sun beat down hotter than ever, and I was glad to be wearing my makeshift cloak.

A strange noise echoed down from above, like a high wind bending a whole forest to its will. I looked up—and made a bubbling, gurgling sound as a strangled gasp caught in my throat. A deep shadow flashed overhead, as if the world's mightiest storm-cloud had decided to show off how fast it could go.

"No no no," I muttered, staring straight up. Crashed rocs look bigger than big. In the air, lazily circling above their prey, the four of them looked *obscene*.

Up ahead, Ramla jumped down and yanked away the blinders that had prevented her donkeys from seeing what was around them. She flapped her arm at Avashti, who promptly started convulsing wildly. Next to him, Vindi seemed unable to do anything but stare straight up and mouth strange imprecations. I drove up next to her, stopped, and jumped down to un-baffle both my donkeys and hers. Strangely, I pulled the whole thing off quickly, elegantly, and correctly, without falling on my ass even once. I suppose that if I failed at everything all the time, failure would become predictable and boring. To be truly devastated, you have to have hope.

The donkeys had already spotted the rocs by the time I jumped back up. Eyes rolling in terror, they took off at a full sprint: My cart lurched into motion, Vindi and Avashti following right behind. The blocky grey decoy that I was hauling bounced and clattered madly, looking like anything but a real elephant. Well, I guess I wasn't the one it had to fool.

Vindi shrieked, pointing straight up. I whipped the reigns

against the donkeys, not that it had any effect. Control over them, at this point, was purely hypothetical. A shadow flashed over me. I ducked, useless as the gesture might be. The roc missed—barely—and slammed into the earth like an earthquake made flesh. The ground actually plunged away beneath me, leaving my cart's wheels spinning uselessly in the air for two desperate heartbeats. Then the ground slammed into me, just moments before a crashing BOOM tried to break my ears. I can say from (much too much) personal experience that it was FAR louder than being struck by lightning. The donkeys shrieked, mouths foaming, sprinting until I was sure they'd have to die from the strain.

"There's too many!" I heard Vindi shout. "There's just too many!"

The river came into sight. With a single elegant move, Ramla jumped onto one of her donkeys and cut the ropes that bound them to her elephant-decoy cart. Her two donkeys thundered toward the safety of the river, and the elephant-decoy—plus all of the soldiers still inside it—slowly rolled to a stop in the middle of the desert. Another shadow passed over me, along with a vast rushing sound as if a truly evil dust storm had just started to understand—and enjoy—its power. I ducked. Wind blasted me as the roc shot *just* overhead, gigantic talons ripping fruitlessly at the fabric of my decoy.

I heard Avashti bellow something as I thundered past Ramla's abandoned cart. I looked back. Vindi shoved her father onto a donkey and cut the ropes... but stayed behind on her now powerless cart. She jumped down as soon as it stopped and started hacking madly at the elephant-decoy, struggling to break it open, trying to free the soldiers trapped inside. My blood froze. So this was how I was going to die. I drew my belt knife, said a quick prayer to nobody—the gods are all jerks and I wouldn't give them the satisfaction of calling on them just so they could refuse to help me—and then I slashed the ropes that connected the donkeys to my own cart. The donkeys raced off. Avashti flashed past me on his own mount, a look of pure astonishment on his face. My cart rolled to a stop, and I jumped down to kick and punch and cut at the elephant-decoy with everything I had.

A metal-bending shriek shattered the air, shaking my eyes so powerfully that I was actually struck blind. When I could see again, the first thing I saw was a looming shadow that drew my gaze straight up. Something the size of a continental landmass plunged straight toward me—until a second, even bigger creature took offense that it wasn't getting its fair share and smashed into the first with a thunderous midair collision. I hastily resumed hacking at the splintered wood.

I heard screams, hoarse and unfamiliar. Vindi had broken open her cart, and shouted at the screaming, fleeing soldiers to free their brethren from Ramla's abandoned elephant-decoy. They didn't listen to her. They just ran, scattering in a host of random directions. I finished hacking a hole in my own cart, leaving the soldiers to their own devices as I sprinted over to Vindi. We reached Ramla's cart at almost the same moment, attacking it with lunatic strength. A gathering windstorm started to fall from above. I didn't look. I didn't want to know just how dead I was.

"RUN!!" Vindi shouted as a huge wooden panel tore off. As one, the two of us sprinted toward the river. Behind us, we heard screams as another eight or nine soldiers scattered. Wind blasted over us. A shadow fell. The earth trembled, and a roc flashed by overhead, a shattered elephant decoy clutched in its claws. We reached the Kairay river. Out of instinct more than logic, we leapt straight into its welcoming waters.

I hit a rock. Of course. Sputtering, I managed to get my head above water. Avashti and Ramla were sitting huddled under some bushes on the riverbank, looking at us oddly. Oh. Yeah. I guess there wasn't really any reason for us to go *into* the water.

Vindi swam for shore with short, powerful strokes, and I was quick to follow. I don't sink, exactly, but I've never really learned to swim, either. See, when the world plays one of its super-fun jokes on me, like hiding a scorpion in my hat and seeing how long it will take me to notice, upon which I run around in circles until I smack face-first into a giant bell that some workmen just happened to leave in the middle of the road, as a result of which I knock myself unconscious in the most musically transcendent way conceivable—*I don't die*. I can lay unconscious in the middle of the street, being run over by carts and pissed on by dogs, for an endless while until I wake up to find that damn scorpion placidly laying eggs in my nose. Having a similar misadventure in water seems like a bad idea. There's this thing that happens to me when I can't breathe: I die. Yeah, I know, not exactly original, but you take what you can get.

"Vindi..." I gasped, splashing through the muddy waters. Something was cutting off my breath. Somehow, my Anteyvan strangling cord had worked its way out of my pocket in all the excitement and become tangled around my neck. I tried to pull it off, which—of course—caused it to get even tighter. I could barely touch bottom even standing on my toes, and the current was threatening to pull me in even deeper. How long would I last *then*?

I sucked in a breath, but—somehow—none of the air reached my lungs. I suddenly spotted the Walnut of Inversion, floating mockingly just in front of me, magically vanishing the air as fast as I could breathe it. Next to it floated the papyrus shell containing the Gooey Orb of Snail-Snotted Doom. I didn't even want to know how *it* was going to kill me.

"Help me… please…"

Up on shore, Vindi peered at me. "I think Saraya's in trouble," she mused. "Again."

"I'd love to take this one," Avashti said apologetically, "but I've got about ten years' worth of delicate papyrus and ink in my pack. Dunking it in river water is *definitely* counter-indicated."

Vindi shrugged and jumped back into the river, reaching me in a few swift strokes. She grabbed the Walnut of Inversion and the Gooey Orb of Snail-Snotted Doom and handed them to me, then unravelled the strangling-cord from around my neck.

"Try to be more considerate," she said. "You were taking *forever* to die."

"Ha!" Ramla cried as we walked up onto the riverbank. "I *told* you we were going to win. Or did I? Ah, who cares! It's an automatic inference from the axiom that *I* always win! So long as you're with me, you will, too. You're welcome," she told us with what was either ingratiating charm or overwhelming smugness. Giving her the benefit of the doubt, I only made *half* of an obscene gesture in her direction. "And not a soldier in sight!" Ramla said, highly satisfied. "We're close, now, real close—at least, if you know the shortcuts that *I* do!"

"You meant for them to die," I growled. "Admit it."

"What?" Ramla said, eyes wide. "Of course not! Why else do you think I secretly built breakaway panels into all the carts, so you could cut them apart more easily?"

"Liar," I said, glaring at her as I rubbed my throat.

"Ha! I love this one's spirit! Such conviction even when she's drastically and completely wrong!"

"That's Saraya for you," Vindi said coolly. "She spends her time moaning about how much the world hates her, instead of using all that time and energy being *amazing*, like you. She's made her choice,

I guess."

"Vindi…"

But the two of them were already heading off together. Avashti gave me a knowing look as he stood, slinging his overstuffed pack across his back.

"I don't want your sympathy," I snapped.

"That's convenient," he said. "I wasn't about to offer any. Shall we?"

I reluctantly nodded, and we fell in behind the other two. We left the Kairay river behind as we climbed high into the arid mountains, following the narrowing cleft that was all that was left of the Valley of Thunder. I smacked my lips, wishing I'd brought more water. It was starting to get *really* hot. I was just thinking about wrapping my head in my blanket/cloak when we arrived.

The Temple of Souls couldn't have been mistaken for anything else. The facade of the enormous building was carved right into the clifflike canyon walls, every inch of its orangey sandstone covered with skillfully engraved murals. Most of them seemed to be depictions of everyday life, but with a number of curious twists. I stared at one which, yes, depicted a huge bunch of grapes driving humans who were pulling a plow, behind which oxen sprouted horns-first from the earth.

"What the hell?" I asked blankly.

Avashti shrugged. "Gods," he said in explanation.

There was a huge open gap where the door should have been. Avashti confidently led us inside. Smooth stone walls soared forty, fifty, sixty feet overhead. There was light, but it didn't come from torches or lamps. It was smeared down the walls in great streaks. Looking closer, I saw that water seeped from the walls, which in turn attracted weird glowing slime molds in vast numbers.

"What the *hell*?" I demanded.

"Gods," Avashti shrugged.

We came to a hallway that was slightly smaller than the huge, echoing chambers we'd seen up until that point. Avashti cleared his throat and stepped up to the very edge of this new hall.

"I am a wizard," he stated in a clear, echoing voice. "Let me pass." Nothing happened. "I am a wizard," Avashti said again, a little impatiently. "Let me pass!"

"Was something supposed to happen?" Vindi asked.

"A floating cart should have come to fetch me. It always has before. Wizards don't have to face the challenges that have been established for lesser—" He caught himself. "—ah, *different* beings."

"Challenges? What kind of challenges?" I said dubiously.

"I don't know. I've never had to face them. Go," he said, shooing us away. "I don't need the lot of you breathing down my neck. Go wait in the other room."

We retreated back into one of the great oversized rooms. We could hear Avashti's voice ringing out: "*I*... am a wizard." "I *am*... a wizard." "I am a *wizard*. Damn it, I'm telling the truth! Let me pass!"

He finally emerged, looking extremely grumpy. "It didn't work," he said unnecessarily.

"Do you want us to leave? Maybe you could get in if we weren't here," Vindi suggested.

"Well... no," Avashti said, thinking it over. "I really want Saraya, especially, to be there when I try to solve her problem once and for all. And I might need you, given that your horns are currently redirecting Saraya's stolen luck back to her. I think we'll have to face the challenges."

We walked back to the smaller hallway. Now that I looked closer, I saw that the floor was covered with peculiar tiles engraved with three-dimensional artworks. One was a smiling baby's face, puffy-cheeked and almost glowing with merriness. One was a stylized sun. One was an incredibly lifelike and noble tiger. One was an idyllic scene of butterflies hovering around flowers. The walls were also tiled, but these pictures were all the same: An angry demon-face with a mouth that was a simple puncture, a black hole into who-knew-where.

"What are we supposed to do?" I said dubiously.

"It's obvious, isn't it? We puzzle out, from context, which tiles we're supposed to step on in which order, and that keeps us safe," Avashti replied.

"Uh-huh. And how to we do that?"

"There you've got me," he admitted.

"What happens if we get it wrong?" Vindi asked. She raised her voice, shouting down the echoing, seemingly endless corridor: "It would be *terrible* if it shot puppies at us. Puppies determined to give us wet, sloppy kisses all over our faces! We'd *hate* that!" Seeing Avashti's startled expression, she shrugged. "Gods," she explained.

"Let's find out what the penalty is, shall we?" Ramla said pragmatically. Reaching a foot forward, she stomped hard on the stylized sun. Nothing happened. Frowning, she waved her hand through the air in front of us. Instantly, half a dozen metal darts shot out of the demon faces. Ramla yanked her hand back, but of course the darts didn't have anywhere to *go*. They ricocheted off the opposite wall, shattering and filling the air with flying, jagged splinters that tumbled in every conceivable direction. I couldn't see that even a 'safe' tile would be a particularly nice place to be if it was being showered with spinning daggers of jagged death.

"Wait." Avashti cocked his head, listening to the clicks and grinding sounds of automated mechanisms reloading and rewinding crossbows. He waved his hand in front of us exactly as Ramla had. Nothing happened. "It takes time for them to reload," he said. "For a few moments, they've got nothing to shoot. Whoever went *first* might be in trouble, but whoever went *second* would be safe."

"Great," Vindi said. "I'm sure the corpse of the first person would be pleased to know that she'd saved everyone."

"Actually, it's a combination of things," I said, opening my pack. "Protecting my friends motivates me, sure. But also the keen knowledge that, in the last few moments before I die, I *will* be respected and loved, and you'll all have to say really nice things about me at my funeral. Plus, you'll have to invent special and touching last words to attribute to me, given that my *actual* last words were, 'EAT FARTS, MORONS!'"

I climbed into all of the extra clothes from my and Vindi's packs, then wrapped one, two, three extra blankets around myself. I could move, kind of, but it wasn't easy.

"Saraya…" Vindi bit her lip, looking worried. "Don't. We'll find a different way. We'll solve the puzzle. You don't have to do this."

"The puzzle may not *have* a solution," Avashti noted. "Not one that we can comprehend, at least. Remember—gods."

"Yeah, but if we—"

"TOO LATE!" I bellowed. "EAT FARTS, MORONS!"

I waddle-sprinted into the corridor. Instantly, the air was filled with the snap and swish of pointy metals darts shooting through the air. Some hit me—and, thankfully, were stopped by all of my extra padding. Others swished past and hit the far wall in a furious rainstorm of snaps and clangs. I could hear the footsteps of the other three following right behind me, staying in the "safe" part of the corridor. I didn't hear the thump of any dead bodies hitting the floor. It was working!

The storm of darts showed no sign of letting up as I jogged on and on. My clothes were actually getting heavier from the sheer mass of metal stuck in them. Worse than that, some of the new darts struck the old ones and drove them deeper in. Sharp points were beginning to pierce my skin. It *hurt*… and was accompanied by a weird, burning, silly-dreamy sort of sensation that bloomed wherever I was wounded. My whole left leg started to go numb, leaving me to limp along as best I could.

"Oh, great," I muttered. "They're… poisoned? Drugged, at least."

"*What?*" Avashti shouted.

There wasn't any point trying to answer. I jogged on and on, metal darts thundering into me as I panted and gasped and staggered and—

I reached the end. Well, not the *end*-end, just the end of the first corridor. A second corridor continued on at a ninety-degree angle. The walls and floor of this new corridor were covered with a very familiar sort of tile, but at least the elbow *connecting* them was safe. I flopped flat on my face and just lay there, gasping for breath. Vindi arrived, and Avashti, and Ramla. Vindi immediately knelt to check on me, her eyes worried.

"How about it?" I rasped. "Do you like me again?"

"You idiot," she said, worry and affection battling for control of her voice. "Just so you know, I hate you even more for scaring me like that."

"Worth it," I managed to gasp.

"This…" Ramla paced back and forth. Her eyes were worried, her normally immaculate hair all over the place. She had the look of a woman just barely holding back panic. "This is not acceptable. Let the gods shower you with treasure. I don't care. I'd rather be alive."

Vindi glanced at her. "We're halfway, probably, assuming there's only two corridors. Forward or back, what does it matter now?"

"Actually," Avashti said delicately, "there are three."

Ramla pointed dramatically at the wizard. "So *you* say. Maybe it's a trick. Maybe there's a thousand. The gods built this place. Who knows what they think is funny? We have to turn back now. We have to leave while we can. No matter how much gold she has, a dead woman can't spend it."

"It's not about wealth," Avashti said softly. "The princesses of Kairay mean to drain the luck out of Saraya, to leave her for dead or worse. They mean to give themselves dominion over everything, forever. *That's* why we're here."

"So we don't even have a good reason!" Ramla said, exasperated. "Wealth? That I can understand. I can hold a piece of gold in my hand. I can buy stuff with it. Stopping Princess I-Don't-Care from gaining control of Who-Knows-What? No. Go ahead and die for nothing if that's what does it for you. Me? I'm getting out of here. Should you recover your senses, feel free to join me."

"You're not going anywhere," Avashti said confidently. "Not without our help. What say we take a rest before we tackle part two?"

He laid down and closed his eyes. My whole body was prickling with pins and needles as I forced my fingers to obey and began picking darts out of my clothes. Vindi sat next to me and helped. Shrugging, Ramla snooped through my pack, and Vindi's, and finally Avashti's. Her eyebrows rose when she saw what Avashti had hauled all this way—stack upon stack of the papyrus documents he'd spent so many years meticulously crafting. Everything was there… all of the contracts and writs and indexes that would allow him to negotiate with the gods and get something like what he wanted. Ramla held Avashti's pack in her hands. She glanced at me. She glanced at the pack. She glanced at me.

"Ramla?" Vindi asked.

"For what it's worth, I *do* like you. I hope your inevitable death is both swift and painless. Bye!"

Ramla ripped a fistful of pages from one of the books and flung them into the hallway we'd just come from. Darts fired, filling the air with flying metal. Ramla sprinted eight steps, ripped out another handful of pages, and flung them in front of her again. More darts fired.

"STOP!" Vindi shouted. "WE NEED THOSE!"

"Wha…?" Avashti sat up, blinking sleep from his eyes. I tried to stand, but the poison hadn't worked its way out of my system yet, and my legs flopped bonelessly out from under me.

"Get up, get *up*!" Vindi cried, yanking on Avashti's shoulders. Ramla was almost out of sight, a snowy blizzard of torn pages filling the air around her. Years of work. Years of sleepless nights and unceasing labor, deep thought and meticulous design. All gone. Vindi waved her hand in the corridor. Darts shot from both sides, bouncing off the walls and filling the air with broken metal. It was too late. The crossbows were already reset.

"It's over," Vindi said dully. "She's gone."

"What happened to my documents?" Avashti said with a terrible calm, looking at the shattered, torn papers that covered the entire length of the corridor.

"Dad… they're gone," Vindi said. "Ramla destroyed them. All of them."

I think it was a sign of how disturbed Avashti was that he didn't even object to her calling him her father. I stood, my legs finally agreeing to hold my weight.

"I don't think we can catch her," I said. "Our only option is to go forward."

"What's the point?" Avashti said heavily. "We might as well dress up like pomegranates and do a moonlit parasol dance for the gods. It's over. We'll never get them to do what we want now."

"Welcome to my life," I said with a faint smile. "You want to know a secret? *Failing doesn't make you a failure*. Trying and failing, that's called life. It's when you *stop trying* that you're truly and finally a loser. Me? I always look for new angles, ways to turn life's sick jokes into unexpected wins. Let's go and get *something*, and see what we can make of it."

"Ramla really was completely selfish, wasn't she?" Vindi mused.

"Yup," I agreed. "Is there maybe anything you want to say about *me*, now? Maybe something about how great and selfless and wonderful I am?"

Vindi thought it over. "When it's really hot out, you kind of smell like cinnamon for some reason."

"I'll take it," I decided. Pulling my de-darted clothes tighter around me, I took a deep breath and waddle-sprinted into the second corridor.

VI

As Avashti had said, there were two more corridors. At some point in the middle of the last one, when I was nearly out of my mind from all the poison, giggling and attempting to cartwheel through the blasting hail of darts, it occurred to me that Ramla might have had the right idea. We made it through, though. I'm still not sure how. Avashti and Vindi spent a good many hours picking the darts out of my skin and giving the poison time to dissipate before we finally went on.

"Be careful," Avashti said. "The Gateway Chamber, well, has its own rules. Maybe it's best to let you experience it for yourself."

"The Gateway Chamber?" Vindi asked.

Avashti nodded. "The Gods don't condescend to appear physically in our reality, for the most part. Instead, the part of them that's *least* likely to drive us insane may manifest here. Sometimes I can negotiate with those... facets... of the gods. Sometimes I have to open up a gateway and travel to a different and transcendent Realm that is ruled and shaped by its source God. Or it may just sit there, covered in tiny turtles and dripping with sheets of ever-flowing honey. Gods don't have to make sense."

We arrived at the Gateway Chamber. It was huge, hollowed out of the stone like a vast empty sphere. Our hallway intersected it about halfway up: To step inside would mean taking a nasty plunge of eighty feet or more. The walls of the chamber were covered with long, thin rods of stone all pointing inward. Once, long ago, I saw a gilded sea anemone in the market, such a rare and unlikely creature that it commanded a price as mythic as it was. This chamber had much the same feel, but with the spikes pointing *in* instead of *out*.

"I don't get it," Vindi said plaintively. "Where are the gods?"

"Ah," Avashti said, and stepped out onto thin air. It held his weight. Apparently walking on nothing at all, he strode six paces forward, then took one *huge* step and pivoted until he was facing straight down. It looked like he was walking down an invisible wall, but his hair and clothes hung toward his feet, untroubled by anything as silly as gravity. He turned again and again, shifting which dimensions served as his own personal "up" and "down" so fast that I nearly got sick just from watching him.

"I want to try!" Vindi cried, jumping into the abyss. It held her weight, too. Moving with increasing confidence, she started rotating herself around a speechless variety of axes.

"Oh, hell," I muttered. I know how it works. The only reason stupid things work for other people is to trick me into trying them, too, with predictably disastrous results. Remind me to tell you about the time Vindi got free money from a fairy-bandit's hive by throwing rocks at it, concluding with the epic story 'Saraya discovers that fairy-bandits are *way* worse than swarming, stinging bees'. On the bright side, I got to experience the fun exercise of running all the way to the river. And also, the less fun exercise of being swallowed by a fish. (Connoisseurs of fish vomit will be delighted to learn how I got out).

"Come ON!" Vindi cried. She ran over to me, grabbed my hand, and yanked me out into the void. I took several stumbling steps, caught myself, and slowly stood up straight. I was standing on nothing, plain and simple. Meanwhile, Vindi went through one rotation after another until she was standing upside-down directly below me so she could do a stomp-dance on the soles of my feet.

I gritted my teeth. "Could you try doing something a little *less* calculated to result in my immediate and overtly hilarious death?"

"Try having fun for once," she advised me. "It's fun. No fooling!"

I carefully leaned forward. This was the part where I plummeted to my pathetic and wildly undignified doom. Presumably my underwear would contrive to get hooked on one of the bristling wall-rods and get yanked up over my head on the way down. Predictably, I plunged forward—but stopped when my feet found purchase on a new "floor" at a bizarre angle to the first. Releasing a shaky breath, I shuffled further into the Gateway Chamber.

As I moved, I began to see gods—or their manifestations in our world. They seemed to occupy their own peculiar dimensions, and were only visible to someone looking at the right angle from the right location. As a result, they seemed to appear and disappear as I moved. Many of the gods looked like plain marble statues. Others were collections of random and mis-matched objects, like one which combined a flaming hoop, an entire ocean (it hurt the eyes figuring out how it fit into such a small space), and a jar of bees. Another one looked like a furtively lurking bowl of fruit.

"How do we ask them for stuff?" Vindi asked eagerly, her head pointing straight down.

"Carefully," Avashti said, his body pointing sideways and describing a slow and grandiose rotation. "Preferably after long years of painstaking study, and with a comprehensive map of their doctrines at hand."

"How do you ask them for stuff if you've lost all that and have nothing but your wits to go on?" I asked. Avashti just looked at me, his mouth twitching slightly.

"Pray," he said.

I found myself standing in front of a stone statue that was more scowl than face. First thing I'd seen in this damn place that made any sense.

"Hey there, Mister God. I'd like a small suicide device that I can conspicuously refuse to use. A really spectacular one, please. Blood and guts everywhere."

"No! Stop! She's kidding!" Vindi shouted. "What she *really* wants is a box that generates an infinite glory of endless butterflies!" She tried to run over to me, only to discover that she was stuck to an invisible wall some fifteen feet away. She jumped and hopped and spun, trying to get on the same plane as I was.

"Suicide device," I murmured. "Suicide device. Suicide device…"

Space warped and bent, like water ripples shifting reality itself. A handsome wooden box appeared in front of me, of a size to be held comfortably in a single hand. I picked it up, eyebrows rising. With great care, I cracked it *just barely* open. A butterfly squeezed out, its wings a bright sulfurous yellow crossed by bands of green. As much as I hated to admit it, Vindi had outdone herself this time. The butterfly was glorious. It fluttered over to my right arm. Flapped twice. Clamped on with six razor-sharp legs, its compound eyes suddenly glowing with a hellish red light, and then STABBED me with a murderously sharp proboscis.

"NOT AGAIN!" I bellowed, slamming the box shut. Vindi finally reached me. She tried to help by the simple expedient of punching me. On the fourth blow, she actually got the butterfly. It didn't help. The glowing-eyed corpse seemed perfectly happy to keep stabbing into me and extracting my blood.

"Vampire! Vampire!" I bellowed. Vindi grabbed my left wrist, where I was still wearing the quasi-silver bracelet. She yanked my arm over and began punching me with my own hand. On the sixth blow, she managed to crush the butterfly with a substance that looked like, but wasn't, silver. Whatever it was, it worked. The damned thing finally stayed dead, or inanimate, or whatever it's called when vampiric butterflies are involved. Releasing a shaky breath, I tucked the Box of Infinite Beauty (And Vampires) next to my other suicide devices.

"Nice to know you're on my side again," I told Vindi.

"I was never on anyone else's," she said stoutly.

"Really? What about Ramla?"

"Never heard of her. What? What's that? I think Dad's calling."

I looked over at the wizard. Avashti was some forty feet away, sitting cross-legged in midair. He was talking to a faint haze in the air, gesticulating grandly to emphasize his points. Vindi crossed over to him, or tried to, the weird messed-up dimensions of this place making it impossible to go anywhere in a straight line. Shrugging, I followed.

"Got anything?" Vindi asked when we finally reached the wizard.

"Being sufficiently precise takes a great deal of time," Avashti said defensively. "I'm working on it."

"But you'll get what we need?" she pressed.

Avashti sighed. "Honestly, Vindi? Without *any* of my plan books, without any of my pre-written contracts, it's a foregone conclusion that I'm going to fail. Spectacularly. The only reason I'm even here is because our backup plan isn't finished and, quite frankly, might never be. It's just too complicated." He shook his head. "The longer I can keep hope dangling from its thread, however thin and tenuous, well, the longer before I have to face reality."

I glanced at the wavering disturbance before him. "Tell me something. What are the odds that that *thing* would agree to reverse what it did to me if we covered it in vampire butterflies?"

"Again with the rampant whimsy," Avashti said disapprovingly. "As a matter of fact, this isn't the god that originally stole your luck, all those years ago. The one who did? She's... well... challenging. I never should have approached her in the first place."

"You can do that?" I asked, puzzled. "Mix and match gods? Can *this* god undo what *that* one did?"

"It isn't easy," Avashti admitted. "It's like taking your broken watch to a different watchmaker, only this one builds his timepieces exclusively out of fruit and doesn't understand why anyone would use metal. Jamming figs into the gears, well, it would be a minor miracle if you got something that actually told the time. Still, what choice do I have? What I did to you all those years ago..." He shook his head. "I couldn't live with myself if I made that kind of mistake again. I can't face *her*. Not again. The risk is just too great."

Avashti went about his work with infinite patience, speaking to the god-thing in a quiet, firm voice. It was stultifying to watch: He couldn't just ask for something, but endlessly looped back to clarify even the tiniest details of what he'd just said, and then looped back to clarify *that*, and then clarified what he'd said to clarify what he just said. I sat down on empty air, chin on my hands, and watched. After a while, Vindi left to sprint as fast as she could around a large dimensional fistula, describing breathtaking loops in the air. I left as well, retreating to the safe, solid stone of the entry corridor, where I could sit with my back to the wall and wonder how I could be bored in such a miraculous place.

I'm not sure how much time passed—a lot, I think—before I heard someone approaching from back down the corridor.

"Turn off, please," a woman's voice said, followed by a series of clicks. Shuffling steps approached—two sets?—but no darts fired and no shattered metal flew. And then that repeated phrase: "Turn off, please." I waved vigorously at Vindi and Avashti. Vindi came immediately, and Avashti—who seemed good and ready to take a break—wasn't far behind.

"What is it?" Vindi asked. "Talk to the wrong god and make the wrong wish? Are you covered in fire ants from the waist down?" She looked momentarily addled. "I can sympathize. Word of advice: If you ask for 'wealth', specify that you want 'wealth' as HUMANS define it, as opposed to suddenly being soaked in glorious, delicious honeydew."

"I, uh..." I raised an eyebrow. "I *am* going to ask about that later. But for now, someone's coming."

"Turn off, please," said the voice. More clicks. Still no metallic death-storm of thundering darts. I guess there was a way through that even Avashti hadn't known about.

Two figures emerged from the corridor. The first, to my astonishment, was Princess Shivaka. She wore a simple green gown, attractively set off by gilded, braided cords crossing her arms again and again, crystal rims and sparkling gems worked in at regular intervals. The other figure, tall and dashing but for his clouded, dreaming eyes, was her husband, Prince Dakar.

"GET HER!" Vindi bellowed, then glanced at me to see if sheer volume had tricked me into obeying.

"No, that's all right," I said. "You get the stab-party started. I'm sure that watching *you* hack her to bits will inspire me to join in. Eventually."

"I'm sorry about… what happened," Princess Shivaka said contritely, her eyes downcast. "I know a simple apology isn't worth much. I'm not sure what more I can do, here and now… give you a crystal rim, perhaps?"

"NO!!!" I shouted, jerking away.

Princess Shivaka looked at me strangely. "As you will. I just think that if you understood *why* I did what I did…"

Prince Dakar stepped in front of her. He didn't seem to know who we were, much less where he was. Given his roaming, dreaming eyes, I'm not sure he cared.

"This is a merry little party," he said genially. "Ah, but there's a solution, you know, if no one comes to your parties: Glue tiny, festive hats to spiders! Then your guests have already arrived. Problem solved! They drink very little and always bring cobwebs, which—given that 'cob' is another word for a male swan—means, I think, that we must applaud spiders their ambition." He beamed at us all. "Are we having cake, now?"

"Before, when we were courting, he used to tell me stories," Princess Shivaka said in a quiet, ragged voice. "He was as sharp as a barrel of nails, he was. You could tell him any story you'd ever heard, and he'd take it apart and put it back together, on the fly, and use the same components to tell you a better story you'd never heard before. I loved him for his wit, his kindness, his gentle humor. I… regret… what I tried to do to you. But after so many years of failure, so many years of having to look at what's left of him… at a physical reminder of what I lost… can you blame me for taking extreme measures to save him?"

Realization dawned on Vindi's face. "You needed perfect luck… so you could finally cure your husband. That's why." She snorted. "Some enemy *you* are. In stories, everyone's either a noble hero or a wicked murderer. Why did you have to be so *complicated*?"

"If it's a villain you want, well, I have one for you," Shivaka said ruefully. "Gamal betrayed me. She had reasons of her own for pretending to help me... as I found out, to my sorrow, when she ordered her soldiers to imprison me in my own suite. I suppose *her* goal, if she could steal your luck, would be to replace me as heir, dominate her husband, and claim dominion over Kairay forever."

"But you escaped?" Vindi said, fascinated.

"I did," Shivaka said modestly. "There are still those who are loyal to me. I came to the Valley of Thunder, where I found a dozen or so of Gamal's soldiers wandering the desert with haunted eyes. I don't know what you did to them, but I don't think I've ever seen such traumatized men and women. They almost begged to switch sides and join me. I had to leave them outside the Temple, of course..."

"This is all very affecting, I'm sure," Avashti said, "but I need to know about a more pressing matter: How did you pass through the Temple of Souls without setting off any traps?"

Princess Shivaka smiled ruefully. "Let's just say that the royal family didn't pay all those wizards all that money to build this place without getting *something* in return."

"I see." Avashti rubbed his chin. "And this ability to turn off the traps, would it work for Gamal?"

"Most certainly." Princess Shivaka gazed at each of us in turn. "We're safe here, for now... but time is short. Once Gamal arrives with a large and well-equipped force, we won't have a chance. We have to get out of here, now, before it's too late. I can protect you. I can spirit you away to a secret place, a place of comfort and safety. Let this be my penance... or the beginning of it, at least."

Avashti thought it over. "You may have a point. Why face a bunch of intractable gods when we could enjoy the personal protection of a royal princess?"

"We have to help Saraya," Vindi said loyally. "We have to *try*." She glanced at me. "You've always tried your hardest to protect *me*. I can't count the number of times you selflessly tackled me away from friendly, happy dogs that were licking my face!"

"You never know about dogs," I said ominously. "Sometimes they attack when you least expect it. I mean, every one of them bit *me*, didn't they?"

"You'd do anything for me. Inconveniently, I've never been

asked to die for you, but this seems like the next best thing." Vindi pointed imperiously at her father. "Fix Saraya!" she declaimed, then brushed her hands together. "There. I've done *my* part!"

Avashti nodded ruefully. "I hate to admit it, but Vindi's right…"

"HA!!!"

"Inconceivably, and most inconveniently, I do love you. No matter what, I have to try."

Princess Shivaka held up a restraining hand. "Saraya needs to stay here and get help. Sure. Avashti needs to stay too, since it's his expertise you need. But why throw away a life you could save? I could take Vindi far from here and hide her safely away. Let me do this for you."

"Well… it *does* make sense," Avashti mused, glancing at his daughter. "Worrying for your safety is a distraction I could do without."

"Nope. Not gonna happen," Vindi said. "I'm here for Saraya, whether she likes it or not. In fact, I'm going to sing loudly and slap her in the face, just to prove that I'd love her even if she were super annoying."

"Wait," I said, frowning. "How does you slapping me prove that *I'm* annoying?"

"Transitive property. The more annoying I am, the more it proves that I love you."

"I don't think…"

"Come on!" Vindi said with gusto. "Let's kick some gods in the face and see what happens!"

"This is a bad idea," Shivaka said. "I can save Vindi. You know I can. What kind of love would it be, letting her die just because —"

"Too late!" Vindi cried. She grabbed Avashti and me by the hands and yanked us into the Gateway Chamber. We both staggered out onto empty air, which thankfully continued to hold our weight. Looking resigned, Shivaka took Dakar's arm and followed.

"If I can just find my way back…" Avashti said to himself.

I solemnly shook my head, which wasn't easy given that I'd just taken a wrong step and seen the whole world flip upside-down around me. "You're doing it wrong," I said.

Avashti scowled at me, standing sideways in midair. "Remind me—my memory isn't what it used to be—which of us here is the wizard?”

“Doesn’t matter,” I said, spitting to the side and watching it suddenly and inexorably shoot straight up once gravity got a hold of it. “One of us is the all-time grand master of getting shit on by life, and it sure isn’t you. Listen. When a person gets burned, the smart thing to do is to avoid all fire forever—right? Or. Or, you can build a dog out of fireworks, light it off, and chase it as it flies screaming around the room until you finally get to bite it on its flaming, sparkling ass.”

“*What*?” Vindi demanded.

“That metaphor wasn’t perfectly clear?” I said, puzzled. “I’ll try to make it simpler: We have nothing to lose. Nothing. We can’t possibly screw things up any worse than they already are. So why jump off a cliff trying to grab a copper grain? I say, if you’re going to jump off a cliff anyway, grab at the sun. If you’re hoping for a miracle, why the hell not shoot for a *big* miracle, one that’ll actually make a difference?”

Avashti gave me a guarded look. “And how does this apply to our current situation?” he asked.

“All this time, you’ve stayed away from the goddess that screwed me up,” I said. “But here, now, when we have absolutely nothing left to lose, you’re still taking us back to the same tired old god who’s failed you so many times before. No. We’re going straight to the goddess who started all this, and we’re kicking her in the face until we get some kind of reaction.”

“That—” Avashti blew out a breath. “—is a strategy I would consider profoundly unlikely to be crowned with success.”

“Same with doing things your way. But if the miracle happens —if we actually win—we get *everything we want*, as opposed to another inadequate, halfway solution.”

Avashti glanced sidelong at his daughter. “Vindi? What do you think?”

“We should try it Saraya’s way,” she said stoutly. “Plus, if she really does go around kicking gods in the face, there’s a non-trivial chance she’ll be turned into a dog.”

“And?”

Vindi smiled. “I’ve always wanted a pet.”

Avashti looked at Shivaka and Dakar. “What do *you* think?”

“This seems like an exceptionally bad idea,” Shivaka said. “Saraya tells us that there aren’t any consequences, that things couldn’t possibly get any worse. That’s where she’s wrong. Dying is the *easy* way out when you go around taunting gods. Allowing me to hide you away and keep you safe would be far smarter." She looked right at me. "You say that you love Vindi. Prove it. Save her life."

"Um," I said, trying to keep my face from revealing just how deeply her words had cut.

Dakar wandered out in front of her, looking confused. "Am I falling?" he asked, befuddled. "It seems to me, the times when there's nothing under my feet are generally the times when I'm falling. Birds are exceptionally good at falling. By flailing around with their arms, they frequently manage to fall *up*. I've tried to imitate their form, but with little success. I wonder, if I paid them generously in seed, would birds condescend to give me falling lessons?"

"We're going for the whole thing," Vindi said decisively. "Take us to the god that screwed Saraya up. It's time to finish this."

Avashti led us along a nonsensical route to a statue that was almost disappointing in its sheer normality. The marble bust depicted the face of a beautiful woman with stars in her eyes. That was it. No screaming lizards giving birth to themselves while long-bearded snails watched approvingly.

"*Some* gods have really stopped trying," I muttered.

Avashti looked uncomfortable. "I visited her realm once before. I think I remember the opening words…"

The wizard cleared his throat. He didn't make any mystical gestures, or speak in a strangled voice from the deepest pits of hell. He simply spoke to the statue, verbally winding forward and back as he added details and closed loopholes, gradually building a word-picture of *exactly* what he wanted. Slowly, a hole in the world faded into existence just beyond Vindi. She glanced at me. I shrugged. She glanced at Avashti. He nodded.

"One," he said. "Two. Three…"

As one, the three of us stepped forward. There was no sensation of travel. One moment we were in the Gateway Chamber, and the next we were standing on a windswept plain of stubby, orangey-tan grass. There were weirdly shaped mountains in the distance, more like towering pinnacles or spires than proper mountains. Overhead, instead of anything familiar like a sun or clouds, the dome of the sky was filled from edge to edge with a gigantic, beatific face— the same face we'd seen on the statue.

"What now?" I asked.

Shivaka and Dakar appeared behind us. Avashti said a few

more words, and the portal slowly faded away into nothing.

"It looked a lot different, last time," the wizard told us. "For one thing, it was a forest. The trees were unbelievable. Bigger than big. Huge. I climbed one of them until I was close enough to poke her in the eye, just about. She *had* to pay attention to me, once I was that close. Not sure how we can reach her from all the way down here."

"So what do we do?"

The wizard frowned. "Let me think."

"*I'll* tell you what we're going to do," Princess Shivaka said pragmatically. "Wizard, enchant the grass to be bigger. Make it as big as the biggest tree."

Avashti sneezed mightily, his face turning red. Vindi and I stared at him.

"Also, don't do it here, where the grass could spear us," Shivaka told Avashti. "Go over *there*, and… uh…"

Avashti collapsed to the ground, his face red. Vindi was at his side in an instant, grabbing his wrist.

"His pulse is all over the place," she said, shocked. "Something's wrong. Something's *really* wrong."

"Get back on your feet," Shivaka ordered the wizard. "You'll be able to breathe more easily if you're squatting or face-down. Take off your belt. It's too constrictive."

I dropped down at his other side. Sweat poured down Avashti's face, and his breath came in wheezing gasps.

"Saraya—" Vindi said, still clinging to his arm. "*Help me.* I think he's dying."

Princess Shivaka stepped closer, obviously concerned. "Avashti, listen to me. What you'll do now is—"

"SHUT UP!" I snapped, seeing that the wizard was trying to speak.

"Not… first time… came to this goddess," he gasped. "The time I accidentally stole Saraya's luck… not the first time. First time, wanted to escape Her Lordship's service. Goddess gave me what I wanted. Sort of. Gave me a deadly new allergy. Either I'd be released from service, or I'd be dead. Either way, escape. Technically a solution, right?"

"But what are you allergic *to*?" Vindi demanded.

"Sounds like a joke," he said, oddly reluctant to explain. "Darshik never believed me. Said I was lazy."

"Tell us!"

"That goddess, she's got a real weird sense of humor. Or none at all. Hard to tell. Doesn't have to make sense, does it, magic?"

"TELL US!"

Avashti's breath sighed out. "Authority. Deathly allergic to authority."

"That's for *real*?" I demanded. "You weren't just making it up to get out of work?"

Avashti managed to smile, however weakly. "Wouldn't you like to know?"

I looked up at Princess Shivaka, who looked shocked and dismayed. "Give him one more order… just one… and I will punch you so hard your head will fly right off your body," I said pleasantly.

"Again with the threats," Vindi said, exasperated. She looked up at Shivaka, smiling hesitantly. "I'm sure you'll act differently, now that you know."

"Of course. I wouldn't dream of making his condition worse." Shivaka fidgeted. "So… ah… what *should* we do?"

Avashti slowly sat up, his complexion returning to normal, his breath coming much more easily.

"Well, we don't have any trees to climb. We can't rely on magic, either." Avashti squinted at the distant horizon. "If we want her to notice us, I think we'll have to get to those mountains and climb high enough that she can actually hear us shouting at her."

"I guess that makes sense," Vindi said, glancing at Shivaka.

The Princess frowned. "I still think if would be quicker and easier to enchant the grass. If you chose to, that is," she said cautiously.

"Without my plan books, that would take forever and fail spectacularly," he said crisply. "We make for the mountains."

"Looks easy enough," I said. Little did I know.

We started walking. Despite the absence of sun, it was very bright and very hot. The grass changed at an almost visible rate, adapting to its surroundings with incredible speed. Some of the plants huddled in on themselves, becoming hard, spiny little knobs. Some went the other way, growing big leaves they could wear like a hat, so as to provide shade. The worst came when I accidentally barked my shin on a rock, blood dripping on the plants I was stepping over. I should have known what was coming. Grass rustled and stirred, growing wiry little vegetable arms. Hungry for the precious water inside my body, the plants began to stir ominously. I didn't pay too much attention until a sharp rock whizzed up and whacked into the back of my head.

"Maybe we should hurry," I said nervously. "Ow! Damn you to hell, plants! Quit it!"

"Should I be alarmed?" Avashti asked. "I can feel tendrils latching onto my ankles, in a valiant—if badly misguided—effort to throw *me* at Saraya. You know what the worst part is? I really need to relieve myself, which would be a spectacularly bad idea just now."

"We could still leave," Shivaka said. "You, wizard—you could open the portal from anywhere, couldn't you? Even here. We still have time. Gamal won't have reached the Temple, not yet."

When no one answered, she shrugged and fell silent. We trudged onward. Well, the other four did. I sort of danced and pranced to avoid the patter of rocks being thrown at me. Avashti wasn't much help. He was working on our backup plan, puzzling out the tricky problem of using the Lens of Becoming to give me good/bad luck. Vindi had packed a single book, a collection of animal fables, and Avashti had commandeered it so as to write a florid, endless list of notes in the margins of the dried papyrus. This time, it was Vindi who had to steer him by the elbows.

Something hit the ground in front of me. A raindrop? I looked up. There were neither clouds nor darkness, just that enormous face, but it was unquestionably raining. I shielded my eyes. It was starting to come down *hard*—blasting down so thick I could hardly see Avashti in front of me.

"!" he shouted, grabbing me and turning me around so he could shove his book into my pack.

"What?"

He cupped his hands to my ears. "Wubba!" he bellowed, or words to that effect.

"Maybe we should stop and rest!" I shouted back.

We hunkered down in a circle, soaked in no time by the blasting rain. Vindi shrugged off her pack and put it down. My left wrist startled to feel weird and tingly. Frowning, I held the quasi-silver bracelet up to my eye. It couldn't be lightning. I don't think there *was* lightning in this weird halfway place. The rain simply fell straight down without—

The firmament split open. An explosion blasted into my ears. *Fire* poured through my flesh. Yup. That's what being hit by lightning feels like. When I could see again, I was twenty feet from where I'd been, there were scorch marks all up and down my left arm, some of my hair was missing, and there was a very strong scent of metal in my left nostril.

"Zirbla!" Vindi shouted into my ear.

"I'm sure you did," I replied inanely. Taking her hand, I returned to hunch rather uncomfortably next to the others. Meanwhile, the plants were adapting to their new reality as quickly as they had the old. As rivulets expanded and joined together into little meandering streams which overflowed and joined into a general and rising flood, the broad-leaved grasses simply grew their leaves fatter and fatter until they floated like little boats. The spiny knob-things popped free of the ground and floated to the surface, counting on stabbing into my flesh like burrs so that I'd carry them safely above the rising waters. The other, more motile vines were overcome with more water than they knew what to do with, swelling and swelling and coming dangerously close to bursting. One of them found a little turtle crawling past and burrowed into the creature's flesh. Suddenly, the turtle started vomiting water like a gushing fountain, looking startled as it disposed of the plants' excess for it. Other plants latched onto mice and frogs and voles, and the whole of the flooded plain was soon dotted with a vast diversity of plant-bound animals vomiting water straight up.

"Someone get Vindi's pack!" Princess Shivaka cried, pointing as the rising water threatened to swamp it. She was *right next* to it, but I guess princesses aren't accustomed to lifting things. Makes you wonder if she employed a servant with a long wooden stick whose sole purpose was to lever one cheek off the ground when she needed to fart.

"This is getting stupid," I said. I grabbed Vindi's pack—and it promptly burst, ripping apart at the seams. To my horror, several bundles of travel bread—our only remaining food—tumbled into the water and melted into goo.

"Oh no. Oh no. I'm sorry. I'm so sorry."

"Saraya…" Avashti forced himself to stop, simply sitting waist-deep in the water and batting at the vegetable boats that kept bonking into him. The rain grew lighter and finally stopped. The sky was as bright as ever: There didn't seem to be any day or night in this place, just the face of the goddess smiling down on us exactly the same as before.

"Princess Shivaka," Avashti said, "do *you* have any food?" She reluctantly shook her head. Avashti glanced at me. "And now, thanks to Saraya's carelessness, it seems that neither do we. This trip was going to be hard enough as it was. How long do you think it'll take to reach those mountains… two days? Three? Tell me, how long do you think we'll last now that we have nothing to eat?"

"So I made a mistake," I shot back. "You want to sling insults and hand out blame? Go right ahead. But keep in mind, since you raised me, it's on *you* that I'm not a glorious glowing perfect heroine. Stagger in wonderment to realize it, but I MAKE MISTAKES!"

"It isn't Saraya's fault," Princess Shivaka volunteered. "Vindi's pack was right next to me. I should have noticed that the seams were loose."

"It's *my* fault, too!" Vindi cried, getting into the spirit of the thing. "I guess I shouldn't have kept my collection of unsheathed swords and dragon's teeth in the bottom."

"All right, *that* time she was joking," I decided.

Avashti took a deep breath, forcing himself to speak in quiet and measured tones. "Fine. We have no food. It's a challenge to overcome. So be it. Now… as a matter of laughably little concern… I don't suppose any of you could find me something to eat?"

I picked up a water-vomiting turtle, examined it, and set it back down. I tried nibbling on one of the big, boat-like leaves. It tasted terrible.

"We'll figure it out," I said. "*One* of these plants has to have fruit, or grain, or tubers, or *something*. We'll get there."

"Or we could leave now," Princess Shivaka noted, "before we starve to death, after which our corpses will be murdered *again* when my sister-in-law finally catches up with us."

"We keep going," Vindi said decisively. She wrapped a soaking-wet blanket around her shoulders and picked up everything else she could salvage from the wreck of her pack. Between us, we managed to stuff everything in *my* pack—the only one we had left—or in our pockets. Then, taking a sighting on the still-distant mountains, Vindi led us at a steady march across the flooded plain.

It was impossible to tell time in that weird place, which only made the rapid shifts in the local flora all the more startling. Now that there was light *and* water, the plants seemed determined to overtop each other, each trying to grab more light than its fellows. Taller and taller stalks sprouted broader and broader leaves, until we found ourselves walking through a bizarre forest that was like looking up at lily-pads from below. It was a weird, green, shadowy place, where thick stalks shot up to a perfectly flat, thin ceiling of leaves nearly a hundred feet overhead. The spiked orbs adapted to the darkness by becoming parasitic, stabbing their spines into nearby trunks while huge, showy flowers gouted from their now-transparent bodies (the flowers on the burrs that stabbed into *me* smelled disturbingly like meat). Even wildlife got in on the action, starting to glow as a way of luring in their prey. Believe me, you haven't lived until you've seen a snapping turtle mesmerize a duck with pulsing, spinning lights above its eyes.

"Finding our way is going to be tricky if we can't see the mountains," Avashti mused. "A person could get *really* lost in here. I don't suppose either of you packed a compass?"

"Sure did," Vindi said proudly.

"Good girl. Let's see if it still works."

Vindi didn't have her pack any more, but after a quick search she found that she'd stowed it safely in one of her pockets.

"The symbols changed," she said, surprised. She squinted at the compass, looked up, and finally pointed into the deepening gloom. "That way is 'Q'. I'm not sure how to pronounce the other directions."

"We head 'Q'," Avashti announced. As we marched on, the water soaked into the ground and left us walking across squishy mud, which slowly firmed into damp earth. Princess Shivaka took the compass from Vindi, seeming as fascinating by its construction as the weird symbols on its face.

"Is this local? Imported?" she asked.

"It's a compass," Vindi said, shrugging.

"This is quite delightful," Prince Dakar said. "It reminds me of a painting I used to enjoy, until I became trapped in it and couldn't escape. Come to think of it, I'm still there, aren't it? Oh my. This is embarrassing. Do you think I should try to figure out which bodily fluids best dissolve paint, or would I be in danger of forevermore being known as 'Seven Portraits of a Vomiting Man'?"

I sidled closer to Princess Shivaka. "Do you really think Dakar can be saved?" I asked quietly.

Shivaka managed to smile, however hesitantly. "He was... he *is*... a good man. I refuse to believe he's gone forever. Someday, we will be together again. It will happen. Yes."

"I almost wish you'd managed to steal my luck," I mused. "Gamal wouldn't have been able to catch you by surprise *then*."

"I was too trusting," Shivaka said regretfully. "I should have known she was going to turn on me. It's kind of obvious in retrospect.”

I nodded ruefully. “So, if you *did* have perfect luck, you’d fix Dakar, and then… what? Give my luck back to me?”

“Why would I do that?” Shivaka said, amused. “Your friend Vindi, when she was at her luckiest, was in no position to fully exploit one of the greatest and most profound gifts the world has ever known. I am. If I were that lucky, I could enact enlightened, wise, constructive policies across all of Kairay. Imagine how much better the world would be, if someone who actually *cared* got to have her way! But why stop at Kairay? There are so many people who need me. So many places suffering under dire despots and terrible tyrants. I could help them. If I truly consider myself a good and moral person, I’m *obligated* to expand my influence as widely as possible. Oh, don’t worry—I’d take good care of you,” she assured me. “I’d keep you in a nice, safe padded room. And you’d lead a happy life, knowing how much your sacrifice had helped everyone else.”

“Ah,” I said wryly. “I forgot who I was talking to. If you want something, you’re entitled to have it. Yes. Of course. How silly of me to expect anything else.”

“Was anything I said unreasonable?” Shivaka asked. “If you had the power and position that I have, and still chose to let everyone around you suffer forever, what sort of person would that make *you*?”

I didn’t have a good answer, so I decided to pretend that I hadn’t heard the question. Avashti batted in irritation at the increasingly gaudy parasitic flowers all around us.

“Which way are the mountains?” he demanded. “Who has the compass?”

“Here,” Princess Shivaka said, handing it to me.

“Well—” I began. I don’t know what happened. I guess I squeezed it wrong. The compass more or less exploded, metal bits spinning into the darkness and vanishing. One especially pointy bit jumped right at my eye. I yelped, trying to bat it away—

“NOT THE NEEDLE!” Avashti bellowed. “IT’S THE ONLY PART WE—”

I tried to stop myself, but my last half-hearted gesture flicked the needle high into the air. We all stared upward. A glowing bird flew past, making a peculiar bubbling noise which stuttered when the needle stabbed into it and stuck there. The bird kept right on going, swiftly vanishing into the distance.

“I’m not angry,” Avashti said carefully. “That was a *mistake*.

It could have happened to anyone. Just... give me a moment, all right?"

The wizard grabbed a flowering parasite and shouted wordlessly as he shook it to bits. He stomped around in a little circle, squishing confused turtles deeper into the mud. He ripped his shirt halfway open and bellowed at the sky.

"Not angry," he repeated, panting for breath. "No food? No compass? What fun. More challenges! Let's go."

Vindi and I exchanged glances. "I think maybe *I'd* better walk next to him," she said.

"Good idea."

Avashti peered at the forest, which looked exactly the same in every direction. "We were going *that* way... I think. Try to walk in a straight line," he said. "Until this phase passes and the trees shrink away to nothing, we'll have to go by memory."

We trudged onward. After a while, those weird, flat-topped trees started to sway as a breeze kicked up. It grew stronger and stronger, swiftly becoming a full-on gale blowing right into our faces. One of the great trees suddenly toppled over, and then another, and then another. I assumed the rest would soon follow, but I'd overlooked just how adaptable the local life was. The great trees somehow turned the tables on their parasites, forcing those gaudy flowers to stretch out longer and longer until they were more like wildly colorful vines, all speckled and bearded and bedecked with all manner of frilly projections. In no time, the vines stretched from trunk to trunk and bound them together: With thousands of flexible, elastic vines joining them, the trees could stand tall in the wind, bouncing around but not breaking.

"Well," I shouted over the wind, "it looks like— OW!"

Something hard smacked into my face. Picking it up, I stared in consternation at a tiny turtle whose shell flared up at the edges into something like wings. When the wind was *this* strong, I guess it didn't take much of a leap to become airborne.

"Saraya brings up an interesting point," Princess Shivaka shouted. "When we reach the goddess, how are we going to get her attention? Just yell?"

Avashti leaned close so he could speak without shouting. The rest of us put our heads together in a little circle, all except Dakar, who kept making little jumps as if wondering why *he* was having so much trouble learning to fall in a non-downward direction.

"Yelling might work if we got close enough," Avashti said. "*Might*. But to be sure, we'll want the artifact that got her attention last time." Avashti pulled a cord from around his neck, at the end of which was a clear, many-faceted crystal. The interior appeared to be hollow, and the oozing motes inside of it were obviously alive. Their colors ranged from a vivid, pustulant yellow to a grotesque, otherworldly violet to an eye-bending orange that I've seen in some of Kairay's more sinister fungi.

"Where did you get that?" I said, fascinated.

"I made it. Not long after she was born, I decided to use wizardry to make a night-light for Vindi so she'd sleep better," he said drily. "This is what I got."

"Congratulations. You succeeded brilliantly. One look at it, and she'd scream long enough to run out of air and fall senseless into bed… and passing out is the same thing as sleeping peacefully, isn't it?"

"What are you talking about?" Vindi asked. "Look at them in there, slurping around being cute and making friends! Awww!"

I looked up from our little circle. I still couldn't tell which way was which… and I didn't remember which way we'd been going, either. The wind had fallen off almost completely, so I couldn't even follow the simple directive, 'march INTO the wind'.

"Does anyone remember which way we were going?" I asked plaintively.

Princess Shivaka shook her head dubiously. "Maybe we should get some sleep," she said. "By the time we wake up, the trees will probably be gone."

Avashti reluctantly nodded. "I suppose that makes sense."

"You take this," Vindi said, stretching out a damp blanket for her father. "I'll sleep on that gigantic flower over there."

"Take care it doesn't swallow you," he said sternly.

Vindi snorted, hands on her hips. "What's it gonna do, pollinate me?"

"Just take care," he said gently.

I spread out my own blanket. I suddenly felt very tired. Who knew what time it was in this crazy place? It could be well past midnight for all I knew.

"I'll take the first watch," Princess Shivaka said. "It's about time I did *something* useful."

Avashti frowned. "Do you think a watch is really necessary?"

"Probably not, but let's face it… we don't know what these creatures will turn into."

"*I'm* here, aren't I?" I said, closing my eyes. "Whatever they become, they'll have eggs and an insatiable desire to lay them in my nose. I can tell you that much for sure."

I guess I fell asleep. The next thing I knew, Avashti was standing over me, his face pale with suppressed anger, Vindi hovering worriedly over his shoulder.

"Wha?" I asked. There was something hard in my hand. That was new. Looking down, I saw Avashti's crystal—the one thing that was guaranteed to get the goddess' attention—clutched loosely in my hand. It was broken. Crystal shards were scattered over the ground nearby, and the living motes were simply gone.

"Saraya?" Avashti said dangerously.

I sat up slowly, staring at the broken crystal in my hand.

"This isn't how it works," I said softly.

"I doubt it will do me any good," Avashti said crisply, "but I would still like an explanation."

"I have to be conscious. I have to see it happen. That way, I get to experience the full, gut-wrenching, existential horror of helplessly watching the crystal tumble out of my hands, bounce off a rock, and slam itself up my nose—whereupon it shatters, so that I'd spend the rest of my life distracted by the colorful motes swimming around in my eyes. That's how it could happen. Not like this."

"People do weird things in their sleep," Princess Shivaka offered. "It wasn't your fault. These things happen."

"It just seems so *unlikely*…" I fell silent, thinking. Around us, the forest loomed as stifling as ever, though the vines had turned into colorful, spiralling trees, and the trees had turned into floppy vines. Vindi tried to lead Avashti away, but the wizard brushed her off, still glaring at me. My eyes slowly rose to Princess Shivaka.

"We've been having bad luck the whole time we've been here," I said slowly. "The compass burst apart when you handed it to me. That could be plain bad luck, it's true. It could have been me… or it could have been you. You could have sabotaged it before you handed it to me."

Princess Shivaka smiled. "And the moon could be made of cheese. A lot of things could be true. Your point?"

"Vindi's pack burst when I picked it up. That could be plain bad luck, it's true. It could have been me… or it could have been you.

You could have torn the seams when we were all distracted by the lightning strike."

"That, too, is true," Princess Shivaka said lightly. "I didn't, mind you, but I grant you that it's theoretically possible."

Avashti was scowling as if he didn't know *what* to believe, while Vindi stood frozen in place. I nodded to myself.

"But some of the things that happened could *only* be you. Only you could have talked to Darshik and learned about Avashti's allergy. When we got here, you started giving him orders right away."

"I stopped as soon as I saw what was happening."

"You stopped as soon as I threatened to punch your head right off your body. Then," I said, showing her the shattered remains of the crystal, "*this* happened when we were asleep, every one of us... except the one person who promised to take the first watch."

"I fell asleep, too," she said wryly. "It's not my fault you walk in your sleep."

"I don't think I did. I think it was you. Each and every time, it was you."

"You surely don't... ah... you surely can't..." Princess Shivaka glanced at Avashti, whose hands were slowly curling into fists, and at Vindi, who looked both shocked and dismayed. "You know, I'm actually relieved that you figured it out," she said brightly. "All of this sneaking around really isn't my style."

"You've been sabotaging us?" Avashti demanded. "Why?"

"You're trying to cure Saraya," Princess Shivaka said simply. "If her *bad* luck goes away, so does my shot at having unnaturally *good* luck. I can't let that happen. If I truly mean to help people, I have to preserve her curse no matter what the cost." She smiled at me. "You know, I really didn't think you'd figure it out. I was sure that a lifetime of bad luck would have taught you to blame yourself, first and always. Shows what I know."

"How could you?" Vindi said, heartbroken. "It doesn't even make sense. What use is it, wasting our time on a trip to nowhere, if all you're doing is preserving this gift for Gamal to steal?"

"Ah, yes, that," Princess Shivaka said. "I really don't enjoy lying, you know. The fact is, Gamal didn't betray me. I betrayed her. Her greed and avarice have no place in the wonderful new world I intend to build. Yes, I *claimed* she was a threat, so that you, Vindi, would come with me—"

"Me?" she said in a small voice.

"Well, your horns *are* the artifact we need," she said reasonably. "Once we have you *and* the Lens of Becoming, it'll only be a matter of time before we can pull off the transfer. Instead of Saraya's luck being reflected uselessly back to her, it'll be transferred directly to me. Speaking of which… Darshik! NOW!"

She pulled a glassy green sphere from her pocket, a wizardly artifact of some sort, and tapped it twice. With a bang and a flash, the royal wizard appeared in front of us. He grabbed Vindi. Shivaka grabbed Dakar. Darshik shouted garbled words and a portal faded into being behind them. Shivaka stepped backward and vanished instantly. Darshik followed. The last I saw of Vindi was the shocked expression on her face, and then she winked out, too. The portal vanished as quickly as it had appeared.

"Make a portal, quick!" I grabbed a shard of the shattered night-light crystal to use as a weapon. I grabbed it the wrong way around, of course, and blood started to drip from my hand. "There's only two of them. Two and a half, if you count Dakar. We have to catch them before they leave the Temple of Souls and get back to her soldiers!"

Avashti tried. I could tell that he was trying. He concentrated, he said the words, he went through the whole ritual, but the portal stubbornly refused to appear.

"Damn that faker!" he exploded. "I don't know what he did, but this is *his* fault—it has to be!"

"Darshik? He blocked you?"

"No. Darshik lacks the intellect, the originality, or indeed, the advanced nervous system which distinguishes actual human beings from disgusting, lowly insects," Avashti said savagely. "It was that damned book of his that told him what to do. *It* blocked me. *Damn it!*"

Avashti paced back and forth. I took stock of our situation: No food, no compass, no wizardly artifact, no escape—oh yes, and no Vindi, either.

"How long until you can open a gateway?"

"I don't know," he said raggedly. "A while."

"I was just thinking… as long as we're stuck here, we might as well try to fix *my* problem. They won't have any use for Vindi's horns if there's no stolen luck to redirect. Princess Shivaka would let her go. I think she would. She's not evil. Just… misguided."

"We'll never make it to the mountains," Avashti said savagely.

"If only there were giant trees, like last time. I could climb right up them, and… and…" He stared up at the spiralling, multicolored forest that soared a hundred or more feet overhead. "I've avoided improvising for so long," he said quietly. "It only brings heartbreak, not doing things the slow, meticulous, proper way…"

"Avashti?"

He sighed. "We've seen how fast the life here adapts," he said. "What if we *encouraged* the trees to become giant?"

His plan was simple. Best of all, it seemed likely to work. Each of us climbed one of the brilliantly colorful trees. They were actually fairly easy to scale—you could almost *walk* up that slow, spiralling incline—and huge bundles of glorious flowers gouted from the trunks to provide handholds. Once we reached the tops, we simply harvested huge flat leaves and held them over our chosen trees, putting them in the shade, encouraging them to grow even taller as a way to get past us. Avashti's tree responded the way he wanted, growing taller at a visible rate. Mine started to sweat beads of sweet liquid, which summoned massive numbers of ants that seemed determined to devour anything in their way.

"ANTS!" I bellowed, leaping over to Avashti's tree. Sparing me a disgusted look, he kept moving his big, shading leaf back and forth, encouraging his tree to keep growing taller and rewarding it with sunlight when it did. Not-so-slowly, our tree shot up higher and higher. The goddess' face grew ever closer, that same beatific expression on her face. I wasn't sure I wanted to look down. As a rule, I try to avoid climbing trees. There are so many fun ways they can turn on me, from broken branches to poison sap, from spontaneously bursting into flames to whatever the hell made that one family of owls so angry at me.

"I think this is close enough," Avashti murmured. He settled himself in the tree's highest branches, took a deep breath, and looked up at the smiling face just above him.

"YEVNEA!" Avashti bellowed, which I'm going to assume was a name, and not a sneeze he'd swallowed down the wrong pipe. "Grant us the boon of your attention!"

"Should I throw garbage at her?" I helpfully asked.

"Saraya. This is a *god*. Let's try being serious, shall we?" he said, exasperated.

One of the goddess' gigantic eyes slowly moved. It seemed to focus on Avashti.

"Mighty Yevnea," Avashti said loudly, "we ask you, please, to REMOVE the boon you gave my daughter! Undo what you did before!"

"Also, don't inhale," I implored the goddess. "I don't care if your boogers are made of candy and diamonds, I still don't want to see what's inside your nose."

Yevnea gazed impassively at us. Her gigantic eye slowly closed, and then opened again, in perhaps the most unlikely wink I'll ever witness.

"I… ugh," I said, as my head started to pound. "Is everything whirling around in circles, or is it just me? I… uh…"

Avashti, somehow, reached out and grabbed my arm before I could fall sideways out of the tree. "I did it again," he said, pale-faced. "She's doing it. She's removing her boon… by killing you. Once you're dead, it's over."

"Not your fault," I managed to say, though all I could see was a brightening white light. "You didn't… she… but there's not any. Not any. Do you see?"

"I TAKE IT BACK!" Avashti shouted. "STOP REMOVING THE BOON!"

I don't know if she answered. I can't imagine she did. The light grew brighter and brighter and…

I blinked, which was sort of big news. Wherever souls go when they die, I doubt they have bodies—or eyelids. I blinked again, just for the fun of it. It was great. With a vast effort, I lifted my head. Slowly, the stone corridor just outside the Gateway Chamber came into focus. Somehow, we were back in the real world again.

"What…? How did we…?"

"It was the only way I could save you," Avashti said gently, crouching at my side. "I opened a portal and got us out of there. Fortunately, changing universes was enough to break the connection."

"So… Yevnea didn't fix me? My luck is still as bad as ever?"

"Yes. I'm afraid we failed rather spectacularly."

"Nuts to that," I said, shakily clambering to my feet. "If Princess Shivaka has Vindi… how long has it been? Can we catch up?"

"Oh, she's had plenty of time to get back to her soldiers," Avashti said grimly, "but I'm going after them. I have to try. What choice do I have?"

"Agreed," I said. "Oh, by the way, this is the part where I die some ridiculous, amusing death. Go ahead and tell the world the tale of my pathetic demise. If you tried to protect my honor by lying about it, the rumors would only grow twice as ludicrous and three times as filthy as what actually happened. When you have luck like mine, there's just no winning."

Avashti glanced sidelong at me. "If you're going to track Vindi with me, maybe you should try being the grim and *silent* hunter," he suggested.

"Nope. Ridiculous and covered in honey-soaked feathers, that's me. Let's go!"

"Hopeless," Avashti sighed, and fell in behind me.

VII

I don't suppose there was any chance Princess Shivaka was still waiting for us, convenient at hand in the Temple of Souls, but I broke into a full-out sprint anyway. Avashti looked at me like I was crazy, shook his head, and followed at a fast walk. The first (or last) of the trapped corridors gave me pause, but as I stood on its edge, a hovering, ibis-shaped cart of solid gold floated up and waited for me to climb aboard. Apparently the Temple only cared about keeping people *out*. I hopped into the cart, silently cursing my golden steed for taking such a slow and leisurely trip up and down the trapped corridors.

When was the last time I'd been without Vindi for any length of time? It was hard to remember. When I proudly rented a plot in the city garden for myself, only to have it unexpectedly wiped out by an extremely tiny volcano, there she was to lend me half of hers. When my effort to make pancakes went disastrously wrong, resulting in a mixture whose scent inexplicably attracted scorpions, there she was to patiently rub salve on my stings. There have only been two constants in my life: One, everything is bad. Two, except for Vindi. I would never give up on her. Simple as that.

The cart finally stopped at the edge of the great entry hall. I vaulted over the side and ran out into the canyon. It was full day, and the sunlight blinded me for a moment. I blinked until bright orange sandstone and picture-scribed walls came back into focus. And also, a ring of maybe a dozen filthy and desperate brigands who surrounded me, swords drawn, looking anything but amused.

"Yeah, see, you don't want me," I said persuasively. "I have a severely malformed skull due to all the head injuries. It would look terrible sitting on your writing desk with a candle stuck on top. If you want a graceful skull with all its original teeth, I suggest you take it up with Princess Shivaka." I snapped my fingers. "Hey, here's an idea! Why don't you hunt her down, catch her, and hold her for ransom? Riches for everyone!"

They just stood there, glaring at me. I considered repeating what I'd said, only louder, in case they were the sort of people who turn to crime because they're shunned by society for being different, which is to say, extremely hard of hearing.

"I… AM NOT… MADE OF TREASURE," I bellowed at the woman nearest me. Her eyes narrowed.

Avashti came puffing out of the Temple of Souls, blinking against the sunlight until he could see again. About half of the swords present shifted to point at him.

"Oh," he said.

"This is Avashti the Wizard," I said graciously. "He's *extremely* rich, or was, until Princess Shivaka stole his philosopher's stone and the secret of transmuting base metals into gold. Hey, another reason to track her down! How convenient!"

The woman next to me waggled her sword in a semi-threatening way, seeming to indicate that we should proceed down the canyon in front of her. I wondered if it would be possible to invent a whole language consisting entirely of sword waggles. Then again, trying to speak it would probably make a lot of people angry and get you roped into any number of duels. I'll count that as a 'maybe'.

"Get moving before it occurs to them to start stabbing," Avashti muttered into my ear. We walked down the canyon, the ring of brigands moving with us. I watched closely, waiting for one of them to trip, or stumble, or maybe sneeze—anything I could exploit, if only for a moment. Luck wasn't with me. Big news, I know, but there you have it.

We emerged into a much wider stretch of canyon. A very large, very weird mirage occupied most of the space there. It was easily the biggest mirage I'd ever seen, and amidst all the eye-bending shimmer stood what appeared to be a chicken the size of a roc.

"I think my eyes are playing tricks on me," I muttered. "What do *you* see?"

"I don't want to talk about it," Avashti said tightly.

One of the brigands put her hands to her mouth and made a credible hawk-scream. The mirage melted away, and I found myself staring at one of the weirdest vehicles I'd ever seen. It looked like a disc of stone cut straight out of the Kairay river, with hundreds—even thousands—of articulated metal legs carrying it where it wished to go. I say it was cut from the river because that's exactly what it was—a huge round platter of water that somehow never fell over the edge. A large island took up most of the disc, lush and green and covered with towering trees thickly swarded with vines.

"This was made by wizardry," Avashti said confidently. "They were probably asking for a fishing boat and got this by mistake, but you have to admire the ambition."

The brigand waggled her sword at us again. I considered trying to invent an equally expressive language, based on dance, that would allow me to say "up yours" by shaking my butt at her, but Avashti was already on the move. I followed him up a ladder and onto the disc, where a series of stepping-stones led us across to the island. The brigands swarmed up after us, but then seemed to lose interest, settling into various hammocks and tree-houses in the little grove that was apparently their home. One fiddled with a bunch of bronze levers poking out of the ground: The water around the edge of the disc began to writhe and steam, rising into a shimmering bubble that—from the outside—was presumably the same protective mirage that made this incredible vehicle so difficult to see.

The brigand woman waggled her sword at me. I was starting to get tired of this. I spotted a trail winding into the island's sole grove of trees. Shrugging, I followed it, Avashti right behind me. In the center of the grove was a slim tower notably finer than the crude tree-houses of the brigands. For one thing, it appeared to be completely covered with pearls. Lounging in front of it, lying in a shimmering hammock spun from multicolored silks, was about the last person I was expecting.

"Princess Gamal?" I said blankly.

"It speaks!" she said, impressed. "One wishes it hadn't, as it lacks the wit—or indeed, the fundamental grammar—necessary to make a point without spitting crumbs all over the place—but we must make allowances. We don't cut people's heads off until they are no longer *useful* to us."

"What do you want?" Avashti said guardedly.

"The same thing as you, I imagine. Revenge against my simpering excuse for a sister-in-law," she drawled. "You can tell this is important to me, because I've chosen to expose myself to the filth that comes out of *that* one's mouth," she said, indicating me.

"Bunnies," I said, just to mess with her.

"And senseless inanities," Princess Gamal said. "We mustn't forget the senseless inanities. She's incredibly annoying *that* way, too."

"What do you want?" Avashti repeated, his tone growing slightly desperate.

"We're on the same side, you and I," Gamal said. "Shivaka and I had a plan. A good plan. We pretended that my mother-in-law wanted *you*, wizard, sent into the Cave of Wonders. Ha. Shavala II doesn't even know you exist, and why should she, when Kairay has so many obstreperous neighbors that require ceaseless diplomatic soothing? So Shivaka and I had you dumped into the pit. Then your girls came running to us, as we anticipated, and we had them dumped down there, as well. Win-win. Either we'd get the Lens of Becoming and everything we needed to triumph, or we'd lose a handful of game pieces we really didn't care about."

"Wait," I said unhappily. "Princess Shivaka was in on this from the beginning? She was part of it all along?"

Princess Gamal smirked. "You need to toughen up, girl. This is a game that's played for keeps. Shivaka did what she always does: Looked all sad and upset when I explained my plan, then finally sighed and looked away. Gives her a great excuse, doesn't it? *I didn't do it. Gamal did! So very sad, this horrible thing I hated to see done but didn't lift a finger to stop.*" Gamal's smile faded. "It was a good plan, too. Then Shivaka had to go and betray me. I almost admire her for it. *Almost.* Didn't know she had it in her. So now I have to catch her and get back what's mine. We have a common purpose, you and I. Seems to me we might be allies in this."

"How can we trust you?" Avashti said cautiously.

Gamal snorted. "Lopping your heads off now, while personally satisfying, would tend to diminish my chances of future profit. Don't trust my words. Trust my greed. *As long as you're useful to me, you're safe.* Now, do you want a free ride across the desert or what?"

"Well…" Avashti glanced at me. I reluctantly nodded. "I suppose we'll accept, for now. Though I wonder why you didn't disable the traps in the Temple of Souls and come after us there."

Princess Gamal stared at him. "Disable the traps? How? Her Lordship, the esteemed Shavala II, could do that. Her firstborn heir could do that. A mere second son's wife? Not hardly."

"But Shivaka said…" I stopped, wincing. "Shivaka lied."

"*Now* we're getting somewhere." Princess Gamal reached lazily to the side of her hammock, where a number of bells stood on a small table. She considered, selected one, and rang it. After a few moments, we felt a lurch, and our strange vehicle started to move. I was impressed. From the speed with which the canyon walls scrolled past, even a horse would have been hard put to keep up with us.

"Where are we going?" I asked.

"Are you *trying* to annoy me with your stupidity?" Gamal snapped. "Shivaka has your friend, who has—or is—the artifact that redirects your luck. Shivaka has the Lens of Becoming. Shivaka has Darshik—"

"It would be equally useful if she had a half-rotten mango," Avashti said distastefully. "Wait. A mango doesn't blather endlessly about how great it is. I may have to reconsider my priorities."

"I like this one," Gamal said approvingly, nodding to Avashti. "Anyway, we need to find Shivaka and stop her before she transfers *your* luck to *her*. Do you have any more genius-level questions for me? Want to know whether fire is hot or rocks are hard? I think you'll be surprised. Specifically, I think you'll be surprised by the extremely steep price I charge for those and other interesting facts."

"We need to find Shivaka," I said helplessly. "Sure. Fine. But where is she? Where are we going? Back to the Lair of Lapis?"

"Ah. That. No." Princess Shivaka swung idly in her hammock. "You may have noticed that I command a small band of brigands. No, no, don't beg me to open your veins and take your blood in payment, that interesting fact is on me. The simple problem with being the wife of a second son is that I don't always get what I want." A darkness crossed Gamal's lovely face. "A woman as high-born as myself deserves to be kept in proper style. My mother-in-law failed me. My sister-in-law, that limp little smirk on legs, goes around pretending that *simplicity* is a *virtue*. Bah. Can you blame me if I acted to get what I deserved, by using my brigands to tax a mere few caravans and trade routes? Eventually, I was able to hire wizards to make this secret river lair, which, as you can see, turned out… different… from what I'd asked for. Different, but useful." Gamal reached over to her table, selected a bell, and rang it. A brigand immediately brought her a drink in a fancy silver goblet, bowed, and left. To go practice stabbing, one would assume.

"Where was I?" Gamal asked. "Ah. The river lair. Yes. When I ran out of space, I hired even more wizards to make me a new lair. Bigger. Better. They were… less successful." Gamal shrugged. "I couldn't figure out what to do with the place, so I sold it to Shivaka. It's the one place that's hers and hers alone, and given that she has no imagination whatsoever, I can guarantee she'll be there."

Avashti frowned. "So… we're heading for a wizardly artifact of colossal size and unknown power?"

Gamal smiled. "Do you see, now, why you have nothing to fear from me? I want the two of you walking in front of me every step of the way. I intend to have advance warning of any danger, in the form of watching for your heads to explode. But don't think we're going in blind. I can tell you *exactly* what our destination does. I wanted a place that would hide my merry band away where no one could find them. What the wizards gave me, instead, was a region that turns absolutely *any* closed container into its own pocket universe. You could jump into a bottle, if you wanted, and find its interior as big as a palace. We," she said, "are heading toward a gigantic wizardly artifact known as The Universe In A Nutshell."

"Sounds like fun," I said faintly.

"That's six," Gamal said pleasantly.

"What?"

"Since I'm prevented from having your head now, as you surely admit I deserve, I'm counting the number of deaths you owe me," Gamal said simply. "Of course, since I would never be so plebeian as to murder you the same way twice, I have to get more and more inventive imagining all the different ways of actualizing your incipient corpse-ness. It's kind of fun." A beatific smile crossed her face. "Oh, yes, that will do nicely. But do I have enough plums?"

"Um…"

"Enough. I'm exhausted from having to look at you for so long. Go. Don't come back. When I want you, you will be summoned."

I glanced at the ends of her hammock in case there was an easy way I could untie them and drop her on her ass. Sadly, they were fused to the trees themselves—more wizardry, I suppose. I shrugged and walked away, Avashti looking thoughtful as he followed me. I found a mossy hillock away from the assorted brigands and sat there, peering through the steamy mirage-bubble to try and guess where we where. Gamal surely knew where we were going, but I didn't feel it wise to depend on her. A wizardly artifact as huge as the one we were after couldn't be anywhere near the city of Kairay—it would have been noticed—but that still left all sorts of possibilities. As I may have noted before, the desert is kind of a big place.

I gradually became aware of Avashti sitting next to me,

seemingly unaware of the tears on his cheeks. I froze. As long as I can remember, Avashti has always been there for me. He's as reliable as bedrock, and as strong. Seeing him like *this* was more terrifying than having a steam explosion hurl snakes at my face. Well, not the cobras, but it was scarier than the *other* three times.

"Vindi will be fine," I assured him. "She always is."

"I know," he said quietly. "Intellectually, I know. Could anything be more obvious? But *believing* it is a different matter. Being a parent... you don't know what it's like, seeing your baby for the first time. Holding something so tiny, so precious, and knowing that half your heart now resides outside your body."

"Princess Shivaka is decent. She won't do anything terrible."

"I know. Intellectually, I know. But telling myself that doesn't stop the images from unfolding before my eyes."

"They can't have much of a lead on us anyway, as fast as we're..." I forced myself to shut up. "But that's just logic and reason, isn't it? I'm not sure what to say."

"I'm not sure there's anything you can." Avashti sighed. "And what am I going to do, anyway, when we get there? I don't have any gods to ask for favors, and even if I did, I couldn't make them obey without any contracts or writs. Here, at the end, my life's work adds up to precisely nothing. Princess Shivaka has a mob of soldiers bristling with blades. I have two questionably useful fists, yes, at the end of weak and shaky arms, and the rest of me isn't so great, either. Have you noticed the way I break into a sweat when anyone even *suggests* walking all the way to the river?"

I stared into the distance, watching the rocky hills of the Valley of Thunder slide past. "Every fight I've ever gotten into, I knew I was going to lose," I said quietly. "But I flew in there anyway, with what some would call 'a flagrant and almost alarming disregard for personal safety'. Because some things are *worth* fighting for. Like the time that drunken soldier decided he'd grab a barmaid and carry her off. I could have stayed out of it. I could have quietly turned my back on everything I believed in. But I didn't. I ended up with two black eyes, a fat lip, three broken ribs, and half a concussion (don't ask). She slipped away in the uproar. And I'll tell you one thing: I've never slept better. Well, not literally, but you know what I mean." I put my hand on Avashti's arm. "We're going to fight for Vindi. Not because we know we're going to win, but because she's worth fighting for. Once you give up on silly things like 'staying safe' and 'not dying', you can just sail in there and start thrashing around like a crazed weasel. You never know. Sometimes, just being desperate enough can get you the win.”

Avashti managed a faint smile. “I can’t stop imagining what I can’t stop imagining… but… thinking about your weird compulsion to fling yourself into losing fights does, at least, *distract* me from my anxiety. Thank you. Knowing that you care that much about me… it doesn’t make everything better, no, but it helps.”

“I don’t *care* care,” I clarified. “I just like getting presents on my birthday, which means keeping you around. See how that works?”

“I love you too, Saraya.”

“I didn’t say that!”

“I know,” he said, smiling. With a renewed sense of purpose, he pulled Vindi’s book out of my pack, the one whose margins he’d filled with so many notes and ideas. Avashti was soon lost in thought as he tried to figure out how to intensify my bad luck to be so bad that it was good. I had a feeling that I could be struck by lightning and he wouldn’t even notice long enough to look up and laugh. His focus was that deep, his concentration that absolute.

The hour grew late. Clouds bloomed across the sky, then flowed off to the east and disappeared. The stars came out, first a few, and then a vast infection speckling the night with their shimmering blemishes. One was lower and brighter than all the rest, and moved while the other stars remained fixed. I watched it for a long while before suddenly realizing what I was looking at.

“Avashti,” I said, shaking his arm. “Avashti!”

“What?” he said, startled.

“Look. See that light, right there? That has to be Pinky!”

“Vindi’s firecat?”

“Right. And the fact that he’s moving means they must still be in transit! See? I was right to encourage you. They couldn’t torture her while they’re still moving!” I blinked. “Uh… which isn’t to say that they *will* torture her once they stop. Oh great—I just put a whole bunch of new images in your head, didn’t I?”

“You’re not helping,” he admitted.

“What if I offered to hit myself over the head with weasels and dance drunkenly at you? I mean, I doubt you’d be able to think about anything *else* for a while.”

“I’d… like to see that,” Avashti admitted. “But not just now. I can distract myself more fully by losing myself in my work.” He frowned thoughtfully. "This good/bad luck thing… it's a lot trickier than I'd hoped. I'm not sure I can pull it off without the plan books back in the tower house."

"Aw, you don't need 'em."

"A commendable sentiment, if misguided. They contain the concentrated knowledge and wisdom of a lifetime. Without them…" He shrugged. "All I can do is my best. It's certainly a puzzle that demands my full attention."

"Get to it, then. Don't even think about Vindi being dumped into a huge tub of rats!" I paused. "Er. Or… um… a huge tub of puppies. Don't think about that, either."

But Avashti, to my vast relief, had already buried himself in his work. I lay down and stole what fleeting snatches of sleep I could. I'm not sure Avashti ever rested. Every time I looked up, there was an Avashti-shaped hole in the stars.

The next thing I knew, it was morning. A hairy brigand bristling with swords brought us a simple breakfast, his unhappy glare letting us know just how he felt about having to serve us. I waited for him to get out his sword and waggle an expressive and poetic tirade against his employer's uncaring dictates, but apparently he wasn't feeling it. I silently offered him a fork, in case a sword lacked the subtlety he needed. He stared at me in disbelief before stalking off in the other direction.

"So, have you cracked it?" I asked Avashti. "Have you figured out the good/bad luck thing?"

He raised an eyebrow. "Are you suggesting that I'm not clever enough to work out the answers to everything in the universe?"

"Given that mosquitos still exist, yes, I am."

He hid a smile. "Well, you're right, for once. I made progress. A great deal of progress. But without my plan books, and the accumulated work and wisdom of a lifetime, I surely didn't get it *right*." He sighed. "We just have to hope we can find Vindi and free her in time. They have the Lens. They have Vindi's horns. They have… excuse my language… Darshik. All they need is for Darshik to be competent, which, admittedly, *could* happen. Eventually."

"Don't worry. We'll win," I shrugged, and then, in a loud whisper, added: *"I'm faking confidence to keep you from panicking."*

"You are, as ever, the soul of consideration," he said laconically.

An hour or so later, the mobile island slowed and finally

lurched to a halt. Avashti and I walked over to the ladder and waited to be let down. The brigands ignored us completely. I was about to suggest that we find Gamal and demand some answers when the princess herself finally showed up. Today, she was wearing a suit woven together from alternating plates of gold and jade, wired together in a cunning manner that, I couldn't help but notice, clicked like every devil in hell was setting off firecrackers all at once.

"What are you waiting for?" she asked. "Let's go."

"*You're* coming?" Avashti said, astonished. "Like *that*? I mean… ah, wouldn't you rather have your brigands do the fighting for you while you stayed safely behind?"

"Normally, yes. But in this specific case, I have the signal advantage of being a high noble. Even if my swallowed burp of a sister-in-law should catch me, there's nothing she could do but slap me on the wrist and let me go. My brigands have no such protection."

"Neither do we."

Gamal smiled languorously. "I know."

"Well, do you maybe want to wear something *quieter*, then?" I suggested. Princess Gamal stared at me. I fidgeted uncomfortably. She suddenly flung her arms out to the sides. Two brigands helped her out of the treasure-suit, beneath which she wore silent and form-fitting silks of simple black. Gamal smirked at me.

"Do you have any other stupid questions, child?"

"She hasn't been a stupid child for years," Avashti said stoutly. "She outgrew at least half of that equation years ago."

My eyes narrowed. "Which half?"

"You have a curious way of saying 'thank you for defending my honor, Avashti!'. I'll assume you meant to compliment me, but swallowed an olive the wrong way and could only quack like a duck instead, which, due to my bad hearing, sounded oddly like you being insolent." He cocked his head. "Strange, how often I have to assume that. I didn't know you liked olives so much."

"Go to hell, Avashti."

"*That* time, you swallowed a squirrel."

The three of us climbed down the ladder and passed through the mirage-bubble into the outside world. I looked keenly around, trying to get a fix on where we were. The ground was arid, desolate, and almost devoid of life—but broken and hilly, with grey stone ranging almost to blue. We were somewhere to the west of Kairay, I think. There was a small oasis nearby, where a scant few trees and

bushes grew vigorously next to a minuscule pond. Beyond that lay
The Universe In A Nutshell. It had to be. It was huge, at least from
side to side, a flat-topped pedestal of stone honeycombed with
passages and pits. It looked like someone had set out to make the
world's most intricate cave, gotten bored halfway, and forgotten to put
the top on.

"That's it?" I whispered, forgetting that I was asking a question
with a patently obvious answer. I'll never know how Princess Gamal
compacted so much scorn into such a simple look. "That's seven," she
said—and then smiled languorously, which was worse.

The three of us crept over to the relative safety of the oasis and
peered through the bushes at The Universe In A Nutshell. Well,
Avashti and Gamal did. I had some slight difficulty with a huge
walnut tree, slipping and sliding on the fallen nuts that carpeted the
ground. On the plus side, I managed not to fall. On the minus side, I
flailed around hard enough that I managed to wrench my back *and*
kick off my shoes.

"Are you done clowning?" Princess Gamal said waspishly as I
struggled to put my shoes back on without bending over. "Good. Pay
attention. The artifact's power extends this far, I think. Any closed
vessel becomes its own pocket universe. Observe." She opened a
small kit crammed with powders and salves, gold dust and gems, and
took out a vial of what appeared to be an ointment heavily impregnated
with mother-of-pearl.

I made a face. "You brought *a make-up kit*?" I demanded.

"It doesn't hurt to remind lesser beings that I am, quite simply,
better than they are. By the way, my compliments on hiding yourself
under clothes that best resemble a shapeless sack. They help.
Otherwise, there'd be nothing to distract from the hideous visage with
which nature cursed you."

"Are you calling Avashti ugly?" I demanded.

"You think you're being funny. Someday, your
misapprehensions will be corrected. Now, watch."

Gamal pressed her hand against the mouth of the vial. What
should have happened, of course, was nothing. Instead, her flesh
collapsed in a queasy and patently impossible way and simply *flowed*
inside. She disappeared with a pop and the vial fell clattering to the
ground. Avashti and I exchanged startled glances. I picked up the
vial.

"Do you know the best way to decant a princess?" I asked. He shrugged. I held the vial upside-down and slapped the bottom one, two, three times. Princess Gamal reappeared with a second pop, now smeared with glistening pearlescent goo.

"I blame you," she said, scowling darkly. "I only meant to do my arm, but *someone's* hideous and excessive ugliness distracted me."

"Next time, I'll dash the mirror out of your hand," I said helpfully.

"That's eight," she said. And smiled.

Wiping off the ointment, Gamal led the way back to the edge of the oasis. Although the Universe In A Nutshell had many openings where passages simply ended in mid-air, there was an obvious main entrance—and it was bracketed by half a dozen guards. They looked anything but bored or distracted.

"We're too late," Gamal said irritably. "Shivaka is already here. Who knows? Maybe she's already won."

I took out a coin and started flipping it, promising myself a yummy treat for every tails—and a piece of rancid fish for every heads. I lost, but not heavily.

"We're okay," I said. "For now."

"Fine. The next step is to remove the guards so I can get inside," Gamal decided. "You, wizard. Shout as loud as you can and run to the left." She glanced oddly at Avashti as he began sneezing compulsively. "You, meatpile. Hoot and holler and run to the right. Presumably, the guards will be so busy tackling the two of you to the ground, they won't even notice when I walk in."

Avashti looked at me. I looked at him. Princess Gamal scowled, deeply irritated. "You *do* know that the penalty for disobeying a direct order from nobility is—"

"No," I said. "Like hell am I getting myself caught for *you.* Even if your plan wasn't a massively idiotic, guaranteed failure—"

"Not that your plan isn't fabulous," Avashti interceded, "but if we got caught, we wouldn't be able to walk in front of you checking for traps. Remember? You meant to have proper warning by watching for our heads to explode?"

Gamal's eyes narrowed. "You have a better plan?"

I looked at Avashti. Avashti looked at me.

"We could… maybe… something with kites?" I suggested.

"That's nine."

"Well, what are our assets?" Avashti said, looking around. "What do we have? Let's think about this. We have ourselves, your make-up kit, the oasis…" His eyebrows rose as he regarded the fallen nuts scattered beneath the walnut tree. "Wait. Does *any* empty vessel become a pocket universe?"

"Are you *trying* to find out the penalty for failing to listen to nobility?" Gamal snapped. "Come with me to the Lair of Lapis. Believe me, I'll enjoy the ensuing demonstration *much* more than you will."

"Listen. If one of the walnuts was hollow… wouldn't *it* become a pocket universe? So, if we threw dozens of hollow walnuts at the soldiers, mightn't some of them hit the soldiers hole-first and suck them inside?"

"It doesn't work like that," Gamal said uncertainly.

"Let's try it!" I cried, standing with my arms outspread. "See if you can get *me*!"

Avashti smirked. He picked through the fallen walnuts, looking for ones that were hollow but still possessed a certain physical integrity. He stood. He took aim. He pelted me with a handful of nuts.

"Well," I said, "*that* was a waste of—"

One last walnut plinked off my forehead. A vast force sucked me upward, compressing and twisting me in ways I hadn't felt since the *other* time I got swallowed by a fish. Just like that, I found myself inside a rugged cave about thirty feet across, dark but illuminated with craggy lines of reddish light where the walls were thinnest.

"Um…" I said, my voice echoing back to me. "Avashti? Gamal? Hello? Does anybody—"

Another weird, wrenching force seized my body and I was suddenly standing back in the world again, feeling a little faint. Avashti stood next to me, looking very pale, holding a walnut in one hand and vigorously smacking it with the other. He stopped once he saw me.

"You didn't have to be in *that* much of a hurry to let her out," Princess Gamal noted.

"It worked!" Avashti said, astonished. "You know," he told me, "I could still hear your voice, for all that it was high-pitched and kind of far-away. I could hear everything you were saying."

"You could? Damn it! I should've said something nasty."

"Why?"

"Oh, c'mon! A foul-mouthed walnut swearing up a storm? Even you have to admit that would be hilarious."

Princess Gamal shook her head. "It worked, yes, but barely... and at the last possible instant. The chances of getting all six soldiers are too low. I won't do it."

I frowned, trying to figure the odds if we didn't have her. It didn't look good. "Look. We need all three people throwing nuts," I argued. "Like you said yourself, the odds are too low otherwise. What I think we should do—"

"I don't care what you think," Gamal sneered.

"What a coincidence!" I snapped. "I don't care what you think, either!"

"The penalty for talking back to me is—"

"You think I care?" I interrupted. "I've already earned my punishment. Dead is dead—you can't punish me any worse than that. So I might as well richly and fully earn the punishment I'm destined to receive. You're pathetic. I hope you choke on your own bile and die. But first, you can watch me throw walnuts at a bunch of soldiers. I'm going out there, with you or without you."

"It's too risky," Avashti said nervously. "Alone, or with only two of us, the odds just aren't there. We have to think of something else."

"No. The plan is good. What we don't have is *time*." I slapped my hand to my chest. "I'm going out there and I'm going to give it everything I've got. The world thinks it has me beat. Hell, I do, too. But you know what? The moment I give up is when my tormentor suddenly becomes right. I'm going to keep going. I'm going to fight until I can't fight any more. Vindi deserves it. Hell, she deserves better than *I* can do, but this is what I've got. I'm going out there."

"It seems demented... but..." Avashti sighed. "I'll go, too."

Princess Gamal shrugged. "I *will* be rather put out if we lose simply because there weren't enough people throwing. Very well. I'll go."

"Did I get through to you?" I said wonderingly.

Gamal snorted. "Not hardly. This has nothing to do with your stultifying little speech. It's logic. You won't do things the right way, which is to say, my way. Therefore, my *only* chance is to do things your way, no matter how stupid you may be." She smiled coldly. "It helps that I can't really be punished if I'm caught. Now," she said, "we're going to need a *lot* of hollow walnuts to do this right. You two conduct the search. I'll supervise."

From anyone else, that would have been a joke. It wasn't for Gamal. She really did supervise, standing over us red-faced screaming 'GO FASTER!!!' and 'FIND MORE!!!' I'm sure she thought she was helping enormously.

Some time later, the three of us walked openly up to the main entrance to The Universe In A Nutshell. The guards stared at us. I'm sure they'd been told to watch for people trying to sneak in. Seeing us walk straight toward them, not even trying to hide, was apparently something they had no instructions for.

"We have you now!" one of the guards shouted. "You're in our grasp—don't even try to run away!" He paused as if hoping we'd do just that, and thereby redirect the encounter into something he was prepared for.

"This *is* amusing," Princess Gamal drawled. "You're trying to give *me* orders?"

"YOU WILL OBEY!!!"

She gave him an appraising look. "So volume equals authority, does it? Tell me, if I commanded you to apply your sword to your foot—which, believe me, from the looks of it, could only be an improvement—how loud would I have to shout before you obeyed?"

"NOW!" Avashti bellowed. The two of us grabbed handfuls of walnuts from our pockets and started pelting the guards with them: Gamal rolled her eyes, but finally joined in. To the astonishment of their fellows, three of the soldiers vanished almost instantly, sucked inside of the hollow vessels. A fourth disappeared mere moments later. Unfortunately, there were still two soldiers left when our supply ran out. They were too shocked to draw their swords—but how long would that last?

Princess Gamal turned and pragmatically started walking back to the oasis, abandoning us to our fate. Avashti stood petrified, staring in terror at those half-unsheathed swords. I screamed, 'NUT YOU, MALEFACTORS!!!' and flung myself to the ground, grabbing handfuls of fallen nuts and flinging them at the two men.

"What?" one of them said, right before he disappeared.

"STOP!" the other said, alarmed. "STOP, OR I'LL—"

He disappeared, too. I stood up and bowed to Avashti, who looked like he was about to pass out from terror. Tiny voices emerged from several of the nuts, desperately demanding to know what was happening. Princess Gamal turned around and came right back, showing no shame whatsoever over her cowardice. I suppose to her, it was simply plain good sense.

We cautiously entered The Universe In A Nutshell. It was a truly weird place—rugged and cave-like up to about five feet, with nothing but blue sky above that. We immediately had a choice between left or right: We chose left. We didn't encounter any people as the passage wound back and forth. We passed heaps of woven baskets, innumerable glass bottles, and piles of brass kettles with ornate lids, but that was all. There was absolutely no sign of human habitation. The passage curved around and emerged back at the main entrance.

"It's a loop?" I mused. "Then where is everyone? Did I miss a side passage?"

"You're not being tricky enough," Avashti said, tapping the side of his head. "How many containers, how many pocket universes, did we just pass? They didn't stay in the world as we know it. They went inside."

"But which one?"

"Ah, you've got me there."

We turned around and went around the loop the other way. I kept a sharp eye out for any side passages, just in case, but there weren't any. It looked like Avashti's explanation was the only one. The problem was, none of the thousands upon thousands of vessels we passed had a big, flashy sign pointing to it proclaiming 'TO DEFEAT EVIL, TRY THIS ONE!!!' The problem with villains is how *inconsiderate* they can be.

"We can rule out the baskets," Avashti said.

I glanced at him. "How so?"

He slapped his hands on one of them. A cloud of dust burst from it, making visible the golden rays of the sun. When it finally cleared, there were obvious handprints on the basket.

"They're too dusty. If one of them was in heavy use, we'd know."

"Ah," I said. "That makes it simple, then—only two choices! A zillion bottles, or a zillion and a half kettles. Easy."

Princess Gamal glanced at Avashti, unimpressed. "Solve it," she ordered him. "You have two minutes."

We walked the short distance back to the entrance. Avashti paced around in a tight circle, muttering to himself and gesturing with both hands. I took out my coin and flipped it a couple dozen times, relieved to see that we still hadn't lost. Whatever Darshik was trying, it didn't seem to have worked yet.

"All right," Avashti said, "I've got it. I think."

"See?" Princess Gamal said. "I chose the tool, I told it what to do, and now we have an answer. I'm a genius."

"I don't have anything to write on, but I *should* be able to keep this all in my head," Avashti explained. "If I assign every container numeric coordinates, I can do a transform on the ones we've checked to differentiate them from the ones we haven't."

"I'm resisting the urge to start shouting random numbers as loud as I can," I admitted.

Avashti stared at me. "I thought you *wanted* to help Vindi."

"Oh, I do! But messing with you is an instinct that goes very deep indeed."

"Incredible," he muttered. He led us back into The Universe In A Nutshell. When we reached the first stack of kettles, he closed his eyes for a moment and murmured more numbers. Finally he nodded, picked one, and flipped its lid open.

"We can get out on our own, right?"

Gamal shrugged. "Probably."

"It's not worth the risk," Avashti mused. "You, Princess Gamal, stay here and stand watch. We'll shout when we want to be let out. You should be able to hear us."

"Given the way those walnuts were swearing, I would certainly think so. But you're overlooking a simple fact," Gamal said. "I don't take orders from nobodies. Let the girl stay and stand watch. To judge from her looks, she enjoys brainless drudgery."

"You're completely right," I said, smirking. "Go. Have fun! I'll stay here."

Gamal glared at me, her eyes narrowing suspiciously. "You think you're being clever again. What are you planning? Out with it."

"It's really quite simple. If I get to dump you out, then I get to decide what I dump you out *into*. Like, for example, a bowl of dog turds." I looked avidly around. "Now I just need to find some dogs."

"You wouldn't," Gamal breathed.

"Given the previously mentioned absence of dogs, we're never going to find out, are we? But I'm sure I can think of something equally intriguing to dump you into."

"I'm staying right here," Gamal decided. "Get out of my sight before I change my mind."

I leapt up and stomped on the open kettle with both feet. In a normal world, I would have crushed it flat or bounced off of it. Instead, I whirled around in a tight circle as my legs squished rope-thin and *flowed* inside. I had just enough time to stick my tongue out at Gamal, and then the world changed.

I fell four or five feet to the bottom of a huge round chamber whose walls were made of hammered brass. It looked to be about two or three hundred feet across. In front of me—

"ARRRG!" Avashti bellowed, landing HARD on top of me. We went down in a heap, hitting bottom with a dull metallic thud.

"Ow! Get off me!"

"At least we know that Vindi's not *here*," Avashti said unnecessarily.

"I wish it were that easy. Look."

The two of us got up. In front of us was what looked like an alchemist's laboratory. It had a work bench, measuring tools, ceramic crucibles, you name it. But there were also about a thousand stained and corroded vials, each and every one of which was presumably its own pocket universe.

"Can your coordinate system account for *this*?" I said grimly. "Worlds within worlds within worlds?"

Avashti shook his head. "You'll have to check them out. Go as fast as you can."

I glanced at him. "Why me? You're the wizard."

"So what?" Avashti said, smiling ruefully. "I'm good at sitting quietly and writing out contracts. You… you're the one who's smart, relentless, and daring enough to fly in and seize *action*, whereas I'd stand paralyzed trying to think of the exact perfect move while I got stabbed to death."

"No, no, I'm not clever at all. I'm really extremely stupid and weak and—" I stopped myself. "Sorry. Instinct. When people start singing my praises is right when I'm likeliest to trip and get my head stuck in a termite nest." I uncorked the first vial, hesitated, and glanced back at him. "If you're sure it should be me…"

"Of course I'm not sure!" Avashti snapped. "I've already lost one daughter. Every instinct in my body is screaming at me to protect you, to keep you safe. Sending you to your maybe-doom instead of going myself is, I think, my own special version of hell. I don't know what I'm doing penance for," he grumbled, "but I hope I had fun doing it."

I smiled at Avashti. "A coward… a coward would run away.

On the other hand, a *weak* man would give in to his impulses and leap in front of me. A man would have to be strong, big-hearted *and* brave to do he knows is right, regardless of the cost to himself. If I occasionally chance into doing the right thing, it's only because I had such a good example while I was growing up."

"Stop making fun of me," Avashti grumbled.

"I was being sincere! It is, admittedly, one of my less-explored capabilities, but it's there."

Taking a deep breath, I jammed my hand into the first vial. I was sucked inside and immediately landed at the bottom of a huge, cylindrical shaft with gently glowing glass walls. There was nothing at all inside—just foul-smelling brownish boulders that might have been some sort of chemical residue.

"DONE HERE!" I shouted. "I'M READY FOR THE NEXT —"

Before I could even finish the sentence, I found myself tumbling out of the vial and into the big brass chamber. I landed on my butt—*hard*. Rubbing my backside—and wondering just how beat up I was going to get checking *thousands* of vials—I uncorked the second one and stuck my thumb inside.

The world I was sucked into looked almost exactly the same as the first, but someone else had obviously been there first. A cart stood innocently in the center of the chamber, and it was piled high with about a thousand hollow drinking-gourds. Empty vessels. Pocket universes, every one.

"Oh, come *on!*" I cried. I guess Avashti took that as a sign to get me out, because I was immediately dumped back into the brass-kettle world.

"Find anything?" he asked.

"More universes," I said, disgusted. "Shivaka *really* didn't want anyone finding her, did she? We're going to have to come up with a different way. Blundering around at random isn't going to do it."

Avashti paced back and forth, his brow wrinkled with thought. "We need information," he said to himself. "We need to know where they are."

"There's no way," I said flatly.

"There's always a way."

"Fine," I said, exasperated. "How about this? We go back to the main entrance and hide. We wait for an evil minion to come by, twirling his mustache and prancing around with joy over how evil he is. Also, he doesn't see us, because he's too busy dancing evilly. We snag his cloak on a broken bottle, which *just happens* to pull out a thread which conveniently unravels while he walks—*without breaking or coming unstuck!*—so we can follow it like a guide-line straight to his destination. How about that?"

"You may be on to something," Avashti mused.

"Were you listening? The last time I proposed a plan that ludicrous, a meteor fell out of the sky and hit me on the head, as if the universe itself felt insulted that I was offering it *that many ways* to make me fail."

"Was that the meteor that set you on fire," Avashti asked, "or the one that— you know, it doesn't matter. We need someone who knows where Princess Shivaka is, someone who can take us straight to her. Maybe, just maybe, one of the door guards is that person."

"So… we let them take us prisoner in hopes that they'll bring us to Shivaka for judgement?" I hazarded. "What if they just stick us in some random bottle to be dealt with later?"

"We aren't going to be their prisoners," Avashti slowly said. "We're going to be their guests."

"We are?" I said dubiously.

"They won't even see us. We'll be hidden inside a pocket universe." Avashti snapped his fingers. "We just need to hide in something they'll find irresistible, something they'll *want* to take with them."

"It's so obvious when you explain it that way," I said laconically. "How about we knock them out and fill their pockets with walnuts? Which we explain by leaving a note on each individual walnut that says, 'YOU'RE HUNGRY. THAT'S WHY.'"

"I haven't figured that part out yet." Avashti paced back and forth, thinking hard. "We have to work with what we have. Fine. What do we have? Ourselves, of course, if not much else." He paused, as if considering some strange new idea. "But then, if any closed container becomes a pocket universe…"

"Avashti…?"

With one swift move, the wizard stuck his thumb in his own mouth and sucked on it. His flesh flowed, twisting and knotting as he got pulled inside of the vessel formed by his own body… about halfway, at least. What remained was flesh-colored, about the size of my fist, and *extremely* disturbing to look at. It quivered, bulged, and then—with a *pop!*—turned back into Avashti again.

"What was that as painful as it looked?" I asked, awed.

He staggered, unable to speak for a few moments. "It was… different," he said in a rough voice. "Harrowing, you might say. Could I do it again? Yes. For Vindi. If I had to."

"One little problem. You're hideously ugly." I paused for three long beats. "…when you're in that form. Why would they take you with them?"

"I have an idea. Let's get out of here."

I shouted for Gamal to let us out. The universe twisted and spun and I found myself tumbling through the air… right onto a pile of extremely pointy walnut fragments. Amazingly, none of them broke my skin. At least, not until Avashti fell on me from a height of about three feet.

"Not as satisfying as I'd hoped," Princess Gamal mused. "Go back in. I'd like to try dumping you in some dead bushes I found. Plenty of thorns. Lots of burrs."

"No," I said decisively.

"Don't be so quick to refuse! I think you'll really enjoy how happy it makes me, seeing you thrash around getting cut to ribbons."

"Princess Gamal… do you still have your make-up kit?" Avashti humbly asked.

"Yes. So?"

"That's how we'll make this work," he explained. "After Saraya and I collapse ourselves into knots, you'll use your make-up kit to cover us with gold and gems and make us look like treasures. Then you can release the soldiers from their walnut prisons, apologize for what you did, and give them a pair of sparkling treasure-lumps as a form of restitution."

"It'll never work," I said, shaking my head. "What gift looks like *that*? I don't care if it's covered in gold and gems, it's not going to fool them."

"Ah, but it will," Avashti said decisively. "See, you've only received gifts from poor people. Their gifts *have* to be practical. Otherwise, what would be the point? The gifts given by nobility, though, are *supposed* to be meaningless and weird, so as to prove that they're far beyond any mere day-to-day concerns."

"Hmm. There's something to that. How about it?" I asked Gamal. "Do you have any gold or gems to spare?"

"No."

I stared at her. "You don't have any gems at all?"

"What kind of question is that?" Gamal said irritably. "Of *course* I have gems. Thousands of them. But I don't have any to *spare*. I'm using each and every one of them to prove my innate superiority to losers like you."

"Avashti, explain it to her *again*," I said tiredly. The wizard did so. Princess Gamal listened attentively.

"I don't like the part where I voluntarily give away money," she noted. "Is there anything we can do about that?"

"Not really."

"And the part where the two of you turn into something small, weird, disturbing and squishy. Since that pretty much describes the way you look *now*, how am I supposed to tell whether it worked?"

My eyes narrowed, but Princess Gamal strode away before I could devise a properly epic comeback. She led us back to the main entrance, where thousands of walnuts lay scattered on the ground. Six of them were still shouting at us. I looked at Avashti. He looked at me.

"Here goes nothing," he said, sticking his thumb in his mouth.

I did the same. Nothing happened. I sucked in just the slightest bit. Suddenly… well, I can't describe what it was like, because it wasn't *like* anything. Even so, it was *really* disturbing. I think the only reason I didn't scream was because I couldn't figure out what to scream *with*, which in turn made me want to scream even more. It was incredibly claustrophobic, blind and sick, sweaty and *wrong*. How can you properly panic when you can't even run around in circles, screaming 'DAMN IT, VINDI, THIS IS ALL YOUR FAULT!!!'

Speaking of which. *This is for Vindi,* I thought to myself, and then, *which, basically, means that it* is *all her fault! What a horrible person, being so loveable and kind that she'd forcibly compel me to want to* do *things for her!*

I couldn't see what happened after that. I assume that Gamal adorned us with gold and gems. I assume that she shook their walnut prisons until the six guards were freed, knowing that they wouldn't dare try to detain a high noble. I assume that she apologized and gave the two of us as gifts to the guard commander, who took one look at all of that nice, shiny gold and hastily pocketed us. The only question was, would he run straight to Shivaka to report?

In my dark and twisted prison, I heard the bleating sounds of someone speaking, filtered through what I had left of ears. Then there was quiet, accompanied by surges of motion as my host walked somewhere. What seemed like a very long time passed, and then the movement stopped and more strangled speech sounds rang out. If the guard was talking to someone, did that mean he'd arrived? Should I come out?

To hell with it. I tried to spring back into the World, intending to land poised and ready to fight. It didn't quite work that way. It was more like I barfed myself out of my own mouth, and I popped back into the world pale and weak and sweating, unable to speak or even move for a moment. The guard stared at me in shock. I was in yet another huge brass chamber, and before me stood a second guard—one I hadn't seen before—who was keeping watch over a blueish glass bottle.

Those long moments of shock turned out to be my salvation. "NUTS TO YOU!" I shouted, pulling hollow walnuts from my pocket and poinking them against each guard's forehead. With some extremely disturbing slurping sounds, they vanished. Then I realized that the original guard still had Avashti in his pocket. Grimacing, I shook his nut until he came tumbling back out again.

"What... what... what?" he demanded.

"COME OUT!!!" I bellowed. With a sudden *pop*!, Avashti burst out of the guard's pocket and appeared next to me, looking incredibly queasy.

"I didn't think it could get any worse," he breathed. "I was wrong. I threw up. I won't tell you where I think it went."

"NUTS TO... oh, hell, I already used that one," I groused, and poinked the guard in the head with the same walnut as before.

"*What*?" he cried as he flowed inside and vanished.

"Where are they?" Avashti asked, looking cautiously around.

"In here," I said, indicating the blue bottle. "Are you ready?"

"No," he said honestly.

"Me neither. Let's go before we have time to realize how stupid we're being."

We jumped, banged into each other in midair, and missed the bottle completely.

"All right, one at a time," I said. "Me first."

I jumped again, and this time got sucked feet-first into the blue bottle. I landed hard at the bottom of a huge, glassy blue well full of reflections. Princess Shivaka stared at me, Prince Dakar ignored me, and six guards reached for their swords. Hollow gourds scattered beneath my feet, but for once I didn't have to worry about a whole new set of pocket universes: A large tent had been set up just behind Shivaka, and a loud voice was chanting inside of it. I couldn't be sure, but I thought it was Darshik.

"Listen—" I said, just as Avashti predictably landed right on top of me.

"Let Vindi go right now!" he roared, scrambling to his feet. "I'm a wizard! I can breathe fire!"

"Dad!" shouted a voice from inside the tent. "Save yourself— I'm fine!"

"Take them," Princess Shivaka commanded. I reached into my pocket for more walnuts, only to be tackled by a soldier. I banged my head *hard* on a bump in the glass and immediately lost interest in fighting. Two soldiers were already sitting on Avashti, while the remaining three stood over us, hands on their swords. So much for a daring rescue.

"I need your help," Princess Shivaka said, crouching down to look Avashti in the eye. "Darshik has been… unsuccessful… in completing his assigned task."

"Why would we help you?" I demanded, trying to sound strong and derisive rather than shaky and close to throwing up.

"I would hope that you'd help me out of altruism," Princess Shivaka said. "Once I have perfect luck, I'll be able to do a great amount of good for a vast number of people. But I'll accept a more craven reason. You see, I truly believe in my cause. The suffering of one is nothing compared to the suffering of thousands upon thousands." Princess Shivaka sighed. "I hate saying this… and I've treated her well up until now… but I *will* order Vindi tortured if you don't cooperate."

Avashti blanched. I gazed at him, trying to divine whether he'd completed our backup plan.

"Do what you have to do," I said quietly. Avashti slowly nodded, his eyes troubled. The guards helped him up: Bracketed by a soldier on either side, he walked slowly into the tent.

The chanting stopped. There was quiet murmur. After a while, a different voice chanted. It stopped. More chanting. Hot and cold crept across my body, and strange tingling sensations, and then it was done. The tent's flap opened. Avashti came back out. Walking beside him, rubbing wrists that must have been tied up until recently, was…

"VINDI!!!" I cried.

"We failed you," she said hollowly.

"Really? Let's test this." Princess Shivaka tried to flip a coin. Predictably, it shot out of her hand and straight up my nose. I sneezed mightily, spraying something disgusting all over my feet. Meanwhile, my shoulders jerked hard enough to break off a crystal rim I'd somehow overlooked, causing it to spin gently across the room and land in Princess Shivaka's outstretched hand.

"Uh-oh," I said.

Darshik emerged from the tent, holding the Lens of Becoming and a weird sort of brass wand.

"What strange fortune," the wizard said, obviously pleased. "I wasn't even trying to, but somehow I transferred the artifact from *her* to *this*. The girl's horns do nothing. *This* is the artifact that redirects Saraya's luck, now."

"I see," Princess Shivaka said, pleased. "In that case, we don't need her any more, do we? Let's go."

"What about…?"

"They don't matter. Leave them."

Princess Shivaka took hold of a profoundly confused Dakar. She and Darshik and their soldiers performed a parody of jumping in place: As one, they were sucked up out of the bottle, leaving the three of us behind. I walked over to Vindi, intending to hug her. She reached for me at the exact same moment and ended up punching me in the face. Well, you know how these things go. We got there eventually, and I reached over to grab Avashti, too. After a long, long time, I finally stepped back and looked the wizard up and down.

"How about it? Our backup plan… did you pull it off?"

Avashti sighed. "No," he said frankly. "I was almost there, but… something went wrong. Your luck is Shivaka's, nothing more and nothing less."

Vindi looked at the empty room around us, frowning. "Do we just… leave?"

"I guess." I snapped my fingers. "Oh, but don't let me forget to pick up those two walnuts in the next room. Don't look at me like that! I'll explain later."

Vindi just shook her head. Together, the three of us prepared to jump up and out.

VIII

It was a long trip home to Kairay. Kind of a weird one, too, considering the sheer uneventfulness of it. Well, other than the part about halfway through where I got hit by lightning out of nowhere, now that my luck was back where it had always been destined to end up. Vindi begged me to take off the quasi-silver bracelet before it attracted yet *another* strike, but—as I explained—I was far too devoted to her to throw away her gift. Also, it had melted to my wrist and I was physically incapable of removing it. But let's go with the first explanation, which was far more liable to get me pie.

Anyway. Long trip. Uneventful. Weird. I mean, we'd faced off against rocs, gods, princesses, evil ravenous walnuts, you name it —and now what? We had to take a long and dusty walk. The end. The occasional oasis provided water and food, so we didn't even have the dramatic pathos of slowly starving to death.

We stopped at another oasis to rest and eat: Vindi looked strangely at me as I swapped figs with her, having waited until she took a bite to prove that hers was neither diseased, infected, nor rancid.

"I'm not going to stand for this," Vindi said. "I'll never stop fighting until we've beaten Princess Shivaka and gotten your luck back. We'll recruit everyone in Kairay to our cause! She can't stand against the united might of an entire city!"

"Yeah. About that." I bit into the fig—and nearly broke my jaw on something incredibly hard. It seemed the fig had actually grown *around* some foreign object. I pried it open—and stared. I actually recognized the object inside of it. When I was sixteen, an escaped donkey slipped on a frog, spun like a whirlwind, and accidentally kicked out one of my teeth. That tooth had just been returned to me in the most unlikely and disturbing way imaginable. "We're not fighting Shivaka," I said.

"Well, sure, maybe *you* wouldn't get anywhere," Vindi

admitted. "But Avashti and I, we'll do whatever it takes to get you all fixed up. How could we not? We love you!"

"Eh," Avashti said, wavering his hand back and forth.

"You just wait," Vindi said. "Everyone in Kairay will rally to our cause!"

"And what will you tell them, exactly?" I said gently. "That their beloved leader is destined to be a successful ruler, enjoying a charmed reign that makes them ever fatter and more prosperous? Face it. No one's going to take my side, and frankly, they'd be stupid if they did. A river at flood raises all boats but mine."

"Well, it isn't fair, what she did to you," Vindi protested, her face reddening.

"How very true! Which means that everything has gone back to normal." I shrugged and started to eat my fig, carefully nibbling around the embedded tooth. "Besides, Shivaka has a point. Just imagine… that kind of power, in the hands of someone who'd use it wisely and well? I'd kind of like to see that."

"You're overcome with grief," Vindi said dramatically. "You aren't thinking clearly. We'll talk about this later."

"Good idea," I said laconically. "Wait until my next massive head injury renders me pliable and stupid, and *then* spring your aggravated idiocy on me. Maybe I'll even go along with it!"

Avashti gazed wistfully into the distance. "It was a nice reprieve, having you mostly fixed," he told me. "My house hasn't caught fire, partially collapsed, or inexplicably developed an intelligent mold hybridized from Leaf Riders and mushrooms in nearly three years. True, those disasters tended to be localized in the vicinity of your room, but the screaming woke me up at night."

"I'm an adult. I can pay rent," I said. I stuck my hand in my pocket, which had a sizeable hole where my money had been. "Or maybe I can't."

"I wasn't asking you to," Avashti said. "Of course you'll stay. Things are just going to be a little more *challenging*, is all."

"Considering all the trouble that comes with me, wouldn't you rather I left?"

"Well… the thing is… I like to keep interesting specimens close at hand," he said cagily. "Makes them easier to study."

"Uh-huh." I glanced at Vindi. "Didn't he used to be a better liar than this?"

"No, he was always pretty pathetic," she said thoughtfully. "I think he just loves you more than he used to, so pretending he doesn't care is more of a lie than it used to be."

"Would *you* like to start paying rent?" Avashti said menacingly to his daughter. She just grinned and stuck her tongue out at him.

I waited for Vindi to take a bite out of her next fig before snatching it from her hand. Which meant that the incensed Leaf Rider which had been trapped inside saw *me* when it came furiously buzzing out. But that might be a story for another day.

* * *

Once we got back to Kairay, life settled into a routine, sort of. Inspired by the weird mirage-bubble around Princess Gamal's moving island, Avashti found enough scraps of failed wizardry to improvise a similar force-shield around the tower house. From the outside, it was an impenetrable sphere of deepest black, impossible to see into or pass through. If you whistled the exact right pass-code, you could enter; after the third time an unexpected bee-sting on the lips caused me to accidentally whistle the barrier into a vengeful and voracious Star-Mantled Ultra-Lizard, I made very sure to only travel together with Vindi. From the inside, the barrier was hardly visible at all, little more than a heat ripple in the air. When I asked Avashti why he needed it, he said darkly, "for enemies".

Avashti spent long hours alone in his tower laboratory, working out how to intensify my luck into something so bad it was good. Of course, since we didn't have the Lens of Becoming *or* the redirection artifact, the whole thing seemed like a case of putting up the umbrella just *after* a roc had pooped like a waterfall on my head. Oh well. At least he had something to occupy him.

A week after we got back, it was announced that Her Lordship, the esteemed Shavala II, had slipped on a mango and hit her head on a horse—a statement so patently ridiculous that everyone assumed it was a euphemism for something far more naughty. Though uninjured, Her Lordship was inspired by her harrowing experience to semi-retire, making Princess Shivaka the effective ruler of Kairay.

A week after that, Shivaka accidentally conquered the neighboring republic of Bas when a filing error caused them to ship their entire treasury to her, instead of the ceremonial peacock of peace they'd intended.

A week after that, Princess Shivaka started to ramp up a massive campaign of conquest. Her victories were practically bloodless: Every time Kairay sent soldiers to a neighboring kingdom,

183

they were blessed with the discovery of an unlocked door in the battlements, or opponents who'd gotten so drunk that they forgot to show up for battle, or a King who'd just hit his head, and—seeing double—surrendered immediately when he saw twice as many soldiers as he expected. Everywhere I went, spirits were high. Anyone who wanted a job had one, either by joining the military or by replacing someone who'd gone. It was a fat time.

About a month after we got back, Avashti took Vindi and me out of the tower house and to the very edge of the force-shield, refusing to answer any questions or explain what he was doing. None of the passers-by could see us through the shield, of course, but they could hear us just fine. I had the weird thought that—if Avashti was bringing us here—it must be because he *wanted* to be overheard.

"Are you all right?" Vindi asked, concerned. "Is something wrong?"

"Just conducting a little test," he said, steepling his fingers together and trying to sound mysterious. "Certain people may deserve what they have. Or they may not. One way to find out is to plant certain information and see what response it elicits."

"What?" Vindi asked, confused.

"Don't try to explain stuff to her," I advised the wizard. "Her head is like rock. Doesn't absorb a thing."

"Hey!"

I snorted, looking Vindi up and down. "Then why, in open defiance of common sense, facts, and reality itself, do you *still* insist that I need to stand up and fight against Shivaka?" I turned to Avashti. "Three days ago at dinner, figuring she'd only understand if I answered inanity with inanity, I replied to her with a three-act play using talking bread as puppets. I'm not sure which was more disturbing… that the bread somehow caught fire while I was holding it, or that she seemed to find crudely improvised puppets *which were on fire* far more persuasive than she finds me."

"I do enjoy seeing you catch fire," Vindi admitted. "Um. Because it gives me the opportunity to put you out, I mean. Whew! Saved it. Good one, Vindi."

Avashti glanced at me. "So you're saying that I should *definitely* set you on fire each and every time I need to explain something to Vindi?"

"I don't like where this is going," I muttered.

Vindi smirked. "I do."

"At any rate—" Avashti raised his voice. "—we got away easy, didn't we? I could have made Shivaka's luck *so much better* than I did. What she has is shiny and fun, yes, but temporary and soon to fade. And when it goes, it goes forever. I wonder what she'll do when she's just the same as us poor slobs?"

I stared at him. "What the—?"

Avashti held up a forestalling hand, gazing fixedly at a couple of strangers wearing poor and much-mended clothing. Come to think of it, I'd been seeing them rather a lot lately. They murmured to each other, and the woman left. I stared. She was still limping, like she always did, but it was the wrong leg. In all the excitement, I guess she forgot.

"Spies?" I said under my breath. Avashti nodded.

"Let's go back to the house and see what happens," he whispered back.

It was an uneventful day. Avashti made dinner, and the three of us wiled away the time afterward telling stories in a pleasantly lazy food-haze. Well. *I* told stories. Vindi was fully occupied trying to help me with the inevitable aftermath of my attempt to feed myself— namely, the Exploding Soup Incident.

"Stop struggling," Vindi said, unwinding a long strip of linen. "*This* one is fine. I checked it myself."

"That's what you said about the last bandage," I noted, "before we—which is to say, I—discovered the ants which had built a nest between its layers. Something tells me they weren't amused when you wrapped them around my arm."

"I'd like to know how you cut yourself so badly on soup, anyway," she said, exasperated.

"I blame vegetables. They're pointier than they look."

She didn't have a chance to reply: A sudden ruckus shattered the quiet of Kairay at twilight. Citizens (depending on their location) either stared in amazement or dove out of the way as a line of horse-drawn chariots thundered down the street, illuminated by nearly enough lanterns to turn twilight into day. In the lead chariot, unsurprisingly, was Princess Shivaka, sitting next to the wizard Darshik. I was far more surprised to see Princess Gamal sitting demurely in the chariot just behind her.

"Hey. HEY!" I shouted, trying to make myself heard over all the noise. It wasn't any use: I had to wait until the chariots rolled to a stop in front of the tower house. "Hey, Gamal!" I shouted, "what the hell are you doing there? Are you gonna knife her in the back or what?"

"That's all over," Gamal called back. "Were you even paying attention? Did you notice that we lost? I'm pragmatic. If I can't have *all* the treasure, well, joining the winning side means I can have *some* treasure. I love my sister-in-law," she said laconically. "I hope she rules forever and ever, and gets richer and richer, and grows fatter and fatter until she can crush her enemies just by leaning on them." She glanced at Shivaka. "So long as I make myself useful to her, perhaps some of that fortune will rub off on me."

"You're an inspiration to us all," I said sardonically. "I'd call you a worm, but I don't think they'd appreciate the insult. Most worms, presumably, have some slight semblance of decency."

"Oh, you're a brave one, you are, shouting insults from inside an impassable black bubble. Why don't you come out? All this yelling is undignified." She stroked her slender neck. "I'm willing to… guarantee… your safety."

"Charming as always," I said, "provided you have a thing for cats in heat with razor blades strapped to their legs."

"Enough of this," Princess Shivaka said shortly. "I have heard certain rumors that you, Avashti, can make my luck even better. Darshik has confirmed that this is true. Now, I can't give you commands for reasons we both understand…"

"Because he'd be useless to you if he was rolling around on the floor, frothing at the mouth from an allergic reaction?" I guessed.

Shivaka glared in my general direction. It was weird, being able to see her so clearly, while knowing that she could see nothing but a featureless black orb.

"Enough. Avashti, come out now!" She bit her lip, forcing herself to walk back the command. "That is, a man of good sense, remembering our generosity toward those who help us, would choose to come out now. You have much to offer us. The war effort needs every wizard it can get. And we, in turn, will not forget your loyalty."

"Logically, if I can't even hold *you* off, I'm not strong enough to fight in your war," Avashti answered. "If you can get me, you don't want me. And if I *am* strong enough for your needs, you'll die horribly if you try to get me. The only sensible course of action is to go away forever!"

Princess Shivaka stood up in her chariot. "Am I to understand that you are refusing to help me? Keep in mind that there are two ways to draw bees from a hive. One, with flowers, which reward the bees with nectar and make them happy. And two, if that doesn't work, with smoke. I can drive you out as smoke drives out bees, wizard."

"Don't bother to try," Avashti advised her. "I can leave any time I want. I only need to reverse time—which, believe me, is both easy and fun—and go out last week, before you knew you needed me."

He turned to Vindi, lowering his voice. "You have my disguise, in case I actually *do* need to go out?"

Solemnly, she held up a fake beard. It looked exactly like his real one.

Avashti sighed. "Shall I assume that, if I groan and roll my eyes, you'll assume that I'm praising you in a lost and dead language known only to wizards?"

"Thanks, Dad!" she said brightly.

"Here," I said graciously, unwrapping the bandage from my arm. "Let me bleed on you. You can go out disguised as a doctor. Huh. Or maybe a butcher. Wow. I didn't know I *had* that much blood."

"Please know that the plan to force you out, should you make me use it, was not my doing," Princess Shivaka said. "It was Gamal's idea. I've stated my reservations, but she continues to insist that there is no other way." Shivaka paused, looking uncomfortable. "I will permit her to begin if you have not come to your senses by tomorrow morning."

"We're mooning you!" I shouted. "You can't see it, but we're mooning you!"

"What are you *talking* ab…" An enlightened look came over Vindi's face. "Oh! I get it." She raised her voice. "Wow, Saraya, what a horrifically insulting ass you have! Super disgusting and hairy!"

"Thanks," I said laconically.

A sudden murmur drew my attention back to the street below. A stumbling figure had emerged from one of the chariots at the back. Moving forward, it revealed itself to be Shivaka's husband Dakar, looking genially addled as always.

"Prince Dakar?" I called.

"Ah!" he said, pleased. "Aren't you the girl who sends me birds with messages written on them? I remember you. You sent me an ibis with the legend 'WHY NOT?!' painted upon its belly, which I have taken very much to heart. Note my shoes, which, despite being neither stylish nor much admired, do make me happy." He looked down, astonished to discover that his feet were bare. "That ibis is a thief," he said solemnly. "Has anyone seen a bird waddling about in gem-encrusted shoes?"

Princess Shivaka squeezed her eyes shut, pained. "My beloved... how many times must I tell you to stay in your room? Gamal advised me to install locks. For your own comfort and safety, I may have to allow her to do so."

"Wait," I said incredulously. "Let me get this straight. Instead of using your newfound powers to cure him, you're keeping your husband *locked in his room*?"

"I wouldn't expect you to understand," Princess Shivaka said sadly. "Wouldn't I be a hypocrite, if I were unwilling to make the same sacrifices that I demand of my people? It seems I'm not destined to be happy. The war effort requires wizards. All of them. More than all of them, really. This is where I define my legacy: Should I divert my wizards to help Dakar, something that would benefit only the two of us... or should I instead sacrifice my own happiness to improve the lives of so many more?"

"Who *cares* about some stupid war effort?" I cried. "Why not stay here in Kairay and *make people's lives better*?"

"It isn't that simple," she said. "I have plenty of war advisors. More than I could ever want, really. But building a whole new society to the benefit of all? I have no one... *no one*... who can give me advice there. There simply isn't an infrastructure of ministers and advisors to support it. It's going to take time to figure out what I need to do. I can spend that time sitting on my hands doing nothing, or I can spend it expanding my sphere of influence so that—when the time comes—I can help *everyone at once*. What kind of monster would help a mere hundred, when she could so easily help a hundred thousand more?"

"Right. So conquering as many nations as possible is more important than curing Dakar. Keep talking," I said coldly. "If you keep going long enough, I'm sure you'll find a way to out-Gamal Gamal."

"I wouldn't expect you to understand," she said, her voice breaking.

"I've written an execution order for that thief ibis," Dakar shouted—if this is even possible—in a conspiratorial tone. "But, even considering how tasty a meal he'd make, I'm not sure I want to set the precedent. Cook and eat just one prisoner, and suddenly everyone starts screaming about cannibalism. It happens every time."

"Just… take care of him," Princess Shivaka ordered Gamal. "I can't stand to see him like this. I can't. Not right now."

She raised her hand and her chariot rumbled away, trailing a billowing cloud of dust. Princess Gamal had her own chariot pull up next to Prince Dakar: She waited there until hers was the only chariot left.

"What are you doing?" I asked, genuinely puzzled.

"I've had enough of your insults," Princess Gamal sneered. "You think you know better than me? Well and good. You now have a royal guest to look after. I'm sure someone as monumentally clever as yourself will have no trouble curing him!"

She raised her hand and her chariot rolled off, leaving Prince Dakar standing, alone and baffled, in front of our house.

"She *abandoned* him?" Vindi demanded.

"Looks like it," I said. "Shall we let him in?"

Avashti frowned. "What if he's a spy?"

"I'll make you a deal. If he *is*, as punishment, I'll eat a bowl of soup. Vegetables and all."

"Given your penchant for ruining my clothes with your blood, I'm not sure what that's supposed to prove."

"Shows what you know. C'mon, Vindi. Let's fetch him in before he gets his head stuck in a frog."

Together, she and I headed down to see what we'd gotten ourselves into.

* * *

The next morning was much like every other morning I've ever experienced, give or take an addled royal prince poking delightedly into everything.

"I like this palace," Dakar said, sitting down at the breakfast table. "Such effort, such expense surely went into making it look so ragged and worn-down. And the food! The chefs must have labored for *years* to perfect such a cunning imitation of unadorned simplicity!" He suddenly looked straight at me. "Do *your* birds wear shoes?" he said urgently.

"Can you take him somewhere? Please?" Avashti said, exasperated. "I've nearly finished the good/bad luck transform, but I must have total concentration to perfect the last few details. They're incredibly fiddly, but absolutely crucial."

189

I raised an eyebrow, which—thanks to an oddly specific skin condition—promptly fell off. "Wait. You're not done? Why did you feed that story to Shivaka's spies if you weren't ready?"

"I misjudged," Avashti admitted. "I never imagined that she'd come based on a single overheard conversation. I thought it would take dozens. I thought… I *knew*… I had plenty of time."

Vindi put down her spoon, staring at her father. "Wait. You made a mistake… and you're *admitting* it?"

"Of course," Avashti said, surprised. "I always admit my mistakes. For example, please enjoy this list of every mistake I've made in my entire life prior to this one." He paused. "And if I ever make a *second* mistake, you can be sure I'll add it to the list."

Vindi and I set about clearing the table. Vindi also took on the duty of extinguishing me each time I caught fire, which I appreciated. Prince Dakar followed us around, happily chatting about nonsensical things. An amusing, if daft, fellow? I wasn't so sure. There was a hint of desperation in his ceaseless nattering, as if some part of him deep inside knew that something was very wrong. If you took a man who was accustomed to solving every problem with sheer cleverness, and trapped him in his own dreams, I think his efforts to talk his way free might sound something like this. That he couldn't pull it off may have been a greater tragedy than every failed little joke the universe has ever played on me.

"What's going on out there?" Vindi asked, distracted by movement outside the window. Soldiers in Kairay colors spread out as they marched toward the tower house, taking up positions in a broad circle around the force-shield. At their leader's signal, they began shouting weird and nonsensical things:

"Avashti! Princess Shivaka COMMANDS you to blow bubbles and sing the good-night song!"

"Avashti! Princess Shivaka COMMANDS you to dream of elephants and knit her a real, live camel!"

"Avashti! Princess Shivaka COMMANDS you to spit straight up and catch it in your mouth, in imitation of the world's most hideous fountain!"

Vindi and I exchanged puzzled glances. Just then, Avashti staggered down the stairs from his laboratory. His face was red, his breath labored, and sweat beaded his brow.

"You're allergic to *that*?" Vindi said, horrified—but it was obvious that he was. Avashti slumped to the floor, unable to walk any farther. Together, we dragged him as far from the window as we could. Vindi fetched some bedsheets and wrapped them around his head, trying to block out the sound. It helped, but not enough. The mere fact that they were *there* was enough to trigger him.

"We have to get you out of here," Vindi told her father.

"That's what they want," Avashti said, his voice strained. "Smoke me out. You better believe there'd be action if I went outside the force-shield. But I haven't finished my schematics... not ready..."

"I don't care. I'm not letting you die. We have to get you out of here."

"Look. It's not that bad. They're plenty far away. See?" Avashti managed to smile at her, though the effort seemed to exhaust him. "Now... be a good girl. Go and... sell something. Or buy something. Don't need you standing over me fretting all day."

Vindi looked at me, her eyes bright. I gave her a tiny, almost imperceptible nod. With Dakar's help, we managed to move Avashti to his bed. I wish I could say we left him resting comfortably. That rasping breath, that fever, that cough... I'm rather a connoisseur of diseases, and if things continued to develop along the same lines, I was fairly sure he had less than two days to live.

"What are we going to do?" Vindi asked as we reached the breakfast table. I made her sit down, then sat across from her. Dakar took the head of the table, looking very solemn as he folded scraps of papyrus into little paper boats.

"I have no idea where I am," Dakar said suddenly. "Is being lost always this much fun?"

"What are we going to do?" Vindi repeated.

"We're going to save him. Obviously."

"And defy Princess Shivaka, who now pairs all the power in Kairay with all the luck in the world. Now *there's* a lost cause," she said hollowly.

"Sometimes, I think lost causes are the only ones worth fighting for," I mused. "Then again, maybe that's because any cause I support becomes lost the instant I start fighting for it. Sometimes, lost causes are fun. Sometimes, they're a way to spit in the face of my oppressor to prove he can't break me. This time? Someone I care about is going to die if I fail. That's all I need."

Vindi sighed. "So how are we going to sneak him out of here?" she asked.

I thought it over. "I don't know that we should," I admitted.

"We have today, hopefully, to go out and find a better solution. If we're willing to leave him here alone, that is, to suffer."

"Let's say we do venture out into the city," Vindi said. "What would we even be looking for? How do you cure an allergy that's actually a curse from the gods?"

"Forget curing him. That's beyond us. We have to think sneakier than that. For example: Can we get rid of the soldiers?"

Vindi thought it over. "I could try to assassinate Princess Shivaka," she said hopelessly. "With luck, every guard in the city would abandon their posts as they ran to defend her. What? It could work."

"No, it really couldn't," I said flatly. "With luck? Really? Right now, *she* has all the luck. If you tried to cut her head off with a sword, you'd trip and accidentally slice up a grapefruit all nice and neat for her morning meal."

Vindi grumbled. "There's so much we don't know. If only some friendly god would reach down from the clouds and give us all the answers."

I looked at her strangely. "Maybe they have."

"What?"

"Darshik's book of prophecy," I said. "The answers are in there. They have to be. All we have to do is find him and steal the damn thing!"

Vindi snorted. "To save my father's life? All right. I'm in. Just tell me one thing: How do we find Darshik? He could be anywhere."

I thought it over. "There must be something special, something magical about wizards," I reasoned. "If so, there must be a way to track it down from a distance. Could you ask your father?"

Vindi made a face. "You want me to ask him about *Darshik*? I think he'd pop a vein and die right then just to prove a point."

I nodded thoughtfully. "In that case, there's only one place to go: The Great Library of Shubara. We find out how to locate Darshik, we steal the book, we save your father. End of story."

"I like it!" Dakar said heartily. "I mean, I really wasn't listening, but your tone of voice is *very* exciting. You sound like adventure!"

Vindi nodded. "I guess we don't have a choice, do we? Let's see if we can sneak out of here."

As it turned out, we didn't need to. Although the soldiers

obviously noticed us when we poked our heads through the great black orb of the force-shield, they made no move to stop us. I guess Vindi was no longer considered valuable now that her horns didn't do anything, and no one had ever cared about me. We'd taken the precaution of throwing a blanket over Dakar, but he obviously wasn't Avashti, so they didn't pay any attention to him, either.

"Is this the latest fashion?" Dakar asked. "Being unable to see? If so, consider me well ahead of the curve and ready for the monsoon ball!"

We hurried to the nearest alley. No one raised the alarm, or bothered to follow us at all. Is it strange that I felt a little disappointed?

"All right," Vindi said as she freed Dakar from his blanket. "The Great Library of Shubara it is."

IX

The basic problem with being a scholar is that the pay is terrible. I can say with confidence that knowing the color of every king's eyes for the past thousand years doesn't make starving to death any more inviting a prospect. The solution employed by the Great Library of Shubara, simply, is to solicit donations from wealthy patrons. Problem: Wealthy patrons expect a return on their investment, perhaps the Secret of Immortality. If you lack morals, you can give your patrons a recipe heavy with mercury and arsenic, which protects you from their ire simply by poisoning them to death before they have time to complain. The Library of Shubara takes a gentler tack. Simply, the Great Library is actually a warren of secret passages, rotating panels, hidden rooms and cryptic doors so cunningly arranged that any given scholar can hide from six different patrons at once, on the theory that you can't make demands of people you can't *find*. Once, I ducked in to see if the librarians could make change for a silver crescent. (I wanted to buy some novelty flowers that came with furious Leaf Riders glued inside, ready to attack anyone who smelled them. What? It was Vindi's birthday—I had to get her *something*). I emerged six hours later covered in cobwebs and so disturbed by what I'd seen that I couldn't speak for ten days. I'm still not sure whether I should be offended that Vindi so gratefully accepted my silence as her birthday present.

Vindi, Dakar and I paused in front of the Great Library of Shubara. The facade was made of stone, and very impressive, with carved friezes depicting humans cracking open the heads of the gods and slurping out knowledge.

"This is a bad idea," Vindi said uncomfortably. "Why are we even here? My father needs us."

"True. He does. We could go home and watch him suffer, helpless to *do* anything about it—or we could try to help him. We need to find Darshik. Hopefully, the librarians will know how to find a wizard."

"I know, I know. It's just—"

"When *I* need to find a wizard, I just start setting things on fire," Dakar said helpfully. "Eventually, my wife hires a wizard to seal my hands harmlessly inside orbs of living water, leaving me free to ask him the vitally pressing question of whether our insides have a color, given that there isn't any light to see them by. People tell me our insides are the color of red and yuck, but you can't fool me. Stabbing a man with a sword introduces a contaminating foreign substance into his guts, rendering the results of the experiment... unpredictable. For example, when I stab myself with the endearingly floppy sword my wife gave me a few months ago, it merely tickles."

Vindi glanced at Dakar. "Come to think of it... it might go faster if it was a *royal prince* asking. Do you think we could use *him*?"

I frowned, tripped up by that simple little word... *use*. Dakar was a human being. Would it cost so much to treat him like one? I took Prince Dakar by the shoulders, trying my best to look him in his erratically wandering eyes. It would have been easier if I'd been able to dislocate my shoulders and tie myself in a knot, but you do what you can.

"The wizard Avashti is sick," I told him. "Maybe dying. To cure him, we need to find the wizard Darshik and steal his book of prophecy." I frowned. "Hopefully that damn book hasn't told him we're coming. Anyway, we're trying to save Avashti's life. Will you help us?"

Prince Dakar nodded. "I think I like you," he told me. "You treat me like... what's the word? I have many of them, but they're all bats, and they hide lint in my pocket and then fly away laughing when I get mad at them. Friends! You treat me like a friend. You can count on me to avenge your death! Just tell me who to stab with my endearingly floppy sword."

"Is... that a 'yes'?" I asked cautiously. I waited. Vindi waited. Dakar smiled and poked me with his sword. It tickled.

"Let's just go inside and see what happens."

"So be it," Vindi said dubiously.

We pushed through the front doors. They were fashioned from interlocking brass plates, and stretched at least thirty feet overhead. We found ourselves in a huge circular room that smelled of papyrus and ink, dust and lamp-oil. It smelled like *secrets*. Book-lined walls whirled around us in an ascending spiral, climbing two, three, four levels before disappearing into the gloom overhead. Many lamps hung from the walls, illuminating the plush—donated?—furniture that cluttered the main floor. I heard the muted sound of a distant door slamming. That was all. We were alone.

"WE NEED TO SPEAK TO SOMEONE!" Vindi shouted. "IT'S IMPORTANT!"

I took a deep breath. "WE AREN'T HERE TO COLLECT ON YOUR DEBTS, WE PROMISE!"

"I DON'T UNDERSTAND WHY WE'RE TALKING LIKE THIS, BUT I LIKE TO FIT IN!" Dakar bellowed.

We waited, but there wasn't an answer, not even the clatter of someone running away. Irritated, Vindi led us onward. We hurried along the curving hallway, which gradually rose and became a second-story balcony winding around the central shaft.

"Could that be a secret switch?" Vindi asked, pointing to a metal sconce that was hanging askew. I tugged on it—and it promptly broke off in my hand. I tried to put it back, and somehow caused the wall to come crashing down. Not all of it. Just the books—every single one of which landed on my left big toe, one by one by one.

"Ow! Ow! OW!!!"

"Look! A secret passage!" Vindi cried, pointing so wildly that she knocked the very last book from the shelf. I prudently yanked my foot out of the way. The book, 'A Complete History of Rubber', bounced off the naked stone and clobbered me in the eye.

Vindi led the way. We found ourselves in a veritable labyrinth of secret passages: The three of us edged sideways through narrow slots between walls, climbed ladders, slid down poles, spun through rotating secret panels, and climbed up and down demented little half-width flights of stairs.

"Ah-HA!" Vindi bellowed, flinging open a pair of curtains. Behind was a painting of an elegantly dressed man baring his rump at us.

"You have to give them points for originality," she admitted.

"More importantly," I said, "when they hired the artist to make that painting, did they have to hire a model, too… and how much did they pay him to just stand there like that?"

"Come on."

"Wait. Move your head from side to side. It really follows you around the room, doesn't it?"

"Come *on*!"

We continued to make our way through the warren, never seeing a soul, never getting any closer to anyone who could help us.

"Uh, Vindi…? Maybe we should…"

"*No,*" she said fiercely. "Don't say it. Don't say we should quit. I'm going to save my father. I am. The day I quit is the day you can start digging my grave, because it means I'm dead."

"My side hurts," Prince Dakar complained.

"We have to rest," I agreed. "My side doesn't hurt *yet*, but after I stumble into a torch and catch fire and you put me out, primarily, by punching me—thank you, by the way—I anticipate that I *will*. Rest now. Then you can punch harder, later."

"This… isn't… RIGHT," Vindi groaned. "My father could be dying for all I know. But am I at his side, taking care of him? No! I'm running around some weird abandoned crazy-person jail, accomplishing nothing, doing nothing. This isn't right."

I reached over to take her hand. "What more can we do?" I asked gently. "We have to start somewhere. Stating, 'I want my father to be cured!' doesn't entitle you to a solution. You have to put in the work, *try* things, and take the risk that you'll fail. Even birds can't simply say 'I want to fly'. They have to knit themselves a cloak of feathers and fling themselves into the sky, which, frankly, has to be riskier than it looks." I glanced speculatively upward. "We have no idea what sort of weird and hurtful things grow out the tops of clouds."

"Are we shouting again?" Dakar asked hopefully. "What's happening?"

"We can't find any scholars," I told him. "The scholars at the Great Library of Shubara. We can't find them. Also, Vindi may or may not be a nude, lazy bird."

Dakar nodded somberly. "You can't catch a bird by leaping at it, can you? But set out the right kind of seed, and they'll come to you."

"And what kind of seed… uh…"

Dakar offering me his cupped hands, which were literally overflowing with coins. It was more money than I'd ever seen in my life, which may not be saying a lot, but has to mean *something*. Vindi stared at both of us, her eyes wide.

"Just how much of this do you think he understands?" she whispered.

"I don't know. Less than everything… but a lot more than Shivaka gives him credit for. Dakar… are you *sure* you want to do this?"

"Do what?" he asked, absently scratching his neck and sending a minor rainstorm of coins clattering to the ground. I started to go after them, then speculated on what would happen if they ALL got stuck up my nose simultaneously. I made Vindi gather them up instead. It took a while, but the three of us eventually found our way back to the main room. There was a small table near the door, with four deeply-stuffed chairs around it. We sat down. Vindi let the coins fall on the table with a prolonged, noisy and musical clatter. She didn't say anything else. She just waited.

To my right, a set of bookshelves hinged open. A bearded scholar poked his head out of the secret passage behind them, his eyes fixed on the coins that lay scattered in front of us. A hatch in the floor popped up, and a young woman stuck her head out. Another table abruptly stood up, revealing itself to be a wizened old man with huge, swooping, owl-like eyebrows, whose body was encased in curiously blocky pieces that looked *exactly* like a table when he rested on all fours. The three scholars cautiously approached us, with many a wary glance at the scattered coins on the table.

"You're… prospective patrons?" the bearded man asked.

"Not exactly," Vindi said. "We only have one question: We need a way to track wizards, to find them at a distance. Can you help us?"

"That's it?" the woman asked cautiously. "Nothing else?"

"That's it."

"Ah. Querants. IT'S A PAYING JOB!" owl-eyebrows shouted. Instantly, about a dozen scholars appeared out of nowhere. At owl-eyebrow's direction, they went to work researching our query. It was enjoyable, watching them take on their task: The whole thing was elegant and yet demented, like some meticulously orchestrated dance arranged by an idiot. Teams ransacked walls of books and heaps of scrolls, working in perfect unison as they hunted down odd references and curious details. Finally, owl-eyebrows returned—still wearing his blocky faux-table costume, I noticed.

"I have your answer."

"What is it?" Vindi said eagerly.

"Not yet," he said, indicating the coins that still lay scattered across the table. "Payment first."

"Done. Take it!"

At his gesture, several of the other scholars swooped down on us. When they parted, the table was gleaming and clean.

"Your answer," he told us, "is that wizards cannot be tracked. They are just the same as everyone else, and there is no special way to find them."

Vindi stared at him. "That's it? That's my answer?"

"That's it."

"You mean you *failed*?"

"No. Not at all. We succeeded in conclusively proving that the thing you requested does not exist. Our duty is to find what's true, whether you approve of it or not."

"I don't believe it," Vindi muttered. She headed for the door, but I paused as an intriguing new idea occurred to me. What had Princess Shivaka said? She had more war advisors than she could ever want, but she *didn't have anyone to advise her on doing good*. Here I was, standing in the Great Library of Shubara, surrounded by a dozen or so of the most knowledgeable people in all of Kairay. Could *this* be what she needed?

"Hold on," I said. "How would you like to advise Princess Shivaka herself?"

"She listens to *you*?" he said dubiously.

"Maybe. Maybe not. But if I presented her with a panel of advisors, fully complete and ready-made, wouldn't she at least have to consider my idea?"

Owl-eyebrows thought it over. "Our services are available… for a fee."

"Well, see, the Final Purpose of money is to be spent," I said. "It you're doing it right, it doesn't exist! By giving you a heaping pile of Nothing, please consider that I've done you the favor of pre-spending your money *for* you."

Owl-eyebrows glanced sidelong at me. "Interesting premise. Sadly, I am a masochist. Please do punish me with actual, physical money."

"Can't blame a girl for trying," I shrugged. "Who knows? It *could* have worked. Smart people can be really stupid about money."

"Money?" Dakar asked genially. "Do you need money? I think I have some in my pouch, here, somewhere under all these coins. They really do get in the way, don't they? One moment."

Prince Dakar tipped out his coin pouch, which looked to be about half full, and sent the remaining half clattering onto the table. Owl-eyebrow's eyes got very, very big. Dakar peered into his coin pouch, looking confounded.

"Empty," he reported, sounding disappointed. "And I was so certain there was something in there."

"Ah… can I have that?" I asked Dakar, gesturing to the coins. "Please?"

Dakar looked confused. "Why are you asking me? They're not *mine*. For one thing, they've signally failed to sing, dance, or cook me treats, conclusively proving that they are not my friends."

"We haven't done any of that, either," Vindi pointed out, looking worried.

"In my daydreams, you have," he said reassuringly.

"Uh, sure." I looked at owl-eyebrows. "I want your three best scholars on call for the Advisory Council. This payment should cover a full year."

"Two scholars, six months."

"That wasn't a negotiation," I said pleasantly. "Vindi, pick those coins up… *slowly*. One at a time."

Owl-eyebrows twitched as he watched a fortune ever-so-slowly being taken away from him.

"Fine!" he shouted. "It's a deal. Now put it back!"

I nodded to Vindi. She opened her hand and let the coins clatter back onto the table. As owl-eyebrows gathered it up, the three of us headed for the door, trying to figure out what we were going to do next. Well, Vindi and I did. I think Dakar was still wrestling with the concept of nudity in birds.

* * *

As we walked across the dusty courtyard in front of the Great Library, I could see that Vindi was holding herself together only with great difficulty. I gestured at Prince Dakar to give us some space: Instead, he tactfully crouched down and pretended to be a frog. The theory being, I suppose, that a frog was incapable of understanding Vindi, and she could therefore say anything she wanted in front of him without embarrassment. I looked around. Tall and solemn buildings surrounded us on all sides, but we were pretty much alone. I stopped, putting my hands on Vindi's shoulders and forcing her to stop, too.

"All you going to be all right?"

"I'm fine. Really."

I looked her in the eye. "Vindi."

She shook her head, her eyes strangely bright. "Are you going to keep me here—murdering my father through inaction, I might add

201

—until I break down and weep some highly performative tears for you?"

"Got it in one. Start weeping."

"Saraya—" Vindi smiled tightly. "I don't know how you're so strong. I don't know how you keep going. We had a brilliant idea, we worked hard to implement it, we overcame challenges and we got exactly what we wanted—and we still lost."

"Let me tell you a secret about life," I said. "Nothing is ever easy. Nothing. Making toast? Hardest thing I ever did. Set myself on fire half a dozen times, and let's not even bring up the fact that a fine powder dispersed in air—like cinnamon—becomes extremely explosive. But here's the thing: Running into a wall is stupid. Isn't it? But your head heals. Bricks don't. Practice enough stupidity, and eventually there's no wall any more. See what I'm saying?"

Vindi glanced at me strangely. "Why are you hitting the wall with your head? There's such a thing as hammers."

"It's a metaphor," I said, exasperated. "This failed. We'll try something else."

"Like what, Saraya? What can we try? My father's going to die. I failed him."

I paced back and forth. "Well… we may not be able to find Darshik and his book. What does that leave? Sneaking Avashti out of the tower, or removing the soldiers that are hounding him."

"They'll be watching for him to try and sneak out," she said dubiously, "but grabbing armed soldiers and dragging them away sounds like an even more questionable idea. Unless we *draw* them away? One of us could start a fire and scream for help. You're good at that. Setting things on fire, I mean, conditional on your being inside them at the time. I hereby charge you with making me toast. You owe me a favor for the time you failed spectacularly at eating an orange and I didn't even laugh at you."

"I used to eat oranges *all the time*," I said, disgruntled.

"Exactly. And one of those times, I didn't laugh at you."

I shook it off. "One fire wouldn't do it," I mused. "To occupy every soldier in the city, we'd need unrest to break out in a hundred different places at once."

"And how do we do that?" Vindi asked dubiously.

"We can't—not by ourselves. We'll need help." I glanced at Dakar. "Do you have any money left?"

"I am rich in friends," the prince said stoutly, then shot me a furtive look. "The real test will be when I try to spend you. Do you think you're worth a whole beer?"

"Well, his clothes might be worth something," I said dubiously. "I'll amend my earlier statement. We'll need *cheap* help, and lots of it."

Vindi grimaced. "Then we need to go where people are numerous and desperate."

"The East Quarter?"

"Exactly."

We headed east. The Kairay river runs generally from west to east, and it's no coincidence that the rich and the poor are distributed in the same way. Where the river enters town, it runs clean and clear. The farther it runs through the city, the more of society's offensive and unfortunate runoff it accumulates. In the East Quarter, they say that the stench alone has been known to take human form and nauseate people to death by dancing around naked in front of them.

The houses got poorer and poorer as we walked, growing closer and closer together. Soon they merged into larger buildings, dilapidated and crumbling, each housing any number of families. When we reached the Kairay river, I was startled to find a maze-like warren of floating garden islands all bound together by chain-link bridges. A lone tree grew from the center of each island, each trimmed in a unique and distinctive way—to serve as landmarks in an otherwise confusing maze, I assumed. Each tree held an elevated platform with a single old man or woman acting as lookout. Meanwhile, there were all kinds of people on the islands themselves, mostly fishing. A lot of the people who lived here were displaced persons from other city-states, who—as far as Kairay was concerned—officially didn't exist. I scowled. *These* were the people Shivaka should be helping. They didn't have much choice but to fish. How else could they feed their families, when they couldn't legally work?

"Hey! Here's an idea!" Vindi called as she led us across the bridge to the first island. "We're going to slip some money under the table and pretend we didn't see it change hands! Real paying work! I promise! Who's ready to earn some honest coin?"

The fisherfolk didn't answer. They just picked up their nets and buckets and quietly evacuated to the next island over.

"Huh?" I asked, the leaves of thriving yams tickling my legs.

"We hear it all the time," said the old man in our island's tree. He had a great mane of dust-colored hair, and a meandering scar that crossed an empty eye. "The *esteemed* citizens of Kairay assume we're stupid, or worthless, or both. They make all *kinds* of promises, yes. But then they "forget" to pay us, or offer work so demeaning and dangerous that no one else would touch it. It's hard for people like us, people who don't exist, to get justice. Bad folk know this. They come here all the time, looking for victims to exploit."

"Well, uh…" Vindi glanced sidelong at him. "We weren't going to ask you to set fires or foment unrest or anything like that. That would be far too dangerous. No, we wanted… um… a large numbers of searchers to comb the city for Darshik the wizard, so they could tell us where he is. We'll pay real coin! I promise!"

"Promises made to *us* are generally worth the breath they're spoken with," he commented.

We tried to follow the fisherfolk to the next island, only to find that they'd unhooked the chains and cast the bridges away behind them. Not only that, but others had snuck up and unhooked the bridge we'd used to get here in the first place. The three of us suddenly found ourselves trapped on a tippy garden island that was floating slowly downstream, through some water I *really* didn't want to go swimming in.

"Help?" I said, appealing to Vindi and Dakar.

"If we fall in and start drowning, they'll have to jump in and save us," Vindi reasoned. "I mean, they aren't monsters."

"Are you volunteering?" I asked, watching her carefully as she edged closer to me, hands outstretched.

"I don't think they'd find it believable if *I* fell in. Aren't you willing to do this one easy, fun little thing for me?"

"No!"

"Come on, Saraya," she said, hurt. "It's me, Vindi—you know, the person you claim to love like a sister?"

"Sisters come in all kinds. For example, there's the kind that grows out of your back like a parasitic wart and giggles wetly whenever it gets hold of a knife. I could be one of those."

"Just one quick little splash," she wheedled. "Don't you love me?"

"Dakar?" I asked.

"Are you asking if *I* love you?" he said, startled.

"No! Do you have any *ideas*!"

"All the time," he said. "But no one sends me a bird with the word 'Salubrious' written on it, no matter how many times I ask."

"Ideas about our current situation. Here. Now. Today."

"When people refuse to help me, I generally attack them with frogs," he said thoughtfully. "They run around in terror as my army of dank minions advances, croaking ominously. When I call off the attack, it proves my good intentions and requires my former adversaries to love me!"

"Sound advice, as usual."

"I don't appear to have an army of frogs *on* me," Dakar mused, checking his pockets. "It seems I must spend the next thousand years training frogs. *Or.* I could spent a single day befriending a single frog-trainer, someone who'd already done all that work *for* me. Either way."

"Is he being insightful again?" Vindi complained.

"We could spend forever trying to recruit individuals," I mused, turning to look at the one-eyed man who was still sitting placidly above us in his tree. "*Or.* We could recruit someone they all know, someone they all listen to. Win *him*, and we win *them*."

We walked the short distance back to the center of the island. The one-eyed man stayed in his tree, his gaze patient and unalarmed as he watched us approach.

"What's your name?" Vindi politely asked him. "What do you do here?"

He gave her an evaluating look. "Jebiam," he said, bowing from the waist. "I teach people not to die. Those that listen, I teach to make a living. I know which Kairay citizens will actually pay for work done. I know which to watch out for. I can match up locals who need work with those who need work done. But mostly, I teach people not to die."

"We need help," Vindi explained. "To save my father's life, we need to find the wizard Darshik…"

As she told her tale, a handful of other community leaders came down from their trees and crossed over to us, tossing over hooked chains so they could reattach the bridges to our island. Those who joined us were mostly older folks, usually scarred or maimed in ways that spoke of the kind of work available to displaced persons. I found it strangely impressive that, after all their suffering, they'd dedicated themselves to the betterment of their people instead of becoming bitter and withdrawn.

"So you need swarms of obedient, invisible nobodies to track down this wizard for you?" Jebiam said cynically. "Surely this wouldn't offend the rulers of Kairay… for example, those with the power to order us dispersed and our floating gardens destroyed?"

"But we can pay you!" Vindi insisted. "Right, Dakar?"

She looked at the prince, who was sitting on the island's squishy, gently bobbing surface. His pockets were all turned out, his coin pouches wide open. They were all empty.

"Money? No. I have none. I don't remember *spending* it, and so I must—regretfully—conclude that that thief ibis has been here again," Dakar mused. "Sadly, I have no choice but to deal with him. I will send my frog army to conclude the matter."

"You don't *have* a frog army. Remember?"

"I don't?" Dakar said, his face a study in shocked dismay.

I snapped my fingers. "We have something better than coin! We can offer you a position advising Princess Shiv—" A bat suddenly flew into my throat and lodged there.

"We can offer you a position advising Princess Shivaka herself," Vindi said, helpfully punching me in the gut. The bat had already flown back out again, with the result that I took a full-body punch from my best friend to absolutely no effect. Well, I shouldn't say *no* effect. It did make me bite my tongue.

"Advising the Princess?" Jebiam said, sounding disgusted. "Can't you at least tell *plausible* lies?"

"No, really!" Vindi insisted. "See, it's like this…" She explained the Council of Advisors we were forming. Jebiam and the others listened closely, occasionally nodding. "…and think of all the good you could do for your people! One right word in the Princess' ear could bring about the changes you've been fighting for for years!"

"But there's no guarantee she'd even accept this Council of Advisors, or listen to our advice if she did," Jebiam pointed out. "You demand a vast amount of labor, in exchange for the mere *hope* that she'll accept us. She may not. We may get absolutely nothing."

"Such is life," I said simply. "You have a *chance* to make a real difference in your community. You can make a grab for it, yes, knowing that you might miss. Or you can sit here doing nothing, waiting for an absolute guarantee that will never come, watching the suffering around you continued unchanged."

"Why would she even want us for this Advisory Council?" Jebiam said suspiciously. "You've already recruited real scholars and librarians, people who know everything. Why would you need *us*?"

I snorted. "Are you kidding? What have those scholars ever

done, here in the real world? Sure, they know the average weight of a thrice-dried fig, but so what? Community leaders like you are the ones who have actual experience helping people, fighting for people, making life better for people. Scholars *think*, and that's good... but you *know*, and that's a kind of cleverness that we very badly need. Join us. Please."

"I need you most of all," Prince Dakar said to Jebiam. "I esteem Saraya far too highly. I am rich in friends, yes, but I need smaller denominations, people I merely respect, if I'm ever to purchase that beer I've been wanting."

"Look," Vindi said, grabbing Prince Dakar and showing our audience his signet ring, "we have Shivaka's own husband with us! Doesn't that prove that what we're saying is true? Or at least plausible?"

Jebiam exchanged looks with the other community leaders. "Well..." He grimaced. "Perhaps I'm playing the fool yet again..."

"It's always foolish to hope," I agreed. "Mind you, knowing that has never made my heart any less the idiot."

Jebiam smiled. "We will help you. Yes. We'll send people out on this task of yours. It'll take some hours to hear back, of course..."

"Of course," Vindi said, looking grim. "Nothing is ever easy, is it?"

"We're going to find Darshik," I said. "Let's assume that. Now we just need to figure out how to get that damn book away from him."

"If you're looking for advice," Jebiam noted, "you might go and ask the sages."

"Sages? What sages?"

"Exactly," he said, smiling thinly.

* * *

Following Jebiam's directions, the three of us made our way to an especially dense section of greenery surrounding the Kairay river. It was as though a gigantic whorl of vines had risen out of the ground for the express purpose of poking us with thorns.

"I bet there *are* no sages," Vindi said morosely. "Jebiam just wanted to get rid of us, to cover for the fact that he lied and no one is even trying to help my father."

"No one ever listens," Dakar agreed, then looked troubled. "Which means that I don't, either. Wait. What did I just say?"

"You heard what Jebiam said," I told her. "The sages don't want people mobbing them, demanding easy answers for every little problem in life. Absolute wisdom requires absolute freedom, or some garbage like that. So they hide. But if we can get them to tell us how to tackle Darshik, we'll be two-thirds of the way home."

"Home. We should be at home. Saraya…" Vindi crouched down and put her hands on her knees, starting to hyperventilate. "What if we're too late? What if it's *already* too late? What if Dad collapsed just this instant, dying, eyes filling with tears as he wondered where his daughter was… and why she didn't care enough to even stay with him?"

"Get a hold of yourself," I said sternly.

"Then do something! Help me! Distract me!"

I pulled back and slapped her. Vindi stared at me.

"That was *not* what I meant."

"It was an accident! You know how rotten my luck is. If you want proof that I didn't mean it, I hereby offer to slap you for real as a point of comparison."

"That was no mistake. Your hand was open!"

"Momentary spasm. Oops. There it goes again," I said, making an obscene gesture at her.

Vindi's own hand curled into a fist, but she stopped herself with a visible effort. "No. I forgive you. I do. Plus, it *was* distracting."

"Then maybe you want to un-fistify your hand?"

"My what?" she asked blankly. Just then, predictably, I stepped on a rancid pile of donkey dung. My foot shot out from under me, and I plunged downward and punched myself on her fist, *hard*. When the shimmering lights had cleared, I found myself lying on the ground, Vindi hovering worriedly over me. At least my head had landed on something soft. Then I sniffed, smelling what I'd landed in. Oh. Oh no.

"Argl," I said. "Wubba? Smork."

"Come on," Vindi said tightly. "Let's get this over with."

"As far as I'm concerned, it's already over," Dakar assured her. "See? I'm helping! Let's go for pancakes."

The three of us approached the thorny green wall. I winced. Jebiam *had* insisted that this was the right path, and I was going to get thorns in me one way or another, wasn't I? Didn't really matter how. Throwing an arm across my face, I put my head down and charged forward, plowing straight into the spiny morass.

"What are you *doing*?" Vindi said, horrified.

"Thought… they'd be magic," I said, gritting my teeth against the pain of fifty thousand simultaneous punctures. "Thought they'd jump out of the way or something."

"There's a tunnel right down there! Didn't you see it?"

"Oh." I looked down. "Sure. I'm smart. Saw it plenty. Just didn't *notice*."

Vindi got down on hands and knees and scooted into the tunnel. I yanked myself free of the thorns and got down to follow her, Dakar coming right behind. It was a weird and winding path we followed, bright and green and with curliqued tendrils whirling away on all sides. Suddenly we reached a clearing. About half a dozen men and women sat cross-legged on large boulders, gazing serenely into the distance. An equal number of somewhat younger people sat on the ground at their feet, fidgeting and scratching and trying not to look sullen.

"Are… um… are you a sage?" I asked a woman who appeared to be floating a hair's-breadth above her boulder perch.

"I am Mari," she said, her voice somehow distant and yet pure.

"And you're a sage?"

"I have spent a lifetime and more devoting myself to quiet contemplation, deep meditation, and pure thought. Some small wisdoms may have found me. And some insights. Your efforts to find the wizard will fail. I have seen this. Those you have sent to look will not find him."

"Then where is he?" Vindi said excitedly. Mari just sat there, looking elevated and inspired and all that crap.

"Maybe I should try slapping *her*," I mused.

"It wouldn't help," said the middle-aged man sitting at her feet. "Tarik," he said, introducing himself. "Apprentice sage. I meditate. I think. I contemplate. Not that it does me any good," he said scowling. "Bunch of serene bastards. Some day I'm going to set them all on fire and see what happens." He shook his fist at the sky. "Damn you, gods! See what you're doing to me? You could prevent this, you know. All you have to do is let me transcend utterly. One instant of pure oneness with the universe, that's all I ask. One!"

"We need to know where the wizard Darshik is," Vindi asked Mari. "Can you… I don't know, cast a spell and locate him for us?"

"I have no magic," Mari said calmly. "I merely extrapolate

small truths from what I know about the world. Certain things inevitably imply other things. As thunder proclaims the rain, so does every detail about you proclaim the wizard that your helpers seek, but will not find."

"So extrapolate where he is *now*," I suggested darkly, taking a menacing step toward the sage.

"I wouldn't try it," Tarik said sadly. "Ultimate knowledge makes a person curiously good at keeping from being drowned in a great big bowl of soup. Believe me. I know."

I took another step toward Mari. She dropped a rounded betel nut on the ground, which, of course, given my luck, I promptly stepped on. To my credit, I wheeled my arms and didn't fall down. To my debit, I forgot about the vines just overhead and ended up swiping my hands across an unbroken carpet of thorns and burrs.

"AAAARGH!"

"I warned you," Tarik said, smirking.

"Please help us," Vindi begged the sage. "Please. If you know as much as you say, you must know how important this is."

Mari just sat on her rock, utterly transcendent, above and beyond all things. Vindi glanced at Prince Dakar.

"Dakar? Help?"

"Some folks think that a talking dog would be an exciting thing to stumble upon," he said. "I think it depends on what the dog says. What if it just yelled discouraging things at you all day long? Talking, in a dog, by its nature, is *unusual*. But that doesn't make it *valuable*."

Vindi frowned. "We should stick... her head... in a dog?"

Mari smiled down at us. "I would, of course, be happy to lead your Advisory Council—"

"No," I mused. "I really don't think we want you. We're dealing with real problems in the real world. We don't need people who've spent their whole lives doing their absolute best to leave the world behind. Come on," I said to Vindi. "Let's get the hell out of here."

"I will send messages to your Council," Mari said placidly. "You will heed them. I have foreseen this."

"Isn't she annoying?" Tarik said conversationally. "I keep waiting for her to get so serene that she wouldn't even notice me sneaking up on her with a head-sized sack and a *lot* of cumin. Sadly, we haven't gotten to that point yet. I know *I'd* be a hell of a lot more enlightened if she weren't always saying spooky-but-inevitably-true crap like that." He seemed to realize something. "It's *her* fault I'm not a sage yet!"

"You think you *deserve* it?" I said, astonished.

"I've worked really, really hard," he said defensively.

"Which does nothing to answer my question."

"Your searchers will fail," Mari said faintly, "but *you* need not. Two roads stretch before you. Take the one garlanded with flowers."

"Whatever, crazy. Come on, Vindi. Come on, Dakar."

"Also," Mari said, "I *would* tell you to watch your step, except that doing so, I anticipate, would make things even worse when my words distracted you and you fell in at just the right angle to break your arm. Thus, I will *not* warn you. You're welcome."

"What?" I said, baffled.

"Precisely."

I turned to leave. The sages did nothing to stop us. I'm not sure they even noticed we existed. Their apprentices… well, thinking about them and what they'd done with their lives made me sad. Staring resolutely ahead, I decided to just not to think about any of them. Which worked fine, right up until I fell down that sinkhole.

* * *

We'd hardly started toward the East Quarter when a lanky boy in torn trousers ran up to us, looking addled.

"You're the ones that hired us?" he said, panting for breath. "Jebiam said to tell you… no luck. Nothing. And we've looked everywhere. We'll keep trying, but…" Seeing the dire expression on Vindi's face, he gulped and ran off.

"Give it time," I murmured.

"We don't *have* time."

"Vindi…"

"Saraya."

"Dakar!" Dakar said, patting himself on the head.

"Saraya… what do we do? What do we *do*? The whole East Quarter thing, it's not working." Vindi paced back and forth, her eyes strangely bright. "I managed to keep from screaming… barely… because we were *doing* something. Making progress. No matter how slow or indirect, we were *doing* something to help my father. It's over. We should go home."

"It's *my* fault," I said sadly.

"For once, blaming you isn't going to make me feel better." Vindi paused. "I'm still going to do it, mind you. But until we *accomplish* something…"

"No. I'm serious. It's my fault. Any side I'm on loses. It's just what happens. Throw me down a pit and carry on by yourself. I guarantee everything will go much smoother."

"I'm not going to do that," Vindi said gently.

"Thank you."

"Pits are too messy. I was thinking of bashing you over the head with a huge boulder of honey-infused hard-candy. You know, so at least you could die a delicious death."

"*Someone's* been reading my dream journal!"

"But until I can afford a piece of candy that big, you're just going to have to stay alive," Vindi decided. "Come on. I don't know what good it'll do us, but we're going to have a talk with Jebiam. If *he* can't help us, well, maybe it's time to go home and have another look at those soldiers."

"Maybe it is," I agreed.

We headed back toward the East Quarter, though our path was neither fast nor easy. Dakar wanted to look at everything, and tended to wander off in unexpected directions despite our best efforts to cajole him along. Vindi's mouth grew thinner and thinner as we took one wrong turn after another, and I was concerned that she'd lose what patience she had and abandon Dakar and me to our fate. Fortunately, she wasn't quite there. Not yet.

The street we were following ended, splitting in two directions. The east branch, the one we needed to take, looked normal. The west branch, which headed in precisely the wrong direction, had piles of smashed and dying flowers heaped along the sides. I stopped, staring at them. Mari the Sage had said to "take the road garlanded with flowers"—but how much did I want to trust her?

"Saraya?" Vindi said uncertainly.

"I'm going west. Do what you need to do."

Vindi grimaced. "I don't suppose it'll hurt. What's a little *more* time while my father desperately gasps for breath?"

We headed down the flower-infested street. Before long, we came upon a large, boisterous wedding. Well, that explained the flowers. They'd gone out of their way to observe every tired old tradition you could think of: Women chased down the bride, tackled her to the ground, and strapped tiny cones (which focus good luck) to every part of her body. The groom, coming to her defense, was captured by the men of the party and forced to try on cones of various sizes as if they were hats. Afterward, children took turns bashing the cones with sticks, most of them splitting open to spill out clay spiders and lizards and vermin, until they found the lucky cone which contained candy and prizes and was therefore the correct size to assure a prosperous marriage. The wedding party mobbed the young couple, ostensibly pasting the broken cone back together, but actually pelting the two of them with every color of paint-powder they could find. Yawn. Wake me up when something *interesting* happens.

"…isn't Damas in want of an apprentice?" said a cheerfully moon-faced old grandmother, holding court among a large number of men and women.

"He is. And my daughter, why, she has three sons too many! If he took on one of them…"

"No," the old grandmother said thoughtfully. "Damas thinks a little too much of himself, he does. Let him struggle on his own for a while. Let strife carry him to maturity."

The others nodded, accepting her judgement. A dour-faced woman raised her hand.

"My daughter's taken it into her head that she'll marry for love…"

"So let her," the old grandmother said. "But help her find work in the shop of your preferred choice. Demand everything and you'll get nothing; but give her an invisible push in the right direction, and who knows what might happen."

I snapped my fingers. "That's it! The final piece! The Advisory Council has scholars, sages, and community leaders. What's the one thing we *don't* have? The earthy wisdom of matriarchs and patriarchs who've taken on all of the squabbling, vexatious, disagreeable people who call themselves 'a family' and guided them to a better place, with nothing but words and wisdom for weapons!"

"We don't have *time*," Vindi said tightly.

"But Vindi! I'm saving the world!"

"Get her name, then. You can look her up later."

The old grandmother hadn't missed a word of our exchange, watching us with curious eyes.

"Name's Obara, though I don't know if I should be admitting it so freely," she said, throwing her head back with a laugh. "They're still looking for me in Bas, they are, for excessive drunkenness and criminal perversion. What's this all about, and with *him* wearing a royal signet ring, no less? Should I be worried? Should I hop on my grandson's shoulders and yell at him to start running?"

"See, what's happening is that I'm putting together a panel to advise Princess Shivaka…" I went through the whole thing. Obara listened closely, nodding once or twice.

"I'm busier than busy," she finally said, "but for something as important as that, yes, I could make the time. I know some others you should consider, too. They're almost as smart as I am! What's the matter with her?" she asked, indicating Vindi. Vindi was hopping from foot to foot, making odd little sizzling noises as she seethed with impatience.

"It's about her father…" Something about Obara's wide-open, sympathetic face made her a very good listener, and I found myself telling her the whole story, even as Vindi started to look like she was moments from exploding.

Obara nodded thoughtfully. "And these soldiers, do they know what your house looks like, or did they just park themselves around that big black bubble and start shouting at it?"

"What does *that* matter!" Vindi cried.

"Wait until nightfall and then *move* the black bubble. The soldiers won't even realize your house is no longer protected. They'll just position themselves around the bubble and shout at it, never knowing it contains precisely nothing."

Vindi and I exchanged awed glances.

"She's right," Vindi said. "I mean, it's an awful risk to take… if someone came along who *did* know what our house looked like, it would all be over. But if they *didn't*, we could hide in plain sight!"

Without another word, Vindi took off running, heading toward the distant hulk of the Grand Emporium, the landmark that would lead us home. I stayed long enough to get Obara's address, and had her send a messenger to Jebiam telling him he could call off his search. Then I took Dakar by the hand and set off after Vindi.

* * *

Getting out of bed the next morning wasn't hard. Not when, after helping move the force-shield the previous night, I'd flumped my head down on my pillow with the precise force required to get a mosquito STUCK IN MY EAR. The wretched thing hummed its delightfully horrible lullaby directly into my skull all night long at unpredictable intervals. All… night… long. I got some sleep. I think. Some of the more vivid "dreams" may have been hallucinations.

"Burn all mosquitos," I said, holding my knees and rocking

back and forth as Vindi joined me at the breakfast table. "Burn them. Burn them all. Burn them with fire."

"Saraya…" She glanced at me, stifling a yawn. "Should I ask why there's so much jam in your left ear?"

"In the dark, I couldn't tell that the knife wasn't clean. To hell with mosquitos. Fire will cleanse them. Fire will make them pure."

"So—" Vindi paused as Prince Dakar joined us, wearing the same clothes as he had the previous day.

"I must compliment the tailors for so cleverly imitating my last outfit," he mused. "They even got the stains right!"

Someone else came through the door. Vindi and I stood at the same moment. Avashti wasn't red-faced, wasn't coughing, wasn't sweating. He looked fine. I looked out the window. Sure enough, the ring of soldiers was still shouting commands at the faceless black bubble, unaware that it had moved.

"Dad—"

"She's kidding," the wizard assured Dakar. "We all know that wizards don't have families. She's the result of a demented breeding experiment which unexpectedly produced a sphinx with the head, body, arms and legs of a young woman. She's not very good at riddles, either."

"I love you," Vindi said, hugging her father.

"See? Not enough clues. I think the answer is 'walnuts wearing party hats', but it's impossible to be sure."

"I love you, too," I said, hugging them both.

"Now *that's* just obtuse."

"I'm part of this!" Dakar said, hugging all three of us. "See? I am loved. I am. No one can question that."

Avashti finally fought his way free—though he didn't fight too hard, I noticed—a hint of a smile touching his face.

"Thank you for saving me," he told his daughter. He glanced at me. "Knowing your luck, I'll say 'thank you for *trying*'." He glanced at Dakar. "Thank you for reminding us all that love is awkward, weird, and inconvenient, and involves total strangers squeezing us for no reason while saying disturbing things."

"I'm helping!"

"And now that I can finally concentrate again, I need to finish my work," Avashti said. He gave his head a little shake. "So many years I spent striving for perfection, and now I have no *time*…"

"Yeah!" Vindi said. "Fly up there and improvise!"

"An approach which, indeed, is fit for idiots and the mentally deficient," Avashti said gently. "The key, I think, is to gather everything one knows and everything one has learned, and do your best... for a time. The work will never be perfect, but at some point, it'll be *good enough*. Instead of wasting two *years* trying for perfection, do something good-enough, and then spend two *months* fixing the problems it causes."

"That's the spirit!" Vindi said cheerfully. "Can I watch?"

Avashti shrugged. "I suppose. If you keep quiet. Saraya, given your penchant for suddenly exploding, I'm afraid I have to bar *you* from the laboratory."

"That's all right," I said, shrugging. "I still have to work out the details of my Advisory Council idea before I present it to Princess Shivaka."

"Let me read the letter before you send it," Vindi suggested. "Wait. Better yet, let me *write* it. I don't know what it is with you and papyrus that leads to wanton and excessive paper-cuts, but I don't think she'll be impressed if your letter is just a bunch of faceless red sheets drenched in blood."

"I don't know that I want to be sending a letter," I mused. "Shivaka might be more inclined to listen if I presented the Council to her in person."

"Don't," Vindi said somberly. "I'll tell you a secret... I like her, too, and not just because she's orbited by actual real-life Handsome Princes panting eagerly at the prospect of bumping into a nobody like me and proposing marriage to her on the spot... but Princess Shivaka, she's a little too quick to 'do what she has to do', no matter what it means to the people who get in her way. She might think your Advisory Council is a good idea. But what if she doesn't? Don't take that kind of risk. We need you."

"Eh," Avashti said, his hand wavering.

"Stay here, where it's safe," Vindi said, clutching my arm. "We'll send a letter, you and I. I promise. Which you'll dictate and I'll write, so as to avoid all the drama with the paper-cuts."

"I don't know what all the fuss is about. It hardly even hurt, last time. Well, until all those lemon slices fell on me."

"Stay," Vindi said. Gazing at me for a long while, she finally followed Avashti up to his laboratory.

* * *

Have you ever had an idea you just couldn't get out of your

216

head? My morning was a lot like that, except that I finally got the mosquito by means of repeated stabbing. Then I could focus on my Advisory Council idea. A letter… a letter would be too easy to ignore. I had to *show* my idea to her. Sure, her efforts to force Avashti out of his tower by using his own lethal allergies against him weren't a great look, but we work with what we have. My mind made up, I stole money from Avashti's secret cache, then went outside and hired a bunch of local kids to carry messages for me. That done, I went back in and gathered what I needed for a trip across town. My pack immediately ripped, of course, spilling everything on the floor. If anything, I was amused by how lazy and inept the universe was getting. Really? That's the best you can do? You couldn't even wait for me to be six miles out, with nowhere to put my stuff and no way to carry it all?

Shrugging, I took Dakar by the hand and headed out on foot, figuring I'd simply get what I needed along the way. It was actually a fine day for a walk. Not looking so clever now, huh, Fate? Once I got thirsty, good luck making the Kairay river disappear.

As it happened, the river was right where it was supposed to be —but cottony seeds covered the surface, which had caused a massive fish kill, which made the whole river smell like a choice slice of fermented vomit. Maybe the universe wasn't losing its touch, after all.

It was late morning when we arrived at the Lair of Lapis—or rather, the great stone gate piercing the towering hedge that surrounded it. I was extremely pleased to see that the messages I'd sent had worked: My entire Advisory Council (except for the sages) were waiting outside the gate, their expressions ranging from frank curiosity to abject terror. I led them and Dakar up to the gate, where a bored-looking soldier sat with his nose in a book.

"Names?" he asked without looking up.

"Saraya Sindahar and Prince Dakar, plus guests."

"Your purpose in— Wait. Really?" He stared at Dakar, amazed. "Everyone's been looking for you, my lord!"

"Really?" Dakar asked, vitally interested. "That would seem to have been your first mistake. If you never start looking for something, it never counts as 'lost'. At the very least, I've been where I am. Why didn't you start by looking there?"

"You'll be escorted in immediately, of course—"

"What about me? And my Advisory Council?" I asked eagerly.

The guard glanced at a list of written instructions. "Well… yes, of course. You'll all be shown in."

He blew six piercing blasts on a whistle. Six pairs of soldiers appeared. They took up positions on either side of our group, swiftly guiding us across the grounds and to the Lair of Lapis. It hadn't rained, but the palace was wet—who had the chore of washing it, and how often?—and its gemlike gleam was even more breathtaking now that it looked like a shimmering fairy vision, a glowing daydream of treasure made real. We were handed off to a gang of palace guards. Dakar was led off in one direction, while my Council and I were taken in another.

We climbed three flights of stairs and arrived at what I'm assuming was a strategic map room. It didn't have anything so plebeian as sheets of paper spread out over tables: Instead, someone must have been tasked with hauling dirt and stone, moss and clay all the way up to the fourth floor so that artisans could sculpt a hundred-foot-wide miniature of the entire area. I think the most impressive parts were the actual working rivers.

"Saraya!" Princess Shivaka cried, waving happily at me. She hopped lightly over the winding, muddy serpent of the Kairay, trailing advisors as she came to grasp both my arms. "I suppose you're not too happy to see me," she said, her face falling. "I can't say that I blame you. What I did to you… I'm not proud of it. I never want to get inured to that kind of pain. Someday, I hope, you'll look at the thousands upon thousands who've been made happy and whole by your sacrifice, and you'll come to forgive me."

"That's actually what—" Coming out a nowhere, a bat flew into my open mouth. Gagging loudly, I finally managed to spit it out. It smacked wetly into Shivaka's gown, bending a plain twist of gold into a gorgeous and amazing artwork.

"That's actually what I'm here about," I said, gesturing to the Advisory Council, most of whom were huddled together and staring wide-eyed at their surroundings. "I couldn't stop thinking about what you said earlier. You don't need any more *war* advisors, do you? Every idiot with more fat than brains thinks he knows how to best throw away the lives of other peoples' children. No. You need *life* advisors, and that's what I've brought. Allow me to introduce them…"

I went through the roster of scholars, community leaders, venerated patriarchs/matriarchs, and sages (or the notes they'd sent, since none of them had bothered to show up in person). Shivaka nodded, smiling and greeting each person by name.

"I'm glad you came to me," she told me. "It's amazing, seeing how selflessly you're working to help others, when you could have gotten sullen and angry and obsessed with revenge. I'll say it: I'm impressed."

I shrugged. "When you trip over a bug and fall face-first into donkey dung, beating up the bug is a waste of time. So is trying to insert a plug into every donkey in Kairay, for that matter. I speak from experience. What matters is what you do *now*." I smiled at Princess Shivaka. "You can help a lot of people in a lot of ways. All you need is a panel of advisors to help you figure out how."

"It's really quite inspiring, how selfless you are," Princess Shivaka said warmly. "Would you like a reward? A government pension, perhaps?"

"Pass," I said. "They'd end up screwing up the paperwork and accidentally establishing a fund to compensate the owners of dogs that happened to bite me. Which, perversely, would provide motivation for dog owners to make *sure* it happened."

"Well, if you're certain," Princess Shivaka said, shrugging. "Thank you so much for bringing them! I wish I could use your idea, I really do, but it just doesn't work for me."

"What?" I said, astonished.

"Your Advisory Council. I'm not going to use it."

"But… why not?" I asked. "You have advisors for literally everything else. Well. *Almost* everything else. I hope." I looked appraisingly at her. "Do you have an Advisor of Going-To-The-Latrine?"

"Are you asking for a job?" she asked archly. "For what it's worth, I think you'd be good at it."

"Just my luck," I said drily.

"It's really quite simple," she said. "I seized power for one reason: I know better than those who held power before me. I can do good where they would have reached for personal gain. Now you're asking me to throw that away, to obey others and give up everything I worked so hard to accomplish."

"Not *obey*," I said patiently. "I'm asking you to listen. To consider. To choose the best ideas, which could well be yours if yours are best, and implement only what you choose. Get *advice*. You do know how advisors work, don't you? Or if I took that Advisor of

Going-To-The-Latrine job and told you what to do on your pillow before you went to sleep, would you feel compelled to obey?”

“I’m sorry,” Princess Shivaka said, “but you really are going to have to trust that I know best. Give it time. I think you’ll be pleased with the results.” She turned to the soldiers that still surrounded my Advisory Council. “Show them out. Oh, and do see that they’re paid for their time, will you?” Princess Shivaka glanced at me, smiling. “No, no, *you* stay. I’m afraid I have to imprison you. Please don’t take it personally.”

“*What*?”

“I hope and trust you’ll understand,” she said. “If not today, then someday. Your imprisonment won’t last long. Given my luck, you’ll bring me what I *actually* want sooner rather than later.”

The Advisory Council was shown out. A pair of soldiers came up on either side of me and grabbed my arms. I glared at Princess Shivaka. She refused to meet my eyes, her cheeks coloring slightly. So she was capable of shame. Good to know.

“Listen—” I said desperately. Just then, I heard two sets of footsteps coming down the hallway outside. One of the two whispered to the other, and my heart stopped. It was Vindi.

“…amazing that we’ve gotten so far so easily… and look, the door’s not even guarded…”

“STOP!” I bellowed. “DON’T COME IN! IT’S A TRAP!”

With a bang and a flash, Vindi leapt inside, followed closely by Avashti.

“Ah-HA! We’ve come to rescue… uh, you?” She stopped, seeing Shivaka and her dozen or so guards for the first time.

“Avashti,” Princess Shivaka said pleasantly, walking over to put her hand on the wizard’s arm. “How lucky that *you* chose to come to *me*. Darshik says you can make me even luckier than I am now. Perhaps you’d like to volunteer to make the attempt?”

“And what if I don’t?” he said guardedly.

“Why, that’s your right, isn’t it? I’m not a monster.” Princess Shivaka sighed. “My sister-in-law Gamal, on the other hand, has all *sorts* of commands she’d like to give you. I wouldn’t like it,” she said regretfully, “but neither would I stop her.”

“Torturing me with my own allergies? Bah. If I die, you get nothing,” Avashti said sullenly. “Try again.”

Princess Shivaka looked deeply regretful. “Need I remind you that I also have Vindi and Saraya in custody? I have no idea what

Gamal might want to do to them. I don't even like to think about it. But neither would I stop her."

"DON'T LISTEN TO HER!" Vindi shouted. "DON'T DO IT!"

Avashti gazed evenly at both of us. "I think… I think I'd like to volunteer. Yes. If you promise to release us all, afterward."

"Very well. Take him to Darshik's chambers," Princess Shivaka commanded. "Tell Darshik to watch him *very* carefully. Try anything, wizard, anything at all, and I'll turn my back while Gamal has a visit with your girls."

I didn't see what happened next: At Shivaka's gesture, the guards dragged Vindi and myself through the Lair of Lapis, out across the grounds, and finally threw us on the ground outside of the gate.

"Their names are to be stricken from the list," the guard with the most medals said. "They are not to be allowed inside again."

We stayed just outside the gate, unable to get back in but unwilling to leave. Several times I felt weird pulses of hot and cold and a tingling, prickling sensation that swept across my skin, but it always fled before I could be sure that something was actually happening. Finally, as the sky began to dim, Avashti was escorted out to us, looking dead tired. Vindi and I grabbed him by the arms, earning odd looks from the guards as we escorted him away from the Lair of Lapis.

"What happened?" Vindi demanded.

"I made Princess Shivaka's luck better," he said simply, "and Saraya's worse. With any luck… pardon the phrase… the universe will now do *anything*, no matter how ridiculously unlikely, to punish Saraya in the short term." He glanced at me. "The question is, what do you mean to *do* with this power?"

"We're taking her down," I said quietly. "Shivaka dismissed my Advisory Council. She threatened Vindi. She threatened all of us. No. This ends now."

"What can we do?" Vindi asked. "You said it yourself. Any side you're on loses. How can we beat *her*?"

"Any side I'm on loses," I said slowly. "It's obvious, isn't it?"

"What?"

I grinned, thumping my hand to my chest. "I've got to take *Shivaka's* side. Congratulations. Reach out and shake my hand! You've just met the woman who's going to conquer the world and give Shivaka everything she ever wanted!"

Looking stunned, Vindi reached out and shook my hand. Avashti snorted.

"Great plan," he said, and he didn't even sound like he was being cynical. "So what do we do first?"

X

Vindi, Avashti and I crouched under some bushes just across the road from the Lair of Lapis (or, at least, the great hedge surrounding it). The gate guards didn't pay us any attention, which was fine with me. Considering the messages I'd sent, things weren't going to stay calm for long.

"I still don't think this is a good idea," Vindi said nervously. "When have any of us shown an ability to actually succeed with a crazy plan? When I was captured and held in The Universe In A Nutshell, you came for me…"

"And failed."

"When *you* were captured and held in the Lair of Lapis, we came for you…"

"And failed."

"Exactly. We're not good at this. When things go wrong— and how could they *not*—you're going to get hurt, bad."

"You just have to look on the bright side," I said maliciously.

"Using my own words against me?" Saraya said, amused. "Let's see who has a higher tolererance for syrupy mush, shall we? Ahem. 'Act with purpose and love, and the world will follow'!"

"Quit it!"

"Make me!"

"AVASHTI!!"

"Girls, girls," he said tiredly. "We have a plan to oversee. A stupid, complicated, ridiculous plan. Honestly, if you're so keen on getting Prince Dakar's attention, just truss up a plover, paint the word 'insouciance' on it, and fling it over the hedge with a catapult. Odds are he'll find it sooner or later."

"We need him, and we need him now. You know why."

Avashti grumbled under his breath, but didn't contradict me. We knew exactly what Princess Shivaka was up to, since a military operation of that size could hardly be concealed: As stupid as it seemed, she'd sent her entire army across the desert to attack Naiber. Naiber was a fine target—big and rich, with numerous ports on the ocean—except that its army was ten times bigger that Kairay's, with the added benefit that they got to stay at home instead of stretching their supply lines across an entire desert. I'd have called Shivaka a raving lunatic if she weren't blessed with the sort of luck that would let her stub her toe, but only if she tripped over a magic wish-giving djinni.

"If I want to win this war for Princess Shivaka," I said, "I need two things: I need to beat her to Naiber, and I need the authority to run things once I get there. Prince Dakar can help with the second part. No one there has the authority to question his commands—nor will they, until Shivaka arrives. If I tell him what to say, and he says it, I can command our entire army!"

"And he'll fall in line and do what you say?" Avashti said dubiously.

"That's what I intend to find out. And it starts by testing this 'so bad it's good' luck you've been boasting about."

"That's it," Avashti said, getting up. "I'm leaving before the stabbing starts."

"Don't you dare!" Vindi said warmly. "Real friends would be *first* in line to stab Saraya!"

"What?" I demanded.

"Well, look at your luck. You're going to be stabbed. It's inevitable. The only question is by whom: Strangers who take it seriously, or friends who'll do their best to stab you *less*."

"Yeah, that's about what I've come to expect in life," I said wryly. Rolling his eyes, Avashti crouched down next to us. As he did so, a bright, pulsing light caught my eye. I glanced up. The firecat had been following us for hours, floating serenely across half of Kairay despite my best efforts to disbelieve it.

"Um… Vindi?" I said. "Just a suggestion, but could you send Pinky away? Getting hit by lightning isn't part of my plan, which means it'll be the first, second, and third thing that happens to me."

She glanced up. The firecat hovered twenty feet overhead like an especially menacing grapefruit, showing absolutely no inclination to leave.

"Shoo!" she said, flicking her fingers at it. "Get! Whoosh!"

Pinky drifted down until it was a mere ten feet overhead.

Vindi turned her palms up in surrender. I edged around to her other side, trying in my debonair and casual way to hide behind Avashti. He snorted and shoved me back under Pinky.

The gate guards suddenly straightened up. Coming down the dusty road, at long last, were the people my latest messages had summoned. There were shabbily dressed folks from the East Quarter, each hauling a bucket. There were fresh-faced young women, convinced by their family matriarchs to seek a love match by hauling heavy scaffolding on their backs (I would have loved to overhear *that* conversation). Following them as moths follow the moon, there came dozens of love-struck young men, bearing heavy packs of their own. I smiled and walked directly out in front of the gate. One of the girls offered me a crystal rim which had been donated by Obara herself. I shuddered, but forced myself to take the wretched thing.

"What's going on?" the guard demanded.

"This fell off of Princess Gamal's dress," I said, showing him the crystal rim. "She declared that no one—*no one*—save her could touch it until and unless she came back for it. I decided to brave her wrath and attempt to return it for a reward."

He looked on in puzzlement as Vindi and Avashti directed my helpers, guiding them in the construction of a rickety scaffolding all around me. On top of the scaffolding were balanced tippy troughs. The East Quarter folks dumped their buckets out into them, buckets filled from the nastiest, smelliest parts of the Kairay river. Vindi took the crystal rim and tied it to a pull-string, leaving it dangling in front of my face. One pull, and I would be doused in fifty gallons of incomprehensible fetor, starting with a stinking slime of human refuse and ending with the vomit I'd inevitably contribute if I had to smell that stuff close up.

"Any of you fine, upstanding soldiers want to make a grab at this crystal rim?" I asked playfully.

The guard scowled at me. "You know we can't touch that thing. No one can. Not if Princess Gamal expressly forbid it."

"No one here has the authority to subject me to the ultimate humiliation and punishment? No one at all? You mean there's no possible way I could be doused in shit?"

"We could pull the string itself," he suggested. "Or we could throw rocks at the troughs. We don't *have* to touch the crystal rim."

"Oh," I said, trying not to show how badly his words had shaken me. "But... would Princess Gamal *believe* you when you claimed that you didn't touch it?"

The soldier stroked his neck, perhaps imagining what it would be like to have it cut in half. "I… ah… she *might*?"

"Ha. You know the answer as well as I do. So it seems I'm completely safe!"

The guard gazed at the troughs, possibly trying to tip them over with willpower alone. "We can't send for Princess Shivaka or Princess Gamal," he reluctantly admitted. "They've already departed on the Naiber campaign. Her Lordship, Shavala II, is at her holiday estate. The only person here who could touch it is Prince Dakar."

"Too bad," I said, gesturing to my helpers. Under Vindi and Avashti's direction, they quickly built a second set of scaffolding next to the first. The young men filled the troughs from their packs, piling in rotten eggs, pustulant meat weeping with slime and maggots, and milk curdled to the point of being a chunky, squishy semi-solid.

"Boy, I sure hope the one and only person with the authority to touch this crystal rim doesn't show up," I said loudly. "That would sure be some bad luck, wouldn't it?"

A butterfly fluttered down and landed on one of the troughs, which started to tip. Vindi sprang forward and grabbed the splintering wood. A bird landed on the trough opposite it, which also started to tip. Avashti sighed, rubbed his nose, and finally stepped forward to steady it moments before I would have been doused.

"It's not working," Avashti murmured.

"Build the last set of troughs," I commanded. "Fill them."

Vindi stared at me. "Saraya, no!"

"Do it!"

My helpers jumped to obey while Vindi reluctantly directed them. The last set of troughs was filled with a fine mix of old knives, rusty nails, and broken glass. Avashti cautiously released his trough and stepped away, pulling Vindi with him. I waited where I was, my smile growing progressively stiffer and stiffer. Something should have happened by now. Why wasn't it working?

"It figures," I said darkly. "You know what a plan is? It's a way to get my hopes up, so that the subsequent litany of failures will hurt all the more. This isn't going to work. It was never going to work. It… um?"

A cloaked figure dragged itself toward us, walking with a lurching sideways gait and taking great care to always face left. It carried a strange device, like a dozen crossbows all braided together.

As it neared, the hood of its cloak fell slightly askew. A rotating orb of fool's gold "looked" back at us. Guards stared. My helpers took a step back, amazed.

"Adversary?" Vindi said, astonished.

"Archon," it replied in that odd and musical voice. "Unless your mis-identification was intentional and meant to engender amusement? Evaluating. Uncertain. Best to cover all bases." Archon threw its head back and screamed with laughter, which snapped off instantly as it looked back at her. "Permit me to explain. A kite, by chance, blew into my cave. By further chance, it tangled itself into the shape of a woman being bitten by an alligator as she tried to use the privy, which reminded me of Saraya. A grain of sand slipped into my gears as I calculated the odds that I was missing something by not seeing the world. Oddly, the answer this time came out to ninety-six percent, when it had always previously been zero-point-three. Of course, I would never violate the sanctity of my position by abandoning it…"

"…but I would," Archon said smoothly as the mechanism turned to the right. "See this?" it said, hefting the weird device it was carrying. "Wizard weapon. They call it The End Of Fate. Blasted my way out with it. I'm eager to experience all of the sins you promised me, now that I'm here. I… oops."

Adversary stumbled on a rotten egg and The End Of Fate went off. There was a sound like the world's largest lute being plucked, and a shadow the size of a small house arrowed toward the Lair of Lapis. Where it passed, the earth was thrown twenty feet in the air. A slot was blown in the hedge, and a great rip tore itself across the manicured grounds. The shadow slammed into the Lair of Lapis itself: Stone peeled away like water, collapsing to earth with a vast rolling thunder. The damage didn't go deep, but the Lair of Lapis was left with a vast cleft sliced all the way down its face.

"What's this?" Prince Dakar peered out from the second floor. "Ah! My friends have come to see me!" He slid down the piled rubble and ran straight toward us, his face alight with joy. I winced and braced myself, knowing what was coming as he reached us. The crystal rim dangled just in front of my face. One tug was all it would take…

"What's this?" Prince Dakar said, fascinated, as he reached up and started to pull one of the troughs toward himself. "Is there something inside of it? Ooh! Is it prizes?"

"NO!!" I bellowed, throwing myself at him. I knocked Dakar out of the way just as the trough tipped, dumping a steaming cataract of foulness and slime over my head.

"How unfortunate," he mused, reaching toward a second trough. "Still, I bet *this* one has candy!"

"STOP!!"

I grabbed the trough, yanking it away from him—but I overshot and pulled it too far the other way, dumping an unholy stew of maggots and meat over my head. Prince Dakar raced from trough to trough, absolutely certain that *one* of them must contain something wonderful. I raced after him, wrestling trough after trough away from him and dumping one indescribable horror after another over my own head. Rancid, lumpy milk splattered my hair. Broken glass poured down my back. Fetid eggs smashed open and ran into my eyes. At long last it was done. The crystal rim hung exactly where I'd left it, untouched.

"If this is how the world is, I don't like it," Archon noted, looking me up and down. "What a strange and disorganized place, where people apparently bathe in sewage for no adequately explained reason. What do you think?" It turned, becoming Adversary. "The level of sin on display may be awe-inspiring, but it isn't *fun*. I don't like it," Adversary admitted, then turned to become Archon again. "It had best be admired, perhaps, at a distance. Shall we go home, and blast the tunnel shut behind us?" It turned again. "Officially, for the record, I'm going to say 'No—let's stay!' That way, I can call you a coward with a straight face after we go home." "I can accept that."

"Take care!" Vindi shouted, waving wildly and blowing kisses with both hands. Archon/Adversary waved back, then shuffled away toward its cave. The gate guards, glancing dubiously at one another, stayed where they were. My helpers, seeing that the show was over, drifted away toward their respective homes. Trying (and failing) to wipe off some of the gunk that covered me, I smiled at Prince Dakar. Bad move. Some of it got in my *mouth*.

"We need your help," I told him. "Your wife, Princess Shivaka, means well but is doing ill by conquering everything and helping no one. We mean to take away her charmed luck. We mean to force her to stay here, in Kairay, and deal with things that actually *matter*…"

I explained the broad outline of our plan while Dakar listened attentively. Vindi tried to shoo Pinky away, which only seemed to draw the firecat closer. Avashti frowned thoughtfully.

"Saraya," he told me, "you know Dakar doesn't understand you, right? *Tell* him what to do. Give him a choice, and you risk losing everything."

I smiled tightly. "Maybe I should. But people have been using him for years. I won't be one of them. Let him decide for himself, as best he can."

"Be reasonable. The *world* is at stake. What if he decides that he wants magic fairies to turn him into a gigantic cake?"

"Such is life."

"I'm not sure I followed everything you said," Dakar told me, "but you *are* my friend. Yes. This I know. Whatever it is you need, I will help you. Also, I would like to eat this giant cake you speak of."

"Huh," Avashti said, puzzled. "Did you just have a moment of *good* luck?"

"What?" Vindi said, craning her neck to stare at me. "Is that even *possible*?"

In her distraction, Vindi lost control of Pinky. The firecat drifted straight toward the quasi-silver bracelet that was fused to my left wrist, and which had developed a positive talent for channeling lightning strikes in the most painful way possible.

"Oh, I think everything's about the same as always," I sighed, just before I got hit by lightning. Again.

* * *

The next thing we needed, of course, was to somehow reach Naiber ahead of Princess Shivaka. She had almost a full days' lead on the three-day journey, and she could travel fast since the rest of the army was already there. Fortunately, Prince Dakar had a fresh supply of money, and was happy to spend it however I wanted so long as he got cake. He was puzzled and distressed over the cakes' lack of gigantic-ness until I pointed out, if he held them *right* up to his eye, they'd *look* as big as mountains. Which also meant that he couldn't move them to his mouth without their turning small again, which meant that he stumbled around in circles with cakes pressed to his eyes, railing against the cruel fate that prevented him from actually eating them. So I bought a *third* cake and fed it to him myself. I don't know—maybe I *am* going soft.

As day faded into twilight, the special tent I'd commissioned was finally completed. It was a very unusual tent, in that it had a floor and a much stronger system of internal beams and supports than tents usually boast. In fact, it was so overbuilt that sitting inside it was kind of like sitting inside the joists at a construction site, if the builders were crazy enough to tie everyone down with an excess of strong but flexible rope.

"Do we really need to be tied down?" Vindi asked curiously, pulling her left wrist from her restraints.

"Hey! Get back in there!"

"I was just asking," she said, sticking her wrist back into the bundle of rope.

"Let's review," Avashti said acidly. "We're a day and half behind Shivaka, so—instead of grabbing the fastest horses in the stable and tearing out as if we'd been kicked in the ass by the left foot of the devil himself—"

"Why the left foot?" Vindi wanted to know.

Avashti sighed. "It's a disembodied foot that wanders the land seeking out children who won't eat their vegetables. Don't tell me you haven't heard the stories?"

"You've neglected our education," Vindi accused him. "I think you'd better tell us the story right now. Oh, and do the voices!"

"Yes, do!" Prince Dakar said cheerfully.

"What kind of voice does a disembodied foot have, anyway?"

"ENOUGH!" the wizard roared. "Anyway, as I said, instead of taking off as fast as we could, we spent long hours hiring this weird overbuilt tent made, and then tying ourselves down so we could *lie* in it." He turned to me. "Face it… you'd depending on a series of coincidences so crazy, *no* amount of luck could make them happen."

I shrugged. "We could never catch Shivaka with horses. We need to grab at the moon, however unlikely it is that we'll catch it. Tell me—seen from above, what does this tent look like?"

Avashti gave his head an impatient little shake. "I know, I know. It's grey, with flaps and an imitation trunk and everything Ramla's elephant decoys had. I helped design it, remember? But no rocs have been sighted in Kairay for months."

"I aim to change that." Freeing myself from my own restraints, I walked over and picked up a glass bottle containing half a dozen glowing, furious Leaf Riders. "One of the things Dakar's money bought us. Sniffing the fumes of ruddy-backed Leaf Riders makes people *impressionable*. Whatever they see next, that's going to be in their dreams for days to come. Romantic, sure, when a dopey-in-love couple stares besottedly at each other. Unintentionally disturbing, when they stare besottedly into each other's *eyes*. But what if you sniff the fumes and then see the wrong kind of stuff?" I rested my foot dramatically on a heavy trunk. "Bones and viscera, *days* old, that a friendly butcher hadn't gotten around to throwing out. But they're safely locked up in this heavy trunk, right? It would take a *almost unimaginable, titanic force* to open this and hurl its contents in my face!" I walked over and rested my foot on a second trunk. "Horrible, disturbing, and downright deranged devil masks." I went to a third. "Fireworks. Not disturbing on their own, but their tendency to set me on fire without provocation or warning makes me nervous." I walked to the trunk in the last corner of the tent. "The strangest, ugliest, and most horrible scorpions and millipedes and hornets and render-ants the neighbor kids could catch and stuff in vials. Pretty sweet, huh?"

Avashti struggled against his bonds. "Even if you *do* manage to get a roc to carry us away, how do you mean to steer it?"

"Ah! Remember how I asked you to bring your electro-magnetic apparatus from home? A roc will know to fear pain. If we can attract—and steer!—a firecat, we can steer the roc. It'll be Vindi's job to attract Pinky. It'll be *your* job to steer it."

Vindi brightened. "You mean I'm allowed to think about Pinky, now?"

"I had a pet, once," Prince Dakar said thoughtfully. "At least, I think I did, although I only saw him when it rained. Don't believe what people tell you: Worms are capable of love."

"Firecats," Vindi said, deep in concentration. "So frisky. So floaty. So adorably lethal."

"This is not going to end well," Avashti grimly predicted.

I sat down, wriggled back into my restraints, and waited. And waited. And waited some more. Dakar began to snore gently. Vindi's breathing grew slow and even. I knew I had to get up and shake them all awake, but I was so, so tired. Maybe if I rested my eyes for just a moment…

I woke with a gasp. The tent was aglow with morning's dim light, at least until a shadow the size of the universe passed over it. I jumped up, realizing too late that—while everyone else was still safely tied down—I'd somehow wormed out of my own ropes in my sleep.

"WAIT!" I screamed. A screech echoed down from above with all the authority of a thousand sheets of metal being torn in half. Vindi woke with a snort, looking extremely confused. I started to run toward her. There was a sudden blast of monsoon-force wind, and that colossal shadow again darkened the sky. Talons as broad across as a man pierced the top of the tent. All at once, the tent leapt into the air, slamming me forcefully to the floor: Through a gap in the fabric, I spotted clouds spinning past—*below* us. The other three were now wide awake: Safely tied down, they were able to deal with their predicament by the simple expedient of screaming. Well, that and a *little* bit of vomiting. I, on the other hand, spun around the interior of the tent like a bouncy-ball trapped inside a spinning pegboard. The bottle containing the Leaf Riders flew straight at me. The cork popped off and it slammed into my mouth right as I took a deep, gasping breath. I got a *huge* dose of fumes. Whatever I saw next was going to be in my dreams for *months*. Maybe longer.

"Everything is normal and fine!" I screamed as the tent spun wildly, shaking violently with every flap of the roc's wings. Four heavy trunks flew threw the air, smashed together, and spewed their contents in my face all at once. Screaming… might not have been the best idea. I got stuff in my mouth. *Lots* of it.

"Vindi!" I shouted over the noise and commotion, in between attempts to spit bugs and rancid meat out of my mouth. That might not have been the best idea: The weird rotational forces of the spinning tent caused them to fly right back in. "Firecats. *Firecats*!"

"Yes! Right!" she said numbly. "Pinky. Pinky. Pinky…"

I made a grab for my tie-downs and missed. With a loud ripping sound, the back of the tent tore off. I gasped. The ground was *incredibly* far below us, the Kairay river hardly more than a twisty, glinting line across the desert. The tent tilted and I slid toward that ragged opening, nothing but air between me and an endless plunge to the most spectacular death anyone could ever hope for. I grabbed a joist and it broke. I grabbed a rope and it snapped. I slid helplessly closer and closer to the opening. Eight feet. Six feet. Two. My feet slid off the end, hovering over an endless precipice of empty air. I could see two incredible wings coming down, booming like thunderclaps at the bottom of each stroke.

"VINDI!" I screamed.

"SARAYA!" Avashti shouted, struggling madly against his bonds.

"FIRECATS!" Vindi bellowed, her eyes closed.

"DAKAR!" Prince Dakar happily contributed.

My knees slid over the edge. My hips started to follow. My whole body began to tilt, the wind tugging me inevitably to my doom…

A glowing ball of electricity appeared in the open air behind us. It had to be Pinky, the firecat somehow keeping pace with the legendary bird. There was no question that the roc knew what it was, or at least knew enough to fear the pain of a firecat's sting: The huge bird quickened its pace, turning to head in a more easterly direction, almost the exact opposite of the way we wanted to go. I started to slide over the edge, screamed, and caught the trailing end of a rope.

"VINDI!" I shouted. "MAKE PINKY GO LEFT! UP AND TO THE LEFT!"

"I don't know how!" she cried, her voice shaking.

"I'm a wizard. This is my job," Avashti said in the hushed tone of a man who knew, now, how he was going to die, and had come to terms with it. He slipped one arm out of his restraints, dug into his pack, and came up with a bunch of metal wires and devices. He narrowed his eyes in concentration, nodded, and reached over to begin assembling them around Vindi's head.

"Just keep thinking about Pinky," he told her. "Exactly the same as before. Don't stop."

Whatever he was doing, it seemed to work. The firecat moved up and swung around to the left. The roc went into a short dive—which, thankfully, tilted the tent forward and allowed me to slide back inside, tears of relief streaming down my face. The roc swung around and headed west, taking us exactly the way we wanted to go. See? As long as I'm not involved at all, we can be completely successful!

Or maybe not. A bristling ball of lightning floated into the tent. I stared in disbelief. No, the first one was still there, exactly where Avashti had directed it. Vindi had somehow managed to attract a *second* one.

"Shoo! Go away!" I shouted. The lethal ball of electricity floated toward Vindi, whose eyes were still shut, and Avashti, who was too busy to even notice it. I had only moments before one or both of them died. My words, my commands, meant nothing to the firecat. It was plain bad luck it had shown up at all, but…

Bad luck? I dove at Avashti's pack, grabbed some metal he hadn't used, and hastily jammed it over my head like some demented, spiky crown. The firecat hesitated.

"This isn't gonna be fun," I muttered, sitting down as far away as I could get from the other two. The second firecat hesitated a moment longer, then drifted toward me—and the metal crown I was wearing.

"WAIT!" I shouted, just before the second firecat began orbiting my head and zapping my skull with a rapid-fire series of lightning bolts.

"Is that as fun as it looks?" Dakar asked.

"Glarble," I said, foaming at the mouth.

"I see. Less fun than magic giant cake that somehow puts itself in your mouth when you least expect it. Thank you, by the way. But *more* fun than being covered from head to foot in stinging scorpions. But less fun than being covered from head to foot in *singing* scorpions. Ah, but what about musical scorpions that love to sting people so hard that they scream in harmony? I have to think about this."

Far below, the ground suddenly ended, replaced by a vast sparkly bluish surface. Astonishingly, we'd already reached the ocean —and, from the looks of the huge city at its edge, we'd also reached Naiber.

"Glurg!" I ranted, foam dripping down my neck. "Guh… Avashti! Back and down! Back and down! Land!"

He frowned and bent to his work. Pinky shifted. The roc shifted. As the only one not tied down, I flew bouncing off of the joists again. In the great hole where the back of the tent had been, the whole world spun around until nothing was visible but ocean. We must be heading back toward land. I gulped with relief: At least the tent was tilted safely forward as the roc descended.

Well. So I thought, until the *front* of the tent ripped open, too. Wracked by ceaseless bolts of electricity from the second firecat, twitching and flopping and barking like a dog, I slid helplessly toward the great plunge. Land flashed beneath us, and trees. Individual trees? We were *much* lower than we had been. In fact…

"JUMP!" I bellowed, rolling forward. I fell out of the tent, plummeting through the air for a single breathless moment before I slammed bodily into the ground. The metal crown flew off my head… and landed, quite improbably, on my ass. The second firecat continued to orbit, shocking me with one rapid-fire zap after another.

"Whee!" Saraya shouted, crashing through the many layers of a tree's canopy before landing quite gently on her feet. Prince Dakar did much the same. I didn't see Avashti… at least, not until he crashed down right on top of me.

"Vindi," I managed to groan. "Look. Over there. Goats."

"Goats!" she said, enchanted. With no one left to attract it by thinking about it, the second firecat drifted swiftly off to the east.

I stood, wincing and popping my shoulder back into place. All four of us looked wide-eyed, wind-torn and ragged, but we were basically in one piece.

"I don't believe that worked," Avashti said drily. "In fact, I'm fairly sure it didn't. I'm dead, aren't I?"

"I love you, too," I told him, working my shoulder and looking around. "Well, I'd say we've got a whole day before Shivaka gets here. What say we go and conquer Naiber for the glory of Princess Shivaka?"

"Hooray!" Dakar cried. Avashti shook his head ruefully. Vindi came over and gave me a big hug. All of the stressful and impossible things we'd been through seemed to hit her all at once and she started laughing hysterically. I'm not sure I could have told her to shut up. I was laughing like crazy, too.

* * *

The main bulk of Kairay's army was encamped on a hill just outside of Naiber, awaiting the arrival of their Princess before they began the attack. Naiber was strangely quiet, all its citizens pulled back behind the city walls. The four us of couldn't have looked very imposing as we limped through the army camp, ragged and wind-torn and with hair (in Avashti's case) spiralling simultaneously in about fourteen different directions. I wielded Prince Dakar like a magic talisman, pointing him at anyone who came to stop us or demand our identities. It was both gratifying and amazing to see one blustering soldier after another shrink away, trying desperately to hide behind their own shadows. We finally reached the command platform. Six old men sat around a huge map, each of them weighed down by so many medals and ribbons that a passing god would have assumed they were made of awards and that their flesh was merely an afterthought meant to hold it together.

"Who the hell are you?" demanded Big Mustache.

"Your boss," I replied, pointing Prince Dakar at him. Dakar obligingly showed his signet ring. These men were made of sterner stuff than the officers we'd cowed earlier; they knew who Dakar was, and knew he had no business running a battle campaign. The thing was, none of them had the authority to overrule him.

"I... see," Big Mustache said unhappily. "We shall, of course, obey your commands... my lord. You'll want to wait for your wife's arrival?"

"Oh, no," I said. "I mean to do my absolute best to win this thing *for* her. I think we'll be starting the attack now," I said, rubbing my hands together. Big Mustache simply looked at Dakar.

"My lord?"

"I am a great believer in peace," Dakar mused. "We must decide how many hugs it will take to end this war. And also, will I be giving or receiving them, and will I first have fresh bread strapped to my arms to make my hugs both soft and delicious? I do hope so."

I pointed at the walls of Naiber. "The bird that stole your shoes is in there."

"That bastard!" he cried. "ATTACK!"

The generals exchanged unhappy glances, but none of them dared gainsay their prince. The four of us walked over to the map. I saw right away that there was part of Naiber that spilled outside of its walls. Well, I was doing my honest best to conquer the place for Shivaka: Why not start with something easy?

"We attack *here*," I said, pointing.

"Says who?" Big Mustache growled.

"Saraya speaks for me," Prince Dakar declared, then paused. "Which is an odd thing, considering that I'm perfectly capable of speaking for myself. Or am I? Perhaps everything I think I'm saying is a lengthy hallucination, and there's actually a frog lodged in my throat, and all *you* hear are melodious croaks that you probably take for a series of spectacular and lengthy burps. Logically, if I want to communicate with you, I should burp at a frog and ask it to translate."

"We attack *here*," I repeated.

Big Mustache didn't like it, but he didn't have much of a choice. He commanded to attack to begin. I pondered the map, made decisions, gave orders. Those orders were passed from signal station to signal station by soldiers in funny conical caps, who snapped colorful flags up and down and sideways in a form of coded communication. Flag messages soon started to return to us. Things were already going wrong: Unexpected squalls popped up and dumped rain enough to turn fields into mud; startled supply-train donkeys floated off into the sky after stepping on hidden fairy nests; a peculiar disease broke out whose main symptom was making our men scream our battle plans to the other side. I leaned over the map, thinking hard, tersely giving orders and trying to hold things together. If I was going to do my honest best to win, that meant persevering through all difficulties.

"*Finally*!" Big Mustache said, relieved. "She's here!"

I looked up, astonished. A line of about a dozen chariots rolled toward the camp, and one of them—gilded and shining in the late afternoon sun—was decorated with hundreds, even thousands of flags all bearing the elegant wading bird of the royal family.

"Princess Shivaka?" I said, stunned. "Here? Already?"

The chariots rolled up to the command platform and stopped. Darshik the wizard climbed down from the first one. He walked back to the second and offered his arm to Princess Gamal. She spotted us and froze in mid-step. Darshik tugged at her arm, puzzled by her failure to come the rest of the way down. She suddenly gave him a dazzling smile and stepped to the ground. Darshik shook his head and walked toward the royal carriage.

"NOW!!" Princess Gamal bellowed, her arms crossed over her head. Abruptly, about a dozen "soldiers" exploded out of their uniforms, revealing ragged and desperate brigands who shouted and howled and brandished their knives wildly. Cursing, the driver of the royal carriage snapped the reigns, causing the horses to shoot off at incredible speed. I caught a glimpse of Princess Shivaka's astonished face, and then she was off and away. The brigands swarmed after her, passing stunned soldiers who didn't seem to grasp the true nature of their former compatriots.

"My merry band of traitors should give us two or three hours," Princess Gamal said dryly, walking over to us. "So. Explain why it would be profitable to me to take your side in whatever it is you're attempting."

"Wait!" the wizard Darshik cried, running toward us. "Foulness and perfidy! Don't listen to them! Her lordship's specific orders—"

"Leave him to me," Avashti said, his eyes narrowing. "This is going to be easy. Like squishing a grape."

"You again?" Darshik sniffed as Avashti walked up to him. Wizard faced wizard. Avashti rummaged around in his pack, finally pulling out a nasty-looking metal wand. Darshik simply pulled out his book of prophecy and started to flip through it, looking for a quick and easy answer to defeating us all.

"GET THE BOOK! GET THE—" I forced myself to stop. Any side I was on automatically became the losing side, right? And my luck was so bad it was good, right? "I SIDE WITH DARSHIK!" I bellowed. I pointed wildly. "Soldiers! I order you to seize Avashti! I

WANT DARSHIK TO WIN!!"

Big Mustache shrugged, flapping his hand to make them obey. Soldiers sprinted toward Avashti, but of course my luck intervened. One of the soldiers tripped and went flying toward him in a crazy, unintentional cartwheel. The soldier accidentally kicked the metal wand right out of Avashti's hand: It spiralled through the air, hit a rock, and kicked up a spray of sparks which just happened to set Darshik's book on fire.

"NO!!" he screamed.

"WATER!" I screamed. "SPRAY IT WITH YOUR WATERSKIN!"

It wasn't much of a fire. If Darshik had trusted me, he could have put it out in an instant. Instead, instinctively doing the opposite of whatever I said, he tried to shake the fire out. Of course, what he actually ended up doing was fanning the flames. The book of prophecy went up in a blazing FWOOMP. Darshik stared, wide-eyed, as pain forced his hand to open and the flaming book tumbled to earth like a blossom of fire which exploded, on impact, into a lotus of ashes.

Avashti finally reached his fellow wizard and dealt with Darshik by the simple expedient of sitting on him. That threat seemed to be dealt with, so I turned back to Princess Gamal.

"So? What have you got for me?" she asked, rubbing her hands together.

"Nothing, until I finish conquering the city. Then we'll have all sorts of treasures to hand out. Shut up for a second and I'll show you."

Princess Gamal gazed at me with narrowed eyes. "Charming. I see you're possessed of your usual mix of disrespectful showboating and personal stupidity. Since I can only kill you once, perhaps the *duration* of your death should reflect my opinion of you. Then again, perhaps not. I'd rather finish the thing and see you dead *before* the universe ends."

"Ha," I said, dismissing her with a flap of my hand. "You're hilarious. I wish I had time to laugh at you as long as you deserve, but… what was that you said about the universe ending? Go be annoying somewhere else."

"Oh, no. I've studied war and strategy. Learned from the best, I have, and taken lessons from all the finest soldiers and generals. *I'll* give the orders now."

"Um…" I exchanged alarmed glances with Vindi. If this was

going to work, it had to be *me* giving the orders, *me* winning the war... or trying to, at least. "You outrank Dakar?"

"No," she said, giving me a nasty little smile, "but if I start contradicting him, don't you think the generals might discover that they have *selective* hearing?"

Vindi nodded decisively. "This is the moment I was born for," she said. She picked her nose and walked over, hand outstretched, as if to wipe it on Gamal's immaculate gown.

"Stupid wretch!" Gamal shouted, backing away. "Who taught you manners, an incontinent monkey?"

"Sorry," Vindi said contritely. "I must be doing it wrong. Is *this* right?"

She picked her other nostril with her other hand, and extended *that* toward Gamal, too. Shrieking, Gamal grabbed a sword from a startled soldier and flung it at her pursuer, missing badly. Vindi kept on coming. Gamal backed away with a stuttering prance that was as close as she could come to running in that clinging gown. Smiling grimly, Vindi chased after her. I had time. For a while, at least.

"All right," I said seriously, turning to the map, "I want one unit to flank the left side, another to approach from the right, and a third to slam up the center..."

A very wise woman once said, "nothing is ever easy". Oh, wait. That was me, after my attempts to light a lantern ended with my head being baked inside a clay statue of a pig made by Kairay's greatest artist, whose works, due to her eminence, were illegal to damage or deface in any way. I had to wear the damn thing for six months until the monsoons came and melted it.

Anyway. Taking that hardly-defended, wall-less portion of Naiber should have been the easiest thing in the world. Just walk in and plant your flag. Done. Instead, one complication spiralled into another, one difficulty followed the next, and the whole thing started to give off the faint whiff of complete and total failure. I kept at it, grimly barking orders, glancing at the setting sun to check the time...

"You won," Big Mustache said, astonished, as the latest message flashed back from the nearest flag station. "I don't know how, but you won. Their leaders are coming to negotiate a surrender right now."

"What?" I said, astonished. "No, no, no. That can't be right. It can't be." I grabbed my chest, trying to ignore a dull, stabbing pain. "It must be... some kind of trick? Lulling us into a false sense of security? Forming up for a secret attack from behind?"

Big Mustache watched the flags intently. "No. You've won. No tricks."

Just to make my joy complete, Princess Gamal came up from the other side, having been smart enough to avoid Vindi in a big loop which eventually brought her back around to me.

"What's happening?" she demanded.

"They surrendered," Big Mustache told her, sounding as amazed as I was. "They're sending their leaders to negotiate terms right now. It's over."

Princess Gamal gazed at distant Naiber, huge and rich and central to a dozen thriving trade routes. She glanced in the direction of distant Kairay… a relative backwater, a desert fastness that would always be ruled by her sister-in-law. She seemed to come to a decision.

"I want to be named their new Minister of Trade and Finance," she said smoothly. "I'll stay here and watch over their money on behalf of my sister. And if I happen to accumulate a little wealth for myself, well, mistakes do happen."

"NO!!" I cried. Avashti, still sitting on an incensed Darshik, gave me a questioning look. Vindi finally caught up to us: Looking at her hands, she seemed startled to discover that they were now clean. She dug around in her nose with both hands, her face growing progressively redder.

"What a time to go empty…" she muttered.

"I… no," I said, sternly reminding myself that I had to take Gamal's side whether I wanted to or not. "No. Gamal is right. I want her to have everything she desires. Do as she says."

Princess Gamal smirked. "You've finally learned to bow to your betters, have you? Don't worry. We aren't offended by your obvious insincerity. Quite the opposite. The fact that you're lying with every word you speak, *but you say it anyway*, is a more profound act of obedience than the most flowery promise."

My face reddened. "I… want… Gamal to win. I want her to have everything. I *demand* she have everything."

"I know, dear, I know," she said, patting my head condescendingly.

The surrender party arrived. There were a total of fourteen men and women, plainly dressed and surprisingly cheerful. Big Mustache took charge, swiftly negotiating an end to the war. I bit my tongue, forcing myself not to intervene. I'd thought for sure I could handle something so simple as *losing a war*. It was so obvious. Take Shivaka's side and watch her lose. Instead, here I was, about to hand her everything she'd ever wanted.

"…and I get to be Minister of Trade and Finance," Princess Gamal insisted. "For life. I want that in writing. I can't be made to go back to Kairay, ever, no matter what."

Big Mustache glanced at her, surprised. "You'll have to surrender your royal charter—"

"Then I'll do it," she said, grabbing Dakar and yanking him closer. "Funny, isn't it, how certain things are just meant to be? I have the papers right here. I meant to grab some maps as I was leaving Kairay, but I accidentally grabbed this Abdication of Royal Charter instead. A happy little accident, wouldn't you say? I'll just sign here… and here… and my dear brother-in-law will witness it. Right? Right. Done."

"We're happy to be a vassal state of Kairay," the leader of the surrender party said, accepting a stamped and witnessed copy of Gamal's appointment. "Ha! I bet Naiber won't be so quick to lean on us after this!"

"What?" Princess Gamal demanded.

"You… aren't from Naiber?" I said cautiously.

"Oh, no," he said cheerfully. "We're from the township of Yamal."

"Yamal?"

"Exactly. Yamal is where the truly destitute folks are forced to live. Naiber won't even let us shelter inside their walls."

"The part of the city *outside* the walls—it isn't Naiber?" I said carefully.

"Nope! Though we're allowed to stay close, you see, on account of the cheap labor we provide. And we're happy to have you, too!" he said to Princess Gamal. "An actual Minister of Trade and Finance! As soon as we get something to trade, we'll be just like a real city!"

"Help?" Princess Gamal said, looking back at us.

Someone stepped up beside me. Dully, I saw that it was Princess Shivaka, back hours too soon. I don't know what crazy luck had brought her here, but it had left her smelling of roses.

"I think it sounds like a *wonderful* idea," Princess Shivaka said firmly. "Good luck, my dear and beloved sister. Fare well! Do write and tell me if they ever get that second chicken."

"Help?" Gamal said again as the surrender party formed up around her. She stared over her shoulder as she and her fellow Yamalitans left, quickly vanishing from sight.

Princess Shivaka looked the four of us over, doing a double take when she saw her husband standing behind us.

"Dakar. Come here."

"There are many kitties in the world," Dakar sadly noted. "Sometimes, the kitty we love the most bites us the hardest. I will stand over here, with my friends, until you stop biting the world quite so hard."

"Then I'll have to treat you as an enemy combatant," she pointed out, "starting when I order you hit over the head with a club."

"Then again," Dakar said, "I suddenly feel like standing over *there*."

Shivaka smiled as Dakar took his place beside her. "And what about Saraya?" she asked her generals. "I suppose she's been trying to drive my armies into the ground?"

"Well..." Big Mustache frowned. "Actually, she's been working *for* you," he reluctantly admitted. "If it weren't for all the terrible luck we've been having, we'd have conquered half of Naiber by now."

"Clever," Shivaka said drily. "Very clever. Using your luck against me, hm? I wouldn't have thought of that. It's all over now, of course." She snapped her fingers, gesturing to her guards. "Remove these three. Don't hurt them, though, unless you have no choice."

Acting on a hunch, I grabbed a sword from the startled soldier next to me and swung it wildly at the advancing guards. Princess Shivaka stared at me.

"What are you *doing*?"

"If experience is any guide, accidentally slicing apart my own face. And guess what? If I die, *you're all out of luck*. Literally."

Princess Shivaka held up a restraining hand, stopping the guards in their tracks. I continued to swing wildly. Any one of them could have slipped under my guard and finished me in moments, but you can't steal luck from a dead woman. She needed me alive.

"Leave her be," Shivaka said shortly. "The wizard and the girl, too. Leave them alone. Don't touch them."

Her generals gave her a strange look, but gestured for their underlings to obey. I let the sword drop until its tip hit the ground.

That was my intention, at least. I'm still not sure how the most beloved stuffed animal of my childhood ended up on the ground just below me.

"Mr. Fluffles! NOOOO!"

Princess Shivaka assumed the reigns of the army and resumed the attack against Naiber. Even without taking her luck into account, she was—quite simply—impressive. She gathered information and synthesized it with unseemly speed, then dispatched her forces with crisp, efficient, and above all *insightful* orders. Yes, as a high noble, she'd enjoyed a comprehensive military education, but she was just plain *good* at this. As the flag stations began to report victory after victory, I realized with a sinking feeling that I'd won nothing but the best possible seat to witness my enemy's total triumph.

"Send more supplies to the west, I command you!" I hazarded. The generals ignored me. So I tried shouting everything Shivaka said word for word, figuring that fortune would turn against her commands if they came out of my mouth. It took fewer than three sentences before Princess Shivaka turned to me:

"I can almost certainly have you detained without killing you," she said sweetly. "Would you like to find out?"

With ill grace, I shut up.

"What are we going to *do*?" Vindi whispered. Avashti got up off of a defeated and depressed Darshik and came over to my other side.

"Saraya?" he asked.

"Oh, and while I hate the necessity," Princess Shivaka said over her shoulder, "your continued opposition—not to mention the abduction of my husband—is most unacceptable. Consider yourselves exiled from the city and realm of Kairay. Forever."

I stared in the direction of Naiber. Kairay's armies advanced steadily across the plain, sending dust billowing into the air. The late-day sky was a relentless blue, providing the perfect weather for an invasion, save for a tiny puff of cloud which dawdled over the ocean. I absently fingered the useless odds and ends in my pocket. Bits of bread. Coins... how had *those* gotten back in there? Mocking me, of course. My fingers touched my Anteyvan strangling cord. I paused, an idea slowly congealing in my mind.

"Can you summon that cloud? Bring it right overhead?" I murmured to Avashti.

"Well..." The wizard took off his pack and pawed through the mess of wires and wizardly artifacts inside. "Probably. I think. I might be missing a few things."

"Vindi. Can you fetch him what he needs?"

"Won't I get run through with swords?"

"The guards have orders to ignore you. Shivaka is about to become far too distracted to reverse that order."

"I'll try," she promised.

I sighed and pulled the Anteyvan strangling cord out of my pocket. I had to be all-in if this was going to work. I couldn't pretend, couldn't stop halfway. I had to be willing to die for my cause. I looked at Avashti, who was building a bizarre metallic device as Darshik, who was still lying on the ground, sneered and criticized his efforts. I looked at Vindi, who was already running errands for her father, grabbing bits and pieces from startled soldiers and from Darshik's own pockets as he irritably swatted at her. Yes. All of us "lesser" folk were nothing to Princess Shivaka, forgotten and kicked aside while she pursued her war efforts. If I won, she'd have no choice but to finally start helping us. Win or lose, it was worth it. This was the only way.

I wrapped the Anteyvan strangling cord around my neck. I winced. I began to pull it tight. Avashti and Vindi were deeply involved in their work, and didn't notice me walk away. I couldn't let them see what I was doing. They'd only try to stop me.

Metal barbs dug into my skin. I couldn't breathe. Spots of light pulsed in front of my eyes.

Princess Shivaka stared at me. "What are you *doing*?"

"Nnnn…" I yanked the cord tighter yet. I was feeling very unsteady, and my legs wouldn't hold me up for much longer.

"You… you're trying to kill yourself, aren't you?" Princess Shivaka said, astonished. "You're trying to deprive me of my luck when I need it most. GUARDS!"

Armed men hulked toward me. Oops. She didn't need to intervene personally, not when she had *them*. How had I overlooked *that*? Bad luck, or rampant stupidity?

A shadow suddenly interposed itself between me and them. I stared in amazement at Prince Dakar. His eyes were pointing in two different directions, but there was still something noble in his posture.

"Saraya is my friend," he said simply. "I stand with my friends. Also, occasionally, with birds I have mistaken for friends. But Saraya is not a bird. At least, she doesn't appear to have feathers, nor has she ever sat on a low branch, singing beautiful songs while she pooped on my head. Though perhaps I should give it time. Many things can happen, if you have patience.”

I collapsed to the ground, pulsing white lights spreading and starting to consume my vision. The guards stopped dead, their every instinct prohibiting them from touching their prince.

“My love,” Shivaka said gently, “you have to move now. Go. Over there. Move.”

“I will not,” he said simply. Princess Shivaka grabbed his wrist and tugged. He swayed, but would not be moved. I stared at him, quietly amazed that someone I knew so little would do so much for me.

“Do I have to do *everything* myself?” Princess Shivaka grumbled. She ducked under Prince Dakar’s arm. Kneeling by my side, she tried to tug the Anteyvan strangling cord from around my neck, which of course made it tighter. I gagged, foam running from the corner of my mouth. She frowned, working her fingers between my neck and the cord. Such was her luck that she just happened to find a weak spot. She pulled, the fabric snapped, and I took a gasping, shuddering breath.

“You really have to stop this,” she said.

“NEVER!” I cried, trying to punch her. I was sufficiently weakened, and striking from such an awkward angle, that I ended up slapping her at half-speed. Shivaka scowled and slapped me back. We got into a quick and vicious slap-fight, Prince Dakar and the guards he was holding off looking on in amazement.

“Enough. Enough,” Shivaka panted. “You don’t matter any more. You can’t stop me.”

“I know. And that’s why I mean to stop *me*. Once I’m dead, it’s all over for you,” I said, pulling the Walnut of Inversion from my store of suicide devices. I wasn’t exactly sure how to use the wizardly artifact, but I tried aiming it at myself and squeezing the sides. With a loud farting sound, the tree behind me deflated as its insides vanished. Grimly determined, I took better aim, pointing the nasty little thing at my head—

“You’re insane!” Shivaka cried, grabbing for it.

“So what if she is?” Prince Dakar said defensively. “Some of Saraya’s best friends are insane, but that doesn’t keep her from cherishing their aid and promising to bring them more pie than they’ve dreamed of in their lives.” A devious look crossed his face. “What she doesn't know is that *I always dream of pie*. So long as she lives, she'll never catch up. In fact—"

Shivaka batted at my hands. I jumped to my feet, still holding the Walnut of Inversion. Shivaka sprang at me. She slipped, and her fingers just happened to stab into my wrist, which just happened to force my fingers to spring open. The Walnut of Inversion shot into the air. I grabbed at it. Princess Shivaka grabbed at it. It did an elegant sort of dance on our fingertips. Prince Dakar craned his neck to look. The soldiers, who weren't even trying to get past him any more, craned their necks to look. I realized that Shivaka had left herself wide open. I couldn't help myself. I pulled back and tried to punch her right in the face. Of course I slipped on a previously unnoticed donkey dropping, my arm swinging wildly as I somehow managed to punch myself. Crying out in triumph, Shivaka snatched the Walnut of Inversion out of the air and flung it at the ground. I guess it was still working, because it caused the earth itself to disappear and vanished instantly down a very small, very straight hole in the ground.

"Why are you still trying?" Princess Shivaka demanded as I grabbed the Gooey Orb of Snail-Snotted Doom from my pocket. "You know you can't win."

"Failing isn't failure. Failing to give yourself the *opportunity* to fail is failure!"

"THAT DOESN'T MAKE ANY SENSE!"

I unwrapped the papyrus shell and tried to pop the gooey orb into my mouth. I wasn't sure what would happen if I swallowed it, but if *one* of those black motes could make a crystal rim, a *hundred* might well make me explode in a shower of combined meat and wealth that would alternately delight and horrify everyone around. Shivaka flung herself at me, knocking the thing out of my hand. A nearby soldier accidentally squirted it with her waterskin and it dissolved instantly. I stared. *Water*? All I'd needed to prevent so much torment and pain was a little bit of *water*?

"All right. You're done for. Or, rather, *I* am," I said, pulling the Box of Infinite Beauty (and Vampires) from my pocket. I actually managed to get the god-device open. Lovely butterflies poured out, attaching themselves to my face and happily sucking my blood. Princess Shivaka grimly started slapping them away. Sadly, her rings must have contained the right sort of metal, because the vampiric butterflies stayed dead. I tried to open the box wider, but I somehow managed to fumble it, drop it, and step on it, whereupon the box shattered into a thousand useless splinters. Oops.

"Well?" Princess Shivaka demanded, breathing heavily. "Got anything else?"

I patted my pockets. Empty. But then, I hadn't actually wanted to die. I'd wanted to distract her. Beyond Prince Dakar and the soldiers, I could see Avashti huddled over a curious glowing helix of twirling metal while Vindi leapt in the air, waving her arms in complicated gestures of need and supplication. The tiny cloud was nearly overhead, dark and threatening. I nodded. I grabbed Shivaka's wrist and calmly pulled her over to the wizard Darshik. I yanked him to his feet, then pulled them both half a dozen steps to the left.

"Considering that this is your final act as a free woman, I can't say I'm impressed," Shivaka said wryly. "One word to my guards, and this will all be over. Are you sure you don't want to make a run for it? Call me soft, but I might even let you go."

"One moment." I glanced at the dark little cloud, which was starting to growl hungrily. I took two steps back and three to the left.

"I'm sorry," the Princess said, "but I'm not willing to wait for you to—"

"One moment. Just one." I carefully positioned Princess Shivaka, who looked at me strangely, and then the wizard Darshik, who just looked irritated. I raised Shivaka's arm over my head, holding her hand in mine. The quasi-silver bracelet was still fused to my wrist, and it glinted in what sunlight reached us. I winked at Princess Shivaka, who scowled at me.

"Would you like to explain yourself?" she demanded.

"Oh, this?" I asked, continuing to hold our joined hands well over our heads. I put my other hand firmly on Darshik's shoulder. Almost without meaning to, I began to laugh. "Tell me," I said, "have you ever been struck by lightning?"

* * *

When I came to, I didn't have eyebrows. Hair, yes, as I could tell from the all-too-familiar scent of it burning—but no eyebrows. Princess Shivaka lay on the ground next to me, stunned but unhurt. The wizard Darshik lay on my other side, his mouth agape, his clothes smouldering. I grinned: I was so used to getting hit by lightning that I'd come to long before either of them.

"How are we doing?" I asked Avashti.

"Working on it," he said tersely. He had the Lens of Becoming and the weird brass-wand artifact, both confiscated from Darshik, and

247

as I watched he began the chants and rituals necessary to transfer my luck. I sat up and looked around. Prince Dakar was still holding off Shivaka's soldiers, none of whom dared touch a high noble. Vindi grabbed a damp rag and helpfully patted my head. Unfortunately, it turned out to be someone's napkin: The dampness was due to mustard.

Flashes of hot and cold swept across my body, and a curious tingling, and then—

"Damn it!" Avashti swore.

"What's the matter?" I said anxiously. "Didn't it work?"

"Sort of. I don't know how it happened, but I transferred your luck to Vindi again."

Princess Shivaka sat up and groaned, rubbing her head. We didn't have much time. Once she started giving orders, Dakar wouldn't be able to protect us any more. In fact…

I paused, my eyes falling on Prince Dakar. Well, why not?

"Vindi," I said, "punch Dakar in the back of the head as hard as you can."

"*What*?" she said, aghast.

"*What*?" Shivaka said, aghast.

I shrugged. "I want to see him fixed. You can cure the crazies with a blow to the head, right? That's the way it works in comedic plays."

"Are you *insane*?" Shivaka demanded. "Do you know *anything at all* about brain injuries? The human mind is so delicate, so unpredictable, so complex that you'd have to be the luckiest bastard in the history of…" She stopped. Her eyes went very, very wide. She gazed at Dakar with a mix of hope and fear in her eyes.

"Do it," I said.

Vindi wound up and tried to punch Dakar. She slipped and ended up hitting him in a much different place, and at a far different angle than she'd intended. His head snapped forward. He blinked. He slowly looked up.

"Dakar? My love?" Princess Shivaka hesitantly asked. "Did it… did it work?"

"I'm not sure." Prince Dakar rubbed the back of his head. "I should hate to be fixed if it meant having to make sense all the time. It was freeing, being able to rant and rave about dogs or birds or worms as I saw fit." He looked tenderly at Shivaka. "Would you still love me, if I occasionally sewed clothes out of feathers and gave them to worms?"

"Yes," she said, her voice barely more than a whisper.

"Vindi," I said. "Help Avashti. Fix me forever."

Avashti shrugged and went to work, waving the Lens of Becoming around and chanting. The soldiers stirred restlessly, but Princess Shivaka was too absorbed in her husband's eyes to give them new orders. Unsure what to do, Vindi settled for poking and prodding her father at random. His concentration was something to behold, but his movements were inevitably altered. Thanks to her luck, they seemed to be altered in the *right way*, by which I mean that my face didn't melt.

"No!" Darshik growled, clambering to his feet. "That's mine. He stole it. GIVE IT BACK!"

I hastily stepped in front of the wizard, grabbed him by both shoulders, and kissed him full on the lips. Given my luck, the results were almost inevitable: He burped right down my throat. Then he farted. Then his face spontaneously caught fire for no reason.

"Better than usual," I noted, stepping back.

Patting out the fire, Darshik resumed his charge, but too late. Heat and cold and strange pangs wracked my body, and the Lens of Becoming actually *melted* in Avashti's hands. By the looks of it, no one would be transferring anyone's luck ever again.

"Is it done?" I asked.

"Not quite," Avashti admitted. "You'll always be less than lucky, and Vindi will always be more. Still, it's about the same as it was a month ago."

"Huh," I said. I took a step toward him… and fell down a sinkhole. The encouraging thing was that it was only half a foot deep.

"Laugh while you can," Darshik said darkly. "My lady? Would you like to order them put to death, or shall I?"

I looked at Princess Shivaka. So did Avashti. So did Vindi.

"They *are* my friends," Prince Dakar said gently, holding her arm.

"I know. Still, they've cost me my chance at Naiber," Shivaka said irritably. "I'll have to withdraw. I'll have to abandon most of the other places I've conquered, too."

"You still have an Advisory Council back in Kairay, if you just ask," I pointed out. "You can still do good. A lot of good. It won't be easy, not any more, but… will *that* stop you from fighting for what's right?"

Princess Shivaka smiled. "I think I understand. And Saraya: About the exile I proclaimed for you and your family…?"

"Yes?" I said eagerly.

"It stands. Stay away from me or I *will* see you dead. Goodbye."

She clapped her hands over her head. An exasperated general called the retreat, flag-men waved their flags, and the whole army began to break camp and depart. No one paid any attention to the three of us. Darshik looked like he wanted to say something, but finally shook his head and wandered off in Shivaka's wake.

"Now that he doesn't have that stupid book, I give it three days before she fires him," Avashti said.

"Since we've been exiled from Kairay…" I mused.

"Go on," Vindi urged me.

"Well, we're right here. What say we take a look and see what Naiber has to offer?"

"We don't have any money, any friends, any property or any prospects," Avashti pointed out.

"Never stopped me before. Shall we?"

Vindi took my right arm. Avashti took my left.

"Yes," Vindi said happily, "I suppose we shall."